A BEAUTIFUL WOMAN . . . A DANGEROUS MOMENT

"Perhaps I can sleep now," Joanna murmured.

So should he if he wanted an early start back to London.

He got up and held out his hand to help her rise from the bench.

And regretted the gesture as soon as her palm slid across his.

Soft heat rippled through him. He should let go, send Joanna back to her bedchamber—alone.

He ran his thumb over the back of her hand. Smooth, soft skin. Was the tremor he felt his or hers?

"Grimm?"

A breathy utterance. An admonition? An invitation?

Ye gods, nothing she said or did suggested she'd come into the hall with seduction in mind. Yet here he stood, spellbound, too damn willing to follow Joanna's lead . . .

"With superb characterization and polished prose, Anton crafts a thoroughly entertaining love story."
—*Booklist* on *The Ideal Husband*

"Anton is a superbly talented writer of medieval historical fiction."
—*The Romance Readers Connection*

Also by Shari Anton

Once A Bride
The Ideal Husband

AT HER SERVICE

SHARI ANTON

NEW YORK   BOSTON

Warner Forever is a registered trademark of Warner Books.

Cover design by Diane Lugar
Cover illustration by Alan Ayers
Typography by Ron Zinn
Book design by Giorgetta Bell McRee

Warner Books

Time Warner Book Group
1271 Avenue of the Americas
New York, NY 10020
Visit our Web site at www.twbookmark.com

Printed in the United States of America

First Paperback Printing: January 2005

10 9 8 7 6 5 4 3 2 1

To my teammates—Diane Berka, Kathie Scott,
Nancy Holzberger and Kathee Kantor.

May you always make average, never suffer another
chop or leave the head pin!

And to Coach Connie Holzberger, for his enthusiastic
support and Cheesecake Bars!

Love you all!

AT
HER
SERVICE

Chapter One

England 1350 ろ

Ivy screamed as only a little girl can—loud and shrill.

Within Lynwood Manor's great hall, Lady Joanna's hands stilled, the herbs she crushed with mortar and pestle momentarily forgotten as she paused to listen more closely to the sounds from outside.

On this early summer's day, the children were playing on the village green, chasing a ball and each other. Their mingled squeals of delight and groans of disappointment clearly signaled how their game progressed. Joanna's seven-year-old daughter was, as usual, among the loudest of the children.

Surely, Joanna thought, she imagined a hint of hurt or a taste of fear in Ivy's last screech.

Then Ivy screamed again, her distress sharp-edged. Heart pounding, Joanna dropped the pestle and ran out of the hall's open door, joining other mothers in their dash across the dusty yard between the manor house and the timber palisade. She burst through the open gate and froze at the sight of three men on horseback, the riders bent forward and low, thundering up the middle of the green and coming straight at her. One had speared a goose, the poor fowl hanging limp and bloodied, a repulsive banner on the lance's tip.

The thieves.

Her fury flared hot and bright. The thieves again raided the village, as they had several times before. However, unlike former raids, this time they arrogantly dared to reveal themselves during daylight, shamelessly displaying their prize, recklessly frightening Ivy and the other children.

Joanna desperately longed to search for her daughter, but as lady of Lynwood she stood her ground, studying the men's faces as they came closer to her. She didn't recognize them, but now knew the faces of her enemies.

She concentrated on the man she judged the leader. Dark-haired and bearded, he bore an ugly, jagged scar on his forehead. He also wore an offensive smirk, as if he knew her identity and scoffed at her attempts to halt his thievery.

The *beast*!

Joanna waved a fist and shouted, "Whoreson! Leave us be! Do you hear me? Leave us be!"

If he heard her command, he gave no sign, merely veered right, leading his men around the palisade to escape into the woodland beyond.

Furious, Joanna spun to order the guards to pursue, but saved her voice when she heard Harold Long, the captain, shout for his men to mount up and give chase.

Praying this time the manor's guards would find and

capture the thieves, Joanna anxiously glanced about for Ivy.

In the middle of the green, near the well, mothers picked up and soothed their little ones, adding their outraged shouts to the children's cries. Joanna went cold at what she heard. The thieves had purposely *terrorized* the children with no regard for whether or not the little ones came to harm.

Fighting panic, Joanna shouted her daughter's name.

"Here, milady!" answered the booming voice of the blacksmith, one of the few males not out in the fields.

Donald Smith strode toward her, Ivy, seeming small and fragile, cradled in his meaty arms. Glistening tears flowed from Ivy's pain-filled blue eyes, streaking her dirty cheeks. Bright red blood dripped from a long, deep gash in her forearm, staining her short gray tunic.

Joanna nearly swooned. She didn't deal well with blood, or sickness, which she'd seen too much of during the past few months.

"The h-horse stepped on m-me, Mama!" Ivy stammered through her sobs. "My arm h-hurts! It bleeds!"

Joanna's hand shook as she pushed strands of golden hair from Ivy's forehead, struggling to banish the horrifying vision of Ivy tumbling on the ground beneath a horse's hooves.

"I know, dearest." She hoped her voice didn't reveal the extent of her horror. For Ivy's sake she must appear calm. "Be brave a few moments longer. Donald will take you into the manor." She looked up at Donald. "Have Maud bind the wound to stop the bleeding while I find Greta."

The blacksmith nodded and bore Ivy away.

Frustrated she couldn't take away the pain or spare Ivy the ordeal to come, Joanna fetched old Greta, the midwife, now the only healer in the village with experience in stitching skin. Along the way back to the manor, she sent the dairymaid out to the fields to inform Wat, the village reeve, of the raid.

Several moments later, seated on the edge of the bed in Lynwood Manor's bedchamber with Ivy draped across her lap, Joanna again struggled for composure.

Terror lurked beneath Ivy's stoic expression. She bit down on a folded towel and buried her face in her mother's shoulder. Cradling Ivy's head, Joanna nodded at Greta, who held a sharp needle and strong thread in gnarled yet steady fingers.

Greta grabbed hold of Ivy's wrist. Joanna tightened her grip on her child's elbow. The moment the needle pierced the forearm's skin, Ivy jerked, gave a muffled scream, then mercifully fainted.

"Hurry," Joanna ordered, feeling her head go light from the smell of blood and her own upset.

"Breathe, milady. Ivy is only cut, not dying."

The midwife's thin voice gave reassurance, but having suffered the grief of burying two children in the days before last Christmas, Joanna held more tightly to her remaining daughter. To lose Ivy . . . Joanna halted the thought from fully forming, unable to bear the swell of grief.

"How long must the stitches stay in?" she asked, amazed her voice didn't tremble.

Greta continued to work—a fourth stitch. A fifth.

"A sennight, at the least. Ivy will have a scar, but has

come to no lasting harm. Given a few days' rest, she will be fine."

Enforcing rest for even a day would be no easy task. Ivy could hardly keep her seat at table each morn, eager to escape to the village to play with the tenants' children. Despite the recent problems, Joanna had considered the village green a safe place for her daughter to play.

No more.

The only way to ensure everyone's safety was to capture and punish the bastards responsible for this outrage—and Joanna was nearly at her wit's end over how to accomplish that feat.

True, she'd thought of one way, but it seemed extreme. Joanna peered into the pale face of the daughter she easily could have lost this morning. Perhaps an extreme solution was now called for.

After what seemed an eternity later, seventeen neat stitches puckered Ivy's arm. A rinse of the blood and wrap of white bandaging completed the process. As they finished, Maud, the manor's housekeeper, cautiously poked her kerchief-wrapped head into the chamber.

"Milady, Wat and Harold are in the hall. Are ye ready to speak with them?"

If Harold was back so soon, then likely the thieves had escaped capture once more. Damn. "Inform them I will be with them anon."

Maud disappeared. Greta gathered up the bloodied towels and her basket of medicinals and followed.

Joanna took a deep breath, kissed Ivy's forehead, and eased her onto the thick feather mattress, hoping the girl would sleep a while longer.

While fears over Ivy's injury eased, Joanna's resolve

to set an untenable situation to rights did not. After a last reassuring inspection of her child, she left the room, leaving open the door connecting the chamber to the manor's hall, the better to hear if Ivy woke and cried out.

The scents of rabbit stew bubbling in a black cauldron on the hearth, and of rosemary strewn among the rushes covering the dirt floor, helped mask the odor of blood drying on her brown, light wool gown. During her mad rush to find Ivy, Joanna's circlet and veil had flown off, and she hadn't given their whereabouts a thought until now, when the two somber men sitting at the trestle table in the middle of the hall turned to stare at her.

Joanna forswore returning to her bedchamber to cover her braided blond hair. If either man thought her scandalous for the mere absence of a veil, so be it. But then, neither Wat Reeve nor Harold Long was wont to judge her harshly.

They occupied benches on either side of the trestle table. Now her trusted advisors, neither had been prepared to assume the positions of authority they now held.

Joanna included herself among the unprepared. The plague of last summer and autumn had cut through both manor and village like a scythe wielded by an indiscriminate mower, taking whichever lives happened to cross the jagged path of the vile sickness. Nearly half of the populace had been lost, in some cases entire families.

Wat Reeve, whom the villagers had elected to his deceased father's position of village reeve, unfolded his long, lank body to stand.

Sturdily built Harold Long followed suit. He now captained the sorely depleted garrison—chosen by the men for his skill at arms, approved by her for his ability to command.

Since her husband's death nigh on seven months earlier, both young men had provided her with good counsel and most often readily abided by her decisions, even when they didn't entirely approve. But, thus far, her decisions had been small ones. The thieves provided the first true challenge to her ability to rule Lynwood, and Joanna disliked the taste of failure.

She eased into the chair placed at the head of the table. The men sat but didn't relax.

"How does the little lady?" Wat asked, his deep voice an odd match to his slight frame.

Likely the servants had already informed the men of the extent of Ivy's injuries. "She finally sleeps. The other children?"

"I visited all the families. The children are bruised and suffered a fright, but are otherwise unharmed, praise the Lord in his mercy." Wat rubbed weary eyes with his palms. "We were most fortunate. When I think of what might have happened . . ."

No one finished the reeve's thought. No one wanting to put the tragedy they'd escaped into words.

Joanna glanced pointedly between the men. "These brutes who harry us must be caught and punished. I will not tolerate a repeat of this morning's incident. 'Tis unacceptable that our children are at risk while playing on the village green!"

Harold pounded a fist on the table. "We have hunted them since they first stole one of Margaret Atbridge's chickens. But with so few soldiers and the planting not yet done, and shearing time coming fast, I fear we will not have enough men available to hunt the ruffians properly for some weeks yet."

"We cannot wait weeks!"

"I am aware of your concern, my lady. I share it! Where before the band struck under the cover of night, they now flaunt our vulnerability. We need more men, more horses and . . . nay, my lady, I do not know from where either can be hired or bought. The entire kingdom suffers the same hardships we do."

She didn't care about the hardships of the entire kingdom, only those in the small portion under her rule, a role thrust upon her without warning or mercy.

The pestilence had robbed her of Elias and Rose, both innocents she missed horribly. But the plague also rid her of Bertrand, whose soul—if justice truly existed in the afterlife—now resided with the devil in the deepest pit of hell.

Joanna gathered her courage to present her decision. As a courtesy, she would first give Wat and Harold a last opportunity to suggest other solutions. Indeed, she trusted their judgment, and hoped either one might offer a less extreme solution.

"This noon the thieves threatened the lives of our children. As you say, Harold, we have not the means to deal with them as we might like. Still, we need a solution, good sirs, and quickly."

Harold leaned forward, palm raised, expression earnest. "Mayhap another appeal to the abbot for assistance is in order."

Joanna didn't hesitate in her answer. Appealing to the Abbot of Holme, Lynwood Manor's overlord, didn't sit well.

"Our last appeal to the abbot gained us no more than Father Arthur. While we had need of a priest, he is helpless against these ruffians."

Indeed, the priest wasn't good for much of anything except spouting nonsense. The man didn't hold a good opinion of Lynwood or anyone who resided there. He had the audacity to wail and moan over the lack of holiness in the kingdom, claiming God had sent the plague to punish the wicked, impious hordes for their sins.

Her toddling son hadn't been impious, or her infant daughter wicked.

"Are you still against an appeal to your brother?"

Appeal to the brother who'd taken the first opportunity to be rid of her upon his inheritance? Who'd married her off to Sir Bertrand de Poitou despite her objections? She'd never again speak to her brother if she could help it.

"I am sure my brother suffers hardships, too. We must deal with this problem on our own."

Neither man would suggest she appeal to the de Poitou family, who'd irrevocably broken ties with Bertrand years before.

Wat shifted in his seat. "If I may take the liberty, Lady Joanna. These scoundrels must know we have no lord in residence, or they would not be so bold. I pray you reconsider your position on marriage."

Wat's suggestion not only pricked her ire but soured her stomach. The men knew she'd had two offers of marriage, both from landless knights seeking to improve their lot. She'd sent both men out the door with firm refusals. If she had her way, she would never marry again. Never place herself or Ivy at the mercy of a man.

Barely restraining her ire, Joanna once more stated her position on what Wat considered a convenient and desirable solution to all of the manor's travails.

"I will not take a husband simply to rid us of a few ruffians."

Wat's mouth tightened. "These ruffians are now more than a nuisance, my lady. In return for our pledge of fealty, the villagers are due protection. You must do whatever is required to meet that responsibility."

She was well aware of her duty to the villagers and manor folk, having witnessed both her father and her husband rule their holdings. Unfortunately, she had no practical experience in the matter because neither man had seen fit to give her the opportunity to try her hand.

They'd both believed women were too softhearted and light-handed to oversee estates. Joanna meant to prove both men wrong, even if neither man was alive to witness her success.

"Certes, the garrison bears the burden of running the thieves to ground, but the villagers could be of aid. I believe a bit of cooperation is in order."

"We are farmers, not soldiers. Do you propose we abandon our plows to pick up swords?"

Joanna nearly shuddered at the consequences should they do so. Not only would some of the tenants hurt themselves beyond repair if given a sharp sword, but the planting must continue with due haste. Because of the plague, too much of last year's crop had rotted in the fields from lack of healthy hands at harvest. Without a bountiful harvest this autumn, all would face starvation next winter.

"Nay, but I do expect everyone to keep a keen eye out for signs of the ruffians and give chase when possible."

"'Tis impossible for the villagers to overtake men on horseback. The responsibility for their capture must lie with the guards."

Harold took umbrage. "Think you we have not followed the louts? They vanish as if plucked from the earth by the wind, leaving no trail! 'Tis uncanny."

Wat huffed. "No one on horseback vanishes without trace. Perhaps your soldiers take their duty too lightly and do not search too hard."

Harold half rose from the bench. "You dare accuse us of shunning our duty?"

"Halt, at once!" Joanna stared at Harold until he reluctantly resumed his seat, then shot Wat a withering glare. "The soldiers do what they can. I have no complaint of them. Besides, what is past is done. We need a plan, good sirs, of how to proceed from now on."

After several moments of silence, Joanna hushed the errant thoughts of self-doubt, squared her shoulders, and forged ahead.

"Since we cannot seem to deal with the situation on our own, then we must find someone who is able. I intend to hire a mercenary to augment our garrison. His sole duty will be to rid us of these brutes."

The announcement raised the men's eyebrows.

"Who, my lady?" Harold asked.

"Logan Grimm, if he is available."

Wat's head jerked back at the man's name, his eyes going wide. "Grimm?" he asked in a harsh whisper.

She could almost hear the thoughts flitting through the men's heads.

Logan Grimm. Legendary mercenary. Reputedly the most fearsome fighter in the kingdom, Grimm charged a hefty fee, but he always won no matter the odds against him. Such a man could track down a band of thieves and dispatch them with ease.

Harold said nothing, only gave her a somber look. Wat found his voice again.

"Milady, is it wise to bring a man of his ilk among the innocent, God-fearing folk of Lynwood Manor?"

Joanna stood up, unwilling to debate her decision further. "A man of his ilk will ensure that Lynwood Manor continues to exist. Harold, you will prepare to ride to London on the morn. I will give you direction and coin before you leave."

With that, she spun around and returned to the bedchamber to see to Ivy, hoping the gossip she'd heard in her father's hall about the legendary mercenary proved true.

'Twas said he was fierce, thorough, and completely loyal to whoever paid his fee. If Logan Grimm could rid her of this band of thieves, give her the peace and security she craved, then by the rood, she'd find a way to pay his fee—somehow.

Logan Grimm nursed an ale in the taproom of the crowded, crude dockside inn he called home while in London, a place he didn't visit often. Usually, he left the service of one lord only to head straight to another. 'Twas rare when he found himself without the prospect of work, rarer still when he suffered a wound from which he must recover.

The inactivity left him more surly than usual, but he admitted the rest had done his body good. The gash on his thigh healed well, if slowly, with the resulting limp easier to hide if he didn't overuse the leg. He would have a scar, but his body bore so many scars he no longer remembered whence they all came. All hazards of his profession.

Luckily, up until this one all his scars came from light cuts. Unfortunately, this sword slice had required stitches. The damn wound still pinched and itched. The only good thing he could say about stitches was that they held the skin together.

As for work, something would come his way. It always did. Somewhere in the kingdom one lord wished to do battle with another lord, for righteous reasons or foul. Either aggressor or defender would seek out and hire Logan Grimm for his skill with a sword.

He hoped not too many lords had learned of how poorly he'd fared on his last job. The dent to his otherwise flawless reputation bothered him more than the irksome stitches.

Habit shifted him on the stool when the door opened. The cries of fishmongers and the stench of muck-strewn streets invaded the inn as three men entered.

The two sailors joined a boisterous group of their fellows. The third man perused the taproom before winding his way through the crowd to the bar. A merchant, Logan guessed, from the quality of his garb. No threat, no prospect.

Logan downed the last of his ale, intending to get up and walk around to keep his leg from going too stiff. He no more than put the mug down on the table he claimed and didn't share, when Abigail, the innkeeper's plump wife, headed in his direction with a flagon in hand. She was, in part, the reason he favored the Red Rooster. She kept his mug full and his bedding fairly vermin-free for a fair price.

He scowled at the woman. "No more, Abigail. If I do not get up and move, I will rot here."

"Not on my stool, ye will not." She refilled his mug. "Man asking for you. Want to talk to him?"

Another reason he liked the Red Rooster. Hugo, the owner, considered it a great privilege to act as Logan's go-between. A convenient and profitable arrangement for them both.

"Has the man shown coin yet?"

"Enough to pay for his ale, and yours."

"Say what he wants?"

"Same as they all want. Healed enough yet?"

Logan shrugged. "Send him over."

Abigail placed a work-roughened hand on her ample hip and narrowed her eyes. "You sure?"

No man had dared to question Logan Grimm's commands for many a year now, for fear of finding himself staring at the tip of a well-honed broadsword. However, a man made allowances for the woman who picked lice from his blankets.

"Send him over."

Abigail ambled back to the bar and pointed Logan out to the man he'd thought might be a merchant. Middle twenties or so. Garbed too fine for a messenger, too drably for a knight or higher lord. Somber. Wary, possibly frightened. Only loyalty to the lord he served, or the prospect of a reward, forced him to pass through the Red Rooster's door to find Logan Grimm.

A quick judgment, but likely accurate.

Over the course of his nearly thirty years, he'd made

few mistakes when judging the men who had hired him or those he fought against. Logan resisted the urge to rub at the wound reminding him of the humbling misjudgment of his last opponent. He'd won the day and earned his fee, but at a price to his pride and reputation.

The man stopped a couple of feet away. "I am Harold Long, captain of Lynwood Manor's garrison. You are Logan Grimm?"

The man seemed too young to have risen to the rank of captain. Still, even given Harold's discomfort, Logan liked the solid tone of the man's voice. He waved Harold to a stool, not to put the man at ease, but because he didn't like anyone hovering over him.

"I am."

Harold glanced around before lowering onto the stool. He leaned forward and folded his arms on the table. "I am most pleased to have found you so quickly. Can you be ready to leave on the morn?"

An urgent matter, then. Of course, when men sought his services the matter was usually urgent.

"For the right price I can be ready to leave as soon as I finish my ale. Have you the right price?"

From the leather pouch tied to his belt, Harold dumped several coins onto the table—a mix of pennies and groats. Logan would wager they added up to nearly three shillings.

"This now, the remainder when your services are no longer required."

Nearly a full week's fee in advance? How unusual.

"How long might that be?"

"As long as needed for you to complete your task. Are you free to hire on?"

Logan took a sip of ale, debating the wisdom of engaging in battle while his leg yet hurt. Damn wounding had happened nigh on a fortnight ago and should stop bothering him soon, he hoped.

"What must I do?"

"Lynwood Manor is harried by a band of thieves. Her ladyship wishes you to dispatch them."

Ladyship. The hair on the back of Logan's neck prickled with warning. "You come at the behest of a woman?"

"Lady Joanna, widow of Sir Bertrand de Poitou."

Logan had no idea who either the lady or knight might be, but he didn't need to know. "Pick up your coins, Harold. I do not work for women, particularly widows. If you like, I can give you names of those foolish enough to do so."

Harold paled. "Her ladyship was most specific that I hire you."

"She does not get me. There are others—"

"Surely her coin is as good as any man's."

Logan glanced at the lovely silver on the table. The coin might be good, but not enticing enough to lure him into working for a woman, especially a widow. He'd done so once. Never again.

"I do not work for women."

Harold gave a resigned sigh, his chin hitting his chest. "These ruffians grow bold. The last time they raided the village, they not only stole a prize goose but injured several children. If they are not caught, the next time someone might be killed."

Logan suffered a brief, sharp pang of what felt oddly like sympathy, an emotion a man in his profession couldn't afford. Perversely, his curiosity prodded him to ask, "Children were hurt?"

Harold's chin rose slightly. "Aye, four of them, including Lady Joanna's daughter. Took seventeen stitches to close the gash on Ivy's little arm."

The wound on his thigh required only ten stitches to close up, and he could still feel the jab of the needle on each one. Seventeen stitches on one of tender age and skin . . . no matter, wounded children or no, he wasn't taking this job.

"Perhaps the lady should apply to her overlord or her family for aid."

Harold glanced away, hesitating before answering. "My lady prefers to resolve the matter herself, if she can."

Logan knew he'd been lied to or, at the least, not given the whole truth. There were deeper problems here. Or was the woman simply mule-stubborn?

Compared to some of his past feats, this might be an easy job. Hell, he might not even have to draw his sword. Too bad a woman was involved.

Harold picked up one of the groats and twirled it through his fingers. "Could we not come to a bargain?"

"Nay."

"Come with me to Lynwood Manor. Meet Lady Joanna. Judge for yourself the character of my lady and her need for your services." He put the coin back on the table. "Should you then decide you cannot accept her offer, these are still yours for your trouble."

Logan arched an eyebrow. "Does your Lady Joanna know you squander her coin so foolishly?"

Harold rose. "Think on it, Grimm. I will return on the morn for either you or the money."

Logan was sure he'd made his position clear. "I have decided. Take the damn coins with you!"

Harold bowed as he took a step back. "Until morn," he said, then nearly ran out of the inn.

Logan scooped up a handful of coins, resisting the urge to fling them at the fleeing captain. He'd not keep the money, of course, but give the coins to Hugo, let the innkeeper return them to Harold when he came back on the morn.

The coins warmed in Logan's fist.

What a foolish man, offering nearly a full week's wage to take a ride in the country, to this Lynwood Manor, wherever that might be.

Logan got up and adjusted the broadsword in the scabbard angled across his back. He should walk out to the stable and check on his horse. The poor beast had been confined to the inn's stable for several days, would likely welcome a long, hard ride.

Like a ride to Lynwood Manor.

He glanced around the taproom, at the men quaffing ale, at Abigail bustling about to keep the mugs full. He could either take that ride to Lynwood Manor or remain there—nursing his wound, spending his hard-earned money on ale and coarse bread and molding cheese.

Rotting on Abigail's stool.

Or he could earn some coin to tide him over until he was fully healed and able to take an offer more to his liking.

Mayhap in Harold's absence the thieves who stole

geese and wounded children had been caught. Perhaps the need for his services no longer existed.

And Harold claimed all Logan had to do to earn the coin was to meet Lady Joanna, not work for her. Mayhap he'd been too hasty, or more likely he'd simply lost his wits. Either way, Logan Grimm strode out of the Red Rooster, resigned to leaving on the morn to meet Lady Joanna of Lynwood Manor.

Chapter Two

The pleasant ride in the country turned into two wretched days of muddy roads and sodden cloaks. When they finally reached their destination, Logan noted the smattering of thatch-roofed huts comprising the village, with a church on one end and a timber palisade on the other. He rode across the notorious green in the center, where the thieves had wounded several children.

One villager braved the foul weather, a woman fetching water from the common well. She looked up as he passed by, her eyes going wide, then narrowing. Logan paid little heed to the usual reaction of surprise and disapproval at his arrival, just as he'd ignored scowls and censure many times before.

Mercenaries weren't welcomed by the common folk, and usually only tolerated by the lords who hired them. Such was the way of the world, and Logan had learned early on not to expect praise or thanks for doing his job. Satisfaction at his success and a hefty purse of glittering coins were all the approval he required.

Of course, in this instance, he would have to be content with the coins Harold had given him. Decent pay for doing nothing.

The woman at the well scurried toward one of the huts, and Logan turned his attention to the palisade. To his delight, a stream of smoke spiraled upward from within the pike-sharpened timbers, heralding a warming, drying fire in the manor's hearth.

Harold waved to the guard at the top of the palisade, who shouted down a command, and soon the gate swung wide. Logan followed the captain across the muddy bailey toward the door of a dreary, smallish manor house.

The place couldn't hold more than three large rooms, Logan judged. Perhaps four rooms if they were small. A solid dwelling, however. Built of the same sturdy timbers as the palisade. Someone had planned well for defense.

The now dead lord? Or a lord before . . . what had Harold said his lord's name was? Bernard? Bertrand?

The lady's name he remembered. Joanna. And the daughter, Ivy. Harold had mentioned them often enough over the past two days whenever a pause in the rain allowed them to talk. Not that Logan said much in return. Not even to chide the captain for apparently being enamored of his lady. Not good for the captain, but not Logan's problem.

He dismounted and handed the reins over to a stable lad in the bloom of his manhood, possessing enough height and muscle that he should have the strength to handle the stallion.

"Mind Gideon's rear hooves," Logan warned the lad. "If he proves unruly, come fetch me."

He couldn't tell if the lad was more wary of him or

awed by the beast, to which Logan owed his life several times over.

"Gideon." The lad ran an appreciative hand over the stallion's sleek chestnut hide. "Strange name for a horse, methinks."

In his travels with various armies, Logan had seen great sights and learned odd things. One had led to the name of his horse.

"In the language of the Jews, his name means great destroyer. Handle him wrongly and he will smash his stall to a heap of splinters."

"I will be mindful."

And he was. Logan watched the lad and horse head for the stable, the lad keeping a firm grip on the stallion's reins but at a respectful distance. Likely Gideon was as tired and in want of shelter and a meal as his master and wouldn't cause problems.

Logan turned toward the already open door of the manor, where Harold waited. Inviting light flickered from within. He pushed back his cloak's hood as he stepped inside, wanting no more than a stool by the fire, a mug of hearty ale, and a slab of meat.

A dozen or so people, male and female, young and old, soldiers and servants turned to stare. Logan knew he must look more a fright than usual, but did nothing to straighten his appearance. Let them stare. Let them be wary or frightened. They didn't want to befriend him, nor he them.

Mercenaries couldn't afford friendship.

Friends were for children to play with on village greens, for elders to trade stories with to pass the time. For people who remained in one place all their lives and weren't con-

cerned about facing someone with whom one had formed
a bond on a battlefield.

His perusal of the group stopped at the hearth, on a
little girl with golden hair and the widest deep blue eyes
he'd ever seen. A white bandage swaddling her forearm
identified her as Ivy, the daughter of Lady Joanna.

His leg wound twitched in sympathy with the seventeen stitches he knew lay beneath her bandaging.

"Is her ladyship about?" Harold asked of no one in
particular.

A soldier came forward. "Lady Joanna is in the village. The blacksmith's babe has decided to be born on
this miserable day."

Harold frowned. "Has she a guard with her?"

"Aye, sir. Two men went with her."

That the lady was guarded seemed to ease Harold's
worry. He proceeded to pluck off his riding gloves. "Inform her ladyship I have returned with Logan Grimm.
Pray tell her she need not rush on our account."

The soldier moved toward the door, and Harold gave
other orders, to someone named Maud for ale and hot
food, to a nearby lad to take their cloaks. All the while,
Logan tried not to stare at the little girl.

'Twasn't her beauty or knowing she hurt that held
his interest, but how restlessness plagued the girl. Ivy
squirmed a bit then went still, as if suddenly remembering someone had ordered her to stay on the stool near the
hearth.

As punishment? Or in deference to her wound? Either
way, she wanted to be up and doing whatever children
did to entertain themselves on a rainy day. He knew

nothing about children, less about female children, yet recognized restrained spirits when he saw them.

The compulsion to rescue the girl from her boredom nearly overcame his good sense. He'd come to Lynwood Manor to meet the Lady Joanna, that was all, and he had no business getting involved in what was none of his affair.

Even though Ivy looked at him without wariness, only curiosity. Even though the half smile she sent his way made him want to smile in return.

He didn't. Instead, he took a seat at a trestle table and relished the generously spiced stew and hearty ale set down before him by a serving wench. Next to him, Harold did the same.

"Do you find the meal to your liking?" the captain asked. Logan glanced sideways, wondering if Harold knew he was being so obvious. "One bowl of good stew is not enough to change my mind."

Nor was the fragrant bread, nor the smooth ale. Nor the heat of the fire or a little girl's smile.

Harold salted the stew that needed no salt. "Of course not. Nor do I expect you will succumb to her ladyship's apple tarts, though they are the most delectable confections in the kingdom."

"I cannot be swayed by food."

"Only money—so I hear."

"Not from a woman."

With a slight shrug, Harold turned back to his meal. To his chagrin, Logan began to wonder when the tarts would appear.

All around him, he could hear the manor folk stirring, their wariness waning. The women at the hearth once more applied spindle and distaff to wool. The soldiers resumed their dice game.

Logan sensed the serving girl's approach. He looked up when she set a tray of small tarts on the table. He should ignore them, just to show Harold he couldn't be influenced. But they looked tasty, and he couldn't remember the last time he'd eaten such treats.

'Twould be a shame to let them go to waste.

The tarts were warm, with the appealing aroma of apple, and a crust so tender it melted on his tongue. He fell deeply under their spell at first bite. He devoured the first one and was about to take a second when the hall's door opened.

Logan's hand paused in the air, observing the entrance of a goddess wrapped in a rich beaver cloak. Obviously gentry, she could be no other than Lady Joanna, and Logan struggled to keep his purely male reaction from becoming perceptible.

Wide eyes of soulful amber graced Joanna's heart-shaped face, her cheekbones artfully sculpted, the sharpness softened by a rounded chin. All crowned by hair the hue of spun gold. She removed her cloak with graceful hands, revealing an unadorned gown of gray, which hugged her beautifully molded curves.

A goddess, but a weary one, evident in the slight slump of her shoulders and the way she tilted her head as if stretching a too-tight muscle in her neck.

Then she spotted little Ivy running toward her, and her weariness vanished. She bent down to capture her daughter in a hug, the joy and contentment in her expression unmistakable.

"Is the babe born?" Ivy asked her mother.

"Aye." With an enchanting grin, Joanna announced to all, "A hefty boy! Neither mother nor babe suffered undue difficulty. Even Donald seems to have survived the ordeal."

A cheer went up, and Logan guessed several mugs of ale would be raised in celebration this night.

"Has the babe a name?" Ivy wanted to know.

"They have not decided on one as yet."

"When can I see him?"

"Perhaps on the morrow if the rain stops."

Ivy looked about to argue, but at her mother's upraised eyebrow, decided against it.

Logan almost smiled, remembering how his own mother quelled nearly every argument with a change of expression. She'd died several years earlier, but he could still envision how she looked the last time he saw her. She'd always hugged him, just as Joanna did with Ivy.

Harold rose, blocking Logan's view of the pair. 'Twas maddeningly tempting to shove the captain aside. Irked by the urge, he turned away and snatched up a second tart, which was as delectable as the first.

"My lady, if you would do us the honor?" Harold called out, waving toward the bench opposite them.

Logan knew he must rise and greet the lady with the courtesy due one of her rank. He didn't often come face-to-face with a lady. The lords who hired him didn't introduce him to their wives or daughters. But as the son of a soldier, Logan had spent his youth in the shadow of a castle and knew enough to bow and mind his manners.

Her footfalls landed steady and soft in the rushes, and damned if his heart didn't beat harder with the rhythm.

An unwelcome happenstance. Best get his refusal done so he could be on his way come first light.

Logan brushed stray crumbs from his tunic and ran his hands down the front of his breeches. All he must do was meet her, exchange a few pointless pleasantries, then turn down her offer. He stood, prepared to bow, and suffered another blow to his senses when Lady Joanna again entered his line of sight.

She halted at the end of the table, placing short-nailed fingertips on its edge. Her head would just tuck under his chin. Indeed, if she stood next to him, her shadow would become lost within his. And for all her beauty, for as straight as she now held her spine and squared her shoulders, she seemed almost fragile. Not in body, but in spirit. A harsh wind wouldn't knock her over, but a softly delivered censure might.

She glanced at him briefly, guessing who he was, giving no sign of what she thought of him. Most women were either attracted to or repelled by his great size and rough looks and didn't bother to hide their reactions. This one gave nothing away, and he had to admire the lady's restraint.

"You have returned earlier than I thought you would," she told Harold, her voice throaty, bringing to mind a hot summer breeze.

"Your directions were most accurate, my lady. I had no trouble finding the Red Rooster. Have the thieves struck since I left?"

"Nay." She tilted her head, dark humor glinting in her eyes. "Perhaps the weather has not been to their liking."

"Praise be, whatever the reason."

She looked at Logan fully then, those amber eyes binding him where he stood. "Well met, Logan Grimm."

He remembered his manners and bowed. "My lady."

"Harold has explained our problem with the thieves?"

"He has."

Satisfied, she waved a hand at the table. "Pray finish your meal. We can discuss your duties later."

Nay, he would get this done. No sense dragging the thing out.

"My lady, by your leave, we may as well speak now." He glanced at Harold, who frowned and held himself stiffly. Aye, the man would be in trouble for his wasteful ways, but that was the captain's problem. "As I told your captain, I cannot accept your offer. If you wish, I can give you names of other mercenaries who might."

She stared at him for a moment, then said, "Oh. I see." Except her expression said she didn't. "If you intended to refuse us, then why did you come to Lynwood?"

Logan wasn't one for noble gestures, but decided Harold should explain his own foolishness.

"You must ask your captain, Lady Joanna. 'Tis his tale to tell."

Having said all he intended, Logan sketched another slight bow, sat down and grabbed another apple tart, hoping Harold wasn't planning to have another.

Harold wished to speak privately, so Joanna led him over to the far corner. With crossed arms and pursed lips she listened to his account of what had transpired at the Red Rooster.

"I beg your forgiveness if I overstepped, my lady." Harold's apology sounded heartfelt. "But I could think of no other way to sway him. I assure you, if I did not believe he could be persuaded to stay, I would not have given him the coin."

That Harold took authority upon himself to spend her coin in such manner was irritating. That Harold thought Logan Grimm could be persuaded to accept the job . . . well, she wasn't sure she wanted to try.

Logan Grimm wasn't what she expected.

Granted, she'd never before seen the mercenary, only heard of him. From tales of his prowess she'd expected a tall, solidly built man, which he was. At least a head taller than she, with shoulders built to carry a broadsword on his back, and arms thick with the muscle necessary to wield the weapon with ease.

He dressed all in black. His shoulder-length hair and wide-set eyes matched his tunic, breeches, and boots, fitting her image of a fierce fighter. Even the depth of his voice, low and rough, and the cut of his jaw, square and solid, weren't surprising.

Yet, for all his dark clothing and great sword, there was something about Logan Grimm that didn't seem, well, mercenary. She'd expected to deal with a man whose appearance proclaimed him little better than an animal, a savage who understood only the language of money and didn't care how he earned it.

Perhaps it was the way Logan spoke, not as an uncouth barbarian but with some polish. His bow hadn't been awkward, but done with a grace worthy of men of higher rank. He wore no facial hair to speak of, merely a dark shadow easily explained by two days of travel. Joanna suspected that the next time she saw him the shadow would be gone, that intriguing jaw cleanly scraped, the olive-toned skin smooth to the touch.

But did she want to see him washed and clean-shaven and again experience a wholly unwelcome awareness in places she would rather not be aware of? Not good. Not good at all.

Perhaps she should accept his decision and send him on his way, consider the loss of the coin as small payment for having him gone. Except the thieves would surely return, and Logan Grimm could rid her of them if only he could be persuaded to stay.

"Did he say why he cares not to work for a woman?" she finally asked Harold.

"Grimm said only that he does not. I suspect he had a bad experience and allowed it to affect his judgment. Is it possible to offer him a greater fee?"

"Nay."

Though Harold seemed to expect further explanation, she withheld comment. The manor's financial affairs were none of his concern. A short silence later, he realized he'd overstepped and glanced down at the floor, then up again.

"Then we must convince Grimm to remain long enough to see for himself that you are neither wily nor unfair."

A grand compliment from the captain of the garrison. She could only hope the rest of Lynwood's people felt the same.

"How do you propose we stop him from leaving?"

Harold smiled wryly. "Get him so drunk he cannot raise his head from his pallet."

"That would be wily."

His smile faded. "I jest, milady."

"I know, but we have no time for jests. If the man truly does not wish to accept our offer, we cannot detain him against his will."

"Then we must make him want to stay." Harold glanced over to where Logan Grimm enjoyed yet another apple tart. "I believe we have already made strides. Good food and ale. We engage him in conversation, ensure he has a clean, thick pallet and warm blanket for the night. I do not think he has enjoyed those simple pleasures for some time."

Indeed, Grimm certainly enjoyed the tarts. Could such comforts influence a man of his ilk?

"We offer the same hospitality to all and sundry. Truly, a mercenary must be accustomed to a hard life. I cannot imagine a few comforts would influence him overmuch."

"Perhaps not usually, but I learned a few things from the Red Rooster's owner that make me believe otherwise."

To Joanna's raised eyebrow, Harold answered, "Hugo was quick to praise Logan Grimm and assure me I made no mistake in hiring the mercenary for whatever job I had in mind. He also informed me I should pay no heed to any tales I might hear of Grimm's infirmity."

She saw no sign of an infirmity. 'Struth, Logan Grimm seemed in the best of health and soundness of body. "What infirmity?"

"His left leg. He hides his pain well, but he limps at times. From what little the Red Rooster's owner told me, I gather he has a wound that heals slowly." Harold crossed his arms and rubbed at his chin. "Nor does he have another offer that prevents him from taking ours. If he can be persuaded you do not intend to cheat him, he may reconsider."

"You believe a woman tried to cheat him of his fee?"

"'Twould seem likely, given his profession."

Joanna followed Harold's logic. Logan Grimm could use a peaceful, comfortable place in which to heal, where he could also earn his fee while he did so. She needed someone to track down the thieves. Quickly. Before they could do more harm to the villagers. Before the funds she set aside to pay the mercenary were gone. Counting the money Harold handed over to Grimm, she could afford an added week at most.

"Will his injury affect his abilities?"

"I think not. He sits his horse well enough."

Joanna pondered her few options. She could either send the mercenary on his way or try this scheme of Harold's. 'Twas irksome to have her original plan disrupted, if not entirely thwarted.

She'd envisioned a much different series of events. Logan Grimm's arrival. His agreement to solve her problem with the thieves. His confidence that 'twould take him only a few days.

She certainly hadn't planned to provide a haven for a mercenary to regain his strength.

"Could not what you propose be taken as wily?" she asked, looking for some reason to devise yet another scheme.

"Perhaps, but I prefer to think of it as persuasion." Harold leaned toward her and lowered his voice. "'Twould also not be remiss if you showed Grimm a bit of attention, gave him a kind word or two."

Appalled, Joanna opened her mouth to tell Harold

exactly what she thought of his suggestion when she saw Ivy slide onto the bench across from Grimm.

The mercenary's eyes narrowed in a clear sign he didn't want company. Ivy, undaunted, merely smiled up at him.

"I am Ivy."

Joanna took a step to fetch her daughter, but the change in Grimm's expression stopped her cold.

"I am Logan," he said in a voice softer than she'd thought him capable of.

"I know," Ivy declared. "Have you had enough to eat?"

"Aye."

The girl and mercenary stared at each other for a moment, then Ivy shifted her attention to the last tart on the tray. Logan gave the tray a nudge toward Ivy, enough of an invitation to accept the offer she'd been hoping for. The little minx!

They said no more. Taking sips from his mug of ale, Logan studied Ivy as if she were foreign to his experience. Ivy, being Ivy, enjoyed the tart, her little legs swinging to and fro, smiling as she ate.

"My lady?"

Joanna took a steadying breath. Harold wanted a decision, and, sweet mercy, she truly had no choice. The thieves must be caught. She needed Logan Grimm.

"Find our guest a thick pallet for near the hearth."

Chapter Three

Joanna's stomach coiled tighter with each step back to where Ivy sat with Logan Grimm.

What was she supposed to say to the man who'd taken her money but now refused to help her? How did one persuade a mercenary to change his mind?

Harold thought Grimm merely needed a bit of cosseting and a few kind words to soften his stance. Given her experience with men, Joanna doubted Harold's conclusions. Both her brother and husband, once they'd made up their minds, refused to budge from a decision—no matter if they were wrong, no matter whom they harmed.

Joanna put her hand on Ivy's shoulder. Ivy looked up, her expression all bright innocence. A mother knew better than to believe such nonsense, especially after witnessing her child's ploy for a treat she should neither have slyly asked for nor received. But now was not the time to scold.

"Ivy, I believe you have lessons to attend."

Innocence faded to a pout. "Wool makes my hands itch."

Joanna crossed her arms and remained silent. With an aggrieved sigh Ivy relented, sliding off the bench to return to the hearth, where she picked up a distaff.

Now alone with Grimm, Joanna eased onto the bench across from him, wishing he could be swayed to her will as easily as her daughter.

Grimm's eyes reflected the black of midnight, that foreboding and dangerous time when demons haunted her dreams and wrought havoc with her sleep. When terrors prodded her from her bedchamber either to look in on Ivy in the nursery or pace the manor's hall.

Of late, too often the faces of the thieves appeared in her night terrors. The goose on the tip of the lance cried out to be saved, inflaming her anger, mocking her inability to deal effectively with the manor's problems.

Before her sat her current problem. Grimm looked at her much the same way he'd studied Ivy, as if he didn't know what to expect. She might need his service, but couldn't bring herself to beg. Joanna saw no other way to deal with him than with courteous directness.

"Harold informs me you refuse my offer because you are reluctant to work for a woman. Perhaps if I knew why, I could put your mind at rest about working for me."

He neither changed expression nor moved an inch.

"Harold informs you correctly. As I told you, I can give you the names of other mercenaries who might be willing."

"Perhaps we could arrange for you to take your orders from Harold. Would that suit you?"

Grimm leaned forward. Joanna resisted the urge to lean back.

"From whose coffer does payment come? Harold's?"

"Nay, but—"

He waved a dismissive hand. "Then no matter who gives me orders, I would be beholden to you for payment. Nay, my lady. I am no longer so foolish."

Stubborn man.

Joanna remembered one of Harold's comments. "I gather a woman tried to cheat you of your fee. I can assure you I would not."

She saw a flash of hurt mingled with anger, his reaction quickly masked. Something more serious had occurred between Grimm and the woman than a dispute over his fee.

"Do you want those other names or no?" he asked, a hint of exasperation in his tone.

Joanna reined in her curiosity over his dealings with the other woman. 'Twas truly none of her affair, and he would no longer tolerate her prying. Grimm wasn't about to budge from his stance. She'd made the attempt to change his mind and failed.

Strange, she should be relieved, but not too surprising given the odd fluttering in her stomach when confronted with those midnight eyes. Grimm was simply too big and too forceful for her to feel comfortable around him, much less in control. Best she hire a different mercenary, one over whom she could exert more power.

"Is there a mercenary you would recommend above others?"

Grimm nodded, his dark hair shimmering raven blue in the glow of the hearth. "Conrad Falke."

The name sounded harsh, and familiar.

"Where might Harold find him?"

"When not in someone's service, he resides in Oxford."

Three days' ride away. 'Twould take more than a sennight for Falke to arrive if he could be found quickly. Not good. And the familiarity of Falke's name nagged at her and must have shown in her expression.

"Perhaps you know of him, too. His services are sought *nearly* as often as mine."

Grimm's boast amused her. He might think highly of Falke, but not *too* highly.

"Perhaps," she allowed. "Likely I heard of Falke in the same place I heard of you. Several years ago, during my father's last days, he often called his knights and favored men-at-arms to gather in the hall to recall past adventures. Many tales involved fighting in battles together, of those men they fought with and the spoils taken."

"Who was your father?"

"Sir John Swithe."

Grimm tilted his head, thinking. "I do not recall the name. Where might we have met?"

Joanna delved into her memories. At the time, she'd been relegated to the hearth with her mother and the other ladies. She would rather have curled up at her father's feet, where she could clearly hear each story instead of catching mere pieces of the tales.

"As I remember, my father told of a great sea battle between England and France. Perhaps you were on the same ship?"

"How long ago?"

"My father died nigh on eight years ago, so . . . I would guess at least nine or ten years. He spoke of admiring your willingness to be first among the men who boarded enemy ships, of how fiercely and accurately you wielded a sword."

Grimm gazed off into the distance, likely delving into his own memories. When his attention again returned to her, she sensed confused amusement.

"My lady, if what you tell me is correct, your father likely spoke of the Battle of Sluys. 'Twas, indeed, a great naval battle between England and France. Unfortunately, your father's memory must have been faulty in his last days, for I was not there."

"Not there?"

"I spent my twentieth summer in Italy, and only heard of the battle when I returned to England—two years later."

"But I remember—"

Or did she? Her father's mind hadn't suffered. He'd retained his keen wits up to the very end. Which meant *her* memory might be faulty. An unpleasant thought.

By the rood, had she made a grave error?

"Have you fought with the king's army in Scotland?"

"A time or two."

More sure of herself, Joanna related a tale as she remembered it. "Then might you be the one whom the king sent to locate a band of the enemy, and managed to rout ten men . . . nay, that was Conrad Falke, was it not?"

Grimm shifted on his seat. "'Tis possible."

Well, at least she now knew why Falke's name sounded familiar. And she was glad the mercenary currently in her hall hadn't performed that particular feat. The tale had been so vicious and bloody.

"Then did you force a line of pikemen to stand firm against a charge of mounted knights?"

Grimm scoffed. "I fight mounted, not among pike-men."

Now she'd truly offended him. Frustrated, Joanna tossed a hand in the air. "I may have only been ten-and-three at the time, but I clearly remember your name mentioned. What might you have done worthy of a tale in my father's hall?"

Grimm's eyes narrowed. "I can hardly answer without either knowing your father or where in the kingdom, or on the Continent for that matter, we might have fought together."

He had the right of it. She couldn't expect Grimm to know what had been said about him in her father's hall. But she should know, and the not knowing bothered her. She definitely remembered hearing his name. How irksome to be unable to recall whatever feat he'd performed to make her think Grimm the mercenary she needed to rout the thieves.

Not that it mattered. Grimm wasn't staying anyway. Still, 'twould probably nag at her half the night if she couldn't put name and feat together.

The hall's door opened. Wat Reeve entered on a gust of wind, spotting her as he struggled to close the door behind him. He wasted no time crossing the length of the hall.

Naturally, he'd heard about Grimm's arrival in the same manner she had. Margaret Atbridge had been fetching water when Harold and Grimm rode through the village, and immediately rushed to the blacksmith's to inform Joanna, who had little doubt Margaret had spread the news farther despite the nasty weather.

Wat honored her with a slight bow. "My lady, I understand the mercenary has arrived."

Joanna noticed the slight emphasis and disapproval on the word *mercenary*. If Grimm noticed, he gave no sign.

All the while Harold was off in London fetching Grimm, Wat had continued to voice his disapproval of her plan to hire a mercenary until she'd finally ordered him to silence on the subject. 'Twas irritating Wat would get his way, though not in the manner he expected.

She nodded toward Grimm, as if Wat hadn't already guessed who sat across from her. "This is Logan Grimm. I am sure you will be pleased to hear he has refused our offer."

Wat's relief was visible. Grimm arched an eyebrow. What the mercenary's thoughts were, Joanna couldn't imagine.

"Do tell." Wat's smile widened. "That does settle our dispute, does it not?"

Joanna tamped down her ire at the reeve for nearly gloating.

"Nay, it does not. Grimm will give us names of other mercenaries who might be available to rid us of the thieves. Just because one mercenary has refused me does not mean my plan has changed."

His delight vanished. "Verily, my lady, on behalf of the villagers I must again protest this plan. Men of Grimm's ilk are not to be tolerated among decent, God-fearing people."

Grimm's eyebrow arched higher, and Joanna's cheeks warmed with embarrassment. How dare the reeve insult any guest, welcome or not, in her hall?

"You will refrain from voicing your opinions before

our guest. Nor do I intend to argue the subject further. If you have no other business in the manor, you may return to your own hearth."

As Wat's spine stiffened, Joanna noticed the absolute silence in the hall. Whatever Wat said would be heard by all.

To his credit, and her great relief, he relented with a brief bow. "I have no further business, my lady. I will see you on the morrow in the southmost field."

He left as he came, hurriedly, letting in the cold and rain while the door stood open. In those brief moments she judged the weather had worsened, the increased dreariness keeping pace with her mood.

Joanna rose, wondering why nearly every man she dealt with of late possessed a contrary nature. Why couldn't just one be agreeable? Well, Harold had been reasonable. Too free with her money, but usually reasonable.

"I asked Harold to find you a comfortable pallet for the night. I would be grateful if you would give Harold the names and direction of any mercenaries you deem suitable. You are, of course, welcome to break your fast with us before you leave on the morn."

Logan lay on a thick, comfortable pallet stretched out in front of the hearth, huddled under a soft, vermin-free blanket. His stomach full, the taste of tart apple yet lingered on his tongue. His leg bothered him some, but not overly, especially considering how much time he'd spent on a horse—in the cold and wet—over the past two days.

He wasn't alone in the hall. Five others, all servants,

also occupied pallets scattered about. All slept. A couple snored.

Despite the noise he should be able to sleep. Experienced fighting men learned early to sleep whenever the opportunity arose. Except his eyes refused to close and his thoughts defied settling.

A man of his ilk, indeed.

In all his years he'd never been heralded as a savior. However, he'd never before been so blatantly proclaimed unfit to mingle in decent company.

The reeve's voiced opinion had left Logan speechless and frozen to the bench—a rare happenstance. He'd done no more than lift a brow. But then, what could he say in his defense? He *was* a mercenary, spilled other men's blood as his livelihood. He had no permanent home, no binding ties to anyone or anyplace. Nor did he want either home or ties.

Which hardly excused the reeve's insolence. By the time Logan thought to take Wat to task, Joanna had firmly censured the man for his lack of manners and sent him on his way.

The lady surprised him.

From the moment she sat across from him, their talk hadn't gone as he expected. He'd anticipated pleas of sympathy to her plight or cajoling intended to lead him to change his mind. He'd heard neither.

Nor did she flirt, or toss a fit, or make inane promises.

He admitted he liked the lady's approach. Direct. Presenting options. All done without rancor, or worse, tears.

Her relating of the tales she heard in her father's hall bothered him, however. Joanna might know of Logan Grimm, but couldn't remember why. By the time she'd finished, he had the niggling sense she felt she'd tried to hire the wrong mercenary.

Try as he might, he couldn't remember meeting her father, Sir John Swithe. Perhaps before leaving Lynwood he could ask Joanna the identity of her father's overlord. Having fought for or against nearly every earl and baron in the kingdom, he might make a connection that way, prodding Joanna's memory of which tale about him she'd heard.

He'd hate to leave the lady thinking she'd made a mistake in trying to hire him. He *was* the most highly regarded mercenary in the kingdom. Unfortunately for Joanna, she hadn't known he didn't work for women. Especially beautiful widows.

Too bad Joanna qualified on both counts.

Logan rolled over, trying not to think about the widow who'd ruined him for all others. Celeste had drawn him into her web with heady enticements of wealth and love, and he'd nearly paid for his lack of foresight with his life. Verily, perhaps not all women were as conniving and deceitful as Celeste, but why take the risk with Joanna?

He couldn't deny his attraction to the lady. She might profess her honesty, but he couldn't be sure of her. 'Twas too similar a circumstance for his liking. 'Struth, his profession provided enough hazards to life and limb without inviting hurt and heartbreak.

Nay, he'd not take this offer. He'd given Harold the names of three mercenaries, any of whom could help Joanna. And if the damn reeve thought Logan unfit for decent company, wait until one of the others crossed the threshold. If Wat found Logan Grimm unfit to grace

Lynwood Manor's hall, he would be twice as appalled at Conrad Falke.

Actually, for Joanna's sake, he should probably tell Harold not to contact Falke. The man could be as mean as a boar. All sword and no polish. Even his fellow mercenaries sometimes avoided his company.

All right, so perhaps he was miffed that Joanna could put Falke's name to a tale but not his. It shouldn't matter. After all, she'd only been ten-and-three. A young girl who should have been more concerned with the neatness of her embroidery stitches than in tales of bloody battles and the names of mercenaries.

The creak of a door ended Logan's musings. Each of his senses heightened, his hand eased toward the hilt of the sword that lay beside his pallet. Then he went still, his eyes narrowing to mere slits.

Joanna's head poked through her bedchamber's doorway. She glanced about, skimming over those sleeping in the hall. He could almost feel her pause on him before passing over. After a few moments, she emerged and closed the door behind her.

She wore a loose-fitting nightrail, no veil, her golden hair down and flowing around her shoulders. An ethereal vision of delicate, angelic grace and beauty.

To his irritation, his loins stirred, reacting to lustful thoughts he shouldn't be having.

A few light steps on bare feet took her to the ale barrel, where Joanna ladled a healthy measure into a mug before easing onto a nearby bench.

She took two sips before she put the mug on the table, crossed her arms in front of her, and put her head down.

Logan knew he should ignore Joanna, close his eyes

tight, and not ponder what demons kept the lady from sleep.

Except his curiosity plagued him until he quietly slipped on his breeches and linen tunic. Joanna didn't look up until she heard him pouring ale into a mug.

Wariness stiffened her shoulders. She touched her uncovered hair, a self-conscious gesture that told him few people ever saw her thus, much less a stranger, never an unworthy mercenary.

Again she glanced about at those sleeping in the hall. Hoping they wouldn't wake, or wishing someone would leap up and save her? As if approaching a skittish horse, he took his time to reach the table, put down his ale, and eased onto the bench beside her. All the while she watched him with wide amber eyes, but he saw no sign that she might bolt. Several seconds passed before the tension eased from her shoulders.

"Is your pallet not comfortable?" she finally asked, in a hushed but clear voice.

"Perhaps too comfortable. I am used to hard cots and harder ground. What keeps you from slumber?"

"Too much on my mind."

"Thieves?"

"Among other problems."

Logan decided not to ask about other problems, knowing his refusal to help her counted among them. Bad enough he inquired about the one he knew of. "How long have they harried the village?"

"Nigh on a fortnight. Four days have passed since their last raid. I would like to believe they have moved on, but I doubt we are so fortunate."

Logan agreed with her conjecture.

"Apparently you have been easy prey. So long as you remain so, they will not leave."

"So I guessed." She waved a dismissive hand. "I came out here because I did not want to think about them anymore. Tell me, will you go back to London?"

Back to a stool at the Red Rooster. Drink Abigail's ale. Wait for another offer. Perhaps some lord requiring his services had contacted Hugh already. Logan dearly hoped so.

"Aye."

"Do you like being a mercenary?"

Like? He'd never had much choice. But Joanna didn't want to hear his life's story, was merely filling the night with questions so she could forget her problems.

"Well enough. I am free to do as I please. The pay is good, the companions usually agreeable."

She sighed, her mouth going soft with a smile. "How lovely to do as one pleases all the time. To have no responsibilities for anyone but yourself." Her smile faded, and Logan felt its loss. "Do not misunderstand. I do not complain. Our life here is good on the whole."

Except life hadn't been good for her for several months.

"Harold said Lynwood suffered badly with the plague."

"True enough. I lost two children . . . and my husband. Others lost more." She shook her head, as if in disbelief. "One would think a mere band of thieves not so threatening after all else we have suffered. But once the whoresons are dealt with, then we can truly get on with our lives."

Logan almost smiled at her rough language, but refrained out of respect for her plight. An uncomfortable twinge of guilt made him uneasy. He was supposed to have been the solution to her most urgent problem, and here he sat, swilling her ale, unwilling to give her a glimmer of hope.

Nay, he wasn't about to accept her offer, but he could give her a bit of aid. What was it about Joanna that softened his stance when he shouldn't? Her courage and determination? The lateness of the hour and a mug of heady ale? Damned if he knew.

"I cannot stay, but before I leave, perhaps I can give Harold suggestions on how to track down your thieves."

She tilted her head, studying him, wary again. "At what cost does this advice come?"

"Consider it paid for."

"Generous of you."

Aye it was, and he wasn't a generous man. But doing her this small favor would allow him to leave on the morrow with a clear conscience.

Joanna yawned, covering her lush lips with dainty fingers. The small action tossed his thoughts back to the lusty images he suffered when she'd come out of her bedchamber.

"Perhaps I can sleep now," she murmured.

So should he if he wanted an early start back to London. He got up and held out his hand to help her rise from the bench. For a long moment she stared at his outstretched show of gallantry—he *did* know his manners—before accepting.

Logan regretted the gesture as her palm slid across his.

Soft heat rippled through him, warming his nether regions. A natural reaction, Logan supposed, to a beautiful woman's touch, especially given his renewed rush of lust.

Long months had passed since he'd run his hands over a woman's supple curves, tasted the honey of a lush mouth, or burrowed into a slick sheath. Willing wenches were easy enough to come by, but for some reason he'd refrained from quick tumbles of late. A mistake. Not satisfying lusty urges had left him vulnerable to an unsuitable woman's charms.

Joanna's hand might be cool, but the flush on her cheeks told him she felt more than gallantry in their contact, too.

Were Joanna's nights long and cold now that her husband no longer lay beside her? Did she miss having a male in her bed to curl up to in the hours before dawn?

Foolish thoughts. He should let go of her hand, send Joanna back to her bedchamber—alone. He ran his thumb over her knuckles. Smooth, soft skin. Long fingers tipped by short nails. Was the tremor he felt his or hers?

"Grimm?"

A breathy utterance. An admonition? An invitation?

Ye gods, nothing she said or did suggested she'd come into the hall with seduction in mind. Yet here he stood, spellbound, too damn willing to follow Joanna's lead if she suggested a tumble in the blankets.

He looked deep into her glittering amber eyes—and saw a flash of fear, quickly masked, but fear nonetheless. By the saints! He'd never intentionally harmed a woman. Skewered a few men, aye, but not injured women.

She'd not seemed overly threatened that afternoon, either by his size or reputation. But then there had been other people bustling around, and a table between them as they'd talked. Now, alone, in the deep of night, Joanna in a slip of a gown and her hand in his, she felt more than uneasy.

And perhaps, given the circumstances, her fear was healthy.

Slowly, he slipped his hand from beneath Joanna's, then took two steps back, removing himself from between her and the bedchamber door. Only when he saw her breasts rise and fall—and no matter how hard he tried he couldn't help but admire the generous mounds barely veiled by her gown—did he realize she'd also held her breath.

He'd done nothing wrong, merely been polite. So why did he feel like an utter bastard?

"My thanks, Grimm. I truly appreciate any advice you can impart to Harold."

Joanna's half-hearted smile didn't make him feel better, but since she didn't appear ready to bolt, he was reluctant to let her go just yet. One question still preyed on his mind.

"Then I am glad to be of service. Tell me, milady, did you happen to remember what tale you heard told of me?"

She shook her head, the smile fading. "Nay. I thought my memory sharp, but I fear I have confused you with Conrad Falke. 'Tis disconcerting, knowing I sent Harold to hire the wrong mercenary."

'Twas more than disconcerting to hear her admit the mistake.

"Perhaps you will yet remember."

She shrugged a shoulder. "'Tis not really important now, is it? You will be gone in a few hours."

"Nay, not important. I am merely curious." He should let it go, but ye gods, to be confused for Falke! "Who was your father's overlord?"

"The earl of Gloucester."

An earl he'd once known, and once fought for. But that had been five years ago, before the earl's death, and too late for any tale Joanna might have heard. Whatever tale she didn't now remember must be from the early years of his profession, when he was no more than ten-and-eight.

For a moment, he considered recounting an exploit or two to shake up her memory. But then she said, "Sleep well," and turned toward her bedchamber.

Abandoned to his senseless curiosity, Logan stood still for a few moments after Joanna closed the door behind her, wishing he'd followed his instincts and pretended to be asleep.

Could she have been more stupid?

Joanna flung the coverlet over her, more to hide under than for warmth. After a moment of unease at being caught in a state of undress, she'd allowed herself to become comfortable in Logan's company.

She'd forgotten he was a mercenary. Worse, she'd forgotten he was a big healthy male. Sweet mercy, he'd proved so easy to talk to she neglected to remember how dangerous a big male could be. Especially in the middle of the night.

Joanna shivered at the memory of other nights, of a husband who lured her into complacency with apologies and assurances, only to use her, hurt her. In the seven months since Bertrand's death the bruises had disappeared, but the deeper wounds to her heart and soul hadn't yet healed.

Her confidence had suffered most, she knew. On occasion, if she allowed Bertrand's voice to intrude, she could hear his derision over a wrongly spiced dish, his sneer over a mislaid mug, his mocking wonder that any woman could make so many mistakes within the course of a day.

In bed, she could do nothing to suit him, so she'd ceased trying. She'd followed his every direction as swiftly and efficiently as possible, never daring to protest when he caused her pain or revulsion.

And yet, tonight, she'd trustingly put her hand in Logan's and felt the heat of what could only be described as attraction. A surprising, unwanted, and dangerous appeal. Which could only bring her trouble. Luckily, she'd felt a ridge of callus on his sword hand to remind her of Logan Grimm's violent profession, bringing her back to her senses.

While she realized he'd gallantly offered his hand to help her rise from the bench, with no intent to seduce or hurt her, she also now knew she shouldn't have complied.

Joanna thanked every deity and saint she could think of that Logan Grimm was leaving on the morn. Such complete abandonment of her good sense must never happen again.

Chapter Four

With a sharp jerk, Logan tightened Gideon's girth strap, preparing to ride with Harold. A short ride this time, down to the riverbank to see where the thieves' trail vanished and advise Harold on how to proceed. From there, he'd be on his way back to London, which he now regretted leaving.

Nothing could have dragged him from his table at the Red Rooster if he'd believed for one moment he would be intrigued by the situation with the thieves. Worse, it irked him he'd made this concession, all because he'd also developed an unhealthy, unwanted admiration for the lovely widow.

He'd not seen Joanna this morn. He'd overheard from the manor folk that she'd left early to meet the insolent reeve in some field, to discuss the planting of some crop. With her she'd taken Ivy, a large basket, and two guards.

Why so early? The twist in his gut said she'd done so purposely to avoid him. Probably just as well, given the events of the night before. Joanna was likely embarrassed, and he would be uncomfortable.

Still, it bothered him that he'd slept through their leaving. Joanna and Ivy must have passed by his pallet on their way to the door, and he'd not heard them depart. Normally he woke at the least noise.

Must have been the heady ale that put him so far under—an excuse he didn't give much credence to but accepted because he didn't want to believe any other.

"I truly appreciate your assistance," Harold said from beside him. "Perhaps you will notice some small sign we missed."

Logan eased his foot into the stirrup, mindful not to wince in front of Harold and the stable lad. That his thigh should hurt like the devil this morn when it hadn't pained him the previous eve was more than annoying. Hefting upward cost him dearly.

"How your thieves can vanish intrigues me."

Harold swung up onto his horse with enviable ease. "'Tis a puzzle we have not been able to solve, and I cannot tell you how much that irritates me. Ready?"

"Lead on."

Logan followed Harold out the gate, allowing himself a small smile over Harold's irritation. They'd talked about the villains over a meal of creamy yellow cheese, fragrant, nearly white bread, and spiced mead. As it turned out, the captain didn't need advice on tracking. Problem was the horses' tracks ended abruptly, as if a heavenly hand reached down and plucked them from the earth.

Impossible, of course.

They passed over the open field beyond the manor and

entered the woodland. Resolved not to dwell upon how his last memory of Joanna would be of her gowned in flowing white and bathed in the soft glow of hearth light, Logan leaned over to inspect the path Harold claimed the thieves used to reach the river. Even now, several days and some rainfall after their raid on the village, Logan noted signs of their passage.

"Three horses?" he asked Harold.

"Aye. We know there are at least three."

"You suspect more?"

Harold paused before he answered. "I have no proof. We know for certain of the three who made the daylight raid on the village. My instincts insist there may be one or more others involved."

Logan knew about instincts, which had saved him from grief several times over. He always listened to the niggling voice in his head, or paid heed to the tightening of his gut. At times the warnings proved false, but more often than not they proved their worth.

"How so?"

"Because of the way of their escape. I suspect someone is covering up their trail, perhaps even giving them shelter. If they are nearby, camped somewhere in the forest, we should have found them by now. We have seen no sign of trespass other than what you see here."

Logan again looked down at the trail. "What of nearby villages? Have the thieves harassed them, too?"

"No villages, merely hamlets, and no, not a one has been harassed as we have." A touch of anger and frustration colored Harold's words. "After the first raid, we sent messengers to everyone within a half day's ride. Naturally, we told them to have a care along with asking them to alert us if they spotted the bastards. In all this time, not so much as a feather has gone missing elsewhere."

"You believe you can trust your neighbors?"

"We have in the past. Lynwood Manor is the largest holding in the area and the only one with a defensive palisade. In times of upheaval, they look to us for protection. 'Twould be to their advantage to cooperate, especially since we are all beholden to the same overlord."

At the mention of an overlord, Logan remembered a suggestion he'd made to Harold at the Red Rooster.

"I am still of the opinion that Lady Joanna should appeal to Lynwood's overlord."

Harold sighed. "Truth to tell, she did, and the result was unsatisfactory. All the abbot did was send us a priest to replace the one we lost during the plague. Father Arthur has been of no aid in capturing our villains."

Logan scoffed. "What did your abbot expect the priest to do? Pray that the thieves might repent their ways and promise to sin no more?"

Harold reined in his horse and looked over his shoulder. "I gather you have little use for priests."

Logan believed in the Lord, often invoked his aid when in dire straits. He never looted churches or abbeys, though he knew of men who'd become wealthy selling off those prized spoils of war. Jewel-encrusted chalices and beautifully sculpted statues taken as booty out of France had no trouble finding new homes in the castles and abbeys of England.

"Priests have their uses; but as you said, unless a cleric is willing to put a weapon in his hand and his backside on a horse to give chase, he is of little threat against villains." Logan leaned forward. "You also mentioned her ladyship's unwillingness to appeal to family. Surely they would be of more help."

Harold shook his head. "Lady Joanna believes she can expect no better response from either her brother or Sir Bertrand's family. She insists we must rely upon ourselves to deal with these villains."

With that, the captain urged his horse forward. Logan followed, trying not to feel too much sympathy for the lady's plight. After all, in his way, he was doing her a service by further looking over the situation—far more than he'd intended to do.

All about him stood tall oaks, sharing the woodland with beech and ash, their leaves rustling in the breeze flirting with the treetops. The air held the freshness of early summer, mingling with the heavy odor of old, damp earth. From in the distance he could hear the river bubble along its course.

Hares scooted along the forest floor. Squirrels chattered their displeasure at the human invasion of their territory. He wouldn't be surprised to see a doe with her fawn amble by.

So peaceful. Tranquil.

The one thing lacking to make the day perfect was sunshine, but the overcast sky foretold of more rain. Logan shifted in the saddle in a futile effort to ease the pain in his thigh, discomfited by the possibility of a wet, cold ride to London.

They reined in on the bank of a small, active river.

"The villains entered here." Harold frowned, looking down at where hoofprints ended at river's edge. "Certes, they must come out someplace but we have not been able to discover where."

Logan glanced up and down the river, noting how the shallow water swirled around rocks and jutting tree roots. On the other side of the river the bank was higher, making it hard but not impossible for horses to climb out. However, the trees grew too closely together for a horse and rider to get through easily. The thieves must have ridden either up- or downstream before coming out. Not an easy feat given the obstacles in the river.

He glanced downriver, judging it the easier course. "How far could they go before being forced onto land?"

"Almost a league, just before the waterfall." Harold tossed a hand in the opposite direction. "They could get a bit farther the other way, but not much. My men and I have searched both ways but found no trace of them."

"Have you made land searches?"

"We have on this side, but not as thoroughly on the other. I have not enough men both to guard the manor properly and conduct as complete a search as is necessary. That is why her ladyship wishes to hire . . . a mercenary, someone capable of both finding and capturing the thieves with little help on our part."

Logan didn't miss the hesitation, or Harold's unspoken accusation.

You were supposed to be that mercenary.

He quickly squelched another pang of guilt and tamped down hard on the thought that this job would be so easy to do.

And Lord have mercy, the puzzle intrigued him. The thieves had to come out of the river someplace; it was just a matter of discovering where, then tracking them.

"You said you sent messengers to those hamlets

within a half day's ride. Do any of them also share this river?"

"Two. The closest is downriver, at the waterfall. The other is upstream nigh on two leagues, on the opposite bank."

"And the others?"

"Scattered about the countryside. I have a map of the shire if you wish to see it."

He shouldn't. He should tell Harold to direct his search toward the area near the waterfall, because that's where Logan's instincts urged him to go first.

Except Harold wouldn't be leading the search for villains if Lady Joanna sent her captain off to hire another mercenary. No matter which of the mercenaries she chose to hire, 'twould take Harold several days to complete the task. The villains could do a lot of damage within that time.

Nor would Logan's curiosity cease nagging at him over why three men on horseback raided Lynwood and not the hamlets, or how they managed to leave a clear trail into the river and no trail at all out.

Logan glanced up at the sky. Definitely looked like rain. Already his thigh ached as if he'd been in the saddle for hours.

Tomorrow might be the better day to travel.

He dismissed as unimportant that if he remained at Lynwood Manor one more night, he would again sleep on a comfortable pallet, savor the quality of the victuals, and possibly enjoy the company of the intriguing Lady Joanna.

* * *

Logan Grimm wasn't supposed to be in her hall, bent over a map spread out on a trestle table. Nor was he supposed to glance up as she removed her cloak, catching her staring at him.

To her chagrin, Joanna couldn't look away.

By the rood, his appearance had improved yet again. Last night she'd thought him a devilishly handsome man. Now he appeared the devil himself, temptation incarnate.

His combed hair was pulled back and tied with a thin strip of leather, revealing the full width and height of his brow, bringing his midnight eyes into prominence. He'd also scraped off his facial hair, baring the sharp, bold set of his jawline.

'Twasn't fair he was still here, prodding forth wanton thoughts she shouldn't be thinking, stirring life into places she'd rather not have disturbed. She'd certainly given Logan enough time this morn to rise, eat, and leave. Obviously, something had happened to delay his departure.

"Ye want me to take those, milady?" Maud asked.

Joanna tore her gaze from Logan's. Chagrined that he'd held her attention for so long, she handed over her cloak and the basket of wild garlic and mushrooms.

"My thanks, Maud. Not many mushrooms this time. We shall have to do without them soon."

Maud glanced at the door. "Where be Ivy?"

"She wanted to see the babe, so I left her at the smith's." Joanna smiled, thinking of the awe on her daughter's face when counting tiny toes. "Donald will bring Ivy back when he comes to deliver the kettle I asked him to mend."

Maud smiled back. "Ye been busy this morn."

Purposely busy, finding as many errands to do as she could to keep her away from the manor until after Logan left. All for naught. But the time wasn't wasted, and if Logan's continued presence meant progress toward the thieves' capture, then she would manage to deal with her unruly reaction to him, too.

"I also saw Wat in the fields this morn. He will be here for nooning."

Their meeting yet bothered her. Wat should know how many sacks of wheat seed were needed to sow the demesne fields, as his father had known, without consulting the ledger. He should also have told her earlier that there was *no* wheat seed in the barn for the late-summer planting. Or was she being too harsh, expecting too much? Thus far, Wat had proved most dependable.

Maud gave an undignified snort. "Eating here again, is he? Is Wat hoarding his victuals, or can he not stomach the taste of his own cooking?"

"Now, Maud. If given the choice of eating your stew or mine own, I would also choose yours."

The praise tinted the woman's age-wizened face rosy, a sight Joanna thought delightful. In the years since she'd come here as a bride, Joanna couldn't remember ever seeing Maud blush.

"Aye, well." Maud cleared her throat and rearranged the garlic in the basket. "I shall have to add a bit more meat to the stew then, what with Wat being here, too. I was hoping Harold might bring us back a brace of rabbits this morn"—Maud tossed her head toward Logan—"but all he returned with was that one."

Meaning Logan, and Maud didn't approve. Because

Logan was a mercenary, or was there something else about the man she disliked?

Joanna decided not to ask. What Maud thought of Logan didn't matter. Besides, the mercenary would be gone soon enough.

"Where is Harold?"

"Said somewhat about fetching another map." Maud turned and took a step toward the hearth, then stopped— and sighed. "I suppose Donald will expect to be fed, too."

Joanna hid a smile. "Considering that he mends the kettles, 'tis the least we can do, I should think."

"Aye, one supposes."

Maud waddled off, and Joanna took a long breath, mustering her courage. If Harold and Logan were discussing where to search for thieves, which seemed a sensible reason for looking at maps, she wanted to know of their plan. And since Harold wasn't there, she'd have to ask Logan.

Or she could wait until Harold returned.

Coward.

Logan studied the map again, no longer stared at her. All the while she crossed the distance to the table, she hoped he wouldn't look up. If she avoided getting too close to him, or becoming entranced by his midnight eyes, her stomach might not flutter or her pulse beat too rapidly.

She halted a bit more than an arm's length away, close enough to see the map of the shire and, damn, just close enough to catch the scent of leather and horse and male.

"My lady."

A soft greeting in his rumbling voice. She'd neglected

to remember its deep timbre and how it thrummed. Sweet mercy.

"Grimm." She waved toward the map. "Is this part of your advising Harold?"

"Nay, 'tis Harold advising me."

The admission surprised her, and she had to force herself not to look up from the map.

"Truly? Why so?"

She heard a resigned sigh.

"Your vanishing thieves have me curious."

Curious enough for Logan to agree to stay and hunt them down? Given her vexing reaction to him, did she want him to?

Aye. She'd already paid him hard coin, and ridding Lynwood of the villains must overrule her troublesome response to his very presence.

Hopeful, she asked, "So why the map?"

Logan's right hand came into view. The same hand into which she'd placed hers last eve. Large, strong, nicked, and callused. Long fingers, short nails. The hand of a warrior. A hand to be avoided.

He pointed to a spot on the map. "This is where the thieves enter the river after leaving the village. Since all the tracks on the path lead the same way, we must assume they used a different route to begin their raid." He traced the river to the waterfall. "I am inclined to believe they came out of the river near here. So what we look for now are likely hiding places in this area."

His now splayed fingers covered a large area of dense woodland, and saints above, she was having a hard time following his explanation, too focused on the scar at the base of Logan's thumb.

Someone had slipped past Logan's guard. With a sword or a dagger? Who? And in what battle? How long ago?

By the rood! She must stop allowing her thoughts to roam where they had no business wandering. Logan likely came by his scar while inflicting great pain, possibly causing a man's death. That was what mercenaries did to earn their pay. Maimed and killed. And Logan Grimm was very good at what he did to earn his pay.

Or so she believed. She still couldn't remember what tale of him she'd heard in her father's hall.

"You believe the thieves hide near the waterfall? So close to the hamlet? Surely someone would have seen them and reported their whereabouts to us."

"Possibly."

His doubt made her look up. "Why would they not? Their safety is also at risk if the villains are allowed to roam free."

"Is it? Only Lynwood has endured thefts. Only Lynwood's children have suffered injury. Does it not seem odd to you that the villains have not raided anyone else?"

Aye, it did. She could think of only one reason why.

She lowered her voice, more because uttering her deceased husband's name came hard than not wanting others to hear. She wouldn't surprise a one of the servants by speaking of his cruelty.

"Bertrand de Poitou ruled this holding for only ten years, but within that time he made many enemies, both highborn and low. Perhaps one of these thieves suffered Bertrand's ill use, and now seeks his revenge."

Logan crossed his arms, tilted his head. "Revenge is generally sought against the person perceived as an enemy. The satisfaction comes from knowing the person suffers. With Bertrand dead, why bother?"

"Because they know if Bertrand were alive, they would never dare steal so much as an acorn. Were Bertrand alive, capture and punishment would be swift . . . and deadly."

"So they torment his widow and child in his stead." He rubbed at his chin. "A rather cowardly way to go about it, but 'tis possible, I suppose."

Except he wasn't convinced. Joanna wasn't sure she was right either, but what other reason could there be?

Harold's arrival interrupted further speculation. He spread out another map, this one showing a smaller area. She recognized every hamlet, every stream and river, every landmark. Somewhere within the familiar area where she'd once walked with no fear of endangerment lurked at least three men who wished her, or her livelihood, harm.

While the men bent over the map and discussed the merits of various hiding places, Joanna listened with half an ear. She knew they planned a strategy for a search, which was good. She welcomed any progress. Still, she couldn't help wishing they would simply ride out and find the whoresons.

Logan ate his midday meal while listening to the storm and enjoying the reeve's discomfort.

The blacksmith had managed to bring Ivy back to the manor before the sky opened up. The little girl was utterly enraptured by the new babe and regaled everyone with tales of tiny fingers and toes and comical facial expressions.

Wat, however, could barely talk from shivering, wet

and cold from his soaking. He huddled by the hearth with a mug of broth in his hands and a woolen blanket draped over his shoulders.

The reeve made no secret of his distaste for the mercenary's continued presence. For each derisive glare, Logan answered with a smug smile, considering the odd battle mild entertainment on a stormy afternoon.

Logan sipped at his spiced mead, resigned to idling away the afternoon in a warm, dry hall. Truly, he and Harold spent so much time with the maps, discussing possible locations where the thieves could hide undetected, the morning had flown by. Not so the hours since, and he knew he'd have to find some distraction to keep his eyes and thoughts off the lovely widow.

Even then Joanna drew his attention, and all she did was tear small pieces of brown bread from her portion of the loaf and ease them daintily past her lips. Occasionally she made some comment to Ivy, but mostly she smiled softly at the girl's proclamations on the marvels of a new babe.

He liked Joanna's smile, thought she should display it more often. It brightened her eyes, softened her mouth, and generally lifted the spirits of all who saw.

Even the spirits of a mercenary who should know better than to muse upon the lady of Lynwood Manor's smile. Such foolishness, wanting Joanna to direct one of those smiles at him. 'Twould only lead to trouble he could well do without. Good thing he was leaving on the morn, putting Joanna and her problems far behind him.

"Have a care where you look, Grimm. Our lady is not for you."

The reeve hovered behind him, delivering a warning Logan didn't need. Still, Wat's insolence pricked his ire.

He kept his voice low, so not to draw Joanna's notice. "Is it a crime at Lynwood to admire your lady's grace and beauty?"

Wat pursed his lips. "For a man like you, it should be."

"Ah, a man of my ilk. So you said last eve. Tell me, reeve, are you always so quick to judge in ignorance?"

The reeve plopped down on the bench, his glare now a mere arm's length away. "I have heard tales of your kind. You are a mercenary, a killer for hire. You have no loyalty except to money, and so no honor. I need know no more to judge you as unfit to scrape the muck from a righteous lady's boots."

No honor? That stung. Logan *did* adhere to his own code of honor, of honesty and fairness, such as it was. The nasty little man's opinion of a mercenary was deeply entrenched, and Logan doubted the reeve would listen to—much less believe—any protest.

And as much as it pained him, Logan had to admire Wat for taking a stance in his lady's defense. Still, he didn't have to like it or put up with the reeve's presumption.

He glared back at the reeve, a look that had put fear in the hearts of hardened soldiers.

"For a mere reeve, you state your opinions rather boldly. You may hold sway over the villagers, may even merit your lady's trust, but you would be wise to keep a civil tongue when speaking to a man who has slit throats for less offensive an insult."

He knew he'd hit his target when Wat paled and rose.

"You are of more threat to our peace and well-being than another onslaught of the plague. A pox on you, Grimm."

Logan kept tight to the bench, knowing if he got up he'd shove Wat's tongue down his throat or his privates up his arse.

"Be gone, gnat, before I swat you."

Wat didn't need further urging.

The plague, indeed! A pox, was it? This from a reeve! A vexing, irritating, self-important *reeve!*

Through the haze of his ire he heard soft footfalls and the swish of skirts.

Joanna's brow furrowed with concern. "Did Wat say something he ought not?"

She meant to make amends for her reeve, if necessary, which she shouldn't have to do. 'Twas the reeve who should make his apology, pay dearly for his heedless comments.

Before him stood the one person at Lynwood, besides Harold, who treated him with a measure of respect and courtesy, the one who should be angriest at him. Who shouldn't be suffering the raids on her village, and added to that, tolerating an insufferable lout of a reeve.

Truly, this was none of his affair, so no one was more surprised than Logan when he answered, "Nay, milady. Verily, you may wish to thank him. He has convinced me to accept your offer."

Chapter Five

Joanna crossed her arms tight against her midriff to quell the fluttering, undecided if she was pleased or not about Logan's announcement. And most confused over how Wat changed the scowling mercenary's mind.

"Wat changed your mind?"

"So 'twould seem."

"I am surprised. You were most adamant about not working for a woman."

"I have not changed my mind on that score."

She set her mind on ignoring his deepening vexation. "Yet you are staying?"

"Aye."

Joanna waited for him to continue, give some explanation, but when it became obvious his revelations were at an end, she decided not to pry further and possibly ruin her good fortune.

Logan might now be in her service, but the man wasn't happy about it. Why goad him into changing his mind once again?

Or was she being too hasty? Aye, she wanted the

thieves caught, but at what cost to both her peace of mind and her coffers?

Joanna admitted she'd likely have no peace of mind anytime soon where Logan was concerned. The man affected her in the most woeful, unexplainable manner. She would simply have to keep her inappropriate reactions to herself. Surely, within a few days, his presence would become familiar, and her fascination would lessen. She'd be able to gaze at those midnight eyes and not suffer added pulsebeats.

The matter of Logan's fee, however, must be addressed, even if he was in a foul mood.

"Then I suppose we should discuss your fee."

"My fee is five shillings per sennight."

Joanna felt herself go pale. 'Twas far more than what she'd expected to pay for a week's service. Her effort to confirm her hearing came out barely above a whisper.

"Five? For each sennight?"

"I will consider the coin Harold gave me as surety against the rest. We will begin the first sennight with yesterday."

Joanna barely heard him. Her legs going weak, she eased down onto the bench, her spirits tumbling to her toes.

"'Tis a knightly sum!"

He shrugged. "'Tis my usual fee. Verily, the service of a mercenary of my reputation is often more highly regarded than that of some knights I could name. Even the king would rather some of them pay scutage and remain home than serve with less-than-favorable results on a battlefield."

"That may be so, but I do not have the royal treasury

at my command. My coffer is not bare, but it is shallow."
Joanna let out a sigh at the gravity of her mistake.
"'Twould seem I not only sought to hire the wrong mer-
cenary but misjudged the cost as well."

He tilted his head. "Did you?"

As much as she hated to admit her errors, apparently
her memory had failed her utterly.

"Certes. I sent Harold to hire you without remembering correctly which tale I heard of you. I also thought I
knew your fee to be two shillings a sennight, not five.
'Tis plain I erred on both man and fee."

Which meant she must send Harold out in search of a
mercenary who commanded a lesser fee.

Damn.

The self-doubt she'd struggled to hold at bay flooded
the very fiber of her being. Perhaps, no matter how hard
she tried, she wasn't capable of holding Lynwood Manor
by herself. Perhaps, as Wat suggested at every opportunity, taking a husband was the prudent course. Even one
of the landless knights who'd courted her wouldn't have
made this mistake.

Had it come to that? Must she sacrifice herself for the
good of her people? Perhaps she'd never had a choice,
had simply been too overjoyed by her freedom to accept
the inevitable.

"There was a time I charged two shillings, but not in
recent years."

Logan's attempt to make her feel less wretched only
served to twist the knife.

Still, she'd not have him pity the poor widow with the
undependable memory and inadequate funds. Scraping
together sufficient pride to get up and plant her feet

firmly, Joanna looked him squarely in the midnight eyes she'd never forget. They might be dark and dangerous, but they also hinted of humor and kindness, qualities she would never have attributed to a mercenary until meeting Logan Grimm.

"I fear I cannot meet your price, but then I imagine you have already surmised as much." An embarrassed half laugh escaped before she could halt it. "I do not suppose Conrad Falke can be convinced to accept a mere two shillings a sennight either."

He answered with a meager smile. "Not Falke. Nor would any of the men I suggested to Harold. You may wish to consider, my lady, that you may not be satisfied with the service of men who command less in wages."

Like with most goods, one usually got what one paid for. She knew that, but what else could she do? Unless . . .

She sat back down, wondering at her own daring.

She had nothing to lose, except, perhaps, another piece of her pride—which was already so badly battered one more bruise wouldn't matter.

"Grimm, do you think you could capture the thieves within a sennight? If I paid you the five shillings, can you warrant—"

"Nay. Too much area for one man to search without knowing for certain how many thieves there are. I may get one or two, but all? I can make you no such pledge."

At least he was honest, she would give him that. Heart heavy, eyes stinging, she accepted what she couldn't change.

"Then I give you my thanks for being forthright and wish you a safe journey to London."

Joanna put her palms on the table, prepared to

summon Wat and Harold and decide what to do next. Logan surprised her once more when he waved her to remain seated.

"Mayhap we can come to some . . . bargain."

She wasn't sure how many times she could deal with having her hopes raised, then dashed, without bursting into tears. And, damn, if Grimm was willing to bargain, why the devil had he not said so earlier? And what made him think she had anything else to bargain with?

Of a sudden she went still and quiet, suspecting what he might demand in payment. Wariness crept along her spine until she noted a lack of either lust or guile in his expression. Logan stared at her, certes, but not as if he wanted her.

She should be grateful and thrilled. Still, Logan was a man, a warrior, and men did not always show their true emotions. Bertrand had been able to hide what he was thinking until it was too late for her to escape.

Cautiously, she asked, "A bargain?"

Logan's eyes narrowed. "You mistrust me. Why? Have I given you reason?"

Where Bertrand had hidden his thoughts, she'd never successfully completely hidden hers. Especially her fear. Oh, how she wished she had somehow learned to hide her fear.

"Not as yet."

"But you expect me to."

"I have learned to be wary of men who propose bargains. A woman usually comes out the worse for them."

Logan snorted. "Not in my experience. But in this case, I believe we both come out the better. What say we leave the fee at five shillings. I have a standard to maintain, after all." He raised a forefinger to hush her refusal. "For those five shillings I will capture your thieves, no matter how long I require to do so, whether a sennight or a full month."

His bargain sounded too good to be true.

"I pay you five shillings, you capture the thieves. That is all. No other conditions?"

"Only if you consider meals and a pallet conditions."

Conditions easily met. Of course, she'd have to cease her late-night wanderings while Logan slept on a pallet in the hall. But the sacrifice was a small one given the gains.

"You are welcome to meals and a pallet. What I do not understand is why you are willing to take a lesser fee than you are accustomed to."

Logan's shrug was supposed to indicate indifference, but the set of his jaw told her otherwise.

"The food is good. The hall is dry, and no vermin scurried over my legs during the night." Even his crooked smile didn't banish her feeling that he wouldn't reveal all. "Perhaps I merely like the company."

Meaning hers, and she would blush if she believed him. "Most of the people of Lynwood are pleasant enough."

"Most all."

His head turned, and Joanna looked where he did. At the hearth. Wat still huddled in a blanket, his expression a mix of fear and anger.

"Mayhap I do have a condition, my lady. When seated at table, I want to be able to look your reeve in the eye."

At the hint of a threat, Joanna took a steadying breath. "I want no trouble between you and Wat. Besides, he usually takes his meals in his own cottage."

"Too bad." Logan's attention shifted again, squarely on her. "What say you, Lady Joanna? Have we a bargain?"

She bit her lower lip, wondering if she might someday regret her decision, but knowing her choices to be few.

"We do, Logan Grimm. You will begin on the morn?"

"I have already begun. I know the lay of the land and have my suspicions on where to search. You will see results soon."

"That sounds like a warranty to me."

"As much of one as I can give."

Which was more than she'd had an hour ago. Noticing Donald headed for the door, Joanna left Logan to his spiced mead.

The blacksmith smiled at her approach. "My thanks for the meal, my lady. 'Tis best I get back to mine own cottage now."

"And I thank you and your wife for contending with Ivy. You heard how much she enjoyed her visit."

"She is always welcome. No trouble at all." Then he jerked his head toward Logan. "Leaving on the morrow?"

There need be no grand announcement. Everyone would learn of Logan's decision soon enough.

"Nay, he has decided to accept my offer and capture our thieves."

"Is that wise, my lady?"

Even the village blacksmith questioned the wisdom of her actions! Hellfire, must she explain her every decision to everyone?

"'Tis our best chance for peace."

Except Logan's very presence caused discord. Joanna glanced toward the hearth and Logan's most diligent adversary.

Wat's blanket and mug lay on the floor. The reeve must have left while she spoke with Donald, and Joanna couldn't say Wat's disappearance upset her. The less Wat and Logan had to deal with each other, the less chance for trouble between them—putting her in the middle. A most unpleasant place to be.

Wat Reeve's one-room cottage stank of mud and wet wool from his breeches and tunic flung over the rungs of the ladder leading to the loft to dry. He debated whether or not to crawl naked onto his pallet and pull a blanket over his head until dawn. What sense pulling out clean garb for the few hours left of the evening?

A heavy rap on his door urged him toward the oak chest at the foot of his pallet. Who the devil would be out in this nasty weather? And why couldn't people leave him alone, if only for one night?

Because he was the reeve, the first person the villagers complained to when a problem arose, that's why.

Unable to ignore the insistent pounding, Wat pulled on dry breeches, fumbling with his strings. "A moment!"

"Then hurry, man. This rain stings."

He recognized Donald's booming voice. Damn. Resigned to more unpleasantness, as if his day hadn't already been miserable, he opened the door and stepped back to allow the huge blacksmith to duck inside.

Wat closed the door against the storm, the wind whistling through cracks in the wattle-and-daub walls he hadn't yet had the chance to repair. While his father managed to complete his many duties as reeve and find the time to maintain the cottage, tend a healthy garden, and raise a family, Wat hadn't yet figured out how to accomplish the same feat—even though he didn't yet have his own family to worry over.

Someday he would. The cottage was simply too quiet. And as reeve, he was expected to take a wife, sire children. One more thing he hadn't had time for yet, nor did he see sense in hurrying to invite the possibility of more pain.

A wave of grief for his parents and siblings washed over him but didn't overwhelm him as it would have a few months ago. Time healed. Grief faded. Life marched forward.

Still, lack of time was taking its toll on the cottage and yard left to him. And if Lady Joanna didn't soon see sense and provide Lynwood Manor with a lord, the entire village would decay.

Donald stood before the hearth, his meaty arms stretched out to capture whatever warmth he could gather from the meager flames. Water dripped from his clothing, creating puddles of mud in the dirt floor.

"What brings you to my door?"

The blacksmith's chest heaved in a sigh. "To ask about what we do now."

"About what?"

"The mercenary."

Wat tamped down his ire as he crossed to the chest, pulled out a tunic, and jerked it over his head. That the mercenary dared to look upon Lady Joanna with appreciative admiration—'twasn't to be borne. Praise the saints Grimm would be gone soon.

"We need do nothing. He leaves on the morrow."

Donald rubbed his hands together. "Not so. Grimm has

accepted Lady Joanna's offer. He means to capture the thieves."

Wat fought panic. All of their carefully thought-out plans—nay, wait. Donald had to be wrong.

"Last I heard, Grimm planned to leave as soon as the storm allowed."

"I just spoke with Lady Joanna. His plan has changed."

Nay, nay, nay!

"He is staying?"

Donald nodded. "So Lady Joanna tells me."

Wat plopped down onto the single stool in the cottage and bent forward, covering his face with his hands. Damn. This was a tangle he didn't need.

What to do? How to keep that interfering, lowbred mercenary from ruining all? Given another fortnight, the plan forged to convince Lady Joanna to marry and provide Lynwood Manor with a proper lord would have succeeded, he was sure. But now, with the mercenary chasing down the thieves—ye gods, now there was a coil he didn't want unwound. Her ladyship would be furious if she ever found out what he'd done.

They'd done, he corrected. Though he'd thought of the plan, he wasn't completely responsible. Three other men had given their approval.

Wat rubbed at his forehead, then lowered his hands, unable to quell the sick roil in his stomach. Grimm must be dealt with so her ladyship never learned of their conspiracy—done for her own good as well as the villagers'.

"We shall first have to tell Edward about Grimm, warn him to keep his men out of sight." The thieves' leader wasn't going to be pleased with this turn of events, but

Wat could see no choice in the matter. "Perhaps Grimm can be bribed to leave."

Donald stared at him as if he'd lost his wits, and Wat admitted grasping at the easy, and likely impossible, answer. Besides, where would he get the coin to bribe Grimm? What little he could spare was promised to Edward and his men to harry the village.

'Twasn't natural for a woman to command a garrison or sit in judgment in the manor court, so Lynwood Manor needed a lord. One to whom all could look for protection in times of travail. One who could decisively, firmly, settle disputes.

The law and terms of Lady Joanna's jointure might give her the rights, but heaven knew a female was too softhearted and weak to rule a manor properly. Even another man like Sir Bertrand de Poitou, who could be harsh indeed, was better than allowing a woman her way. One could never be sure of a female's whims.

Wat took a deep breath. "Then we must ensure Grimm fails. If he cannot find the thieves within reasonable time, then Lady Joanna may tire of paying his fee and send him on his way."

"Perhaps," Donald allowed, but didn't sound convinced. "Or perhaps we should give up this scheme and send the thieves on their way. Their last raid proved too real for my taste. Ivy should not have been injured."

They'd discussed this before, and all agreed that Ivy was as much at fault for her injury as Edward. If she hadn't tossed a rock at his horse, setting it off stride, she wouldn't have been harmed. Still, Wat wasn't pleased that the children had been in harm's way at all.

However, he had to admit the thieves' ploy of a daylight raid, of heightening the appearance of dire threat, pushed Lady Joanna to act. And she had, just not in the desirable direction.

"There will be no more injuries. I will see to that." Wat rose from his stool and put his hands on his hips. "We cannot give up so soon, Donald."

Donald crossed his arms against his massive chest. "I am not the only one who wonders if perhaps we acted too soon. Granted, we all would prefer a lord. What right-thinking man would not? But perhaps hiring thieves was not the best way to go about it."

Wat refrained from voicing that he'd also wondered, but dismissed the doubts as foolish. And untimely.

"We have already paid Edward and his men for their services. 'Tis too late to change our minds now."

"We could tell Edward to take his thieves elsewhere."

A chill ran down his spine at having to tell Edward anything, much less to pick up and leave. Not that he would ever let his disquiet over Edward show, especially not to a man as well respected among the villagers as Donald.

"What say we wait a few days, see what happens with Grimm? I will inform Edward of the mercenary's intent, warn him to remain hidden. Perhaps Grimm is not as capable as her ladyship claims he is."

Donald looked doubtful.

And Wat feared those doubts merited.

Logan knew he couldn't sit on his pallet all night, staring at the banked fire in the hearth, watching the bedchamber door, hoping the lady behind it was also having a sleepless night. He doubted she would come out.

Truly, he hoped she had the sense to slide the bolt behind her, remain safe and secure behind stout oak. The lady of the manor shouldn't be creeping about in the middle of the night, for whatever reason, no matter how safe she felt in her own hall.

But 'twas not only wondering if Joanna might again wander out of her bedchamber during the wee hours that kept him awake and uneasy.

For the life of him, he couldn't remember the last time he'd allowed his ire to prod him into doing something inadvisable—as he'd allowed Wat to prick his anger and change his mind about accepting Joanna's offer. Not only to change his mind, but goad him into making a very foolish bargain.

If Conrad Falke ever heard of how Logan Grimm had lowered his fee, and for a woman at that . . . ye gods. The odds of his fellow mercenary's learning of the bargain were slim, praise the saints; otherwise, Falke would laugh from here to doomsday and spread the tale over the entire kingdom.

Unless, of course, Logan could complete the task within a sennight, collect his full fee, and call the deal done.

Logan frowned into the glowing embers. A few days wasn't much time. Possible, but not truly within reason. Whoever the band's leader was, he'd found a good hiding place.

However, there must be tracks to that hiding place. Horses couldn't take wing while in the river and fly to wherever they were stabled or corralled. All Logan had to do was find those tracks somewhere within an expanse of land several leagues long and just as wide, in some places thickly wooded.

A crack of thunder echoed through the hall, bouncing among the high arches overhead. The storm grew stronger, the rain heavier, all the better to wash out any paths and make tracking the thieves harder.

He almost laughed aloud at the impossible task he'd set for himself, but he refrained, wary of waking one of the servants, who would surely inform Joanna that she'd hired a witless fool.

Perhaps she had. Witless for allowing Wat to goad him into this unholy bargain.

Since he usually tried to be honest with himself, he admitted the twit of a reeve wasn't entirely at fault. Joanna shared the blame. While he'd started out with the intent to tweak the reeve's nose, he'd ended up feeling obligated to repay the lady for her honesty and kindness.

Saints above, he hated that feeling of obligation. 'Twas one of the reasons he'd become a mercenary instead of a common soldier like his father. Free to serve whomever he chose, if he chose, for whatever length of time he saw fit. Not beholden to any lord for his bed and bread for a lifetime.

Logan stretched out on the pallet, taking one last glance at the bedchamber door. Lady Joanna of Lynwood possessed the good sense to remain behind it, safe and secure. And he was glad. Honestly, truly happy.

He wanted no more reasons to admire the lovely widow any more than he already did.

Chapter Six

Logan woke instantly to the touch of a hand on his shoulder. Habit and training took over, placing his sword in his hand and his body at full alert.

Several moments passed before he realized he wasn't being attacked and that he'd frightened Harold to paleness. The captain had scurried back out of harm's way even before Logan rose to sit and stare bleary-eyed at his surroundings.

The manor's servants hadn't yet stirred. Logan guessed the time as just before sunrise.

"The village has suffered another raid," Harold whispered urgently. "I thought you might wish to know immediately."

Logan set aside his sword and began pulling on clothing. "Anyone hurt?"

"Praise the saints, nay."

Dressed, his sword strapped on securely, Logan followed Harold out of the hall. Hazy sunlight greeted him, a hopeful sign for a dry day. Perhaps he would have good fortune in tracking these thieves after all.

As they crossed the bailey to the gate, Logan asked, "Did anyone see the thieves?"

Harold sighed. "Nay. The villagers woke to find possessions missing. Two have lost wood from their stacks, another cannot find a chicken. What concerns me most is the chalice missing from the church. Where before they stole food, now they steal something they can sell for a good profit."

Logan mulled over the information. "They have stolen nothing of value before?"

Harold half smiled. "Do not allow Margaret Atbridge to hear you say her prized goose had no value. But nay, they have confined their thefts to items they need to survive."

The theft of a goose was punishable with a fine. Not so a chalice, especially one made of gold, possibly worth several pounds. For its theft, the thieves subjected themselves to a sentence of hanging.

The villains were getting bolder and greedier, likely thinking that since they hadn't been caught yet, they wouldn't ever be caught.

"Have they attempted to take items from the manor?"

"We are better protected than the village. The gate is bolted at night, and guards patrol the wall walk. They would be bold, indeed, to attempt to enter the manor's bailey."

Logan glanced back at the sturdy palisade. From the wall walk one could see for leagues, except during the black of night. The guards might be able to detect movement around the palisade, but wouldn't see anyone skulking about in the village. Leaving the villagers vulnerable.

Wat stood on the steps of the church at the far end of

the village, facing a man in a disheveled black cassock who must be the village priest. Logan couldn't hear what the priest was saying, but from the man's angry expression and wildly waving arms, Logan could guess. Wat obviously wasn't having any luck calming the priest's rant, and the reeve's obvious relief at their approach struck Logan as comical.

Well, Wat was relieved at *Harold's* approach. The reeve had made it very clear the previous eve that Logan was unwelcome, and the sooner gone the better. Wat was in for a surprise he wouldn't like. Perverse, Logan knew, but causing the reeve any amount of upset almost made his bargain with Joanna worthwhile.

As Logan and Harold reached the steps, the priest's anger didn't diminish. He simply redirected his tirade at Harold.

"Have you heard what these thieves did? They snuck into the church and stole my chalice! I cannot say Mass without my chalice. You must get it back!"

"I am aware of the theft, Father Arthur. We will do all in our power to see the chalice returned to you. This is Logan Grimm, whom her ladyship hired to capture the thieves."

Wat showed no reaction at all.

He knows.

Damn. But then, news traveled quickly in small communities. Harold might even have informed Wat earlier. However, the priest's eyes narrowed at the news, and Logan felt the prick of his displeasure.

"This is the mercenary I heard about? How are we to trust he will not find the thieves' hoard and simply take all for himself?"

Wat's head bobbed in agreement with the priest. "I have the same doubts. We are asked to trust a hired killer with the protection of the villagers. Not possible, I say."

Harold opened his mouth; Logan stopped him with a hand to the arm, casting a quelling glance from the priest to the reeve and back again. He didn't so much object to their opinion of him, but to their deplorable disloyalty to Joanna.

"Have you so little faith in Lady Joanna's judgment that you question her decision to hire the best man possible to bring these thieves to justice? She acts in your best interests, and yet you attack her efforts. A poor show of loyalty in the one who seeks to do her best by you, I say."

Only slightly abashed, Wat chewed on his bottom lip. Both reeve and priest stared at Logan for a moment before Father Arthur regained the courage to speak again.

"You have yet to prove her ladyship's trust not misplaced. By all that is holy, the sinners had no right to enter a house of God and invade the sanctity of the altar. They must be caught and punished!"

"Aye, Father Arthur, we understand." Harold turned to Wat. "Are you aware of any missing possessions other than the wood and chicken—and the chalice?"

The reeve rubbed his forehead as if trying to soothe an ache. "No one has reported anything else to me, but the morning is yet young."

"All right, then. Wat, take Grimm to where we know the thieves struck. I must go back to the manor and report to Lady Joanna. She should have risen by now."

Aye, most likely the lady was up and dressed, busying herself with seeing to preparation of the morning meal. Logan tried not to envision Joanna's lithe form gliding among the tables. Or bent over at the waist, stirring a kettle of pottage, her gracefully rounded backside presented enticingly for a man to admire. 'Twas disturbing that even as he should be hurrying off to look for signs of the thieves that the vision of Joanna should take shape so sharply.

"Harold, have my horse saddled. Do you have a guard to spare to accompany me?"

"I will ask for a volunteer."

Harold took off at a run toward the manor.

The priest wagged a warning finger. "You had best bring my chalice back or suffer the wrath of the divine."

As the priest stomped up the stairs, Logan mused that this was the first time he'd been threatened with divine punishment for a deed he hadn't committed. Which only strengthened his beliefs on the worth of priests.

Left alone with Wat, Logan crossed his arms. "Shall we begin?"

Wat pointed at the wattle-and-daub cottage closest to the church. "Wood stolen from there." He turned slightly and pointed to another cottage. "Wood and chicken taken from there."

The reeve dropped his arm and gave Logan a quick glance. "I wish you luck in your search, mercenary," he said, without a hint of sincerity, then strode off in the opposite direction.

Logan watched the reeve go without any compulsion to call the irritating man back.

The reeve entered a rather large cottage situated on a spacious yard. So he had done rather well for himself. But then, as village reeve, Wat was due considerations to reflect his status. 'Twasn't unusual for a reeve to occupy the largest cottage in the village, or to receive other gifts in return for the performance of his duties.

Logan knew he had no right to judge the man the villagers had elected as their reeve, but damn, why couldn't they have chosen a man less irksome to deal with?

Turning to the task at hand, Logan inspected the muddy area around the chunks of firewood stacked against the first cottage. He noted footprints of two adults, likely those of a man and a woman, both shod in leather-soled shoes or sandals. A child's bare feet. Even the tiny tracks of mice who made their home deep in the pile. Yet, he saw no unusual boot print that led either to or from the cottage that might belong to one of the thieves.

He backed away toward the garden, following various trails made by what he assumed were the residents of the cottage. A deer had run through of late. And a hare. He found the path the child used to take the cow to graze in the common meadow.

No trace of his thieves, however.

His thieves? Aye, they were now his. To capture and haul before Lady Joanna for judgment.

What would her ladyship do to them when they stood before her? Banish them? Would she hang them? Did she have the fortitude to inflict as harsh a punishment as most lords wouldn't hesitate to impose? But he was getting ahead of himself. First he had to catch the thieves.

Logan went on to the second cottage that had suffered thefts. One set of prints dominated the area surrounding the woodpile. Light prints, probably belonging to a woman. But the heavier, larger and fresher prints that led to the stacked wood and back out to the green might belong to the thief.

Logan bent down and studied the impression in the mud. Nothing struck him as remarkable—no crack in the sole, no odd shape to the heel—just that they didn't belong there.

He got up and turned toward the green. In his path stood a dark-haired woman of middling years, her face stamped with fury, wielding a long-handled, black iron ladle. She looked familiar, but he couldn't remember from where.

Logan kept a wary eye on the ladle and strove for a soothing tone.

"Mistress, you have naught to fear from me."

"Yer that mercenary, are ye not?"

That most of the villagers knew the identity of the stranger in their midst didn't surprise him.

"I am. Wat tells me you suffered a theft last eve."

"Four large chunks of prime firewood! The other day they made off with me finest, plumpest goose. The thievin' bastards have taken more from me than anyone else in the village. 'Taint fair, I say!"

Her mention of the goose gave him her identity. Margaret Atbridge. And now he knew why she looked familiar. She was the woman standing near the common well when he'd first ridden into the village with Harold.

Logan gave Margaret high marks for boldly confronting him, ready and willing to protect her property, even if armed with only her courage and a mere ladle.

"I gather you did not hear the thieves approach your cottage last eve."

Her anger changed into disgust. "Nay, I am sorry to say. Like to get me hands on them, I would. Poor goose is probably bones and feathers by now, so no use to her ladyship anymore. Lady Joanna will surely miss me goose's fine goslings. Weren't none better to send to the abbot."

The comment brought home how close were the relationships between the village and manor and overlord. What affected one affected all. Not that the abbot would suffer overmuch from the absence of a goose, but Joanna must somehow make up the loss.

Logan waved at the boot prints in the mud. "Could these tracks be made by someone you know, or might they be made by one of our thieves?"

Margaret squinted at the ground. "Ain't no one allowed by my woodpile but me." She waved the ladle at the intruder's trail. "Bold as brass he comes up and steals me wood. I would wager it was the same man who speared me goose. A mean-looking one, for sure."

An odd thought struck Logan. "Have you something in your cottage you could protect one or two of these prints with? A crate perhaps?"

She thought a moment. "I suppose I might use my wood box. To what purpose?"

"Many of the villagers saw the thieves when they rode through the green, so can identify them after I catch them. But if we compare the mens' boots to these tracks, we might know for certain which one is your particular thief."

He had to appreciate her wry smile. "Aye, that we might. I will fetch my box."

Joanna knew when Logan entered the hall without looking up from the kettle of pottage bubbling in the hearth.

Why she should be so aware of his mere presence she couldn't explain, and sometime during the middle of a restless night she'd decided to cease trying. So long as she kept that awareness to herself, no harm could come from it.

Harold had told her about the previous night's thefts, which made her angry, then informed her of Logan's intent to ride out as soon as he finished looking around in the village.

It also meant he truly intended to begin earning his hefty fee this morning. Praise the saints.

She spooned a healthy portion of pottage into a wooden bowl and set it down next to the thick slice of brown bread and healthy chunk of yellow cheese she'd already placed on the table. With a hearty morning meal and the victuals Maud prepared for his nooning, Logan should have enough sustenance to see him through the day.

She felt him coming near and turned to see him approach in hose-covered feet, having taken off and left his muddy boots near the doorway. With a wave of her hand she indicated he should sit and eat. He raised an eyebrow at the laid-out meal, then slid onto the bench and picked up the piece of cheese.

She eased onto the bench opposite Logan. "Did you learn anything of value in the village?"

"Found some boot prints. They may belong to one of our thieves."

"Is that of help?"

Between bites of cheese and spoonfuls of pottage he explained how the prints might aid in identifying the thief who'd pilfered wood from Margaret.

He swallowed the last of the cheese. "For now, I look for three men with horses in places where they should not be. Those will be our thieves. However, when they are captured, someone who saw them must swear they are the same men who made the daylight raid."

"I can."

"You saw them yourself?"

"Quite clearly."

Especially the man who'd been closest to her, who'd aimed his horse straight at her before veering off. Never would she forget that man's smug smile, taunting her.

"What did they look like?"

"They looked much too pleased with themselves, of that I am certain."

Her burst of ire brought a small smile to Logan's lips. To shut it out, and to comply with his request, Joanna closed her eyes and tried to give him descriptions that might be more helpful. 'Twas hard to draw him pictures with words, and she found the faces of two of the men hazy. But not the third.

"One haunts me more than the others. By his very demeanor I judged him their leader." She opened her eyes to find Logan staring at her intently, waiting patiently for her to explain. "His hair is black and long, in dire want of trimming and washing. His eyes are very dark, might also be black, and are set somewhat close together. High brow. Pointed nose. But what I remember most is the scar that mars his forehead. It runs from here"—she placed a fingertip at the inner corner of her right eyebrow and traced upward and angled across her forehead into her hairline—"to here. I would know him anywhere by that scar."

"Then if you can place them on the green during the daylight raid, and the boot print near Mistress Atbridge's woodpile is a match to one of their boots, we know the same men are performing all the thefts."

"Do you have a doubt all the thefts are committed by the same men?"

He shrugged a massive shoulder, the hilt of the sword in the scabbard strapped across his back bobbing with the movement. 'Twas rare she saw him without his weapon, a tool of his trade, a reminder of his profession. Yet he ate his meal as any other man might, even in a more mannerly fashion than some men she could name.

"I just hope I catch them before they have a chance to sell the chalice. If found in their possession, it would give us further proof we have the right men." He paused a moment, his brow furrowing. "Have you a notion of where in the area they might sell a chalice?"

"Oundle. If any other place is more likely, then Harold might know. Or Wat."

His mouth skewed, as if he'd eaten something that left a bad taste in his mouth. "I will ask Harold."

She rose from her bench when he rose from his. "Where will you search this morn?"

"The river, south toward the waterfall."

"But Harold and his men have already searched much of that area and not found anyone."

"So Harold told me. I intend to see for myself."

She crossed her arms. "Seems a waste of time to me. Would it not be better to go another direction?"

He leaned toward her, just a little, but enough for her to catch the male scent that threatened to muddle her mind.

"You hired me to find and capture the thieves, my lady. Do you now intend to direct my every move?"

Joanna struggled to answer. "Well, nay, but . . ."

He raised a hushing forefinger. "Then allow me to conduct the search in the way I deem fit."

She pursed her lips, forced to admit she truly didn't know the best way to go about the search, and probably shouldn't be giving the man she was paying—and paying well—any advice on how to go about completing his task.

"Very well, then I shall merely wish you good fortune, and pray that your search bears fruit. Quickly."

Logan wore a smile all the way along the path to the river. He couldn't help it; the woman delighted him.

He'd been surprised to find she'd personally set out his morning meal, an unexpected show of hospitality. And damned if he didn't like talking to her, even if the conversation centered on his task and how to go about it.

Then she'd wrapped enough food in an oiled cloth to last him and Clarence, the soldier who accompanied him, two days. Because she believed them doing taxing work, or wanting to be sure they didn't return early citing hunger?

Still smiling, Logan guided Gideon into the river, heading downstream, allowing the horse to chose its own path among the rocks over which the chilly water gurgled on its headlong rush toward the waterfall.

He carefully studied the banks for anyplace where the thieves might either enter or leave the river. Wherever he judged the bank not too steep for a horse to keep its footing, with a space between the trees wide enough to ride through, Logan studied the area thoroughly for signs of passage.

Nary a hoofprint to be found.

After studying the third place possible, Logan began to wonder if he was going about the task wrong. Perhaps Joanna had been right, that searching an area other than along the riverbank might be wiser. Except his instincts rarely led him astray, and though he had made no progress as yet, those instincts nagged at him to continue his course.

The river wasn't straight. In places it took sharp turns and dived deeply east before curving back west, closer to the village. He'd seen how the river coiled on Harold's map, just hadn't realized the distance so far. 'Twas already midmorning, and Logan judged he'd traveled a mere half a league south from where he entered the river.

Slow progress, indeed. At this rate he wouldn't reach the waterfall for several hours yet. A discouraging thought. And his stomach grumbled despite the hefty morning meal. Too, he should allow the horses a rest, out of the cold water. At the next place he deemed safe to get out of the river, they would stop for a spell and have a bite to eat before continuing on.

To his amazement, he happened upon that spot sooner than he'd thought possible. To his chagrin, there stood Wat and another man.

What the devil was Wat doing on the banks of the river? Wasn't the reeve supposed to be supervising the planting?

Wat hadn't spotted him yet, so Logan reined in and waited for Clarence, who'd ridden silently behind him, to come alongside.

"Who is the man with the reeve?"

"That is Robert, husband of the village brewer. 'Twas from his cottage some wood and a chicken were stolen this morn."

The cottage where no thieves' boot prints marred the mud.

"What business would bring those two to the river?"

"The water. Mistress Brewer claims the river water has a better taste than that from the common well, so she uses it to brew her ales and meads. Her husband, and sometimes her son, help her haul it to the village." Clarence pointed. "There, you can see Robert's buckets in the thicket."

Logan saw them. Two oak buckets strapped with black iron.

Chagrined he hadn't thought of the possibility earlier, Logan asked, "I take it there are paths between the village and the river other than the one we followed this morn?"

"Several. One can get to the river by a variety of ways. This particular path winds its way to behind the church."

Naturally. How stupid of him not to have realized that before. And since the brewer's cottage was close to the church, she and her family used the most direct route to the river for hauling water. Which explained Robert's presence on the bank, but not Wat's.

"Does the reeve haul water, too?"

Logan didn't bother to hide his skepticism, and knew Clarence didn't miss it.

The soldier thought for a moment, then answered, "As reeve, Wat is responsible for checking weights and measures used in the brewing. Perhaps he ensures Mistress Brewer uses the water she claims she is using?"

"Would not the manor be best served if he were in the fields where he belongs?"

Clarence shrugged. "I fear I cannot comment on that score. 'Tis not among my duties to keep track of the comings and goings of the village reeve."

Of course not. A soldier's duty concerned the security of the manor, of guarding the gate, not noting the adventures of Wat Reeve.

Wat looked up then, saw Logan, and immediately stiffened. Out of dislike? Or because he'd been caught somewhere he wasn't supposed to be?

Logan urged his horse forward, Clarence doing the same.

Both men on the riverbank watched his approach with open hostility. Ignoring Wat—for the moment—Logan directed what he hoped was an engaging smile at the brewer's husband. While he questioned the reeve's efficiency in his duties, Logan had no doubts about the brewer's skill.

He reined in directly before the man who was married to that fine woman. "Good morn to you, good sir. I am told you are the husband of the brewer."

"What of it?"

He leaned forward in the saddle. "I have taken my ease in some of London's finest alehouses, and in the halls of a few of the kingdom's wealthiest lords. Pray inform your esteemed wife that her brews compare most favorably to all. Particularly her spiced mead. 'Tis among the finest I have had the pleasure to sample."

As Logan hoped, Robert's hostility faded somewhat.

"She will be pleased to hear."

"I also understand you suffered loss from your wood-pile last eve. Did you happen to hear the thieves?"

Robert shook his head. "Nary a sound. Why?"

"Merely trying to place the time of the theft. Again, my compliments to your wife."

"I will . . . tell her."

Logan kept his smile in place as he addressed Wat. "I am surprised to see you here, reeve. Did you not say something about planting oats this morn?"

"Where I go and when is none of your concern, mercenary. Shall we go, Robert?"

Wat spun on his heel and strode up the path. Robert fetched his buckets, but before following Wat, dipped his head in a brief but courteous fare-thee-well.

The action surprised Logan, warmed him, and he returned Robert's polite acknowledgment of their brief exchange. The men were already out of sight when Logan urged his horse out of the river.

Dismounted, he unwrapped the oiled cloth and removed chunks of bread for himself and Clarence. They allowed the horses to graze and drink, and while Clarence rested on a log, Logan ambled along the path Robert and Wat had taken.

There were prints in the mud, of course. Two men. Both leading away from the river. Logan squatted, his eyes narrowed in on those boot prints, becoming uneasy.

He could see where the men walked away from the river, but saw no sign of their walking *to* the river.

How very, very odd.

Chapter Seven

Joanna pushed back the hood of her cloak, turned her face to the midafternoon sun and drew a long breath, indulging in the scents of freshly tilled earth and the promise of continued warmth.

Soon they'd no longer need firewood for heat, only cooking. Earlier she'd ordered all the shutters in the manor opened to allow the stale air out and the fresh air in.

On the morrow several servants would go to the pond to gather fresh rushes to spread over the dirt floors. Unfortunately the scant supply of rosemary wouldn't allow her to sprinkle a quantity over the new rushes, but Joanna didn't mourn the lack. Next year she would have rosemary aplenty, picked from the plants in her new garden.

The plague's aftermath had been hard to bear. Hearts were yet healing from the loss of human life. Hope had arrived with the coming of spring; small joys sprang up with the warmth of summer.

The source of Joanna's joy, her darling Ivy, currently picked daisies along the edge of the field where teams of oxen struggled to pull sharp-edged plows through the rain-soaked earth. Behind the plows walked two men swinging mallets to break up the clods of dirt. Then came the sowers, mostly women, scooping seed from woven baskets, planting oats in the furrows.

Under the watchful eye of the shepherd, lambs romped among the ewes grazing on the stubble of last year's wheatfield. The pigs had been driven into the forest to feed on acorns and crab apples, so the swine no longer indiscriminately rooted about in the gardens, causing trouble among neighbors.

Off in the distance, from the blacksmith's cottage in the middle of the village, she could hear a hammer strike iron on the anvil. The carpenter, she knew, was making repairs to the manor's dovecote. And if she tried hard enough, she might catch a whiff of the bread baking in the manor's oven.

Life was good at Lynwood Manor today, and would be perfect if only she didn't have those thieves lurking about, pilfering fowl and firewood—and now a chalice from the church.

Which brought her thoughts right back to Logan Grimm, who she'd tried not to think about since their talk this morning.

Even while discussing a serious subject, their conversation had been . . . pleasant. Even when she'd questioned the direction he intended to search, he hadn't taken overt offense, merely reminded her to allow him to do what she was paying him for.

Allow him. As if Logan Grimm needed her permission.

He'd assuredly not needed her permission to begin his task by talking with the villagers. She'd been miffed that

Harold woke Logan and told him about last night's raid before informing her, and that Logan hadn't wasted any time going into the village, poking around—and charming Margaret Atbridge.

Margaret had babbled about not only his consideration for her loss and his wonderful suggestion for preserving the thief's boot prints, but also saw fit to comment on the pleasing arrangement of Logan's facial features and the breadth of his shoulders.

The woman had sung Logan's praises so thoroughly it pricked Joanna's ire that the villager had spent enough time with him to notice his quality.

The sound of hoofbeats brought Joanna out of her wayward musings, but not out of her entanglement with Logan. He rode toward her on his huge black stallion. Clarence had veered off, headed for the manor.

To her disappointment, Logan didn't drag a thief or two behind him. Of course, this was the first day of Logan's search. She shouldn't expect miracles.

To her chagrin, she also thrilled at the magnificent sight of a handsome man atop a majestic horse. They made a splendid pairing, a spectacle of man and beast moving in fluid accord, the master firmly in command.

After being married to Bertrand, she should have been unresponsive to the appeal of all men. 'Twas both bemusing and bewildering to realize she'd not been ruined for all others. Especially for this particular male.

A mercenary shouldn't conjure up memories of the bards and minstrels who frequented her father's hall and the market fairs, singing ballads of chivalry and courtly love. Tales of bold knights and fair ladies. Of yearnings begging for fulfillment. Of romance, pure and true.

She'd put those foolish notions behind her long ago.

Why Logan Grimm should hold a strong appeal for her, she didn't know. But he did. Not that she would be nonsensical enough to act upon the attraction. Or even to believe in romance.

Logan reined in with a flourish, the stallion's front legs rising high before pounding down to the ground, reminding her of knights before a tournament, putting their horses through their paces, showing off form and fitness, striving to impress the ladies ogling the strutting males from the stands.

She had to smile at that. Logan was certainly no knight, and she no prize to be won. Still, it tickled her fancy that he'd exhibited a bit of gallantry just for her.

He dismounted fluidly and tossed the reins to the ground, an effective command to a well-trained horse to stay put, as if tied to the earth itself. Naturally, the stallion responded as he ought even when Logan moved away.

Now, if she were the heroine of one of the minstrel's tales, she would award her dashing knight with a compliment at the very least. But she was not, and flights of fancy weren't allowed the lady of Lynwood. Nothing, especially not a flash of romantic musing, must interfere with her responsibilities toward the manor folk and villagers.

One of which was to ensure Logan performed the service he'd agreed to execute. She had every right to ask him how his day had gone—as his employer.

"You are back sooner than I expected."

"Did not take me as long as I expected."

"Find anything?"

"Nothing of import." His half smile warmed her clear

through. "Patience, my lady. I will find your thieves sooner than later."

"I truly did not expect you to haul them in today."

"But you hoped."

"One must always harbor hope or go mad."

He tilted his head. "You say that as one who has flirted with madness."

A confession she would rather not make. Nor was the nastiness of her marriage any of his business.

"A time or two," she admitted, then sought to place the conversation back on firmer ground. "I gather you traveled all the way to the waterfall."

"Near enough." He crossed his arms. "I did learn that the river takes more sweeping curves, and there are more paths between Lynwood and the river than I realized. Having a good look at those paths is tomorrow's goal."

Patience.

"Wat told me he saw you at the river this morn."

He looked across the field, probably for Wat, who had already returned to the village. His scowl made her wish she'd not mentioned the reeve.

"Did he now? I admit I was surprised to see him. I thought Wat was supposed to be here, not playing in the river."

Logan had the right of it. Wat had arrived later than he should have, with no satisfactory excuse for being at the river, merely complaining that Logan had seemed to be taking a leisurely ride, finding nothing, wasting time.

Joanna feared the two were on the verge of an all-out battle, which she wasn't sure how to avert. She certainly didn't like being in the middle of the combatants, and she refused to fan the fires.

"Wat has many duties. So long as he attends them all, I have no complaint."

"Mama, look! I found berries!"

Ivy's shouts of discovery were the diversion Joanna needed from both Logan and Wat. Her daughter crossed the field at a heedless run, one fist clutching the stems of daisies, the other wrapped around what Joanna assumed were now crushed berries. Red juice oozed between the fingers of Ivy's upraised fist, trickling along her arm and discoloring the bandaging wrapped around her stitches.

Sticky mess. Stains on tunic.

Still, when Ivy opened her extended hand, Joanna plucked out a piece of the offering, closed her eyes, and declared them the finest strawberries she'd tasted since last summer.

Ivy giggled and made the same offering to Logan.

He hesitated, but to his credit, managed to find a piece big enough to pick up with his large fingers.

As Joanna had done, he closed his eyes while savoring the taste. When he opened them, he fixed them on Ivy.

"Good. Sweet. Are there more for the picking?"

"Nay. Only these few." And to make sure the adults didn't get any more of the treat, Ivy shoved the rest into her mouth.

Joanna rolled her eyes; Logan suppressed his laughter.

"Too bad," he said with an exaggerated aggrieved sigh. "Your mother makes the most exquisite apple tarts in the kingdom. I am anxious to sample whatever delicacies she can fashion with strawberries."

She almost blushed at the compliment. "Well, there will be no more tarts until after more of the berries ripen. I used the last of the apples the other day."

Both Ivy and Logan looked crestfallen, which made Joanna laugh, which felt good. Happy. A rarity of late.

She gave Ivy's braid a playful tug. "Come. 'Tis time to return to the manor. Those hands need a wash."

Ivy glanced down at her juice-streaked hand, ignoring the dirtier one clutching flowers. "Aye, I suppose."

Joanna shared an amused smile with Logan before he turned and whistled sharply. The stallion tossed his nose in the air before lumbering toward them. Sweet mercy, the stallion was huge, and up close, rather frightening.

Instead of mounting, Logan swept up the reins and fell into step with her, Ivy between them.

Ivy skipped, then ran, the poor flowers taking a beating. Then she walked backward so she could admire the horse.

"What is his name?" she asked.

"Gideon," Logan answered.

"He is big."

"He is supposed to be. He is a stallion."

"Are all stallions big?"

"Most."

"We do not have stallions, only mares and geldings. We used to have one, but Mama sold him after Papa died. I guess he was big, too."

The stallion had been just as mean as his master, and had been quickly disposed of upon Bertrand's death. She saw no sense in keeping a horse even his master couldn't always control, and she'd needed the money.

"Can you ride?" Logan asked Ivy.

"I once had a pony, but he died."

Joanna bit her bottom lip. Ivy didn't know exactly how the pony died, and Joanna saw no sense in telling her. Unlike her mother, Ivy had shed tears at her father's burial, expressed sorrow for a few days afterward. If the girl had any good memories of her father, they were few and hers alone. Let her keep them.

"You miss your pony," Logan observed.

"Aye, I do."

He glanced back at Gideon. "Would you like to ride mine?"

Joanna stopped in her tracks, utterly panicked by the suggestion.

Ivy leaped for joy. "Aye. Ohhh, that would be *wonderful!*"

Oh, no it would not! She shot Logan a withering glare, which he didn't see because he smiled down at Ivy, so she placed a hand on Ivy's shoulder and strove for a calm tone.

"Ivy, the stallion is much too big for you to ride. He is trained for fighting, not carrying little girls."

Ivy immediately pouted.

Logan looked up, confused. "He will barely know she is in the saddle."

"Oh, Mama, pleeease?"

"Ivy, I—"

"Pleeeeeeeese?"

Joanna took a calming breath, envisioning every horror possible if she allowed Ivy atop that stallion. "He might buck and throw you off. Or he might spook and—"

"As long as I hold the reins, Ivy will be as safe atop Gideon as she is on her own pallet, I promise you."

Outnumbered. Outmaneuvered.

Joanna crossed her arms over her midriff, her stomach beginning to ache. Logan seemed so sure of the stallion, and Ivy hadn't had the joy of a ride since her pony's death. But ye gods, if anything happened to Ivy—she closed her eyes, too close to tears for comfort.

She felt his hand near her face before he touched her, perceived the warmth before the heat. Sweet mercy, his offer to Ivy had flung her into terror, and yet she wanted to lean into the man responsible for her fright for comfort.

"Joanna, look at me."

She forced her eyes open.

"I would not suggest Ivy ride if I believed her in any danger. Your fright is unwarranted. Truly, on my word of honor, no harm will come to her. If you like, you can ride with her."

If anything frightened her more than Ivy getting atop Gideon, it was getting on herself. She would shake her head violently to clear away her fright, but the heat of Logan's palm on her cheek, his fingers pressing against the nape of her neck, simply felt too good to shake off.

"You are sure the horse will not object?"

"He would not dare."

"Pleeeeeeeeeeeeeeease, Mama?"

Joanna stared hard into Logan's midnight eyes, seeking further reassurance. Finding it. Still, she could manage only a whisper. "Then she may ride."

He gave her neck a squeeze before he swooped a joyful Ivy into his arms. "Give your mother the flowers so you can hold on with both hands."

Joanna accepted the bouquet gratefully. They would give her something to hold on to so she didn't wring her hands raw.

Logan carried Ivy to the horse. "You must sit still, and do not kick. Can you do so?"

"Aye!"

Joanna suffered renewed doubts. Ivy sit still? Damn near impossible.

Then Logan flung Ivy up onto the stallion's back. Joanna's heart sank to her toes, waiting for the horse to buck, to object, to move. But he didn't. Gideon stood statue still, unflinching, not moving a muscle.

"Lean forward a bit and hold tight to the saddle," Logan instructed. "What say you? Comfortable?"

Ivy fair beamed down at Logan. "Very. I am ready."

Breathe, Joanna.

But she couldn't, not until Logan had a firm grip of the reins, not until horse and rider had taken a few steps and the stallion truly didn't seem to mind.

And Ivy did sit still, her legs unmoving, obviously enjoying the view from atop the stallion.

Then Joanna breathed, and fell into step beside Logan.

"My apologies, Joanna. I did not know it would frighten you so. Next time I make a suggestion to Ivy, I will ask her mother's permission first."

"I would be most appreciative."

"Are you sure you do not want to ride with her?"

Not in her lifetime. Not in any lifetime. Ivy was the adventurous one, and she hadn't come by the trait through her mother.

"No power on this earth could get me atop a stallion."

By the time they reached the gate, Logan couldn't concentrate on anything other than putting one foot before the other. His injured thigh burned so badly all he wanted was to sit down for the rest of the day.

He'd been fine while riding; walking proved excruciating.

Joanna had noticed his limp, but said nothing, merely glanced at him with knowing concern, biting down on her bottom lip to withhold comment. Her forbearance ended as they entered the stable.

"Why do you limp?"

"My leg hurts."

"So I assumed. Why does it hurt?"

Within her tone he heard shades of his own mother when she'd begun to question her young, stubborn son. Tolerant patience. All the while warning him he might as well confess to all because she would learn all anyway, despite his reluctance to tell her.

Must be a motherly trait. Given Ivy's restless spirit, Joanna likely had developed the attribute early in her daughter's life and practiced tolerance often. Except he wasn't a child anymore. Didn't need mothering. Particularly not from Joanna.

He didn't want her fussing over him.

Not quite true. He wanted fussing of a different sort from Joanna. That of a female to a male. Exactly what he shouldn't want.

Celeste had fussed. With wine. With her body. In her bed. He'd barely survived with head and heart intact, and didn't like being reminded of that particular wound.

"An old wound. It hurts betimes."

Logan led Gideon to his assigned stall and reached up for Ivy. She didn't reach down. Instead, she pointed to her bandage.

"I have a wound, too. Greta put seventeen stitches in my arm. Did you have stitches?"

"Aye, but not so many."

"Did it hurt?"

"Certes. Did yours not hurt?"

She shook her head. "Only the first, then I fell asleep. Will it hurt when Greta takes them out?"

She'd fainted, Logan surmised, probably a good thing. As for her question, he honestly couldn't say, so he shrugged a shoulder. "I do not know, Ivy. Mine are still in my leg."

"May I see?"

"Ivy," Joanna said in a warning tone. "Come down."

Logan bit back a smile when Ivy gave an aggrieved sigh, but stretched out her arms and fell into his. So light, she was, and bright, like a ray of sunshine.

As soon as he put Ivy down, Joanna held out the daisies.

"Give these to Maud. We will dry them and use the petals to sprinkle in the new rushes."

He watched the girl skip off, allowing his smile to form fully. "A handful, that one. Adorable. Bright. And not afraid of horses."

Joanna crossed her arms. "I do not fear horses, only stallions. How long have your stitches been in your leg?"

Logan began undoing the saddle fastenings. "A bit over a fortnight."

"Then they have been in your leg too long. Perhaps that is why your wound pains you at times."

Perhaps. He hadn't taken the time to seek out one of London's physicians, nor had he worked up the courage to tug the stitches out himself.

"Greta would take them out for you," she offered.

Logan pulled off the saddle, knowing Joanna was only trying to help. Fussing again.

"This Greta is the manor's healer?"

"Well, truth to tell, she is our midwife, but—"

"Nay." The thought of being attended by a midwife sparked horror in every fiber of his male body. Midwives delivered babes and tended to women's ailments, not men's. "No midwife. Is there another?"

"Nay. That is why I suggested Greta do it."

"I would rather take them out myself."

Joanna winced at his declaration. "Have you ever pulled out your own stitches?"

"Never had them before."

And he'd do his damnedest to avoid them again. Troublesome things, they were.

"I could take them out for you," she said quietly.

Her offer so surprised him he nearly dropped the saddle. All he could do was stare at her. The woman was serious!

"Why?"

"Because you hurt. I have not pulled out stitches before, but have watched the process. We can remove them as soon as you are done here."

She didn't give him time to agree or refuse, merely turned around and left the stable.

Allow Joanna to remove his stitches? He'd have to remove his breeches. She'd have to touch his thigh. Oh, sweet Lord, did he dare?

"Would you like me to finish with your horse?"

The stable lad's question barely broke through Logan's musings.

"Nay, I will do it."

He was stalling, and knew it, but ye gods, he needed time to think about Joanna's latest offer. The mere thought of her hands on him aroused him, sent heat surging to his loins.

He should refuse. But all the while he removed Gideon's tack and settled the stallion into the stall, Logan's leg reminded him that to refuse meant further pain.

He could take the stitches out himself. Cut them open and give them a yank. But what if one got stuck and refused to yield? He nearly winced. Perhaps 'twould be better to have someone else do it who knew something of the process. But Joanna?

There was always Greta. The midwife. He shivered. Nay, not a midwife.

Then Joanna.

Or he could leave the wound alone and hope the pain eased on its own. As he'd been doing for over a fortnight already and the pain got worse. All right, the stitches had to come out, Joanna the best one to remove them.

Except if she touched his thigh, his body would react in ways she wouldn't appreciate, he was sure. Even now his male parts urged him to follow Joanna into the manor, slide off his breeches, allow her to put her hands wherever she damn well pleased to put them. What his body yearned for hadn't been included in Joanna's offer, however.

Logan limped what seemed a very long distance to the hall, and every step was painful.

The stitches should come out. Joanna had offered to remove them. No matter what his body yearned for, he didn't truly want physical intimacy with Joanna, and was certain the lady didn't want involvement either.

He could control his base urges. All he had to do was think of something else while her warm hands caressed his thigh. Or perhaps the removal would hurt so much that his base urges wouldn't have the chance to manifest.

Logan opened the large doors and stepped into the hall.

Every servant in the place stopped what they were doing and turned to stare. Even Ivy, who was wrapping string around the stems of her flowers to hang them up to dry.

Joanna stood before her bedchamber door. Waiting for him.

They all know.

Which meant he couldn't change his mind, turn around, and head out the door. They would think him a coward, and he had a reputation to uphold.

Chin held high, trying not to limp, Logan crossed the room, followed Joanna into her bedchamber, and shut the door behind him.

Chapter Eight

Joanna said a short prayer for her courage to hold. She'd gathered all the supplies she thought she might need and put them on the small bedside table beside her night candle and the psalter she sometimes read when demons threatened.

A basin of hot water, towels, bandaging, small shears, and the pincers she used to pluck stubborn feathers from fowl all awaited her use.

If she removed the stitches quickly, didn't ponder over how she might hurt Logan, and paid little heed to his bared thigh, she'd be fine. She hoped.

Logan leaned against her closed bedchamber door. The sheer bulk of him shrank the room. Did she imagine it, or was his face a shade paler than it should be?

Frightened? Logan? That didn't seem possible. Or was it? She *had* told him she didn't possess a healer's skills.

"Are you sure you would not rather have Greta remove your stitches?"

He rallied somewhat, but still looked wary. "Nay. Let us be done with this."

Her thoughts precisely.

He removed his scabbard and carefully leaned his weaponry against the wall. His belt came off next, which he tossed on the floor next to his sword.

"Where do you want me?" he asked.

The air became thick and heavy. They were alone in her bedchamber, which was bad enough, even though she'd informed everyone of why, not wanting them to speculate.

Now she was about to invite Logan to sit on her bed. But where else could he comfortably sit where she could easily tend him? The stool was too short. Asking him to stand seemed unreasonable.

The last man who'd come anywhere near her bed had been Bertrand. She'd not shared it with another since, though two men had let her know they'd be delighted to warm her mattress and blankets and body.

Sweet mercy, she was only removing Logan's stitches, not climbing into the bed with him. Her pulse beat a little faster at the unbidden, wanton thought that if she wanted to share her bed with a man—which she didn't— Logan mightn't be a bad choice.

"On the bed seems best."

Logan took the few steps to the bedside, then hitched his knee-length tunic up to his waist and reached for the strings on his breeches.

Joanna blushed and turned around, both curious and afraid of what Logan might unwittingly reveal.

The man had the gall to chuckle.

Vexed, she crossed her arms but didn't turn around. "You find my granting you privacy amusing?"

"One would think a widow not so reserved. Surely you know how a man is put together."

Certes, she did. Her father's castle had been filled with males. Servants and squires, retainers and knights. Lack of privacy ensured that betimes even the daughter of the lord caught someone in a state of undress. She also knew not all men were put together in the precise fashion of all others. Some were more generously endowed.

If gossip held true, the bigger the man, the better endowed, and Logan was a very big man.

"I wished to save you the embarrassment of revealing that which you might not wish to have revealed. Nature is not as kind to some men as to others."

He laughed out loud. "I assure you, my lady, that nature has been most gracious to me. Should you ever wish to know how benevolent, you have but to ask, and I will reveal all."

She gasped at his boast. That he should offer to . . . the wretch!

"Have you no modesty at all?"

She heard the thick ropes supporting her mattress groan under Logan's weight.

"'Twas lost many years ago, I fear. You may turn around now. I am settled and modestly covered."

She turned around. Logan sat on the bed, grinning, his hands, palms down, resting on the mattress on either side of him. He'd arranged his breeches and tunic to expose only a portion of his muscled upper thigh.

Then every wayward thought fled. Whoever stitched Logan's wound had done an appalling job of it. The stitches were too long and placed too far apart, and she wondered how they'd managed to keep the wound closed. The skin around the stitches had swelled and turned an angry red. Flakes of blood yet marred the points of puncture. Merely touching the wound would hurt him. Plucking out the now frayed thread might be very painful.

"No wonder you hurt."

He looked down at the wound, then poked at it. "Aye, I should have sought out a healer sooner."

Joanna grabbed the scissors. "I will try to be gentle, but I fear this will hurt."

His grin faded somewhat. His shoulder rose in a small shrug. "I expect so. Have at it, Joanna."

He'd called her by name for the second time, and she wished he hadn't because she liked the way it sounded in that deep, husky voice, making this already too-personal task seem more intimate.

Get it done.

Joanna placed her left hand on his thigh, just below the stitches. His skin was warm and smooth, stretched taut over hard muscle. She steadied her hand and slipped the tip of the shears under the first thread. It didn't snip open as it should.

"The thread is hardened. We will have to soften it first. Otherwise, when I pull on the thread, it might break into tiny pieces, and we may never get it all out."

He reached into his boot and pulled out a silver dagger—shining, sharp, and lethal.

"This work better?"

She couldn't imagine using it. What if her hand should slip?

"Nay. Best I use scissors."

For a moment she thought he might try to slip the dagger's tip under the stitch, but then he tucked the weapon back into his boot.

Joanna dipped a towel into the basin of hot water, wrung out the excess, folded it into a pad, and placed it carefully over the stitches.

"This should work but will take a few minutes." With naught to do for the nonce, she sat next to him, but not too close. "How did you come by the wound?"

"An opponent I thought vanquished had some life to him yet. The next time I run a man through, I will ensure he is truly unable to raise his sword again."

She winced at the crudeness of his description, but knew the ways of a battle. Men fought, men fell, men died. He'd said enough to satisfy her curiosity, and she truly didn't want further details.

"The physician who tended your wound has no right to call himself one. He did a poor job of it. You should have had twenty stitches, at the least."

"For one who proclaims she is no healer, you have strong opinions on the work of others."

She crossed her arms, something she caught herself doing every time Logan pricked her ire. "One need not be accomplished at stitching to notice when it is badly done."

He picked up the towel, frowned at the stitches, and put the towel back.

"A lad of a squire did the mending. I thought him rather brave, and neat, considering the wealth of blood."

"Not a healer?"

"One is not particular when one's leg is split open."

She imagined so, but still. "Why the squire?"

"He was there, and he had needle and thread in his pouch."

Said as though she really should have guessed.

"Did you have a physician look at it afterward?"

"Nay."

She gave him a look that asked the obvious question.

"None was available. They were busy elsewhere with more serious wounds."

Joanna pointed at his. "You could have died from loss of blood. How much more serious did it have to be?"

"The bandaging held the stitches together. I could walk. How much more tending did I need?" His eyes narrowed. "I am alive, am I not?"

She might have told him how fortunate he was to be alive, with his leg still attached, if his petulance hadn't warned her she'd overstepped. She had no right to question what he'd done, no right to preach on what he *should* have done. But so long as he was at Lynwood, she could ensure he didn't take a serious wound.

She pointed to the chest she'd felt no need to open since Bertrand's death. "While you are here, you are welcome to use my husband's chain mail. The shirt might be tight, but will protect you from harm."

"My thanks, but I prefer not to wear mail. Too cumbersome."

Stubborn. Well, she'd offered, but it was his life to risk and none of her concern as long as he didn't get himself badly wounded or killed before he caught her thieves.

Joanna rose up and bent over his leg, picked up the cooling towel, ran a finger over two of the threads and judged them soft enough to try again. Once more she placed her left hand on his inner thigh.

He hissed before she got close with the shears.

She expected to see pain, and nearly shivered at the emotion evident of an entirely different sort. He suffered not with pain, but with desire. Bold and brash. Logan's midnight eyes, smoky with passion, told her exactly where he would prefer her left hand to move, what he wanted her to grasp.

As if to confirm her suspicion, the part of him eager for her caress rose up to form an impressive bulge under his tunic.

Heat flared in her nether regions, responding to his male call to mate. The thrill rushing through her body took her by surprise. Many years had passed since she hadn't been repulsed by the prospect of coupling.

She couldn't allow it, of course, no matter that her body told her she might at last be ready to accept a man's touch without feeling revulsion. No matter that her curiosity urged her to move her hand and reveal what he offered. No matter that her instincts whispered that Logan might be an excellent lover.

Her body might be ready, but she'd be foolish to ignore her heart's plea for caution. She'd endured too much pain and sorrow from her husband to frivolously become involved with another man, to place her body and heart in peril.

Still, she didn't move her hand from his thigh. "Mayhap you would be more comfortable being tended by another."

"Do I frighten you, Joanna?"

"Nay." And it was true. She was wary, but not on the verge of fleeing the chamber. "But if my touch brings you . . . discomfort . . ."

"When a beautiful woman intimately touches a man, he is hard-pressed not to want more." He gave her a disparaging smile. "I will endeavor to control my unruly parts while you finish. One should never vex a woman who holds a pair of sharp shears so close to one's bared skin."

His attempt at humor eased the tension somewhat, and Joanna surmised his lust would wither quickly when she tugged on the stitches. She hoped her own unruly parts would calm with the same swiftness.

She waved the shears. "A wise man."

"One tries, though one is not always successful."

"On my oath, I will try not to do more damage than has already been done."

"'Tis all I can ask."

Joanna slipped the shears under the first thread. This time the thread gave way as it should. As she worked her way through the other nine, two of which weren't as cooperative as the others, she again began to doubt her abilities.

She shouldn't be playing at being a healer any more than the squire who'd stitched his wound. She could be doing Logan a grave disservice. But if she asked him again if she should call upon Greta to pull out the stitches, he would only refuse.

So she put the shears aside and grabbed hold of the pincers.

"This is the hard part," she said just above a whisper. "I am not sure if I should pluck the thread or pull slowly."

"Try plucking. The quicker done, the better."

Probably. Envisioning Logan's skin as the hide of a chicken didn't work well, but she tried to use the same skills. With the thread firmly within the pincers' jaws, she tugged. Logan's leg twitched. The string moved but didn't come all the way out.

Bright red blood seeped from the puncture points, and the coppery smell shot straight to Joanna's head.

"Pull harder, Joanna."

Beads of sweat broke out on her upper lip, not from exertion but from nervousness. This task demanded concentration and apparently a bit more fortitude and strength than she'd thought she would need.

Determined to ignore the blood, she set the pincers closer to his skin and gave a mighty tug. The thread came out intact.

Logan's hiss, this time, spoke of pain, but there was nothing she could do to spare him more. One stitch out, nine more to be removed.

She placed the towel over the punctures. "Hold this. 'Twill stop the bleeding. Ready for the next?"

"Nay, but do it anyway."

With each stitch removed she became more confident. And as each stitch bled, her aversion became more pronounced, affecting her stomach, even though Logan swiftly covered the blood with the towel.

He withstood her tending stoically, never crying out, not even flinching after that first tug. She worked quietly and quickly, somehow managing to pluck out all ten stitches without losing what she'd eaten for nooning.

Her knees unsteady, Joanna tossed the pincers on the table and sank down on the edge of the bed.

"Praise be, we are finished. Are you all right?"

"More so than you, I think. You look about to swoon."

His tone of concern touched her. Her head didn't spin

so fast nor her stomach churn so hard anymore. Still, she took a deep breath to further settle both.

"I shall be fine. Is there much pain?"

"Let us say I am most glad there were only ten stitches and not eleven."

His relief brought on a smile. "I imagine you are. Do you still bleed?"

He peeked under the toweling. "A bit."

"Then we will wrap a bandage around it." She reached for a strip of white linen, then mindful of how her touch had affected him earlier, traded Logan the towel for the bandaging. "Wrap it tightly enough to stay on. 'Twill loosen swiftly with movement."

He looked questioningly at the bandage. "Then why bother with it?"

"To keep the blood in your body and ensure the wound remains closed."

"Oh."

A knock sounded on the door at the same time Maud called out, "My lady?"

Joanna left Logan to the bandaging while she opened the door a crack to answer the housekeeper.

Maud didn't look any too happy.

"What is it, Maud?"

"We have guests for supper."

Guests? How nice! 'Twas rare anyone stopped at Lynwood Manor to pass the time.

"Who?"

"Sir Gregory Marshall and the two squires who accompanied him last time beg hospitality for the night."

Joanna almost groaned, in no mood for the company of Sir Gregory. Dare she hope he was merely passing by on his way to some other destination and hadn't come to press his suit? Not likely. Still, she could hardly refuse the knight a meal and a pallet on her floor.

"Tell Sir Gregory we shall be glad of his company."

Maud gave her a look that said she knew otherwise but would pass along the message as directed.

Joanna closed the door and turned around to see Logan tying the strings on his breeches.

"Sir Gregory Marshall, hmmm?"

"Do you know him?"

"Met him a time or two. Friend or ally of yours?"

Joanna crossed to the table to clear away the supplies, deciding how to describe Sir Gregory, though it was truly none of Logan's business.

"Neither," she decided. Not friend nor ally. More like pest.

"Then what does he want?"

Me. Nay, not quite correct. Gregory would be willing to take her to have what he really craved.

"He wants Lynwood Manor."

Logan huffed. "When last we met he had not enough coin to make such a purchase."

Joanna picked up the shears and pincers, tossed the towels over her arm, and hefted the basin of water.

"He does not mean to come by Lynwood through purchase. Would you be so kind as to open the door?"

He did. "Then how . . . oh. He is your suitor?"

"So he believes."

And somehow she must press upon Gregory—that very night—that she neither wanted nor needed his suit.

*   *   *

Logan hurriedly strapped on his belt and scabbard. Then he paused, wondering why he rushed. To protect Joanna from Gregory Marshall? An absurd notion.

The woman didn't need protection from a knight of good family, even if that knight had little coin to claim as his own. Verily, if Gregory won Joanna's hand, became lord of Lynwood Manor, he'd be doing very well for himself.

Except the mere thought of Joanna's hand in Gregory's rubbed a raw spot on his innards.

All right, so he desired the woman, had come within a hair of pulling her into his arms and down on the mattress. For a moment he'd nearly succumbed to temptation, but his wits—and conscience—saved him.

The last widow he'd pulled into a bed had nearly been the death of him, and he could see shadows of that ill-fated alliance creeping in on him. Joanna might not be Celeste, but he couldn't let his better judgment become clouded by lust.

Lynwood Manor was a decent holding and Joanna a beautiful widow. Gregory was a worthy knight of about Logan's own age, and considered handsome among the ladies—a tall, dark-haired noble who had the misfortune of being a second son. A match between Joanna and Gregory might benefit them both.

Except Joanna didn't seem overly joyful at the prospect of Sir Gregory Marshall's visit. Her heart wasn't engaged. Not that affection was a necessary requirement for marriage. Far from it. Many marriages, especially those among people of higher rank, came about for reasons other than the personal desires of the bride and groom involved.

Whom Joanna might marry was none of his affair. He was but a mercenary in her employ, hired to catch a band of thieves. When done, he would bid her fare-thee-well and leave. With no regrets and no messy ties.

His mind settled on the matter, Logan opened the bedchamber door and stepped into the hall—to see Sir Gregory Marshall gallantly bent over Lady Joanna's hand.

Perversely, Logan wanted to run the man through for having the temerity to mash his lips against Joanna's fingers. Instead, he slammed the bedchamber door behind him, making nearly everyone present jump, including Gregory.

Logan decided he'd accomplished his goal when Gregory dropped Joanna's hand.

The knight didn't take the interruption well. His narrowed eyes fixed upon Logan, then flickered to the bedchamber door. Logan could guess at the thoughts running through the knight's mind, and when Gregory didn't immediately draw his sword to defend Joanna's honor, the knight's reputation slipped a notch downward on Logan's inner tally stick.

Not that Logan intended to be drawn into a sword fight with Gregory, like two men scrapping for a bone to which neither could rightfully claim ownership. But he wasn't about to set Gregory's mind at ease about what had gone on in Joanna's bedchamber, either.

He walked toward the pair, ignoring the hint of ire in Joanna's eyes for his ignoble entrance into the hall, noting how much better his leg felt for the absence of tight stitches. How nice to be able to walk again without limping even though the wound stung a bit.

Logan gave the knight his due, bowing before him slightly. "Sir Gregory."

"Grimm. What do you here?"

"At present I am in her ladyship's service." He shrugged a dismissive shoulder. "Nothing too difficult, merely ridding the area of a band of thieves."

Gregory tapped his gauntlets against his leg, a sure sign of the man's continued ire. "Not your usual sort of employment."

"Nay, but I was between offers, so . . ."

"Between offers, hmm? I heard your last foray did not go as planned. Reports had it you might lose your leg."

If Gregory had heard, apparently the report had spread quickly and thoroughly. Damn. He would have to do something to undo the damage. 'Twouldn't do for the lords of the land to believe he'd lost his leg. Offers for his services would dwindle to a trickle.

Logan smiled. "Nay. A mere cut, is all. And thanks to Lady Joanna's tender care, nearly completely healed. As you can see, all my parts are whole, and I assure you, in working order. My thanks for your concern for my well-being."

Gregory's answering smile left no doubt about his lack of concern. He turned to Joanna, who'd remained quiet during the exchange. Given the furious look she shot him, Logan had to admire her restraint.

Which meant she'd caught his reference to all of his parts being in working order. He probably owed her an apology for that shot, but couldn't bring himself to do so in front of Gregory.

"My lady, certes, you need not have hired a mercenary for so simple a task," the knight said, his tone dripping with honey. "You had but to send for me, and I would have gladly taken care of the problem for you without charging Grimm's steep fee."

Joanna raised an eyebrow at the condescending tone. "Would you?"

Logan heard a warning in those two simple words; apparently Gregory didn't.

"Of course, my lady. I would be most pleased to be of any service you will allow."

Joanna crossed her arms, then raised a fingertip to her lush lower lip, tapping. Seriously considering Gregory's offer?

Given her mood, Logan wanted to scoff, but couldn't, not yet.

Mon Dieu! If she took Gregory at his word, allowed him to take over the search for the thieves, sent Logan on his way, 'twould be the first time he would suffer a dismissal! Dismissed by a woman? 'Twould do more damage to his reputation than losing a leg!

And Gregory knew it, the bastard.

Joanna lowered her hand. "Then you believe I erred in hiring Grimm?"

"Not erred, but perhaps in your zeal to catch the thieves, you went to the extreme. 'Tis easily corrected."

"I did not think my judgment so flawed."

"Joanna, dear heart, you must not be upset over this. Women simply are not accustomed to dealing with—"

Joanna tossed her hands in the air and gave a most unladylike squawk, sending Gregory back a step, making Logan want to cheer. He shouldn't have worried over his reputation, or over Gregory's marrying Joanna. The knight should consider himself fortunate if she didn't poison his meal.

The woman was utterly magnificent in her fury, breasts thrust forward, hands on beautifully rounded hips, exuding a confidence he'd never witnessed in her before. And he thanked the fates Joanna aimed her fury elsewhere, that he was merely an observer.

"You arrogant . . . man! How dare you question how I oversee my holding?"

"Now, Joanna—"

"You are welcome to a night's bed and board. I expect you will wish to leave quite early on the morn, so I will have Maud prepare a packet of food for you to take with you so you suffer no delay."

Gregory's spine stiffened. "You are not being reasonable."

Logan almost pitied Gregory. Almost.

"I see," Joanna answered, her voice deceptively calm. She glanced about the room, spotted who she sought. "Guards, Sir Gregory has decided he wishes to leave *now*. Pray give him escort to the gate."

Gregory gaped, as did nearly everyone in the hall. Joanna ignored them, wheeling around to stride off in the direction of her bedchamber. She stopped midhall, spun around, and shot Logan a glare he probably deserved.

"You I will speak with later!"

Then everyone learned that Joanna, too, knew how to slam a bedchamber door.

Chapter Nine

"Mama is most peeved with you."

Ivy's announcement came as no surprise to Logan. Sir Gregory had left nigh on an hour ago, and still Joanna remained secluded in her bedchamber. He'd expected her to come out long before now and "talk to" him as she'd threatened.

Logan took another gulp of spiced mead before setting his mug on the table.

"Peeved, hmm?"

Ivy slid onto the bench beside him. "*Most* peeved."

Certes, he'd made a remark to Sir Gregory Marshall he probably shouldn't have, but Joanna was excessively upset over a trifling comment if she brooded over it this long. And if Joanna was angry, why not take him to task and be done? As she had with Gregory. Tossed the knight right out of the hall. The astonishment on Gregory's face still made Logan smile.

"Tell me, Ivy. Does your mother usually lock herself away when angry?"

"Nay. Mama *never* gets this angry."

She had earlier, in magnificent fashion.

"Never?"

"Not ever. What did you do?"

Ivy had been present in the hall during Gregory's ouster, but apparently didn't understand what led up to it. Especially his part in that welcome event, which had been modest, indeed.

"Nothing to warrant a sulk of this magnitude."

Her eyes narrowed in confusion. "What is magni . . . tude?"

Logan smiled down at her, realizing he'd used too big a word for so small a girl. Ivy's brightness and manner sometimes belied her age, or so it seemed to him. He knew little about children, about female children in particular, and knew not how to make comparisons.

"I should have said your mother places too much importance on so small a matter."

"Oh." Ivy thought that over. "Then why is she yet angry?"

He wished he knew. Having no answer for the child, he shrugged off the question and changed the subject. "How does your arm feel?"

Ivy glanced down at her bandaged forearm. "It itches."

"No pain?"

"It hurt, at first, but now it just itches, and Mama will not let me remove the bandage to scratch."

He well remembered the irritating itch, and how scratching his stitches made them bleed. Perhaps he shouldn't have been so careless with them. "Is it bad to scratch?"

"Mama says if I scratch them, they will fester and swell and hurt again, so I do not scratch them."

Logan wished he'd known. "I heard you needed seventeen."

Ivy's head bobbed. "Want to see? 'Tis a long cut."

And have Joanna learn Ivy removed the bandage at his urging? She was angry enough at him as it was.

"Nay. Can you just show me how long it is with your fingers?"

Ivy placed her thumb and forefinger on her bandage, spanning her wound. Within those scant inches, the midwife had placed seventeen stitches. Logan's wound had been twice as long and sewn together with ten, and according to Joanna, a badly done ten.

No wonder he'd taken so long to heal.

"How much longer must your stitches stay in?"

She sighed. "Greta says at least two more days."

"That is not so long."

He apparently gave her no comfort, for her expression clouded. "Maud said Mama took your stitches out. Did it hurt?"

Like the very devil, but he couldn't tell that to Ivy and possibly scare her. Besides, hers would probably come out easier. He hoped.

"Not so much. Hurt much worse when they went in."

"Did you cry?"

"Nary a tear." None that anyone had seen, anyway. "I would not worry overmuch on their removal. And think of how much better your arm will feel when they are out."

"Truly? Like your leg?"

"Truly. Just like my leg. Good as new, now."

He'd said something right. Her eyes brightened again.

"Then mayhap Mama will allow me to play on the green again."

"Mayhap."

Logan guessed that might take more time than Ivy allowed. Joanna didn't fear for Ivy's arm, but for her life. Then again, mayhap within two days the thieves would no longer be a worry. The children could again play on the green. The villagers wouldn't worry over the loss of their possessions. Logan could leave Lynwood Manor and go back to London.

He took another long swallow of spiced mead.

From London he could begin to repair the damage done by the false reports on the severity of his wound. Ye gods. A daunting task. 'Twas also disconcerting he had Sir Gregory to thank for alerting him to the problem.

Ivy slid off the bench. "You might tell Mama you are sorry. That is what I do, then her anger goes away."

"Does it?"

"Aye. Except you may have to tell her so more than once. Mama is *most* peeved."

The girl skipped off toward the hearth, leaving Logan to ponder over her mother's degree of pique.

He'd known as soon as the words left his mouth that Joanna might take exception to his comments on the wholeness and working order of his parts. Certes, in the bedchamber with Joanna's hand upon his thigh, there had been no doubt of the truth. He'd gone hard and ready and most willing, and come too close to taking action.

Perhaps needling Gregory over having been in Joanna's bedchamber, a place the knight wanted to enter as her husband, hadn't been wise. But damn, witnessing Gregory kiss Joanna's hand hadn't sat well. Envisioning the two of them tumbling around on her bed, naked, sweating, heating the room—sweet mercy, his gut twisted even though he now knew Joanna would never allow Gregory the privilege.

Logan knew he had no right to interfere in Joanna's affairs. She was a woman full-grown, a widow who knew what to do with a man in her bed and had every right to seek her pleasure with whomever she wished.

Even Gregory.

Except the thought of any man other than himself in Joanna's bed tied Logan's innards in knots. He couldn't remember desiring any other woman to this degree, not even Celeste. While the intensity of his desire might scare him witless, it also refused to abate. His body wasn't listening to reason. All it knew was a craving for Joanna.

Perhaps, if he gave in to that craving, the hunger for her would be satisfied and not pester him anymore. Except she wasn't even speaking to him at the moment.

Maybe Ivy had given him good advice. He could offer Joanna his apology. And then . . . what? He doubted she was in any mood to satisfy his cravings, not now, likely not ever. The best he could hope for was to get back into Joanna's good graces. That would have to be enough.

Hellfire. He shouldn't be feeling guilty or considering playing the gallant. He was a mere mercenary in her service, not responsible for her well-being. All he was required to do was capture her thieves and get the hell on with his own life.

Logan glanced at the door that had been closed too long, downed the last of his mead, and stood up. By God, if he was going to humble himself, there was no better time than now.

He almost made it across the room before Maud placed herself square in his path. The stout housekeeper crossed her arms and pinned him with a warning glare.

"What are you about, mercenary?"

Logan glared back. "I intend to speak with her ladyship."

"Have you not done enough harm?"

The accusation punched him in the gut. "I never meant to harm her."

Maud huffed. "Ye have done more damage than—" She pursed her lips, whatever she'd been about to say cut off. "'Twould be best if you leave her alone."

More damage than what? Or who?

What made Maud, a servant, albeit one of high standing who enjoyed Joanna's good favor, take on the duty as her lady's protector? Was this a long-standing habit or a recent development?

Either way, it pricked his ire. Joanna didn't need Maud's protection. Joanna was decidedly capable of making her own decisions and giving her own orders.

"Why do we not let Lady Joanna decide?"

Maud's mouth thinned to a sour line. "You stay here. I will ask."

She sailed off on her mission. Logan wasn't sure it was a good idea to allow the self-assigned guardian of the door do the asking. His suspicion proved true within moments, the answer clearly readable in the smug expression on Maud's face.

"Her ladyship prefers not to speak with you yet."

"Why not?"

"She did not say."

"I would know why."

"Let it be, Grimm."

He probably should, but knew he wouldn't. He took a menacing step toward Maud. She didn't budge. So he picked her up and set her aside. The housekeeper's shock was so great she didn't move, giving him enough time to get through the door and throw the bolt behind him.

Furious pounding began immediately, followed by vile oaths of retribution. He ignored Maud's ranting in favor of studying the woman seated on the stool, white fabric and crimson-threaded needle in hand.

Embroidering, he knew. On what he had no notion.

Joanna looked up at him, her face pale, her eyes puffy but not red. She must have cried earlier, but now appeared composed. Calm. Damn near fragile.

She set down the embroidery at her feet. "You have a way of upsetting women, Grimm. Now Maud is wroth with you, too."

Said too softly. He didn't like it, not from Joanna.

"Maud's anger I understand. 'Tis yours that leaves me befuddled."

The pounding became harder, as if Maud was now using both fists. She screeched Joanna's name.

"Maud, leave be," Joanna called out, her voice a little stronger, edged with the tone of command.

Better, Logan thought, but not strong enough for his liking.

The pounding ceased. "I tried to keep him out, milady!"

"I know 'tis not your fault. I will speak with him."

Logan thought he heard a disgruntled huff, but 'twas hard to be sure through the closed door.

In the ensuing silence, Joanna's spine straightened, her

shoulders squaring in a physical gathering of body and emotions, reminding Logan of the tactic men used when preparing for battle. Logan readied for the first wave of an attack.

"You had the gall to imply to all and sundry that we did *more* in my bedchamber than remove your stitches. And you wonder why I am upset?"

Her opening volley buffeted at his defenses. He wanted so badly to take her in his arms, soothe away her anger, and make his apologies that he crossed his arms and leaned back against the door to prevent immediate surrender. In her present mood, he wasn't sure how she would react to so intimate a maneuver. But 'struth, he'd prefer she tried to claw his eyes out than burst into tears.

"You and I both know that nothing untoward happened while you removed my stitches, though we also know *more* could have happened."

She raised her chin. "That matters not. I was still shamed."

"So shamed that you hide yourself away and shed tears? I am sorry if what I said caused you a moment's discomfort"—he held a finger up to halt what he guessed would be an objection—"but truly, Joanna, 'tis no one else's business what happened in your bedchamber. Whether we took out stitches or pleasurably enjoyed each other is . . . well, a matter for us alone."

She clasped her hands in her lap and looked away. "I am now lady of Lynwood Manor, and as such must set a decorous example for my people and for my daughter."

"By becoming the ideal of virtue for all to emulate? You are human, Joanna, not Holy Mother Mary."

"That is blasphemy!"

"Only the truth." He shoved away from the door. "I once knew a knight who followed the code of chivalry to the extreme. He knew every word of the rules and adhered to each as if his very life depended upon whether or not he upheld them. When he fell, he fell hard and nearly lost both mind and life. Better to take small stumbles, I say, than fall off the edge of a cliff."

She waved a dismissive hand. "You do not understand. If I stumble, the people suffer. And if they suffer . . ."

She bit her bottom lip.

He'd never been in her position, merely observed how the lords he'd served ruled their people. He supposed that women, with their more tender hearts, might notice their tenants' suffering more than a man might. But neither man nor woman could prevent all of life's afflictions.

"Suffering is a part of life. You cannot prevent all of your tenants' travails."

"I must prevent those travails I can or . . . or I fail them. If I fail them, they will lose what little faith they have in me."

He wanted to tell her she had no worries on that score, but he'd seen for himself that the villagers' faith was weak. Joanna had to prove herself to them over and over again, merely because she was a woman, their lady—not their lord.

'Twas the reason she'd hired him to rid the area of the thieves, to prove her ability to rule Lynwood. Still, he believed she took too much on herself.

"So you martyr yourself on the altar of their respect? Granted, respect must be earned, but at what price to you?"

"Whatever I must pay."

"Pay too dearly, and you will have naught left in your coffers, not even their respect. Joanna, you must cut yourself a bargain. The price you expect of yourself is too high."

She rose from the stool. Though she began to pace, he liked the firmness of her steps. Even a bit of color seeped back to her cheeks. She might stumble on occasion, but possessed the fortitude to come right again.

"A bargain," she said, speaking more to herself than him. "I wish—" She shook her head, banishing her wish.

"Wish for what?"

She stopped pacing, glanced at him. "Wish I could turn back time, have this morning back. I would react differently."

"Why? I thought you handled Gregory admirably."

"You would." She smiled, then took a deep breath. "I should not have tossed him out."

"You are well rid of him."

Her smile widened. "There are others who would not agree. Wat believes Sir Gregory Marshall would make a fine lord for Lynwood Manor."

"Who the devil cares what Wat believes? 'Tis you who would have to marry the . . . knight. If you do not want him, then sending him on his way was the right thing to do."

"Perhaps, but not the way I did it. I should not have lost my temper so forcefully. 'Twas the one thing I vowed not to do after . . . my husband died."

The admission pulled Logan up short, all of the pieces of the puzzle coming together with a mighty, ominous thud.

He knew men who ruled with the force of their voices,

followed by the hammer of fists if the shouting didn't get immediate results. He'd seen peasants scramble in fear when their lord rode through the village, and wives cringe at their husbands' very presence.

Had Joanna's husband been such a man? One who ruled by fear and not wisdom? Who used his fist instead of reason? Very possible, considering her vow. Which she'd broken this morn.

Logan clenched his fists, wishing he could get his hands around Bertrand de Poitou's throat. 'Twas good the man was already dead.

"That is why you hide. You are not so much angry at me, or even Gregory, as you are at yourself."

Her smile faded. "Certes, I am angry at you. 'Twas you who made that ill-considered comment about your parts being whole and working after coming out of my bedchamber, which led to Sir Gregory's questioning my judgment, which sparked my temper!"

A temper she showed him now, and he couldn't help himself from fanning the flame.

"Well, you saw for yourself I did not lie about my parts."

Her hands went to her hips. "Logan."

A warning to desist. Not yet.

He moved toward her, stopping within mere inches. She neither cringed nor flinched, but held her ground, her amber eyes staring at him openly, without any hint of fear. This was the Joanna he admired, and whom he wanted so badly he again crossed his arms to keep from reaching out to her.

"Do you know that you are utterly glorious in your

fury? I thought so this morn, and have not changed my mind."

Aye, there was definite color in her cheeks now.

"Fury serves no purpose. It only makes everyone wretched."

"Only when aimed poorly. And you did not. You hurt no one. Well, perhaps Gregory's feelings, but that does not count. He deserved to be tossed out on his ear for the way he spoke to you. You should make no apology for that, not even to yourself."

She took a deep breath, her lovely, firm breasts rising and falling. "Anger must be controlled."

"And you did. Gregory walked out of here alive and well, his nose not broken, no dagger in his gullet. Had he spoken so condescendingly to a lord . . . well, he would not have or risked life and limb."

"But—"

"Either rule or be ruled, Joanna. If that means you must show your temper a time or two, so be it. Just warn me when you are about to loose an arrow so I am not standing innocently before your target."

She raised an eyebrow. "Innocent? You?"

He smiled, innocently.

Her eyes rolled in disbelief of his temerity, but her small smile confirmed her sense of humor was alive and well. *Damn, but I like Joanna.*

Was that really so bad? Had he been terribly wrong to judge all widows on the experience with one scheming one? Perhaps he'd been unfair, but it changed naught. Becoming involved with a woman of Joanna's rank wasn't wise for a mere mercenary.

He should leave immediately. He'd accomplished his

goal. Joanna hadn't yet said so, but she was no longer as peeved with him, no longer so angry with herself.

Then she tilted her head, her soft smile warming his insides while freezing him in place.

"Why is it I can talk to you?" she asked. "There are people here aplenty who might listen and understand, and yet, 'tis in you I confide. Twice now. Does that not seem strange?"

Her openness had surprised him the first time, when she'd done so in the middle of the night. This time it felt—right.

"Not truly. 'Tis sometimes easier to talk to someone with whom you have no close connection. If I were one of your guards or a villager, you might feel less inclined."

"But should not one feel a measure of trust before venting one's woes? And does not trust come with knowing someone well, their worthiness proved over time?"

"Not always. I often have no time to get to know the men I fight with before I must decide who to trust at my back and who not. Most often I am right."

"But not always."

"No man is always right, but I trust my instincts, and they rarely lead me astray."

She sighed. "I wish I had such confidence in mine own judgments."

"'Twill come with time if you allow it."

Her smile widened. "More sage advice?"

He shook his head. "Merely life lessons learned. If one cannot trust oneself, who can one fully trust?"

And peering into those beautiful amber eyes, Logan knew he could trust himself to remain in her bedchamber no longer.

He bowed slightly. "If her ladyship will permit, I will unbolt the door and allow poor Maud to enter. I would not be surprised if she had her ear pressed to the door, ready to call out the guard at the least alarming sound."

"Maud means well. She tries to protect me from harm."

A long-standing habit of the housekeeper's then, and Logan could guess from whom she'd tried to protect Joanna before. Likely her husband.

"Was Maud successful?"

Joanna's eyes clouded for a moment, then cleared. "Not as often as she would have liked."

Bastard. Logan felt his ire rising all over again.

"And Ivy?"

"That is a mother's task, to shield her children from harm. In that I was successful—until the plague. Nothing worked against the sickness." A single tear formed in the corner of her eye. "Elias and Rose died in my arms, the only succor I could offer either of them, and it wasn't enough."

Elias and Rose must be the children she'd lost. Hearing her despair, his chest tightened, helpless to relieve a mother's grief.

"Your little ones died knowing they were loved."

"So I h-hope."

One moment his control was firmly intact. At the hitch in her voice, restraint vanished.

Logan cupped Joanna's face, palms to cheeks, and thumbed away the tear before it could fall. So soft, so utterly lovely, her skin. Eyes bright, mouth full and lush. She tensed but didn't pull away.

"Your husband. How did he die?"

Her tongue eased out to wet her lower lip. Fully entranced, he knew what was about to happen, and nothing short of the earth opening up and swallowing him whole could stop it.

"The wretch died on a pallet in the hall, alone, knowing I despised him."

He should just cheer. Instead, he gave in to the inevitable.

As he'd feared, her mouth was warm, soft, yielding. Everything a man could hope for and more. The scent of her muddled his thoughts, the kindling of desire heated his loins. Even as he struggled to keep the kiss light, still fearful Joanna might pull away in outrage, she grasped fistfuls of his tunic and leaned into him.

His breath grew ragged as the kiss deepened. Passion flared, and he didn't doubt she could feel the hardening, rising evidence of his desire through their layers of clothing. She trembled, but he sensed no fear, only a response to the lust that simmered within them both.

Logan pushed aside every reason why he shouldn't be kissing Joanna, why he shouldn't still be in her bedchamber with the door bolted. That she was a gently born lady and he a lowly mercenary no longer mattered.

Even knowing he would later pay dearly for indulging the curiosity of his base urges, the price wasn't high enough to end the copious pleasure.

Then she moaned, a low purr in her throat, battering against what meager control he'd managed to retain. All the while he firmly grasped hold of the threads of his reason, he dearly wished he could release them to the winds and let Fate take them.

Joanna clung tight to Logan's tunic, sure that if she let

go, she would melt into a puddle at his feet. She'd experienced one man's kisses, and never, ever, knew a man's kiss could be long, tender, and sweet. Wet but not slovenly. Firm but not hurtful.

She didn't seek release from Logan's masterful mouth, nor inwardly wince at where the kiss might lead. Sweet mercy, she could stand here for hours with his mouth covering hers, partaking in this exquisite feast. With her heart beating too fast. With her senses awhirl with both confusion and delight.

Aye, she liked this man's kiss—a surprising happenstance on its own—but what shocked her most was her body's quick, hot response to the mere touch of mouths. Her woman's places fair ached with yearning to be filled.

By Logan Grimm. Who she didn't doubt would oblige her if she gave him the smallest hint that he should back up a step or two and take them down onto the bed.

She wouldn't, of course. No matter what he thought, she couldn't take a lover and expect her people to accept it without comment. The dairymaid might sport with whomever she pleased, but not the lady of the manor. Her people would think badly of her for taking a mercenary as a lover. Their meager respect would diminish. She couldn't risk that happening.

Still, wouldn't it be wonderful to know what coupling could be like with Logan? To know if his hands would caress her body with the same gentle firmness as his mouth moved over hers. To learn if the male parts he'd bragged on earlier could ease her woman's aches.

That thought took on further meaning when Logan's lips eased away from hers, leaving her breathless and bereft. To make her reluctance to release him worse, he sprinkled light kisses over her face, as if trying to make the separation easier.

Nothing would. Not yet. She pressed her face to his chest and sought to catch her breath. His arms came around her in an encompassing embrace. Not smothering. Not dominating.

Safe. Protected. She damn near cried for the joy of it.

"Joanna?"

Logan's voice was deep and raspy, lacking his usual self-assurance. How strange. But then there had been nothing of the normal in these past few minutes.

"Hmm?"

"I believe I had best leave."

Because he feared she might lose her control, or he his? 'Twas rather gratifying to think Logan might be as affected by a single kiss as she. Either way, he was right. He had to leave her bedchamber. The soonest the best. No matter how much she wished he could stay, explore the temptations she'd pondered over between bouts of guilt for losing her temper.

"I believe you must."

Neither of them moved.

"I will not tender an apology for that kiss."

"Nor would I wish you to make one."

She smiled at his relieved breath and somehow found the fortitude to begin slowly pulling way, his arms releasing her as they separated. "Were you concerned I might toss you out, too?"

"A bit. But then I reasoned that you cannot, at least not yet. I have yet to catch your thieves."

Joanna bit her bottom lip as he unbolted the door and strode out of her bedchamber. Aye, she couldn't toss

Logan out until after the villains were caught. But then she wouldn't have to toss him out: he would leave on his own.

'Twas against all sense to hope Logan didn't snare his prey too soon. Shocked by the thought, Joanna flopped down on the bed.

Sweet mercy, she'd known the man for all of two days and allowed him liberties she'd vowed to permit no man. Only by keeping to her vow could she ensure her own safety. Protect Ivy.

Better she should have kissed Gregory. His kiss wouldn't stir unwanted passion, or leave her weak-kneed and vulnerable. Wouldn't have her wondering about romantic trysts in the moonlight and illicit assignations in her bedchamber. Wouldn't leave her feeling bereft when the kiss ended, wanting another, wanting *more*.

Damn the bards for their songs of love and yearnings. She could very well do without either. She needed no man in her life, especially one who presented a danger to her common sense. A mercenary, no less. A man who lived by no rules or code.

Joanna rose, determined to put Logan Grimm out of her head for a time. Perhaps if she had something to eat and a good night's sleep, she could make sense of it all.

The wetness between her thighs mocked her, warning her that when it came to Logan Grimm very little made sense.

Chapter Ten

Several hours later, unable to sleep, Logan sought respite from the aching aftermath of Joanna's kiss.

Having tried drinking more ale than sensible, then breathing deeply while trying to clear his thoughts, then considering easing the ache himself and knowing 'twould be less than satisfactory, he pulled on his clothes and went outside.

The night was crisp and clear, the bright stars and luminous moon casting shadows about the bailey. Peace reigned, the majority of God's creatures deep in slumber—except him and the guards who patrolled the wall walk.

He'd never before walked guard duty at night and now hoped it might prove of enough interest to banish the memory of Joanna's soft mouth moving beneath his lips, silence her soft purr.

Something had to work—short of stealing silently into her bedchamber and hoping she didn't scream when he slid under her blankets—or he'd go mad.

He took the steps up to the wall walk two at a time,

eager for the breeze that fluttered the green, orange-trimmed flags posted at either side of the gate. He nodded at the guard posted there, then walked a few yards down before stopping between two points of rough-hewn timber.

The breeze wasn't half as bracing as he hoped for, so he leaned against the palisade and forced his attention to the village below.

Again peace reigned. Nary a whisper could be heard, nor movement detected. From this height Logan clearly saw the common well in the green's center, even made out shapes of the grave markers in the small cemetery next to the church at the far end of the village.

Which marker commemorated the passing of Sir Bertrand de Poitou? Probably the largest one. Logan's palms again itched. Aye, good thing the bastard was dead. 'Twas a shame about Joanna's little ones though. The plague hadn't discerned between young or old, innocent or wicked. The sickness took the good with the bad and left the survivors shocked and mournful.

And thankful to be alive. As he was. The sickness hadn't found him, nor did he mourn anyone's passing, his parents having died years ago.

No light shone from any of the cottages' doorways or windows—save one. Wat Reeve's. A faint light seeped into the night from the sides of his door, and Logan wondered what demons kept the reeve awake this night.

At the sound of footsteps, Logan glanced sideways to see Harold coming toward him, a loaded crossbow in his arms. 'Twas surprising the captain of the guard patrolled at night.

Logan smiled at the man he'd come to like. "Could you not assign yourself a better time to patrol?"

Harold smiled back. "One of the guards is ill, so I took the duty."

"A captain should get his sleep. Why not assign another?"

"We all take on added duty these days. Before the plague we were twelve and are now only eight. Besides, 'tis hard for me to sleep anyway, what with the thieves yet on the loose."

A reminder that several people would sleep better when Logan finished his task. Since no hint of censure tinged Harold's comment, Logan didn't take it as criticism.

Logan again peered down at the reeve's cottage. "'Twould seem we are not the only ones concerned over the thieves. Wat keeps us company."

"Not only Wat. I am told the blacksmith, the carpenter, and the brewer's husband are in there, too. Likely sampling the latest of Mistress Brewer's wares."

"Is that common?"

"Common enough." Harold's smile widened. "I imagine all will stagger out soon. Wat has to be in the fields at sunrise. 'Struth, I would not want his position."

From what Logan had observed of other reeves, the men led comfortable lives and made a good wage. Their duties were many and varied, and all struck Logan as rather boring.

"Why not?"

"Too many problems. Take the planting, for one. We have fewer people to put in the fields, and I hear there is no wheat seed on hand for the late-summer sowing. He told Lady Joanna this morn that a trip to the market fair in Oundle is necessary to purchase more."

That didn't sound good.

"Can seed be bought at this late date?"

"Let us hope so."

Not good at all.

"Did he not buy enough last autumn?"

"'Twas not truly Wat's fault. His father made the purchase before he took ill."

Then Wat hadn't received skillful training, didn't have a good model to follow.

"Wat is recently made reeve, then."

"Aye. He lost both parents and his two siblings to the plague. 'Twasn't a surprise when the villagers elected him to his father's position." Harold leaned a shoulder against the palisade, his expression pensive. "You may have noticed that many of us are young and ill prepared to assume positions of authority."

Logan remembered meeting Harold in the Red Rooster, the thought crossing his mind that the man seemed too young to have risen to captain of the guard.

"You include yourself as ill prepared."

He chuckled. "Me most of all."

Logan waited for him to elaborate. When Harold held his peace, he prodded.

"So far as I can tell you have settled nicely into the position."

"I hope so. I would not wish to disappoint her ladyship."

Did Joanna know of Harold's admiration for her? Logan doubted it, not from the way Harold acted when around her. Harold showed her just enough friendliness for politeness' sake, as the captain of the guard would treat the wife of his lord.

Except in this case the wife *was* the lord.

"You do not mind serving a woman?"

"Not at all, at least I do not mind being in Lady Joanna's service." He tilted his head, again pensive. "She operates differently from Bertrand, who simply decided what he wanted, then gave an order. Joanna considers all of her choices longer, even asks those who would be affected by her choice for their opinion before making a decision. All has turned out well thus far, though I think, betimes, she tries too hard to please everyone, which we all know cannot be done." Harold nudged Logan's shoulder. "I hear she even took on a healer's duties this morn. How is the leg?"

Naturally, the news had spread. The youngest village child had probably heard of how Lady Joanna removed the mercenary's stitches. And they likely speculated on what else might have happened behind the bedchamber door. Which he still maintained concerned nobody beyond him and Joanna.

If Harold fished for information, he wasn't going to get any from Logan. Whatever happened between him and Joanna privately would remain private. Besides, Harold's loyalty to Joanna might induce him to do something stupid, like defend the lady's honor, and Logan wanted to keep a good relationship with the captain of the guard.

Logan knew he'd done some fishing himself, but not entirely out of idle curiosity. The more he knew about the holding, the better he might understand why the thieves targeted only Lynwood Manor. That had always bothered him, that and why Wat and the brewer's husband's footprints led away from the river but not to the river.

"Leg is fine. Her ladyship plucked out the stitches as if they were feathers from a chicken."

During Harold's good-natured laughter, Logan's thoughts again focused on one person who wasn't happy with some of Joanna's decisions, especially the decision to hire a mercenary to deal with the thieves.

"Wat is none too happy with some of Lady Joanna's decisions."

Harold waved a dismissive hand. "I cannot see where he has cause for complaint. 'Struth, he has even voiced the opinion that her ladyship should marry, feels 'twould be best if she provided Lynwood Manor with a lord."

The news took him aback. True, Joanna had mentioned earlier that Wat approved of Sir Gregory, but had the reeve actually had the nerve to tell Lady Joanna she should marry? Apparently. The reeve overstepped.

Logan scoffed. "Like that dullard who was here earlier?"

"Oh, Sir Gregory is not all bad, nor is Sir Edgar. Both would be good matches for her. They are of a rank, and either would be able to serve the half a knight's fee Lynwood owes to the abbot. Lady Joanna will either have to find someone to serve the manor's portion or pay scutage when that comes due in summer."

Bertrand must have served the knight's fee, which had given Joanna twenty days respite from her husband. Now she would have to pay the abbot to replace her husband's service, and many times that money went to pay mercenaries.

And who the devil was Sir Edgar? Another suitor?

Would yet another swain show up at the manor door? Hellfire.

Logan made a mental note to hold his tongue should that happen. 'Twas none of his business, just as it hadn't been his place to make comments to Sir Gregory. But damn, he hadn't liked the knight on sight, liked him even less when he tried to lord it over Joanna.

The responsibilities of ruling a holding were endless, some heavier than others. Still, Joanna seemed willing and able to shoulder them all. 'Twould be easier if she had more coin in her coffers, a condition dependent upon a good harvest.

There were never, ever, warranties on a harvest.

But then, Bertrand must not have been the best manager of his lands and finances if his widow now must count every coin. Another mark against the man.

"You have been at Lynwood a long time?"

"Nigh on ten years now."

"As a guard?"

Harold shook his head. "Until he died, I served as Sir Bertrand's squire. Lady Joanna was kind enough to allow me to remain after his death. When the plague took the previous captain, the guards put forth my name, and her ladyship accepted."

Squires didn't usually remain squires.

"You hope to earn your knighthood?"

"Perhaps, but 'twill not happen anytime soon. I have not the money to support the equipage. Neither does Lady Joanna. I would have to enter the service of a richer lord. I know of one or two who might agree to take me on."

A squire turned guard. Even being made captain was a

decline in status for a man who must be of good birth. There were exceptions, of course, but most squires aspiring to knighthood came from the ranks of the gentry or higher.

"Then why do you not leave?"

"I cannot while the manor is in dire straits."

Logan had to admire the man's loyalty, his willingness to put off his own ambitions for the good of others. To serve Joanna during her time of greatest need. Logan couldn't think of a lord he'd served during his many years as a mercenary who had inspired such loyalty in his own heart. There wasn't a one of them he would have hesitated to abandon if he hadn't been paid to stay.

Nor had Logan ever aspired to more than he was, though as a soldier's son and better than most at wielding a sword, he might have earned a higher place for himself through hard work and luck.

But that would have meant remaining in one place, serving one lord. The life of a mercenary suited him better. It paid well, too. Well enough that he'd saved a tidy sum. Someday he would have to decide what to do with it, but that day was far off.

Harold shoved away from the palisade. "I have lingered too long. Shout if you see anything out of place, will you?"

"Of course."

Harold resumed his slow patrol around the wall walk, which Logan guessed would take half an hour or so to complete.

Again, Logan glanced down at Wat's cottage. The man must not be disliked by all if three men found him a fit drinking companion.

Had he been too hard on Wat merely out of dislike, because the reeve hadn't agreed with Joanna's decision to hire a mercenary? Wat's outburst last eve could be forgiven if viewed in the light of loyalty toward his lady, just as Logan viewed Maud's guarding of the bedchamber door.

Maybe Wat was just a young man feeling his way through a position he wasn't prepared for, failing in some ways and overstepping boundaries in others. As was Harold, who seemed to have settled into his duties though yet unsure of himself.

As was Joanna, a lovely woman thrust into a role she hadn't been prepared for and who now surely questioned her decision to hire Logan Grimm. Not because she doubted his ability to catch the thieves, but because he'd taken liberties no mercenary should be allowed.

By damn, that kiss had been sweet. Her taste exquisite, her response wondrous. Too easily they could have taken a further step, to petting and fondling, leading to a romp in the blankets Logan knew would be satisfying for them both. And likely cause problems.

Aye, Joanna's kisses begged repeating. 'Twas a temptation to which he must never again surrender.

"'Tain't right, them takin' the chalice," Otto Carpenter declared to the other men sitting around the small table in Wat's cottage, making a healthy dent in the keg of ale supplied by Robert Brewer. "Ye need to get it back, Wat."

"I will."

Except Wat had no idea how. When he'd asked about the chalice this afternoon, after he and Robert Brewer had ensured nothing remained of the horses' hoofprints near the river's edge, Edward had denied pilfering the chalice from the church, claiming the priest must have mislaid it somewhere. Wat didn't believe him, but couldn't prove otherwise, and considered arguing with Edward dangerous to life and limb.

"Did you get the doves?" Wat asked of Otto.

"Aye, six of them. Left them in a bag out in the woods by the tangled oak, as ye instructed. I finished the repairs to the dovecote, so will not have an excuse to be in there anymore. We will have to find another source of meat for them if her ladyship does not come around soon."

Robert frowned. "Will the doves be missed?"

"Nay," Otto replied with confidence. "With all the hatching going on in there they should not be missed. Cannot see how a body could keep count of them."

Wat scratched his chin. "The sows are having their piglets. Mayhap we could snatch one or two of those."

Donald Smith leaned forward, scowling. "I do not like stealing from our neighbors or her ladyship."

Wat agreed, but saw no other way to keep their bargain with the thieves.

"None of us do. But our plan is taking longer to work than we thought it would."

"How much longer must we hold the course?"

"Until her ladyship agrees that she must take a husband to provide protection for the villagers."

Donald huffed, his big body heaving mightily. "We shall have a devil of a time keeping them in food and firewood if this scheme takes many weeks longer. I still wonder if we did not make a mistake in hiring them."

Wat had heard the comment from Donald before, and therefore considered the blacksmith the weakest of the small band of conspirators. If Donald began backing away, the others might follow, and all would be lost.

"We all agreed this to be a good plan, and we are still all agreed we prefer to serve a lord rather than a lady, and our reasons are sound. Are they not?"

Wat waited for grunts of agreement before he continued. "I say we give it more time."

Robert emptied his mug. "Her ladyship does not seem inclined to marry, however. Did ye all hear of how she tossed Sir Gregory out of the manor today? Ain't going to be no marriage there."

The sick feeling Wat had fought upon hearing that piece of news now returned, souring his stomach more than before. He'd considered Sir Gregory the better of her ladyship's two current choices.

"There is still Sir Edgar. And who knows, perhaps another knight will come along who sees the holding as worthy and is willing to marry Lady Joanna to get it."

"What about Grimm?" Otto asked. "What if that meddling mercenary catches the thieves and our part in this scheme is exposed?"

Wat shuddered at the thought, even as his ire rose. Grimm. A complication they hadn't foreseen. Blast the man! If the mercenary had stuck to his original decision to turn down Lady Joanna's offer . . . well, he hadn't, so he must be dealt with.

"I made Edward aware of Grimm. The thieves will move their camp if he gets too close." Wat sighed heavily. "I wish I knew of a way to get rid of that damn mercenary."

After a few moments of silence, Otto suggested, "Perhaps he could meet with an accident?"

Donald took immediate exception. "I will not be a party to murder."

Nor did Wat relish the thought of blood on his hands. "Is there a way we could discredit Grimm, get her ladyship to send him on his way?"

"I do not see how," Robert answered, then paused. "Unless he does not find the thieves within a reasonable time. Then her ladyship may send him on his way. Never known her to throw good coin down a dry well."

More grunts of agreement, and Wat had to allow that Lady Joanna didn't waste coin on needless or foolish expenditures. Unless one counted the hefty fee she paid Logan Grimm for his services in the first place.

His ale was gone, his eyelids growing heavy, and for all they had talked over the situation, he and his companions weren't any better off or less worried than before. There was but one problem left to solve before he shooed them out the door.

"One of you will have to take over as contact for the thieves when I go to Oundle."

Not one spoke up. All shifted in their seats and avoided looking him in the eye.

"Come now, one of you has to do it."

Donald finally spoke. "Why? If the thieves have agreed to hole up for a few days, there will be no hoofprints to rub out. And if you deliver the goods to them tomorrow, they should require nothing until after you return. 'Tis too risky for anyone else to act as contact. We all have families who might question our absence."

Wat's ire rose up again. He came close to calling them all cowards, but refrained. These were his friends, his companions in this scheme. He couldn't rail at them without repercussions. He could, however, chide them a bit.

"Are you not the lords of your own homes? Must you answer to your wives for every minute of your time?"

Robert huffed. "Now see here, Wat. I must be available to help my wife with the heavier of the work. I cannot always slip away without her notice."

"Mine has the new babe to care for," Donald stated. "And I must be available if one of the guards comes round with a request to have a horseshoe repaired or her ladyship needs a kettle mended. I cannot just up and leave without someone taking notice."

With an agreeing nod, Otto chimed in, "Same with me. Now that I am done repairing the dovecote, I must make repairs to the floor in the church. If I am not performing the task, Father Arthur would surely make comment to Lady Joanna."

Good excuses all. Still, they did nothing to ease Wat's anger at having to do all the work while the others would reap the benefits. But they were right, they would be missed and their absence remarked upon.

As reeve, having no family to mark his absence, only he had the freedom to roam as he pleased.

"I will speak with Edward tomorrow when I deliver the goods, ask that they restrain themselves while I am gone."

"Do not ask them, Wat," Donald warned. "Be sure they follow our orders. 'Tis we who paid them and feed them. And fetch the chalice. 'Twas not among those things we agreed could be taken."

Wat merely nodded his assent, wondering if providing the thieves with firewood and food were enough to keep the men in line. Edward had agreed to those conditions, but Wat felt the thieves were becoming disgruntled with the bargain. And getting greedy. Surely the thieves had taken the chalice. Nothing else made sense.

"When do you leave for the fair?" Robert asked.

"I hope to leave Monday. Likely to be gone for four or five days."

Donald got up. "Are we done?"

"Ale is gone," Robert announced.

"Then 'tis time to be abed."

Within moments they'd said their fare-thee-wells and filed out the door.

Wat heaved a heavy sigh.

This scheme had started out so well.

Their own village ravaged by plague, three men had come to Wat's door looking for work. He'd given it to them, though not in the manner they'd requested. Still, when assured they would never be caught and punished, they'd agreed to play the parts of thieves, their decision made easy when their stomachs grumbled.

But the men were no longer hungry. And they'd taken a shine to the excitement of the raids. Wat didn't want to know from whom they'd stolen the horses they rode.

He banked the fire in the hearth.

He hated being away when the situation was so unsteady. Still, he looked forward to attending the fair, not only to buy the wheat his father should have purchased last autumn, but to enjoy the food, the horse races, the music and revelries.

People from all over the shire would be there. From whores to the lords of the land. Perhaps he could ask around, learn of another bachelor knight looking for property, then inform him of the value of Lynwood Manor and its pretty, available widow.

Wat could hardly believe Lady Joanna had tossed Sir Gregory out of the manor. He'd heard the entire story from several people and concluded it was that damn mercenary's fault.

Dammit, he'd warned Logan to keep away from Joanna, so what did the mercenary do? He allowed Joanna to remove some stitches from his leg, in the privacy of her bedchamber no less. What else had gone on in the bedchamber was a matter of speculation, and everyone was speculating like mad.

Somehow he had to get rid of Grimm. 'Twouldn't do for her ladyship to become friendly with a mercenary. It might not sit well with a prospective husband that she allowed a man of such low rank and bloody reputation into her good graces.

As he removed his tunic, the thought struck Wat that instead of bringing the gander to the goose, perhaps the other way around might be best. If Lady Joanna also attended the fair, 'twould also remove her ladyship from Grimm's influence.

The more he thought about it, the more sense it made. If eligible men could see Lady Joanna, judge her worthiness right away, he'd not have to convince them to make the trip to Lynwood Manor—they would surely do so on their own.

Sir Edgar might even be in Oundle, and have more success at a second attempt to convince her ladyship to accept his suit.

All Wat needed was for Lady Joanna to enter a betrothal agreement before he could tell Edward and his men that they were no longer needed and to move on. Before Logan Grimm's services were no longer required.

Verily, Edward made him very nervous.

But Logan Grimm scared him witless.

Chapter Eleven

Logan left long before sunrise, alone.

After learning about the sorry state of the garrison, he couldn't warrant asking another man to take on extra duty.

Whatever news he had to report back to the manor could wait until the end of the day. He doubted he could get overly lost, having studied the maps enough to know if he traveled east he would come upon the river and could follow it to near Lynwood.

And there were only three thieves. Surely they'd prove no hardship to capture—if he found them.

He rode a straighter path than along the river to the waterfall and the hamlet at its base. A collection of hovels, really. Not as prosperous a place as Lynwood.

And yet, 'twas a pretty spot, surrounded by woodland, the small waterfall gaily pouring over rocks into a large pool. Farther south, just within sight, a mill stood on the bank where the river again narrowed.

As at Lynwood, however, people worked in the fields. Only one team of oxen pulled the plow, a few peasants following behind. Some used large mallets to break up clumps of turned-over soil, the others sowed the furrows.

Off to the side stood a man, his arms crossed over his chest. He watched the planting progress, fulfilling the same duty here as Wat did at Lynwood—ensuring those whose day it was to work in the demesne field showed up to fulfill their duty.

Unlike at Lynwood, young children played with sticks and hoops in the area around the common well, unafraid that a band of thieves would ride through.

Deciding the overseer would serve his purpose, Logan dismounted and slowly approached the peasant garbed in rough-weave brown tunic and breeches. Strands of gray striped otherwise black hair. Deep lines marred his weathered brow. The man's eyes narrowed in a healthy suspicion toward strangers.

Logan gave the man a nod and slight smile. "Good morn to you, good sir."

"Who might you be?"

"Logan Grimm, currently in Lady Joanna of Lynwood Manor's service. I should like to ask you a few questions about a band of thieves that harry Lynwood."

The man rubbed his chin. "Heard about her ladyship hiring you. Mercenary, are you not? Not that I hold nothin' against mercenaries, you understand."

"Understood. I am told your hamlet has not suffered raids as Lynwood has."

"Not so much as a twig missing." He tilted his head toward the field. "'Course, we ain't got much more here than twigs. Lynwood has better pickin's than the rest of us in this corner of the shire."

Then he held up a hand to stave off more questions and shouted at a lad in the field.

"Theo! Not so much seed. And get it into the furrow."

He watched for a while as Theo—an older lad, perhaps ten-and-six—adjusted the amount of seed he sprinkled and improved his aim.

With a grunt of approval, the peasant once again turned his attention back to Logan.

"New man," he said. "Apprenticed to a cobbler in Bristol before the plague took the cobbler and the shop closed. Theo said when they began buryin' the dead in mass graves, he up and left for the countryside." He chuckled. "Do not know how Theo does with shoes and such, but sure can tell he ain't never worked in a field afore."

Poor lad. As in the countryside, the plague had swept through towns, wreaking havoc, disrupting life's plans. Turning apprentices into field laborers. Other of the displaced took to begging to survive. Some once hardworking, honest folk turned to . . . thievery.

Logan squinted at the lad. "New, you say?"

"Nigh on two seasons now. Say . . . you thinkin' Theo might be one of them thieves?"

Not really. The lad certainly didn't look menacing—as if one needed to look sinister to embrace villainy.

Logan shook his head. "Merely considering possibilities. Besides, the lad arrived long before the thieves first struck Lynwood, and they have horses. Is there anywhere about you would consider a good place for three men to hide, someplace where they might find shelter for themselves and their horses?"

The peasant scratched his head and glanced south,

toward the mill, before revealing, "There be a hunting lodge upriver. The tale goes it was used by royalty, back long afore I was born. Fallin' down, now. Might be worth a look, though."

A possibility. Harold had explored the lodge early on and not found anything suspicious, but another look might be warranted, even if Logan's instincts said the thieves hid somewhere south of Lynwood. When the peasant didn't mention the mill, Logan assumed the man didn't think it a possibility.

"My gratitude for your time."

"Hope you find 'em. They ain't bothered us yet, and we like it that way."

Logan mounted Gideon. "Pray let me know if they do."

"Surely."

As he rode away, Logan wasn't sure if he should believe the man. For the thieves to disappear so completely, they must have help. A group of people envious of the "better pickin's" at Lynwood would be the most likely to give aid, especially if the thieves agreed to leave their little corner of the shire alone in exchange for that help.

Too, the man had tried to send him upriver. Because the deteriorating hunting lodge was the first place to come to mind, or because the man didn't want him searching near the hamlet?

To satisfy his own curiosity, Logan rode by the mill, apparently not in use because of a broken wheel. Seeing nothing out of the ordinary, he was about to turn around and head north when he spotted a wide spot in the trees where the grass was trampled. Wide enough for horses to pass through, this path led somewhere. Even if it didn't lead to where the villains camped, he should follow it.

Logan soon came upon the reason for the path. Strawberries. The leafy plants sprawled over the forest floor, brightened by the sunlight filtering through the treetops. The fruit had just begun to ripen, a touch of red here and there.

He immediately thought of Ivy and her enjoyment of so small a pleasure, the juice oozing between her fingers to stain her tunic. Of the lovely smile Joanna wore as she partook of the offered treat.

Joanna didn't smile near enough as she ought.

Logan dismounted, drawn by a perfectly shaped berry of bright red. He scrunched down, breathing in the aroma of damp, rich soil, and picked the fruit.

Some considered eating uncooked fruit unhealthy, but an army on the march consumed whatever food could be found, and he'd eaten many a berry from the bush, and pear and apple from the tree.

Joanna hadn't admonished Ivy for eating uncooked fruit, had taken a bite herself, and enjoyed it.

This one strawberry would make Joanna smile. He could see himself offering it to her, watching her mouth curve upward, a spark of pleasure lighting up her amber eyes. With delicate fingers she'd take it from the palm of his hand, twist off the stem, and place the tip of the berry on her tongue. Then her lips would close around the fruit as she took a bite.

He could see her eyes closing, the delight on her face as she savored the treat. If he took enough strawberries back to Lynwood, perhaps she would make a batch of those wonderful tarts. Then he and Ivy could share a few, neither of them caring about sticky fingers or stained tunics. Joanna would smile leniently at the two of them, perhaps indulge herself, too.

Logan reached for a second berry. Unable to resist, he popped that one into his mouth. The third went into his palm. And a fourth.

Then he wondered what the devil he was doing. Picking berries. Woman's work. He was supposed to be searching for thieves, not gathering fruit to make a lady smile.

What would his fellow mercenaries say if they could see him now? They'd tell him he'd lost his wits, that's what. Chide him for going mad.

For a man with a reputation for fierceness, who didn't hesitate to lead a charge in battle, who never shrank from shedding another man's blood, he was certainly going damn soft over a woman and a little girl. Over strawberry tarts.

Four days he'd been at Lynwood, and here he knelt in a strawberry patch, planning to present them to Joanna just to make her smile.

He'd become involved with a widow, a lady, once before. Not once had he done anything for her to make her smile. His affair with Celeste had developed over the course of a month of flirting and testing on both sides. She'd wanted him in her bed and he allowed himself to be, seduced by her lovely body and flattered by her admiration for his prowess.

For nigh on a fortnight he'd seen himself becoming more than a mercenary. A horrible mistake on his part.

Two days after the siege of her castle ended, victory hers, Celeste had been more than willing to turn him out of her bed, and send him on his way—with only part of his pay, considering her sexual favors worth a full quarter of his fee.

He hadn't seen it coming, not the rejection, not the betrayal. That was when he'd pulled his sword to emphasize to Celeste and two of her knights that her sexual favors weren't worth that big a loss to his purse. Thank the Lord, she'd acquiesced to his demand before he'd been obliged to draw blood.

Hurt, angry, feeling the veriest fool, he vowed never to place himself in that position again. Never take an offer from a woman, especially from a widow.

Then he'd met Joanna.

Aye, the physical attraction was strong. His body responded to her touch in swift, hot manner. He'd lost sleep last night in a vain effort to hold his imagination at bay, banishing visions of what *more* could have happened in Joanna's bedchamber, in her sweet-smelling bed with the door bolted shut.

'Twasn't odd that he wanted to lie with her, to rub his skin against hers, feel the weight of her breast in his hand, bury himself in her depths. Desire he understood. Passion between a man and woman, the sating of those passions, he accepted as a part of life.

The danger didn't lie in wanting to bed Joanna, but in wanting to make her smile.

He didn't return until evening meal was nearly finished.

Joanna knew immediately from the slight furrow of Logan's brow that he was in a foul mood. As if to prove her right, he looked no one in the eye as he slowly crossed the hall—limping slightly but not so bad as before she'd removed his stitches—and fetched a mug of the spiced mead she'd noticed he truly liked. He talked to no one as he took a seat at an empty table.

She thought to get up to fetch Logan's evening meal and ask what troubled him, but then saw Maud striding toward him with trencher in hand. The two exchanged no pleasantries as the housekeeper plopped the broken meats, cheese, and bread before him. Nor did Logan bother to thank Maud for the meal, just grabbed a hunk of bread and popped it in his mouth.

How horribly rude—of both! She should take them to task, but decided to leave them alone, especially Logan. Over the years she'd learned to avoid sullen men, having paid a price for having the audacity to try to cheer them. Her efforts had only made the situation worse.

She'd do well to keep her distance until his mood improved. Still, he looked so miserable she wanted to wrap her arms around him, ease the lines on his brow, tell him all would be well.

A foolish notion. Logan wasn't a child but a grown man, and not in need of her comfort. And if she got too close to him again she'd probably have as much trouble sleeping tonight as last night.

Sweet mercy, Logan's kiss had stirred her in ways she hadn't ever imagined being stirred. To wish for another kiss was foolish. To yearn for *more*—unwise, utter folly. Yet, she suffered, and knew of only one man who might cure—

"A fine meal, my lady. Would that Margaret Atbridge possessed your skills."

Torn from her wayward thoughts, Joanna turned her

attention back to her guest, Father Arthur, thankful he had no idea how far astray her thoughts had wandered.

"I am sure Margaret does her best."

"She makes a fair cook and housekeeper, but none can compare to you."

She briefly wondered at the priest's reason for flattery. What did he want from her? Perhaps she was being unkind, for he hadn't asked anything of her—yet.

"I am delighted you enjoyed your meal."

She refrained from extending an invitation to yet another meal, where she would again have to listen to the man's complaints. Either the brewer's rooster crowed too loudly outside the rectory's window at too early an hour, or Margaret lacked a housekeeper's skills. Surely, dining with the priest once a month was more than sufficient penance to absolve her of whatever small sins she might commit.

"I see the mercenary has returned," he said, his tone laced with the same disapproval she'd heard from others and disliked. "By the looks of him he had no luck in his search today."

Perhaps that explained Logan's sullenness, but Joanna had a feeling something more irksome bothered him.

"He will succeed, eventually."

"By the Sabbath, I hope. Those . . . thieves absconded with my chalice. How can I be expected to say Mass without it?"

Use a mug? She could imagine his horror if she made the suggestion. And now she knew what he wanted of her. Somehow to make up the loss he'd suffered—rather, the church suffered. The chalice didn't belong to the priest, but to the church, which belonged to the abbot.

"Would you like me to send a messenger to the abbot to request another chalice?"

Father Arthur shook his head. "'Twould take too long. I need a suitable vessel to use Sunday."

Logan might find the thieves and chalice within two days, but as that was unlikely, Joanna mulled over possibilities and struck on one she hoped would work.

"I have two goblets which might suit your needs."

"Are they gold?"

"Silver."

"Oh. Well. I suppose they will do."

Irritated once again, Joanna rose to fetch the goblets from the trunk in the bedchamber. They'd been her wedding gift from her brother, only used on what Bertrand considered special occasions, then packed away after his death.

The priest was welcome to borrow them until Logan recovered the chalice, if the whoresons hadn't already sold it—which might not be so horrible. The gold chalice was worth several pounds. Upon being given that amount of money, mightn't they move on to richer holdings? Perhaps. But she wanted them caught.

She'd no more than risen when Ivy rushed up and threw her arms around Joanna's middle. A mother knew this ploy, too. Her daughter's request came quickly.

"Mama, have you decided about attending the market fair?"

Joanna still wanted to strangle Wat for suggesting she attend the fair within Ivy's hearing.

"I told you this afternoon we cannot attend."

"But 'twould be so much fun. Do you not want to see the dancing bear?"

Of all the attractions Wat mentioned, this was the one Ivy had latched on to. And, naturally, Ivy assumed that if her mother decided to go, then the daughter would go, too.

Joanna *did* want to go, but not for the novelty of a dancing bear. The enticements were many—the gaiety, the colors, the freedom to purchase whatever she wished without worrying if Bertrand would disapprove.

Too, she worried about trusting Wat to purchase the seed. She doubted he was as good a bargainer as his father and might spend too much coin either from ignorance or lack of courage. And he'd been inattentive to his duties these past few days, arriving late for meetings they'd planned, or his thoughts seeming far away from the subject at hand. She feared he might become so distracted by the attractions of the fair he would forget his duty altogether.

The best reason to attend would be to sell Bertrand's helm and suit of chain mail. Perhaps to a lord intending to gift them to a newly made squire. Then she'd have coin aplenty to make purchases for the manor, for a new gown or two for herself, and even set some aside as part of Ivy's inheritance.

Either Harold or Logan should be able to tell her what to expect as a fair price. The bargaining she could handle. Would even relish. 'Struth, she would be tempted to sell those goblets, too, if she hadn't just promised them to Father Arthur.

Unfortunately, she might have to trust Wat to buy the seed and make the sales another time. Too many reasons existed to remain home.

Joanna looked into hope-filled eyes and steeled her resolve. "Ivy, your arm is not yet healed."

"Greta says my stitches might come out in two days, so my arm will be just like new, like Logan says his leg is like new."

Ivy and Logan had talked about their stitches? How odd. A conversation she might ask Logan about. Later. When he was in a better mood.

"This is not a good time for us to be away from the manor. There is the planting—"

"We need seed to finish the planting."

"—and the shearing—"

"Can be done when we return."

Joanna could see no common reason would satisfy Ivy.

"'Tis not safe, Ivy. Remember the thieves? The guards are needed here to protect the manor, so they cannot accompany us."

Ivy mulled that over, and Joanna gave her daughter credit for having the good sense not to suggest they travel without guards.

"Logan could guard us."

A novel solution, though impossible.

Joanna chucked her daughter under the chin. "Dearest, Logan is supposed to be looking for those same thieves."

Another pause for thought, then Ivy's eyes brightened.

"Logan could search for the thieves while we travel to the fair. I will ask him."

The girl was off so fast Joanna would have had to run to catch up, and she refused to scold across the hall. Without any hesitation, Ivy scooted onto the bench, knelt beside Logan Grimm, and even put a hand on his shoulder while she rushed into an explanation for her request.

Whence came Ivy's bravery? Certainly not from her mother. No one else would *dare* get as close to Logan, not when he gave every signal that all should leave him alone.

But then, Ivy was young and probably hadn't noticed Logan's irritation, or that he'd not spoken to anyone upon entering the hall, or that he purposely chose an empty table so he could eat alone.

Or maybe Ivy had noticed all those things and still didn't fear the mercenary.

Nor, Joanna realized, did she. Not fear. A reluctance to get too close to Logan, perhaps, but for reasons other than fear for her safety. Deep down in her soul, Joanna knew Logan would never physically harm either her or Ivy. For all his size, for all his violent profession and sometimes abrupt manner, Logan Grimm would never use physical force against her.

Joanna took a deep breath at the revelation. Perhaps it was the way he now looked at Ivy as she chattered, his elbow on the table, his head resting on his fist, bemused. Or perhaps 'twas a leftover sense of safety from yesterday when he'd held her so gently, kissed her thoroughly, firmly, but with tenderness.

She wasn't sure where the certainty came from, but it was there, solid and indisputable.

She'd never questioned her trust in his ability to capture the thieves. Were he to consent to Ivy's pleading—which he would surely resist—she could trust him to guard their lives with his own.

If she could trust him with her life, then why not her body?

Oh, this line of reason would get her into trouble for

sure. She simply couldn't take a lover. Trustworthy or no. She dare not take her responsibilities as lady of Lynwood lightly. And wouldn't Father Arthur toss a fit if he could peer into her mind?

Joanna marched into her bedchamber and flipped open the large trunk's lid. On the bottom lay the suit of mail. Atop it rested several items, most belonging to Bertrand.

A helm. Knight's spurs. A sword of Toledo steel in a leather scabbard of high-quality workmanship. Two daggers—one long and lethal, the other delicate with a jeweled hilt he'd used for eating. The goblets presented to her as a wedding gift by a brother she'd never forgiven for getting rid of her by selling her into marriage. She grabbed the goblets and lowered the lid.

Ivy skidded into the room. "Mama, in what town is the fair?"

"Oundle. Ivy, you must—"

"Is that north?"

"Aye, but—"

"I will tell Logan."

"Ivy!" she called after her escaping daughter. Too late.

Joanna sighed and started after her daughter to make her desist, then made the mistake of glancing at the bed. The bed she'd never wanted to share with Bertrand, in which he'd used her for sating his lust.

The same bed in which she'd tried to sleep last night but couldn't, because for the first time in her life she lusted after a man. For Logan. For his tender kisses and gentle touch. For the pleasure a man could give a woman that she'd heard giggling servant girls openly talk about but had never experienced.

The tips of her breasts tingled with yearning for

Logan's long-fingered hand to caress. Her woman's places heated, preparing for the joining with a large male part in working order.

Joanna bit her bottom lip. Could she? Just once?

"Joanna?"

Logan.

Her heart slammed into her chest so hard it took a moment to catch her breath and regain her composure. Except her senses proved unruly. Gad, he was a fine specimen of a man. And, dammit, a woman simply shouldn't be expected to resist temptation when presented with such an alluring delicacy.

"What?"

"Do you truly want to go to this fair?"

"Well, aye, but—" she waved a goblet-heavy hand in the air. "I told Ivy 'twas impossible for us to attend. I know she must be disappointed that you turned her down, too, but I do not see how—" Then she noticed his expression and could hardly believe what she saw. "You did tell Ivy that 'tis not possible for you to act as our guard, did you not?"

He hesitated. Her heart dropped.

"Not as yet," he admitted.

Sweet mercy, 'twas as she feared. How could a sensible, grown man turn to pudding in a little girl's hands?

"Logan, you cannot seriously consider making the journey. What about the thieves?"

He crossed his arms and leaned against the doorjamb. "I may have been wrong about where they were hiding. When I went to the hamlet at the waterfall, a man there directed me to an abandoned hunting lodge north of here. After I searched the mill and woodland near the hamlet—did you know of the large patch of strawberries there?"

She nodded, all she could manage.

"I found no sign of the thieves, so I took the man's suggestion and went to the lodge. There are signs of recent use, and tracks indicating whoever used the lodge came and went on horseback."

A shiver ran down her spine. "Our thieves?"

"Perhaps. I cannot be certain, but I do know the lodge has been abandoned once more, and the people went north when they left. I have to wonder if our thieves know I am searching for them and are now holed up farther from the manor than before. So, I could continue searching while we travel to and from Oundle."

That sounded sensible, except . . .

"Would that not be dangerous? I could not take Ivy on a search for thieves, and she would be desolate if I left her behind."

He straightened. "You will not be searching for thieves, I will. And I have already spoken with Harold. He can spare one guard to accompany us. Joanna, if I thought for one moment that either you or Ivy would be endangered, I would never agree to act as your escort."

Which she truly should have known all along.

"When did you speak with Harold?"

"Just now. He came in for his meal right after you came in here to . . . fetch goblets?"

Sweet mercy, she'd forgotten all about Father Arthur!

"They are for the priest, to use as chalices until the church's is recovered. I had best give them to him so he can leave before the guards close the gates for the night."

Logan moved out from in front of the doorway. Joanna hurried past him, only to nearly run over her daughter.

Ivy didn't move out of the way. "Are we going?"

The little minx. "Were you listening?"

"Not the whole time."

Ivy was so eager to go. So was Joanna. She found the prospect of spending several days in Logan's company, enjoying the delights of the fair, very appealing. And perhaps, if she could get her courage up during one of the nights spent in an inn where nobody knew her and wouldn't judge, she and Logan could enjoy each other. Oh, the temptation!

But this wasn't a decision to be made in haste.

"We shall see."

Chapter Twelve

Outside, at times the rain came down so hard a man couldn't see beyond a few feet, making a search for the thieves that day all but impossible. Inside, warm and dry, Logan eavesdropped on the battle currently raging in Joanna's bedchamber.

He wasn't alone in his inescapable breach of manners, for everyone in the hall could hear, and no one pretended not to.

Logan sympathized with Ivy, who did *not* want the midwife to get any closer to her with the scissors or pincers, yet all the while he understood Joanna's frustration in failing to convince her daughter to cooperate.

Ivy hadn't resorted to tears—yet. Joanna hadn't resorted to threats—yet. Still, one of the females was going to lose this war, and it made for grand entertainment to listen to the feints and parries of the combatants.

From a distance. Not one of the people lounging in the hall, himself included, had any wish to become embroiled in the argument.

"Ivy, the stitches *must* be removed."

From her tone, Logan could envision Joanna with her spine straight and arms crossed, fast closing in on the limit of her patience.

"I do not *want* my stitches out."

Ivy was similarly resolute, no doubt employing a pout in an effort to break her mother's will. Logan considered pouting a bad strategy. From what he'd witnessed, the little girl's thrust-out lower lip didn't have any effect on Joanna.

"You have no choice, dearest. Now climb up on the bed so Greta—"

"Naaaay!"

Ivy dashed into the hall, headed for the doorway, then skidded to a halt at the ominous rumble of thunder. Unwilling to brave the storm, she frantically sought a hiding place.

Logan likened the girl to a hare being pursued by a hawk, frantic to reach the safety of a warren. 'Twas both comical and sad that there was nowhere Ivy could hide where her mother wouldn't capture her.

"Ivy, come back here!"

Joanna's command widened Ivy's eyes farther, and in that moment her gaze met his. Her plea for deliverance clutched his heart. 'Twas the damnedest feeling to want to open his arms, catch her up, and provide the haven she sought.

"Ivy!"

Joanna sounded closer, as if about to come out of the chamber. Ivy knew it, too, and decided on her best course of action—a quick dash across the hall, then a well-timed duck to scoot under the table where he sat.

Not a heartbeat later, Joanna strode out of the bed-chamber.

Logan took a long breath, knowing he should tell Joanna where Ivy hid, but he hated to betray Ivy altogether. He could hear the girl breathing hard.

"Ivy!"

Ivy pressed up against his leg, seeking succor.

Logan smiled and shook his head, uncomfortable with the position the girl placed him in, yet enchanted by her show of trust. Ivy might not be able to avoid having the stitches removed, but neither could he turn the girl over to the ordeal so speedily.

With quick hand gestures he informed Joanna of Ivy's whereabouts, then indicated she should go back into the bedchamber.

Taken aback, Joanna didn't obey immediately. She also used a silent hand gesture to confirm that Ivy hid under his table. He nodded. Joanna pointed at him, jerked her thumb toward the bedchamber, then emphasized the meaning of her wagging finger with a scowl. He clearly understood. If he didn't get Ivy out from under the table and bring her into the bedchamber promptly, Logan would be in a heap of trouble, too. Then Joanna turned around and obeyed his request, giving him no time to protest.

Everyone in the hall understood the exchange, and every one of them grinned over his predicament, showing him no mercy whatsoever. Especially Maud, whose expression clearly stated she didn't think him capable of handling one little girl.

Logan very much feared the housekeeper right.

He bent sideways far enough to see under the table

where Ivy huddled against his leg, hugging her upraised knees, her head bent forward. A heartrending, pitiful sight against which he steeled his resolve. He tugged at Ivy's golden braid.

"You may come out now."

"Nay."

"How long do you think you will be able to avoid your mother?"

All he got in answer was a sniff.

"I know you are frightened, but it does no good to put off that which must be done. Either now or later, those stitches must come out. Why not now?"

"'Cause."

"'Cause why?"

"'Cause it will hurt."

"Not overly much."

She pressed harder against his leg, his assurance having no effect. He tugged on her braid again.

"At least come up on the bench so we can talk. My neck grows stiff from bending over."

"Mama?"

"She is in the bedchamber."

Ivy slowly uncoiled and slithered up onto the bench, taking a moment to glance toward the bedchamber to ensure her mother truly wasn't in the hall. Forlorn, she crossed her arms on the table and put her head down.

They sat in silence, Logan wondering what to say to ease Ivy's misery. 'Twas then he noticed she no longer wore a bandage, noting the length of her mended cut and the snug, neat stitches. The next time he needed a wound closed he'd know how the stitches were supposed to look. Pray the fates, he hoped he wouldn't need to put the knowledge to use anytime soon.

"Seventeen, hmm?"

She didn't answer, just shrugged a shoulder. Odd for Ivy, this silence. A measure of her fear.

"Remember the other day when you and I spoke of your having them taken out? You know it must be done."

"I know," she admitted, her voice so soft he barely heard.

"Ready to go back in?"

She looked up at him, tears spilling over, her bottom lip trembling.

His heart broke. "Ah, sweetling. Come here."

He'd never held a child across his lap before, so never realized how small yet solid a little body could be, or how lightly a head would rest against his shoulder. Or how utterly impossible it was not to give this particular child a hug while wiping away tears with the hem of his sleeve.

" 'Twill be over quickly, then you will be rid of the irksome stitches and not worry over them anymore."

She answered with a long sigh, not yet ready to surrender. While he'd like to give Ivy more time to reconcile to the inevitable, he worried that Joanna might soon come to check on his progress, then both he and Ivy might be in for a scold. Though he liked the look of Joanna in a fury, he much preferred observing while she aimed her fury elsewhere.

So, how did one tempt this child to do what one wanted her to do? Bribe her? Threaten her? With what?

The answer came in a blinding flash. An unfair shot, he supposed, but at this juncture he was willing to try most any tactic.

"Unless, of course, you do not want to go to the fair. If those stitches remain in your arm, we have no hope of convincing your mother to go."

"She may decide not to go anyway," Ivy complained.

"Perhaps, but we need not give her a sound reason to refuse."

She was silent for long heartbeats, then sat up a bit straighter, her eyes red-rimmed and sparkling.

"Will you come with me?"

She didn't mean to the fair, but into the bedchamber. He'd won, but didn't feel good about it.

"Certes. I will stay the whole time if you want me to."

Ivy twisted around, her arms rising to encircle his neck. He soon came to realize that not only must he accompany Ivy into the bedchamber, he must also carry her. So he did.

Ivy wrapped her limbs around him, clinging like the ivy with which she shared a name. Her face snuggled into his neck, her warm breath coming a bit too fast for his liking.

Reluctantly, he entered the bedchamber. Both women turned to stare. Joanna, who'd apparently been pacing, raised an eyebrow at his surprising success and waved him toward the bed.

Where Greta waited with scissors in hand.

Remembering his own ordeal, he couldn't set Ivy down and abandon her to the mercy of the midwife, so he eased down onto the bed, determined to see this through.

He gave Ivy a quick squeeze for reassurance, a rub on the back for comfort—or as an apology, he couldn't precisely determine which he meant. "Come, Ivy, let us have this done."

He could feel her hesitancy even as her hold on him loosened. As Ivy settled across his lap, he looked up at Joanna. She stood a few feet away, staring at Ivy, her lower lip tucked between her teeth. Then her eyes raised to his and a sad smile touched her lips.

The realization struck that he'd taken her place. Joanna should be sitting on the bed, daughter on her lap, ready to comfort Ivy through any pain. As if she heard him, with a slight shake of head and small gesture, Joanna told him to remain where he was so not to disturb Ivy.

A whimper let all know Ivy wasn't completely reconciled to having her stitches removed, and all Greta had done was reach for Ivy's arm.

"I will warrant you that this part does not hurt at all," he assured Ivy. "All you will feel is a little tug."

Greta huffed. "May not even feel a tug. I have stitched up many a cut over my time and know how to take the thread out. Not like some others."

Logan refused to feel guilt over declining to have a midwife remove his stitches. All his good reasons for spurning the offer faded when Greta gently grasped Ivy's arm and slid the scissors under the first stitch.

His stomach went suddenly unsettled.

Ivy winced when Greta cut the first stitch.

Logan wanted to yell at the midwife to take better care, but his mouth was far too dry for speech.

"That was not so bad," Ivy commented.

"Your mother and I tried to tell you so," Greta countered. "You sit still and we will have these out in a trice. All that clamor over naught. A body would think I was puttin' 'em in, not takin' 'em out."

A second snip. A third. Ivy's little body relaxed, melting against him.

Sweat broke out on Logan's brow. This was ridiculous. The midwife wasn't hurting Ivy. He had no reason for either sweaty brow or palms. Verily, he'd faced a company of bowmen, their arrows notched, with less trepidation.

Fortunately, in a quick, efficient manner, Greta soon had all the threads clipped.

Then Greta reached for the pincers. Ivy tensed.

Logan physically restrained himself from pulling Ivy's arm out of Greta's hand.

Greta plucked out the first stitch.

"Ow."

'Struth, he would have hit the midwife had Ivy's protest been uttered with any strength behind it.

"Like a pinprick, is it not?" Greta wiggled Ivy's arm. "Look, 'tain't even any blood."

Good thing, or he might not be able to hold himself upright through the remainder of the process. He looked to Joanna for reassurance that all was going as it should, and finding the mother calm, tried not to worry so much over the daughter.

Joanna's concern for Logan increased as her concern for Ivy lessened. Sweat glistened on his forehead, his skin taking on an unhealthy pallor. The poor man hadn't reacted this markedly when having his own stitches removed.

He stared at Ivy's arm, and Joanna swore that Logan, not Ivy, winced with every pluck of thread.

Ye gods, the man was a mercenary. He'd probably observed more carnage and death in one battle than she would see in her lifetime. One would think he would be hardened against the sight of a few small stitches being removed.

Apparently not.

Perhaps 'twas because the wound belonged to a child that caused his distress. Sometimes adults, especially parents, became more upset over the hurts of children than they did over their own injuries.

Whatever the reason for Logan's unsettling reaction, she hoped he didn't allow it to overcome him before Greta finished.

Ivy didn't protest beyond the first meager outcry, uttered without enough force to give it credence. The short threads slid out smoothly, without bloodshed.

Logan's had bled. Because of the longer threads? Or from being in too long? At the time, she'd wondered if she were doing something wrong, but from observing Greta's method, now knew she'd done it rightly. Like plucking feathers from fowl.

"There, done," Greta announced. "You will have a scar. That cannot be helped, but otherwise you mended well enough."

Ivy stared at her arm. "Will I have the scar always?"

"'Twill never go away. Consider it a caution against being so careless again."

"No more throwing rocks at horses?"

"Getting out of the way might have been the wiser course."

Logan frowned. "You threw a rock at a horse?"

Ivy looked up at him. "Nay, I threw the rock at the thief, but I missed him and hit his horse. Then the horse stepped on me."

"Oh."

Joanna thought Logan's pallor grayer than before.

Ivy tossed her arms around his neck. "My thanks."

Logan hugged her back, whispering something in her ear that Joanna couldn't make out. Then Ivy slid from Logan's lap and came toward her, and from her daughter's contrite expression knew what instruction he must have given.

"Sorry, Mama."

Joanna gathered Ivy into an embrace. "Apology accepted. Tell Maud that you may now have a strawberry tart."

Ivy dashed out into the hall, calling for Maud.

Logan rose up from the bed, looking a bit steadier.

"My thanks," she told him. "I do not know how you convinced her to cooperate, but I am grateful you did."

"Shared experience, is all. She just needed reassurance from someone who'd recently had stitches removed that she would survive the process."

Perhaps, but Joanna could think of at least one man who'd once had a wound stitched who Ivy wouldn't have run to for reassurance, knowing he wouldn't give her what she needed. More likely her own father would have belittled her fears, certainly wouldn't have sat on the bed with her in his arms to comfort her.

More likely Bertrand would have tossed Ivy onto the bed, ranted about her misbehavior, ordered her to stay put or suffer the consequences.

"Still, I am grateful."

He managed a smile, which told her Logan was recovering from Ivy's ordeal. "Does that mean I am also entitled to a strawberry tart?"

He could have all he wished, but she wasn't about to condone gluttony, nor was she quite finished with him.

"In a moment. Greta, Logan's stitches bled when I removed them. Is that cause for concern?"

The midwife turned to Logan, whose mouth thinned into a straight line.

"Do they still bleed?" she asked him.

"Nay."

"Hurt?"

"Nay."

Joanna almost called him on his lie, but refrained. Logan still limped on occasion, though not so much as before. His measure of hurt might be different from hers.

Greta shrugged. "Should be fine, then. If you have trouble I could take a look."

He eased toward the door, escaping, though not so quickly as Ivy had done. "Will not be necessary. If I do not get my tart soon, Ivy will eat them all."

Stubborn, stubborn man.

Greta might be a midwife, akin to a woman's physician, but Logan's stance against allowing her to inspect his wound made no sense to Joanna. She would let the subject drop, for now, and observe how well he walked. If he didn't continue to improve, she would insist he submit.

Like she'd insisted Ivy have her stitches removed, and had no luck in that endeavor at all.

"Perhaps we could all use a tart."

Logan was out the door so fast she had to laugh.

"Obstinate, that one," Greta said. "Most men are. Good with Ivy, though. One would not expect that of a mercenary."

"Nay, one would not. They took to each other from the first, though. Strange, but I am glad she neither fears nor dislikes him."

As others disliked him, refusing to accept him because they all thought him beneath them because of his profession. Only Harold, a fellow soldier, seemed to approve of Logan.

"You like him, too."

Joanna wondered if she'd revealed too much to Greta of her inappropriate, wanton musings on what she would like to do with Logan. What she wanted him to do to her. The physical attraction had become a living, breathing demon, and there was naught she could do to send it back to the netherworld from which it crept out to haunt her nights and intrude on her days.

"I do," she admitted. "And I had best see that Logan and Ivy do not overdo on those tarts."

Joanna left the bedchamber.

Maud had set out a few of the bite-sized tarts, and Logan and Ivy were huddled over the platter, their delight comical. Joanna slid onto the bench next to Ivy and fetched a tart for herself, admitting the little treats very good.

Ivy licked juice from her fingers. "Can I now play on the green, Mama?"

She'd hoped to evade that issue for a while. Perhaps she still could. "'Tis raining."

"I meant tomorrow."

Joanna forced down the last of her tart, noting Logan had also lost some of his enthusiasm for the treats.

"Nay, Ivy. Not tomorrow, either."

"But my stitches are out."

"And do you remember how you got those stitches?"

"I will not throw rocks at horses again, I vow."

"Nay, you will not, because you are not allowed on the green until the thieves are caught." At Ivy's downcast look, she added, "None of the children are allowed on the green, for safety's sake."

"But the thieves have not come back for *days*."

"Merely three, which does not mean they will not come back."

Ivy looked to Logan for support. To Joanna's great relief, he didn't seem about to contradict her.

"Your mother is right. Until the villains are caught, 'tis best all the children remain where they are safe."

"But I miss playing with my friends."

He had no answer for that, but Joanna did.

"Perhaps tomorrow we can invite some of the children into the hall to play. Would that suit you?"

"Aye."

No enthusiasm to the answer. Ivy didn't look any happier. Joanna admitted she didn't like the situation, either, but the children must be protected.

Wat stood under the twisted oak tree, holding a canvas tarp over his head to stay dry. The weather wasn't fit for man or beast, but this was the day he'd arranged to meet with Edward and must do so.

At his feet lay two sacks, one containing two piglets, in the other several loaves of bread.

'Twas getting harder to provide the promised victuals, especially the meat. The bread came from his own allotment of a loaf a day from the manor's ovens. Every other day a loaf went into a sack for the thieves. No one missed the bread—well, his stomach missed the bread—but the piglets . . . the swineherds were sure to notice and report the loss to Lady Joanna.

But piglets went missing occasionally, having wandered away from the sows while rooting for acorns in the woods. Lambs, too, were known to roam too far from the ewes while grazing, even under the watchful eye of the shepherd.

'Twas being forced to catch the animals, kill, then deliver them to the thieves which began to wear on Wat's temper.

Which was completely Logan Grimm's fault.

Had the mercenary not taken it into his head to accept her ladyship's offer, Wat wouldn't be stealing piglets. The thieves could have stolen their own during a raid, which would impress upon Lady Joanna the necessity of providing Lynwood with a lord.

But Wat had promised the thieves they wouldn't be caught, so they couldn't raid while Grimm remained at Lynwood.

Grimm had to be gotten rid of. Soon.

He didn't hear the horse until it was nearly upon him. Not Edward, the band's leader, Wat noted. Merely Joseph, the one Wat doubted possessed a shard of sense. Which was probably why Edward had sent the dolt to collect the victuals instead of braving the storm himself. Wherever the thieves were hiding these days, Edward chose to remain behind, stay warm and dry.

Wat tamped down his ire. Perhaps that was for the best. 'Struth, Joseph was easier for him to face than Edward.

Soaked clear through and not seeming to mind, Joseph

reined in a few feet away and dismounted. He pointed at the sacks at Wat's feet.

"Them ours?"

Who else did Joseph think Wat went to this much trouble for? "They are."

Joseph picked them up and tied them to his saddle. "That mercenary still around?"

"Aye."

"Edward will not be pleased. He is getting restless with naught to do but pace the floor. This hiding gets old."

"Better to hide than swing from a noose."

"'Tain't done nothin' to warrant hanging. Stole a couple of chickens and a goose, is all, just like you told us to."

True enough, Wat admitted. He and his fellow conspirators had stolen the rest and given it over to the band. Except the chalice. Wat was sure Edward had stolen the chalice from the church—a mistake on Edward's part which might prove useful later.

However, the band had made a mistake for which Lady Joanna might mete out very harsh punishment. "You injured the children. The worst hurt was to Lady Joanna's daughter. For that she may judge a noose suitable punishment."

"Did not mean to hurt the children, only scare 'em a bit. They all should have run, especially the little girls. Never thought one would take a stand."

So Edward had claimed, but then Edward also claimed he hadn't stolen the chalice.

"Well, no matter your intent, Ivy's arm required

stitches, and Lady Joanna is most distressed over the injury."

"The girl all right now?"

Concern? From a thief? What nonsense!

"Her stitches were removed this morning. Hellfire, man, you have more important things to worry over than Ivy's health."

"The mercenary."

"The mercenary. If he finds you, it will not go well for any of you."

Or me, if they tell Grimm who hired them.

"Can you not get rid of him?" Joseph asked.

Wat had spent many hours mulling over how to get rid of Logan Grimm. He'd tried to speak to Lady Joanna about the mercenary, but ever since the night he'd warned Grimm to stay away from her ladyship, every time Wat mentioned the mercenary she gave him a look that pointedly warned that he overstepped the boundaries of his position.

He didn't like the way Grimm looked at Lady Joanna, as if she were available to the likes of a mercenary. He truly hated the way her ladyship favored Grimm, as if he weren't beneath the notice of decent folk.

And if what Greta told him earlier was true, then this morning, Lady Joanna had trusted Logan Grimm with Ivy, her precious daughter, as she would have trusted no other.

"I dare not speak against Grimm for fear of reprisal. He has managed to entrench himself in Lady Joanna's good favor. I can do nothing about him, but you could."

As soon as the words left his mouth, he knew this was the only solution.

"What?"

"Kill him."

Joseph stepped back, a recoil Wat didn't expect. "We agreed to commit a few thefts, not murder!"

"Then make his death seem an accident, or better, arrange for him to disappear altogether. No one will miss him or come looking for him. Verily, until the mercenary is dealt with, none of us are safe!"

Joseph mulled that over. "I do not think Edward will agree."

"While Edward is deciding, you may wish to remind him that it was his horse that landed on Ivy's arm, and who Lady Joanna will punish the harshest if the mercenary ever finds you."

"Perhaps he will not."

"Given enough time, he surely will."

Joseph mounted his horse. "I shall tell Edward."

"Do that, and while you are speaking to him, tell him also that I must leave the village for nigh on a sennight. There will be no more food delivered until I return."

"You would go back on our bargain?"

"Pray remember our bargain did not include the theft of a chalice. 'Tis fortunate for you I convinced Father Arthur to allow Grimm to recover it instead of alerting the abbot, who would surely send a knight or two to run you down."

There had been no such talk with Father Arthur, and the abbot wouldn't bother to send knights. But the thieves needn't know the truth.

With a terse nod, Joseph rode off.

Alone again in the silent night, Wat gripped the tarp tighter to keep his hands from shaking with the enormity of what he'd done. Ye gods! Frustration had clutched his innards, forcing words from his mouth he'd never planned to utter.

Kill him.

But then, hadn't Otto first made the suggestion several nights ago? Hadn't he merely carried through on what his conspirators would surely come to understand was the only way to get rid of Logan Grimm?

Wat made his way home, uncertainty gnawing at his innards.

Chapter Thirteen

Logan saddled Gideon while Oliver, the stable lad, saddled Joanna's mare for an early-morning ride to answer a summons from the swineherds about missing piglets.

With the horse's tack checked, the packet containing several items he might need during the day secured, he left Gideon's stall to check on Oliver's progress.

Nearly done. In a few minutes they'd be off.

The rain had stopped sometime during the night, leaving the air fresh if a bit damp. The rising sun spread both light and warmth over the wet earth, and an accompanying breeze helped begin the drying. 'Twould be a fine day.

Too fine for Joanna to be dealing with yet another problem so early. But then, when one was in charge of a manor, one dealt with the problems at hand, even when they came at dawn on the Sabbath, rousting a body out of bed.

She stood in the stable's doorway, leaning against a jamb, looking down at her booted feet, her eyelids still heavy from interrupted sleep.

She wore a light cloak over her workaday gown, the only type of gown he'd seen her wear, not the silks and brocades most highborn ladies insisted they must don to proclaim their rank to all and sundry.

As a knight's wife she must have, at some time, worn fine garb to attend the court of their overlord. Even abbots gathered their knights together for feasting and fine wine, to ensure the landholders remained loyal and didn't forget to pay the many fees owed. As holder of Lynwood, had Joanna yet made the required oaths of fealty and loyalty to the abbot?

With her delicate beauty, Joanna would turn many a man's head if garbed in jewel-toned silks, as she'd turned Sir Gregory Marshall's head, as well as some knight's named Edgar.

As she'd turned Logan Grimm's head. 'Twas useless to deny it, even to himself. Joanna was a beautiful woman, no matter what she wore, no matter in what mood. He couldn't imagine any male with functioning wits not wanting her, or any bachelor knight worthy of her not seeking a marriage.

Joanna deserved silks instead of rough woolens for her gowns. Gauzy veils instead of linen mantles to cover her head. Jewels to grace her fingers. Soft leather to cover her feet.

Yet here she stood garbed little better than a peasant readying to ride into the forest to speak with the swineherds about missing piglets. He would escort Joanna there and back, acting as her guard, then renew his search for signs of the thieves.

She looked up as he approached her. A lock of hair had slipped from her hastily fixed braid. The golden wisp dangled near her cheek, tempting his fingers to tuck it back behind her ear. He resisted by halting farther than an arm's reach away from her.

"Ready yet?" she asked.

"A few moments more. Is this visit to the swineherd necessary?"

She smiled. "Probably not, but 'tis as good an excuse as any to get out of the manor on what promises to be a lovely morning. Besides, the brothers are new to the position and Tom says Matthew is distraught. He needs assurance I will not cut off his head for a missing piglet or two."

So many responsibilities she'd taken on.

"You need a steward to send on such errands."

"Perhaps someday. For now, there is only me. Ah, we can depart now."

Oliver led the mare from the stall, heading for the mounting block where Joanna waited. Logan fetched his stallion, clearing the stall in time to see her swing a leg over the mare's back and settle into the saddle.

Sweet rump. A tribute to the lady's seat he wouldn't voice aloud, at least not in front of Oliver. In private, he just might, if only to enjoy her blush.

Logan allowed Joanna to lead across the open fields, mostly because she knew to what spot in the woodland she must go, but partly to admire the way the woman handled a horse.

The farther they rode, the more he realized he wasn't the only male admiring a female. Gideon had caught the mare's scent and showed signs of becoming randy, which made the stallion harder to control. Logan admitted Gideon had good taste. The mare was certainly a pretty thing, with a smooth gait and muscled haunches, just as her rider must possess strong thighs to grip the saddle so well.

Logan tried very hard not to think about how Joanna's thighs might feel when wrapped around him, securing him between her legs, urging him onward.

As he feared, when they entered the woodland where they must slow down and he must close in, the stallion pined to close in farther. 'Twas all Logan could do to hold Gideon on tight rein so he wouldn't nip at the mare's rump to let her know he'd be delighted to cover her.

Logan finally pulled Gideon to a halt to allow more space between them and Joanna, disappointing both himself and the stallion. He bent low over Gideon's neck and grabbed a fistful of mane.

Harshly, he whispered, "Not for us, boy. Settle down."

The stallion tossed his head and snorted in protest.

"You think I do not know how you feel? I am nigh on as randy as you are. You want the mare, I want the woman. 'Struth, neither of us is about to get his wish."

"You all right back there?" Joanna called.

She must have heard Gideon complain.

"We will be. Lead on."

Logan rode farther back than he liked for safety's sake, but allowing the stallion another good whiff of the mare wasn't wise. When Joanna pulled up to a log and dismounted, he tied Gideon to a stout tree upwind of the enticing mare.

The swineherd was indeed young, and anxiously twisted the felt cap in his hands. He stood beside a sow lying on her side, piglets latched on to her teats, noisily sucking up their morning meal.

Joanna picked her way through the wet brush over to the distraught swineherd. In a voice too low for Logan to understand the words, she soon had the lad calmed down enough that he no longer mangled his cap.

Cute piglets. Tasty, too. Logan was trying to remember the last time he'd savored roasted piglet when the swineherd's voice rose.

"That is why I sent Tom to the manor, milady. 'Tis not common to lose piglets this early. At this age they tend to stick real close to the sows, don't do much wandering off. I think someone took 'em."

"Now Matthew, why would—" Joanna began to ask, then turned around, her eyes widening with the implication. "Our thieves?"

"Most likely," Logan answered.

Made sense. Instead of raiding the village for fowl, why not sneak off with a couple of piglets?

Joanna addressed Matthew. "Where are the other sows?"

The lad pointed toward the river. "Gathered in that stand of oaks near where the river bends east, right where we left 'em before yesterday's storm. Lots of acorns and a bit of shelter there."

"Then why is this sow here?"

"I think she came looking for her lost ones."

Joanna glanced at the sow, her mouth thinning with ire.

"You have checked to make sure the piglets are not mixed in with the rest?"

"Of course, milady. Tom and me, we counted three times, and the sows, they keep good track of which belong to 'em. Ain't no strays. After Tom got back from the manor, I sent him to look after the others while I waited here with her—" he tilted his head toward the sow "—for someone to come."

So the thieves braved the storm, guessing the brothers would take shelter from the pouring rain, betting no one would see them or hear any squeals of piglet protest. A good wager.

"When you were counting piglets, did you notice signs of horses?" Logan asked.

Matthew shook his head. "Nay, but we weren't lookin' for no hoofprints. Can look again, if you want."

Logan suspected they wouldn't find a hoofprint anywhere, but there was always hope the thieves would one day become careless with their tracks.

"Do that. Send word if you find anything."

Matthew nodded, then grabbed a long pole from where it leaned against a tree. He gave the sow a poke.

"Come on, girl. Let us go back to the others."

The sow slowly rose, shaking off piglets. When she moved, 'twas in the direction of the manor, not the river. Matthew clucked at her, turned her with the pole, and prodded her to a faster pace—at least as fast as she could move with six piglets crowded around, impeding her progress.

Damn. He'd hoped his conjecture of the other day held merit, that the thieves had hid in the hunting lodge, then gone north. Apparently not. They were still close enough to Lynwood to dash out and steal two piglets during a storm.

Four days ago he'd begun searching. While he hadn't expected immediate success, his lack of progress proved vexing.

As Matthew and his charges passed from view, Joanna sighed.

"What?" he asked.

"Poor sow. She must have followed her little ones' scent this far before she lost it."

Which also bothered him. Whoever took the piglets headed in the direction of the manor. Of the village. That niggling sensation of unease over how the thieves managed to leave no trail, of why they only raided Lynwood, now nagged with urgency.

"Joanna, I truly hate to say this, but I am beginning to believe the thieves are getting help."

She cocked an eyebrow. "From who?"

"One or more of the villagers."

Immediately she shook her head. "Nay, that makes no sense. Why would the villagers aid the very men who steal from them?"

"That is what I have yet to figure out. Do any of the villagers hold a grudge against you, or perhaps your husband, or even the abbot?"

"Not that I am aware of." She gave out an unladylike huff. "No one particularly liked or admired Bertrand, but everyone respected his authority as lord. Not that they had a choice. To disagree with or cross Bertrand was to invite swift, harsh retribution. The abbot? We pay our fees and send our tributes, and he leaves us alone. As for me?" She raised her hands, palms upward. "I am sure not everyone approves of all I do, but none have made their displeasure known."

Except one that Logan knew of.

"Wat is not content."

She waved a dismissive hand. "Verily, Wat has his

own ideas about how a manor should function, but I do not doubt his loyalty. He wants what he deems best for the villagers, which means he wants us all to prosper. Surely, aiding thieves would not be a good way to go about it. Do you truly suspect Wat for some sound reason, or is it just because you two rub each other wrongly?"

Her defense of the reeve didn't surprise him, and perhaps his dislike of the reeve colored his opinion. But no matter what he believed, he had no proof, only suspicions.

"I hope I am wrong."

"I am sure you are. These are good people, Logan. They have been through much hardship. We pulled together to survive the plague's aftermath and are making progress toward recovering. I cannot think of one of them who would hinder our efforts."

Obviously, Joanna wasn't ready to think ill of anyone within her realm, so he decided to let the matter drop, for the time being.

"Ready to return to the manor?"

She picked up a leaf—a brown, fragile reminder of last autumn—from the forest floor, her petulance fading as she twirled it in her fingers. "Oh, I know I must, and I will. Father Arthur expects me for Mass. Still, 'tis tempting to delay a while longer. When I go back, someone will present me with another problem I must deal with, and I would rather not." She smiled then. "I sound like Ivy. 'I do not *want* to.'"

Said as Ivy had said about her stitches, knowing of the pain but not how much, fearful of the unknown. Intriguing. Joanna hadn't struck him as afraid. More likely she was just tired, perhaps feeling a bit overwhelmed and sought a distraction.

"What would you rather do?"

"Oh, perhaps go pick berries, or wade in the river, or just stay here and enjoy the peace of the woodland."

"You should do so more often, then."

"But that would be shirking my duties, and for the lady of Lynwood 'tis not allowed."

"Is the lady of Lynwood never allowed to enjoy simple pleasures?"

"When there is time, but there never seems to be a moment to spare these days. Perhaps later this summer . . ."

Her smile faded, the wistful expression turning somber—Joanna again becoming the lady of Lynwood. He wanted the *woman* back, the one in dire need of a diversion.

"Have you decided about going to Oundle?"

"Not as yet."

"How long since you saw a bear dance?"

"Seems a lifetime ago." She again twirled the leaf. "My father always made the trip to the fair and took us all with him. What I remember most is the entertainers. The mummers and jugglers and puppets. And the dancers, garbed in the most colorful costumes 'twas said the women wore in the harems of the infidels."

She laughed lightly at the memory. "They were so exotic in their colorful silks, swirling suggestively so the men would toss coins. My mother proclaimed them too bold and most wicked, but I always thought them enchanting."

Joanna tossed away the leaf, watching it drift to the ground, knowing she'd revealed too much to Logan, again. But this time she didn't question why she could talk to him, merely accepted that she could. Likely he'd also guessed she'd once envisioned herself swirling around in bright colors, enticing coins from the men who gathered around to ogle and lust for the bewitching harem dancer.

He clapped his hands, mimicking the lively rhythm of the melody chasing round in her head. His eyes were dark, his meaning clear—

Dance.

She shook her head, very aware she lacked the grace or boldness of a dancer.

He raised an eyebrow. "Why not? I have a coin."

Despite the thrill that shot through her, she couldn't bring herself to move her feet. "I have not the gift. You would be disappointed."

"Never. Dance for me, Joanna."

Her heart beat faster, lured by the seductive rhythm and Logan's unmistakable challenge. Dare she be so brazen?

Why not? There was no one to see except Logan. No one to disapprove of or frown at a fanciful whim. Sweet mercy, she hadn't given in to a whim in years, not since her marriage.

Joanna untied her cloak and tossed it aside. Logan's approving smile urged her onward.

She closed her eyes, and before her appeared a stunning woman, a gauzy veil covering her head and lower face, framing sultry chestnut eyes. Garbed in purple, scarlet, and saffron wrappings of silk. Barefooted.

To the strains of a flute and beat of a drum, her gold

bracelets flashed in the sun. The strings of bells about her ankles jangled to the rhythm of her dance.

She moved with light steps, her breasts thrust forward, teasing the men who watched and worshiped. A bump of a hip. A fling of an arm. The deliberate removal of a length of silk. All the while she wore a beguiling smile for the crowd.

See me. Want me.

Joanna opened her eyes while in the midst of a movement the crowd had cheered. She danced not for a crowd but for one man who watched her with lust in his eyes. Whose want of her became physically evident. Emboldened, Joanna danced toward him, her daring tingling the tips of her breasts and heating her woman's places.

Joanna dipped and swayed around him, tempting Logan to reach out and snare the object of his desire. He clapped, setting a never-faltering rhythm. She tossed her head back, flung her arms wide, and spun as the dancer had spun, delighting in the freedom and getting dizzy.

The clapping stopped.

"Joanna! The tree!"

She hit the tree with her shoulder, hard enough to halt her dance and fracture the enthralling fantasy. She leaned against the rough bark, her breath coming in gulps, and feeling more alive than she'd felt in an age.

All because she'd accepted Logan's challenge, for a few minutes becoming an exotic dancer with Logan as her captive audience.

Then he was before her, concern warring with the desire that burned in the depths of his eyes. He wanted her, blatantly and without apology.

And, sweet mercy, she wanted him. Perhaps the fantasy could be mended and continued, though in a different manner.

Logan's hand lightly brushed over the shoulder where she'd likely have a bruise tomorrow. Her breath took on a new rhythm, her heart a stronger beat.

"Hurt?" he asked.

"Nay," she said on an exhale.

"You hit hard. 'Twill bruise."

"Probably."

His hand moved from her shoulder to her neck, his fingers warm and long and caressing. If he leaned down but a little, his lush mouth would capture hers and—

"You dance divinely."

"Until the end."

"Even at the end. You remained upright."

"Logan, cease talking and kiss me."

She liked the way Logan obeyed orders. He kissed her thoroughly, with a demand for a like response. She gave it to him, most willing to be led astray. 'Twas frightening and thrilling, and made her feel both powerful and helpless at the same time.

When she sensed him backing away, she grabbed fistfuls of his tunic and through her kiss tried to convey the order she didn't think she could utter aloud.

His arms wrapped around her, one across her shoulders, the other lower. His hand grasping her backside pushed them together so tightly she could measure the length of his hardened arousal.

He understood. Would he obey?

He eased away from the kiss, but not the embrace. "Ye gods, Joanna."

"Please, Logan."

"Here? Now?"

"We may never have another chance."

Did she sound as desperate as she felt? She didn't care, her pride tossed aside with her good sense.

"Then wait here."

Joanna let him go only because she knew he'd be back. He ran toward his horse and fumbled with the pack tied to the saddle.

She held tight to her fantasy, refusing to allow reality to intrude. She wasn't the lady of Lynwood, but a bold and brazen harem dancer. This wasn't a woodland clearing but a cozy hideaway where lovers met to steal a few moments of forbidden pleasure.

Logan spread his cloak on the ground, in her mind becoming their thick feather mattress. He unstrapped his scabbard and leaned his weaponry against the tree, the fierce mercenary becoming her ardent lover.

When he held out his hand, Joanna needed no coaxing to accept his invitation. Eagerly, she slid back into Logan's embrace, greedy for her lover's kiss, his touch, his possession.

Her eagerness drove Logan wild.

Somewhere in the far reaches of his mind a small voice tried to warn him that coupling with Joanna on a forest floor wasn't right, that she deserved better than a quick, heated joining. But as he tugged open the ties of her gown, she moaned, urging him to hurry and silencing the misgivings he didn't want to heed.

She helped him remove her gown, leaving her nakedness veiled by a wisp of a white shift. He caught a tantalizing glimpse of her dark-tipped full breasts before she reached for the hem of his tunic. He helped her bare his chest to the morning breeze, then took them down onto the cloak he'd spread on a too-thin bed of leaves.

The ground was hard beneath his hip, the air cool on his heated skin, his desire for Joanna so potent he didn't care.

Neither, it seemed, did she.

Her fingernails raked through the sprinkling of hair on his chest, then traced the edge of his collarbone, sending a shiver of pleasure clear through him. Her breast seemed to swell in his hand, the nub hardening immediately under the brush of his thumb, her eyes almost closing in bliss.

With a fierceness of purpose, Logan vowed to take Joanna beyond ecstasy. He could give her fast and hard if that was what she wanted, but by damn, he would also give her completion. If she was right, if this was to be their only chance to couple, then he'd make this one time most memorable.

For Joanna.

For himself.

Not that his own completion was in doubt. 'Struth, he would have to exert rigid control to hold his ultimate pleasure in abeyance. He thought he could, but to ensure success he embarked on a campaign designed to bring Joanna to the very verge, so if he slipped a bit, she wouldn't have complaint.

She certainly didn't complain about how he kneaded her breast. Nor did she protest when he took the tip into his mouth, shift and all, and suckled.

"Oh, my. Oh, Logan," was all she uttered in a voice low and thick with ardor, fanning the flame in his loins, deepening the ache in his privates.

His control slipped a notch. To counteract it, he slid his hand down along her side, tugged upward on her shift, then slowly petted the curve of her calf and behind her knee before seeking the soft, hot skin of her inner thighs. She tensed, the muscles tightening but not trapping his hand, not halting his journey to the thatch of hair at the juncture of her thighs.

She hissed when his fingers found the wet, slick entry to her woman's sheath. Her hips rose when he stroked her, her soft gasps assuring him she needed very little preparation for the joining.

The plea of his penis nearly overwhelmed him. With every fiber of his being he wanted to sink into Joanna and stroke them both into a frenzy.

First he had to get his breeches down.

Panting, he rose up on his knees. When his fingers didn't seem to remember how to undo his laces, Joanna came to his aid. He knew her motive was selfish when she not only undid the laces but tugged at his breeches, unleashing his randy parts.

She stared at the length of him. "Whole and in working order."

"And eager to please. Spread your legs for me, woman, before either of us comes to our senses."

She lay back down, tugged her shift up to her waist, revealing the golden hair where his fingers had played, and spread her legs wide.

He entered her an inch at a time, feeling her rise beneath him, welcoming his penetration. Buried to the hilt, he paused, desperately grasping at the shards of his control.

Her eyelids fluttered closed, waiting for him to move,

to escort her on the last leg of this incredible journey to heaven.

Rashly, Logan wanted Joanna to remember fully which man now partnered her on a forest floor.

"Open your eyes. Look at me, Joanna."

She obeyed, her amber eyes sparkling, peering deep into his. Whatever she saw there heightened her need and fed his. Her sheath tightened around the part of him almost ready to burst.

"Logan," she whispered, a supplication.

He answered, slowly at first, then faster and harder. She met each stroke, both taking and giving back, her expression turning to wonderment, and at the pinnacle, to amazement.

She closed her eyes as she went over the edge, the soft pulse of her pleasure taking him with her. He didn't object, too overcome by the heady sensation of accomplishing his goal, by the fierce pounding in his loins, and the awareness that Joanna might have just ruined him for all others.

The last should bother him immensely, but at the moment he didn't give a damn whether or not he would ever lie with any other woman. He admitted he'd been easily enticed, thoroughly entranced by a woman he shouldn't have wanted, much less taken.

Having taken, he was loath to give her up. He couldn't force himself to roll off of her just yet, most content to observe her slow descent from the height of their lovemaking.

Her breath was still a little fast when she opened her eyes and smiled up at him in approval.

"Oh, Logan, what did we do?"

"I would say we did extremely well."

She laughed lightly. "Agreed."

"No regrets?" The words out, he wished he hadn't been so foolish to ask. To his utter relief, her smile didn't fade.

"Nay. 'Twas wondrous."

He agreed with a last kiss, knowing they couldn't remain there much longer. Joanna needed to return to the manor; he must continue his search for the thieves. She would again be the lady of Lynwood; he her hired mercenary.

And in the depths of his soul he knew for certain, even though he didn't yet know how or when, they would again be lovers. This couldn't be their only chance for so spectacular a union.

Chapter Fourteen

Joanna fought off the stunning effects of the woodland fantasy by throwing herself into the tasks she'd planned to do before she'd tossed her common sense to the winds by dancing for Logan.

Before learning that while she might not be an innocent maiden, my oh my she'd been ignorant of what a man could do to, and for, a woman. Before discovering she could feel powerful and weak, earthy and ethereal—all at the same time.

Confused and a little frightened by the new knowledge, she paid little heed to Mass, Father Arthur's droning in Latin unable to hold her attention.

If she walked around in this daze all morning, someone would surely notice and wonder if the lady of Lynwood had lost her wits. So as soon as she returned to the manor, she asked Maud to accompany her into the buttery. Surely inspecting the larder would prove a distraction and allow her thoughts to settle for sorting out later.

She took a deep breath, determined to enjoy the anchoring scents of hearth and home. Now that the lambs were weaned, the ewe's milk was used to make butter and the large rounds of mellow cheese so necessary to the manor's food supply. A quick count of those rounds already stored on the shelves pleased her.

Joanna smiled at Maud. "The dairymaid has been busy!"

"The ewes are givin' us a right good supply of milk, milady. They continue like this through the summer, we will have to find another place to store the cheese."

Or a few rounds could be sold in Oundle—if she decided to go—without placing the manor's stores at risk. The extra coin would certainly be welcome. Except making more cheese meant using more salt, a precious commodity.

"Need we purchase more salt soon?"

"I think not. We should have enough to meet our needs for another month or so, even with the makin' of extra cheese. We start runnin' short, we can add a bit less to the stews, make up for the lack with herbs from the garden."

Planting herbs in a garden, instead of purchasing all of them as Bertrand had done, had been a wise decision. Putting Maud in charge of the garden an even wiser one.

"The herbs thrive under your care, Maud. In particular the rosemary. We may have enough to sweeten the rushes soon."

Maud blushed at the compliment. "'Tis good of you to say so, milady. Don't do nothin' special, just tend 'em."

Joanna made a mental note to find some special way to properly thank Maud for uncomplainingly tending to her duties every day, endeavoring to lighten the lady of Lynwood's burdens where possible.

Joanna next headed for the meadow, walking instead of riding in an effort to spend her abundance of vigor. She only partially succeeded, slowing down to delight in a perfect summer's day. The sun shone bright and warm, the grass waved a brilliant green, the sky glimmered a shimmering blue.

The puffy white ewes grazed on the hillside. The lambs paid less heed to eating than playing.

Next week, as soon as the oat and barley crops were fully planted, the shearing would begin. The ewes would be far less lovely afterward.

"Hail, master shepherd!" she called out.

He raised an eyebrow, questioning her unusual presence, but then smiled back at her. "A good morn to you, milady. Come to count the lambs?"

From that Joanna assumed he'd already heard about the missing piglets and had taken a count of his own charges.

"Any missing?"

"Not a one. Aim to keep 'em all, too."

"I wish you good fortune in that endeavor." She again looked out over the flock, this time focusing on the intent of her visit. "Have we all we need for the shearing?"

The shepherd nodded. "Six men, our usual four from Lynwood and two hired from the hamlet. The smith assures me he will have the shears sharpened in good time. Have ye given any further thought to puttin' a floor in the barn?"

No, she hadn't, and there were good reasons why she should. The cleaner the fleece, the better price the wool merchants paid. The shearers did what they could to protect the fleece from becoming too soiled, but when wrestling with an unhappy, bawling sheep on a dirt floor, cleanliness was nigh on impossible—for either fleece or shearer.

"Too late to do it this year."

"Aye, but there is always the next."

"I will keep it in mind."

Satisfied, Joanna strolled back toward the manor. Along the way she picked a clump of wild violets, thinking they would bring a touch of color to what had always seemed to her a dreary hall.

A tapestry or two would do the hall wonders, both for decoration and as a buffer against winter drafts, but she'd never had the coin to purchase the colorful yarns necessary for a satisfactory weaving.

A scene bloomed in her head of a formal rose garden with a fountain burbling in the center, and little cherubs playing harps and flutes in the clouds—a scene fit for a tapestry.

Smiling at the fanciful vision, Joanna entered the huge thatch-roofed, timber tithe barn that stood outside of the manor's palisade. 'Twas nearly empty but for a generous mound of hay. What had been left of the rings of last autumn's wheat and barley had been carted off to the Abbot of Holme before Easter—along with ten rounds of cheese, three geese, sixteen chickens, and two bushels of turnips.

There should have been sacks of wheat seed sitting near the hay, but apparently all had been used for the early-spring planting, with none left for the second planting later in the summer. How Wat, or more likely his father, had made such a mistake . . . but the error had been made, and more seed must be purchased.

Perhaps she could use the coin from the sale of Bertrand's chain mail not only to pay for the seed, but to purchase lumber for the floor of the tithe barn. Bertrand had scoffed at flooring the barn, insisting the expense wasteful, preferring to use the coin for trips to London to do heaven knew what with only the Lord knew whom.

She'd never dared to question his actions or expenditures, just used the money he allowed her for household purchases as wisely as she could. Her coffers were in a sorry state at the moment, and would be sorrier still after she paid Logan the two shillings she still owed him. But if all progressed as hoped, they'd be healthier come autumn, and she could make whatever improvements to the manor's property she saw fit.

Oh, wouldn't Bertrand howl in protest if she used the profits from his precious chain mail to purchase mundane lumber!

The thought made her giddy, and the only cure for it was to spread her arms and take several spins across the expanse of the barn, dancing so lightly she kicked up hardly any dust.

Excited about the project, Joanna headed for the church, where she knew Otto Carpenter worked, eager to talk to him about the costs involved for lumber and nails and labor for flooring the tithe barn.

Along the way she spotted Margaret Atbridge digging in her garden, and some of her good sprits fell away as she bemoaned the loss of Margaret's goose to the thieves. She could still envision the poor thing hanging from the thief's spear, limp and bloody.

Damn thief. That particular goose had been the most dependable breeder of numerous, healthy goslings from which the manor always purchased the three biggest and plumpest to send to the abbot.

Joanna knew she must talk to Margaret to inquire after the now motherless goslings and decide how to proceed in the future, but that could wait until later, after she spoke with the carpenter.

As Joanna expected, Otto Carpenter swung his hammer in the nave of the church, replacing warped boards with straight and true ones. At least this was one expense she didn't have to bear. The priest paid for repairs to the church out of the stipend he received from the abbot and from the tithe he received from both manor folk and villagers alike. His living wasn't a grand one, but neither need he go begging.

Father Arthur stood a little way off from the carpenter, likely judging the quality of every nail driven into the floor. Because she knew the priest would expect it, she dropped a silver penny into the poor box, lit a votive candle, and knelt before the pretty statue of the Holy Mother. With head bent, she meant to pray, but stopped herself.

'Twould surely be sinful to pray without feeling the least bit pious. Truth to tell, she felt wonderfully, wholly wicked and wanton and couldn't drum up a smidgen of remorse.

As she had for most of the morning, she pushed the details of her woodland tryst with Logan to the far reaches of her mind. What she couldn't banish was the sensation of having her world tilted upright. Of feeling awake and alive.

Happy.

Unfortunately, in the past, happiness hadn't lasted

overlong. Likely, her current contentment would vanish with the onset of some burden.

There could be no more fantasies with Logan, of course. Their lovemaking might have been most pleasurable, but Joanna knew that just because she'd given in to a moment's madness once, she couldn't allow herself to succumb a second time. Logan's kisses thrilled her, his touch aroused her. His possession made her body quiver in anticipation and writhe with bliss.

She'd wanted *more* and gotten it. Unfortunately, she wanted Logan again. And again. A course she didn't dare take. She wasn't a harem dancer, but the lady of Lynwood. She couldn't have an affair with a mercenary and risk losing everyone's respect.

That her heart cried out at the unfairness didn't truly matter. She couldn't risk all on a whim, with a man who would go back to his own life once his task in Lynwood was done.

Joanna refused to think about how much she would miss Logan when he left. His handsome face. His brashness. His unfailing self-confidence. His charming way with Ivy.

His pleasing way with her.

So, for now, she would hoard the joy, allow the pleasure found by a harem dancer and her lover to tarry as long as it would, and try not to feel too bad when it faded away.

Joanna crossed herself and rose. Father Arthur still stood near the altar, hands on hips, staring at the poor carpenter.

"Good day, Father Arthur. How goes the work?"

He wasn't pleased with her intrusion, but managed

civility. "More slowly than I expected, but then, one must not rush the work when one wants quality."

Otto's hammer never missed a beat, and Joanna gave the man credit for his patience with the priest.

"I was hoping to speak with the carpenter for a few moments."

The priest frowned. "Can it not wait?"

It could, but feeling feisty, Joanna strove for a ring of authority to her voice. "What I have to say will not take long. I assure you his work here will not suffer."

Leaving the frowning priest, Joanna strode over to where Otto already sat back on his heels. She scrunched down to keep her words private.

"When you are done for the day, pray come to the manor. I have a project in mind and need your counsel."

"Be after nooning, milady."

"That will suit."

With a nod of agreement he went back to his work, and Joanna hoped the smile she tossed Father Arthur on her way out of the church didn't appear too condescending.

She hadn't intended to pass through the churchyard on her way back to the manor. The place held naught but misery. But two tiny grave markers called to her—

Elias. Rose.

The heartrending grief had eased over the past months, but Joanna didn't think she would ever let loose of it completely.

She divided the violets and placed them on her babies' graves, then dried her tears. They were at peace now. No more sickness or pain or suffering could touch them.

As deeply as she mourned her children, Joanna didn't miss the man whose grave marker overshadowed all others in the churchyard. The exorbitant cost of the tall, ornate stone marker yet irked, but the design and making of it had been specified in Bertrand's will, and she couldn't in good conscience ignore his final wishes.

Well, she could have, but saw no sense in offending anyone by disregarding the lord of Lynwood's last instructions. So he had his way—for the very last time.

In her lifetime she'd been intimate with two men. One who'd possessed the right to do with her as he pleased, the other who'd taken the time to please her first.

The two were similar in several ways, particularly in size, though Logan wore his height and weight in more appealing fashion. Neither man suffered insolence from others, but there again Logan proved the better man by controlling his responses when angered.

Where Logan could find enjoyment in a piece of crushed strawberry taken from Ivy's hand, Bertrand would have shooed his daughter away with an admonishment to have a care for his tunic.

Bertrand prided himself on his prowess in the practice yard and on the battlefield—most knights did. When there weren't battles to be fought, the knights tested their skills against each other in tournaments. For both their own enjoyment and prizes, where fortunes could be won or lost at the tip of a lance. The year Bertrand lost his stallion and chain mail in the joust to another knight, he'd seen nothing wrong in beggaring Lynwood to raise the ransom money to buy them back.

While she'd never witnessed Logan's skills at arms, she didn't doubt them. He relied on his sword to make his living and took great pride in maintaining the reputation he'd built over the years as a fierce and dependable mercenary. Which was why he commanded the high fee of five shillings per sennight.

'Struth, she'd hired Logan on the strength of his reputation—and she still couldn't remember what tale she'd heard about him in her father's hall that so firmly fixed his name in her memory.

She'd been all of ten-and-three when her father died, and Joanna had to admit her memory of that time wasn't as sharp as she might like. How embarrassed she'd been the night when she sat across from the mercenary she wished to hire, recounting pieces of the stories she remembered hearing, not a one of them having anything to do with Logan Grimm.

Joanna took a last glance at her babies' graves, glad she'd put the flowers on them, before beginning her stroll across the village green to return to the manor, the night of Logan's arrival at Lynwood still on her mind.

He hadn't taken offense at her lack of memory, merely pointed out her errors, revealing how young they'd both been at the time she'd heard the tales. Logan couldn't have been more than ten-and-eight when he'd performed whatever task she'd heard about, earning only two shillings a sennight and just beginning to build his reputation.

Had he begun in Scotland? In France? Been hired by the king for his army, or by some other lord for his troops? Had England been at war with either country at the time, or had some baron or knight taken it into his head to claim some piece of another's property as his own?

Joanna shook off the musings. Logan's past was past, his tales his own. Nothing truly mattered except that he was at Lynwood, doing his best to capture the thieves who harried the manor and its village.

Her manor. Her village. Her people. For the tenants she would do whatever she must to ensure that they prospered and kept safe. Including hiring a mercenary who—

Joanna stumbled, her knees going weak under the on-slaught of hearing her father's awe-filled voice as he told a tale of Logan Grimm. Her stomach churned as death and destruction spun out in sickening detail, leaving no doubt that the mercenary had earned his fee.

The horror and viciousness stunned her.

Bertrand might have been a cruel man, but nothing he'd ever done could match the barbarism of Logan Grimm.

When they parted that morn, Logan had been sure he and Joanna parted as lovers. She'd worn a bright smile, her manner playful, seeming content and accepting of what they'd done.

He'd spent much of the rest of the day reliving their lovemaking, humbled by the intensity of her response to him, awed and wary of his response to her.

There had been more between them than the mere sharing of physical pleasure. They'd come together with a swiftness and completeness that took his breath away.

As if their joining were inevitable, predestined.

His body had found its true mate, and Logan very much feared his heart was more than willing to take a reckless gamble.

To fall in love. To place his happiness in the hands of a widow, a lady of gentle birth who'd hired him for the use of his sword.

All day his head had issued dire warnings of the impediments to such a pairing of lady and mercenary. 'Twas utterly foolish to hope for more than a brief affair, ending when he caught the thieves, then departed.

Except his heart countered the warnings with whisperings of how whole he'd felt with Joanna in his arms, how complete he'd felt when joined with her. Of how, if he could win her love, he would win a prize beyond measure.

He'd battled the conflict within him all through his search for the thieves, torn between what he knew impossible and the belief that somehow he could prevail.

For this one woman, for Joanna alone, he would be willing to—what, give up his life as a mercenary? Settle down to one place and call it home? To do what with himself? He'd never overseen the planting of fields, knew nothing of raising sheep, had no notion of how one went about deciding what supplies must be purchased when and at what price.

He'd be utterly useless to Lady Joanna of Lynwood, except, perhaps, when it came to the manor's defense. He knew soldiering. He could make Joanna's world safer by day and provide her with a lover's tender comfort at night.

Considering more than a lover's place in her life would be utter folly. Joanna had already told him she didn't want to marry again, and there was truly no reason why she should unless she wanted to. Especially to a man who had naught to recommend him except a bit of money he'd been able to save. He had no title, no land, and so no worth to a woman who already possessed both.

And still his heart refused to keep silent, urging him to

consider unimaginable possibilities. So he'd returned to Lynwood with the intent of exploring the possibility of a permanent attachment.

Except something had happened between their tryst in the woodland and the coming of evening to alter Joanna's mood completely. She hadn't greeted him upon his arrival. She'd allowed Maud to serve his meal. She cast but furtive glances his way. Her smile had vanished behind a veil of silence and distance.

Regrets over having lain with him? Perhaps Joanna had also done battle with herself on the wisdom of tossing sense and caution to the wind and coupling with a man she desired but shouldn't have lain with.

But they had lain together, taken and given pleasure in stunning fashion. And while he might suffer for not resisting temptation, he would never, ever, be sorry for joining his body to hers and discovering true bliss, or for guiding Joanna to her woman's pleasure.

He'd do it again in a heartbeat, wherever and whenever she wanted. All she had to do was give him some sign, and he'd comply.

Except that tonight the only signal he received was to stay away.

She'd gone about her tasks as she did every evening, seeing to the serving of the meal and the cleanup afterward. Then took time to spend with Ivy. Right now mother and daughter sat before the hearth, Ivy on Joanna's lap, neither of them aware of aught but one another.

Maybe he should take that as his answer. Leave the woman alone. Catch her thieves and go on with his life and put the nonsense of his troublesome emotions behind him.

But then, Joanna had retreated into herself once before, during her upset over losing her temper and tossing Sir Gregory Marshall out of the hall—and, hopefully, out of her life.

Could it be something similar had happened after their tryst? That she was again more angry with herself than with him?

He wouldn't know unless he asked.

Getting up his courage took longer this time than last, only because the stakes were higher to him, and he wanted to wait until nearly all had sought out their pallets before he asked Joanna to divulge the cause of her upset.

Not until much later, when Joanna sent Ivy off to her pallet, did he decide the time had come. He left the bench, strode across the hall, and nearly lost his nerve when she saw him coming and pretended not to.

Well, damn. He'd faced bigger, stronger, meaner adversaries than the lady of Lynwood in her sulks.

"A word, milady?"

"I am quite fatigued. Is it necessary?"

So formal. What had happened to the harem dancer who'd entranced him?

"I believe it is important. Come walk with me."

She raised an eyebrow, as if she didn't believe his audacity. "Where to?"

Someplace private where they wouldn't be overheard. He considered her bedchamber, then thought better of it.

"The wall walk. I have something I wish to show you."

A lie, but it worked. They walked in silence through the night, aided by a sliver of moonlight, across the bailey and up the tower stairs. Logan noted the position of the guards making their rounds, judging he had about ten minutes before one of them would reach where he and Joanna stood.

He could feel the tension in her stance as she leaned against the timber, looking between the pointed spikes at the village below.

"One cannot see much tonight," she said softly. "Perhaps 'twould be better to wait until morn."

"Will you be speaking to me on the morn?"

"I . . ." She bit her bottom lip, whatever she'd been about to say swallowed by her hesitancy to answer.

"Joanna, what happened after we parted this morn? I thought us on very good terms. Now you hardly deign to look at me."

Her answer came devastatingly swiftly. "I made a horrible mistake. What we did this morn should not have happened, can never happen again, and I would thank you to never remind me of it."

He'd been prepared for regrets, but not total rejection. Just as Celeste—nay, Joanna wasn't as conniving. She pushed him away for other reasons. Experience told him he'd need to push her to reveal the source of her upset.

"A shame, that. I considered what we shared this morning an experience of rare quality."

"We rutted on a forest floor."

Her crudity pricked his ire.

"Rutted? Then perhaps 'twas another woman who gave herself to me, and I to her, for I remember making love, not fornicating. Tell me true, Joanna. When you lay beneath me, panting, moaning, coming to your peak, were you not aware of more happening between us than me rutting on you?"

"Does not matter." She waved a hand in the direction of the village. "What was it you wished to show me?"

"Not a thing, and I think you know that. I want to know where my harem dancer has flown so I can track her down and bring her back. I yet owe her a coin."

He knew the moment it came out of his mouth that he'd insulted her, likened her to a harlot who romped with men for money. Still, he took her flash of ire as a hopeful sign.

"Wat was right. I should never have allowed a man of your ilk inside the gate."

A low blow.

"You did not consider me so far beneath you when you danced for me."

"That was before . . . before my memory improved, and I realized I should never have sent for you to begin with."

"Have you been listening to Wat?"

"Nay, to my father."

To her father? Improved memory?

A chill slid up his spine. Apparently Joanna now remembered whatever tale of Logan Grimm had been told in her father's hall, and it upset her.

"What did your father say?"

"You burned a village, much like the one I see below me."

Was that all? His setting a torch to a few thatched roofs disturbed her?

"Surely you know it is not unusual for the village and crops to burn when one lord lays siege to another's castle."

"You torched the village, then rounded up the men and hanged them all."

Now he knew exactly which tale she'd heard, and admitted it wasn't a pretty one.

"I did so at the order of those peasants' overlord. He considered it just punishment for their acts of rebellion against him."

She looked at him then, and Joanna's loathing nearly sent him back a step.

"And the women, did they deserve rape? The children . . ." She took a long breath. "Did the children deserve to be penned like sheep until finally released to fend for themselves? Did any of those innocent children live, Logan? Did you ever once wonder what happened to them as a result of your actions?"

Not until many years later.

He'd done what he'd been paid to do, torch the village and round up the men. He'd heard the screams of the women, but didn't have the right to interfere. He'd known the children were herded into a pen, but he'd been paid and sent on his way before knowing what had become of them.

That he'd felt a pang of remorse when he'd learned of the children's plight wouldn't satisfy Joanna. Nor did he know how to explain that he'd learned never to look back, that it would cripple him to the extent he might never be able to take another offer from another lord.

Would she understand? In her present state, probably not. Perhaps not ever.

"I am a mercenary, Joanna. I do what I am paid to do, no more, no less."

"Then catch my thieves."

He didn't stop her when she fled the wall walk.

No one seemed surprised when a few minutes later, Logan moved his pallet from in front of the manor's hearth into the guards' barracks in the gate tower.

Chapter Fifteen

Joanna paced in front of the hall's hearth, impatiently waiting for the three men she'd sent for.

This morn she must decide whether to send Wat to Oundle on his own or if she should go to the market, too. Thus she wanted to speak with Wat, Harold, and Logan to guide her decision, which she already knew wouldn't be an easy one to make.

So many factors to consider. Her own unsettled feelings among them. Most of which she'd struggled with yesterday afternoon and last night and hadn't yet put to rest. Especially those about Logan.

Last night she'd dreamed of flaming cottages, screaming women, and crying children, and Logan's part in the destruction and cruelty. Bad enough on its own, the dream had taken a nasty turn, with the cottages belonging to her village and the faces of the women and children becoming those of people she knew. She'd awakened sweating and shaken, fearful for her own tenants, distraught she'd not been able to prevent the horror.

After calming some, she'd realized the difference

between her dream and reality. Still, the visions haunted her, taunting her arrogance for believing she alone could provide for and protect those within her charge.

Mingled within the horror of the mercenary hanging men while women screamed and children cried, had been other memories of Logan, sweet and tender, bawdy and brash, of the two of them sprawled on his cloak indulging in yesterday morn's fantasy. Intruding on those were his kindnesses toward Ivy when he allowed her to ride his horse and when he held a scared little girl while her stitches were removed.

How could the mercenary her father spoke of with awe for having performed so barbaric a task also be the compelling, caring man she'd come to know?

She'd tried to doubt her memory, deny Logan could be the vicious mercenary of her father's tale. Not so, of course. When confronted, Logan hadn't denied his part in the atrocity. He made no excuses, gave no explanations, stated only that he was a mercenary who did what he was paid to do.

And wasn't that why she'd wished to hire Logan Grimm to catch her thieves, confident he would do as she ordered because she paid him?

Perhaps she should have listened to Wat, given more thought to bringing a violent man to Lynwood. She knew Harold had also had misgivings, though he didn't express them. But the morning of Ivy's injury she'd been determined to take action against the band of thieves, especially against the leader. As much as she abhorred violence, on that gruesome morning, if she'd held a sword in her hand and known how to use it skillfully, she didn't think she would have hesitated to run the villain through.

But that would have been justice.

Had the lord who'd hired Logan to quell his tenants' rebellion considered his actions justice? Possibly, but the thorough degree of punishment made her shudder, and indeed, whatever the lord's reasons for his deeds didn't truly matter.

'Twas her involvement with a man who could follow those merciless orders that upset her most. That she had lain with a man who could drive a group of children into a pen without remorse left her numb. Sweet mercy, if she ordered Logan to torch Lynwood and hang all the men, would he do it without questioning?

She'd become entangled with a man who could be cold and ruthless. No matter how much she'd tried to keep it from happening, telling herself and him that she couldn't engage in an affair, her attraction to Logan had strengthened with each passing day, until yesterday they'd come together in a union she'd gloried in.

Giving in to temptation hadn't been wise, but she'd been helpless against it.

Verily, the man's physical attributes were praiseworthy. All muscle and sinew sculpted into an enticing, virile male of goodly height and alluring form. That such a man, who could lure most any female to his bed, would want her in return had proved flattering and thrilling.

She might have resisted temptation if not for how Logan made her feel. As though she was beautiful, desirable, and worthy not only of his attention but of his time. No man had given her such a gift before.

So which man was the true Logan Grimm? The ruthless mercenary of her father's tale, or the man who'd graciously kept her company on a night when she couldn't sleep? Then several times over given her reason to admire him. Who prodded her out of feeling wretched when she made mistakes and whose mere presence fed her confidence.

The hall's door opened. Wat entered first, followed closely by Harold and Logan. Wat wore what had become his usual disgruntled expression. Harold simply looked tired.

She couldn't discern Logan's mood at all.

They'd parted last eve with sharp words, and he'd moved his pallet out of the hall. Was he angry? Indifferent? She couldn't tell. He'd closed himself off from her completely, and for that she should probably be thankful.

If Logan kept his distance and she hers, they'd have no more late-night talks, nor walks through the fields, nor fantasies in a woodland clearing.

Her heart bled at the loss.

Joanna swallowed the lump in her throat and waved the men to the table, where they would all break their fast while she listened to their opinions.

Logan took the place farthest away from her, almost separating himself from the rest of them, as if he didn't belong.

Perhaps that was best. When his task was completed he'd go back to his own life, leaving Lynwood and its lady to get on as best they could without him. Given no choice, she would get on. With the thieves dispatched, she'd have the security and peace she craved, the coin given to the mercenary well spent.

"Logan, if you would, I should like a report on how goes the search for the thieves."

If her formality struck him as odd or hurtful, he didn't

show it by expression or comment, merely continued to butter his bread with his eating knife.

"During the past four days I have searched most of the area surrounding Lynwood Manor. I found no trace of the thieves, neither tracks from their horses nor signs of a lit campfire."

Concise and terse, which she should have expected.

"You suspect they are still in the area?"

"I suspect several things for which I cannot offer proof. Until I do, I prefer to keep my own counsel."

Like suspecting the villagers might be aiding the thieves in some way. She still thought the suggestion outrageous. Why the villagers would aid those who robbed them didn't make sense.

"You mentioned finding tracks by the abandoned hunting lodge."

"Several days old, leading north. They could belong to the thieves or perhaps not."

All true. All things they'd talked of before. Except now Logan refused to speculate, and she needed his opinion.

"Would you say they are yet in hiding not far from the manor?"

"I am inclined to believe so, but cannot say for certain."

Irritating, stubborn man!

Wat leaned forward, smirking. "Beg pardon, my lady. I believe the mercenary says he is no closer to capturing the thieves than he was when he began his search. For all he boasted on his ability to complete this task, I ask you to consider that Grimm has failed you."

Joanna felt the kick to her gut. Wat neatly insulted Logan, but he also made her aware he considered her decision to hire Grimm a failure. But then she'd known all along Wat didn't approve.

Harold put down his tankard. "Grimm has not failed yet, Wat. You must consider that while we do not yet know where the thieves hide, we are also now very certain of where they do not. 'Tis only a matter of time before they are found."

"How much more time is necessary?" Wat asked. "How much longer must her ladyship pay for no results?"

"I believe the bargain between Lady Joanna and Grimm allows for extra time at no added cost."

Logan looked pointedly at Wat. "I will not cheat her ladyship. I will find those thieves if I must stay for a month and turn over every leaf in the forest."

His tone made Joanna wonder if he gave assurance or issued a warning. Given the animosity between reeve and mercenary, Logan's statement could be taken as either. No matter what happened, these two would never get along. They had rubbed each other wrongly from the beginning and never made an attempt to become friendly.

She supposed she should be content that they hadn't come to blows.

Wat huffed. "So you say, and yet have found no trace of them, have even suggested the thieves may have left the area."

"Perhaps." Logan reached for a piece of cheese. "Two things I have never understood. The first is why they only harry Lynwood. A man I talked to at the hamlet suggested 'twas because Lynwood possessed more to steal. What think you, Wat? Why steal chickens only from the village when one of the hamlet's chickens would make as tasty a stew?"

"How should I know why they prefer our fowl? I am no thief, nor do I know the workings of their minds."

"Then consider how they have gone about the business." He paused for a moment, as if putting his thoughts in order. "Several weeks ago three men came into the area. On horseback. I am inclined to believe those are stolen horses. Agreed?"

"Most likely."

"So they began their thievery elsewhere, and we might assume they are on the run from whomever they stole the horses. During their travels, a chicken at Lynwood catches their eye, so they sneak into the village in the middle of the night and steal it. They find a cozy spot in which to hide. Now, sheltered and fed, they decide to remain a few days until assured they are safe. That may explain the first theft, even the second, but not the rest."

Wat shrugged a shoulder. "As you said, they are sheltered and fed. Perhaps they do not yet feel safe enough to move on."

"Even though Harold and his guards, and now me, made attempts to find them?"

"Obviously they do not worry about being captured."

Joanna felt the pang of inadequacy. What more could she have done after those first thefts either to capture the thieves or convince them to move on? Because she'd made no definite move, they'd raided again, injured Ivy.

Logan now leaned forward, fixed on Wat. "I find their lack of concern intriguing. They are so sure of themselves they not only remain near Lynwood, but become bolder with the thefts. They go so far as to make a daylight raid, spear a goose, which all admit is a grand prize, allowing themselves to be seen. Why?"

"To taunt us," Joanna said, remembering the smug expression on the leader's face, sure of her conjecture. "They believed they could do so without any reprisal."

Harold nodded. "And they were right. By then they must have known of our shortage of guards. Unfortunately, they were also skillful in leaving no trail."

"Which also concerns me," Logan stated. "We will leave that for future contemplation, however, for 'tis their motives that bother me more."

"Food and shelter," Wat injected.

Logan shook his head. "For all the fowl and piglets they have stolen, 'tis not enough food to keep three men's stomachs from grumbling for this long. They must be getting victuals from elsewhere, either stolen or purchased. Yet we hear no reports from the surrounding hamlets of food or firewood being stolen or of the presence of three strange men on horseback."

"'Tis a puzzle," Harold commented, echoing Joanna's thoughts.

"Indeed," Logan agreed. "I know not why they stay. Begging pardon, your ladyship, but while Lynwood Manor is a nice place, 'tis not overly prosperous. They have nothing to gain here."

Not out in the village. More could be had from the manor, which made Joanna very nervous.

"Could this all be a test for a yet bolder raid on the manor?"

"Perhaps. But again I do not understand why. There are better pickings to be had throughout the kingdom."

Joanna couldn't argue that. "Do you think they have already sold the chalice?"

"Tracks at the abandoned hunting lodge lead north. The

nearest large town where they might be able to sell the chalice to someone who wouldn't ask a lot of questions about where they got it would be Oundle. 'Twould not be remiss to speak to the merchants there who deal in gold. One might even be able to learn from whence they stole the horses. I imagine that man would like to have them back."

Oundle. Logan had reason to make the trip as part of his search for the thieves. Even Wat had reason, to purchase wheat seed.

True, she wanted to sell a few rounds of cheese, but Wat could do so. He could also make it known she wished to sell a suit of chain mail and make any necessary arrangements with a prospective buyer.

As much as she longed to go to the market city and take Ivy to see the dancing bear, Joanna wasn't sure if she should. For one thing, she'd be in Logan's close company for several days, which only the day before might have been a reason to go. No longer.

"The journey to Oundle is part of the reason I wanted to talk to all of you. I need to decide if I should go. 'Struth, I am very much of two minds on the matter."

"As I told you the other day, milady—"

She stopped Wat with an upraised finger. "I am not pleased with how you presented your opinion. You should not have done so in front of Ivy. The poor child is unhappy about not being able to play on the village green. Then you fill her head with visions of sweet cakes and dancing bears. 'Twas most unfair of you to raise her hopes."

He raised his hands, palms up, contrite. "I meant no harm, milady. I saw a chance to broach the subject and did not think of how Ivy might feel if you refused. I fear my lack of dealings with children put me at a disadvantage."

An honest mistake. Forgivable. Yet Joanna couldn't help comparing. She doubted Logan had many dealings with children, either, yet he'd done wonderfully with Ivy.

Just as Wat and Logan had rubbed each other wrongly, Ivy and Logan had found common ground from the moment they met. Over apple tarts. The memory of Logan pushing the last tart on the platter toward Ivy tugged a smile from Joanna's lips, which she didn't allow to linger.

"In the future you will have a care, Wat."

"As you say, milady."

His abashment satisfied her.

"In which direction do you lean?" Harold asked.

Stay or go. That she wanted to go wasn't an issue. Which course would best serve the people in her charge?

"I admit I am torn. I believe Wat can deal with the purchase of the wheat seed. He could also manage the sale of a few rounds of cheese we have to spare. However, one thing I had hoped to do was sell Bertrand's suit of mail—"

"Sell it?" Wat asked sharply. "One would think you would wish to save it."

"To what purpose?"

"Why . . . someday you may have another son. The suit of mail would be part of his inheritance."

Sweet mercy. Not this again.

"Whether or not I ever marry again—and you already know my feelings on that score—whatever inheritance this nonexistent son receives would come from his own father. Bertrand's mail is a part of Ivy's inheritance. Since I doubt she has plans to don it, then the money from its sale could be used to make improvements to Lynwood."

Wat's eyes narrowed slightly. "Such as."

"Flooring the tithe barn, for one. The cleaner the fleece, the better price we receive."

"As I recall, Sir Bertrand thought flooring the barn a waste."

Bertrand thought spending coin on most anything that wasn't absolutely necessary or didn't contribute to his personal comfort and desires a waste.

"I have already spoken to Otto about the costs involved, and believe the expenditure worthwhile. We would not be able to have a plank floor in place before shearing this year, but certainly in time for next. And there are other improvements I would like to make." Joanna took a quick glance around the hall. "A tapestry or two in here would go far to brighten up the place as well as shield us from winter drafts."

"A tapestry?"

He didn't approve of that improvement either. Damn. Why had she ever given Wat Reeve permission to speak freely, even encouraged him at times? Logan had one thing right—the reeve could be very irritating.

Joanna leaned forward slightly. "Perhaps two."

Harold drummed his fingers on the table. "Milady, if we are considering how best to spend the coin from the sale of the chain mail, you might wish to think about hiring another guard or two."

"An excellent suggestion. Whence do we get them?"

"Inquire in Oundle."

"I could." Except she wasn't sure exactly how to go about it. Did one just announce one was looking for soldiers, then hire those who came forward? "Truly, you should do the hiring of guards, Harold. I fear I do not know how to tell a good soldier from bad."

"I do," Logan said. "I could speak with them first, if you like, before sending them back for Harold's approval."

Wat's head swiveled toward Logan. "I do not recall Lady Joanna inviting you to go with us."

"We spoke of it the other day. I offered to act as one of her escort, and Lady Joanna accepted."

"But you are supposed to be searching for the thieves!"

She could see Logan gathering his patience.

"Lady Joanna cannot go to Oundle unguarded, especially if she takes Ivy along. Unless you have suddenly become proficient with a sword, you cannot be expected to defend them against whatever trouble may arise on the road. I meant all along to inquire about the chalice, and see if perhaps the thieves were operating in a wider area than we believed, and we just have not heard of it."

"I still say your duty is here."

"Since Lady Joanna pays my fee, my duty is wherever she says it is." He looked at her fully then, those midnight eyes drawing her in. "What say you, milady? Have you changed your mind?"

No matter what had passed between them, no matter that she'd remembered the horrific tale that caused her inner turmoil, Joanna knew she and Ivy would be utterly safe with Logan acting as their escort.

"I have not. But then, I have also not yet made up my mind on whether or not to go."

"What keeps you here?"

An impertinent question, but one easily answered. "Many things. The last of the oats must be planted, and if

Wat is not here then I should oversee it. We need to ready for the shearing. Should a problem arise, I should be here to deal with it."

"Are there not others you could put in charge for a few days? Surely someone trustworthy could oversee the planting of oats. The shearing will not begin until after we return. And frankly, as ruler of Lynwood, you should not have to deal with every petty problem that arises."

She'd heard all this before from Logan, on the day she'd tossed Sir Gregory out of the manor. Rule or be ruled, Logan had said. Still, her conscience pestered.

"I am also uncomfortable leaving while the thieves are yet about. I should be here if they strike again."

"Your being here will not determine whether they strike, or which goose or lamb they steal, or if they settle for firewood. You told me the other day that your father always made the trip to Oundle. What did he do there?"

"He visited with the merchants, sometimes spent long hours going from one to the next, deciding whose word to trust and whose not. Inspecting their goods. Determining who would give him the better value for his coin."

Logan nodded, as if she were a student who'd come up with the correct answer. "Establishing relationships with merchants, whether they deal in seed or gold or tapestries, must be done by every lord, whether he does it himself or entrusts a steward to do it for him. Since you have no steward, 'twould be worth your while to make yourself known in Oundle as the ruler of Lynwood Manor."

"Grimm is right, milady," Harold agreed. "If naught else, the merchants should also be given the chance to know you, see for themselves that even though Sir Bertrand has died, Lynwood Manor still exists and our needs are much the same. For seed, of course. Iron for the blacksmith. Leather for our shoes. All number of goods that we cannot produce ourselves."

They had a point. She'd been so concerned over her portion of the shire she'd forgotten they were also dependent upon good relations with others in the kingdom.

Logan smiled then, but the smile wasn't for Joanna. He looked beyond her, and Joanna knew who must be lurking there.

Ivy.

Joanna sighed, knowing what her daughter must have overheard and so was about to ask. She'd left the girl in the nursery enduring a reading lesson with Father Arthur, which meant the priest must be standing there, too.

"Mama, are we going to Oundle?"

Why, she didn't know, but Joanna glanced over at Logan, whose smile never faltered as he mouthed the word "go."

Go to Oundle, with Ivy and Wat and a soldier to act as buffer between her and Logan, ensuring she kept her distance. She and Ivy could shop for ribbons and watch the dancing bears. If she were fortunate, there would be no dancers. She could sell the cheese and chain mail, hire guards, and perhaps learn the fate of the chalice.

Joanna wasn't sure which reason decided her, but as she turned around to face Ivy she was confident she did the right thing.

"Aye, we are going."

The only one who cheered was Ivy, tossing her hands in the air with a resounding "Huzzah!"

The decision made and declared, Joanna turned her attention to the preparations necessary.

"Harold, we will need one more guard. Have you someone in mind?"

"Aye, my lady. When do you wish to leave?"

The sooner she left, the sooner she could return. She needed only today to prepare.

"At first light on the morn. Wat, have the cart wheels inspected, and be sure the horses are properly shod. Ivy and I will ride in the cart with you."

Wat and Harold rose from the table, leaving Logan still sitting there, his eyebrow cocked. Expecting an order, too?

"Logan, I leave you to the planning of our route. Do you know the roads?"

In answer he glanced over at Harold. "I will need another look at your maps."

Joanna took a deep breath, mentally listing everything she must do before morn to prepare for her absence of at least five days. So much could go wrong while she was away.

Even as she thought it she brushed the worry aside, the weight lifting from her shoulders. 'Twas bad of her, she supposed, but she was about to do what she'd longed to do since the moment she'd come to Lynwood Manor as a bride.

Escape.

Chapter Sixteen

Not completely trusting Joanna's and Ivy's safety to Wat, Logan followed the reeve out to the stables, at a distance, hoping Wat wouldn't notice.

A successful endeavor.

From within Gideon's stall, where he busied himself going over his stallion's equipage which he knew to be in excellent condition, Logan heard Wat and Oliver drag the cart out of a stall and into the center aisle. After a few silent minutes Wat pronounced the cart in good enough shape to make the journey. He then told Oliver which two horses were to pull the cart and to have them hitched and standing outside of the manor's door before first light on the morrow.

Wat then hurriedly left the stable, and Logan shook his head at the reeve's insolence for only partly following Joanna's orders.

Logan eased out of Gideon's stall. Seeing no sign of either reeve or stable lad, he inspected the cart.

Old. Worn. The planks forming the bed seemed solid

enough, and though the iron banding on the two large, solid-wood wheels bore rust, he saw no cracks or breaks.

Logan turned to the squeal of leather hinges. Oliver came through a door at the end of the building, his arms piled high with leather straps connected with steel rings. Logan stepped aside to allow the lad to pass and drop the heavy load on the dirt floor near the cart's tongue.

Oliver brushed his hands together, smiling a greeting for Logan. "Need Gideon saddled?"

Logan almost hated to disappoint the lad who'd taken proper care of Gideon and delighted in readying the stallion for a ride most mornings.

"A bit later." Logan waved a hand at the pile of leather and steel. "Harnesses?"

"Aye. Ain't been used in months. Got me some straightening and cleaning to do."

"So I see. For which horses?"

Oliver wagged a finger, indicating two stalls. "Those two. Old nags both, but they got some strength to 'em yet. Can still pull a plow well enough, so should have no trouble with the weight of the cart."

The lad stepped up to one of the stalls, gave the horse's head a loving stroke. "This one be ready to go. The other I will have to take to the smith later on. One of her shoes should be replaced."

Logan decided he needn't check all of the shoes, as the reeve hadn't, because the stable lad knew what he was about. Still, Joanna had told Wat to ensure the horses properly shod, so the reeve should have done so.

"I will take her to the smith."

Oliver looked up, surprised.

Logan waved a hand at the harnessing. "You have plenty to do here. Truly, I do not mind."

Nor did Logan have much else to do to keep him occupied all day. He'd ridden damn near every inch of ground within several leagues of Lynwood and found not a sign of where the villains made camp. In the afternoon he would take another trip over to the hunting lodge, but doubted he would notice anything new.

Aye, he wanted a look at Harold's maps to see which roads led to Oundle, but that wouldn't take long.

"Well, if you be willing, I will get you a rope."

While waiting, Logan gave both horses a quick inspection. As the lad said, both had seen better days. The one Oliver declared ready to go appeared blind in one eye, and the one needing a shoe had a slight dip to her back. Singly they weren't good for much, but, as a team, they were apparently able to pull a plow. With steady hands at the reins, they should do well enough with a cart.

Did Wat have steady hands? He'd better, for the cart would carry precious treasure. Joanna and Ivy.

Logan brutally shoved aside memories of last eve, of Joanna's horror and disgust. He'd relived their talk often enough last night, didn't need to torment himself all through today.

He should have known better than to wonder if a lady could accept a mercenary as her lover, should never have allowed himself to become enchanted by a gentle woman—and her little girl.

Not for us, he'd warned Gideon of Lynwood's females, and he should have listened more closely to his own warning.

Rope secured to the bridle, Logan led the nag out of

her stall, raising a few eyebrows as the two of them crossed the bailey.

At the gate, he shouted up to the guard, "Should Harold look for me, I will be at the smith's."

The soldier nodded his understanding, and Logan began the trek across the village green.

There had been no need to name anyone but Harold, the only one who might inquire of Logan's whereabouts. Joanna wouldn't. She'd made her feelings very clear. She considered him brutal, an unfeeling animal who performed atrocities for mere money. True, on occasion he'd accepted his fee for following orders he didn't like. 'Twas what a mercenary did to earn his fee. Whether torching a village or searching for thieves, he did whatever he was ordered to earn his pay.

Logan doubted Joanna would ever understand that his part in that particular event had been a small one. Her heart cried out at what she saw as injustice and cruelty toward the women and children, and condemned him for having any part at all in their suffering.

Joanna might possess a forgiving nature—witness her swift and easy forgiveness of Wat that morn—but apparently she wasn't about to forgive the mercenary for past deeds.

Just as well. He'd had no business striving to establish himself in Joanna's good graces in the first place. Nor would he try again. The fall was too steep and the landing too hard.

Donald must have heard the clop of horses' hooves. From within his shop, he looked up from where he sat on a stool, a whetstone and shears in hand.

Logan didn't bother with pleasantries. "Oliver says she needs a shoe replaced."

"Say which one?"

"Nay."

The smith got up, placed stone and shears on the stool, and ambled out of the shop. The horse stood docilely as he picked up one hoof, then a second.

"Should have guessed 'twould be the one with the odd bend. Won't take but a moment to shape it."

Logan stood by quietly as the smith fetched a piece of iron in the shape of a horseshoe, tossed it into the glowing coals, and applied the bellows. Like the stable lad, the smith knew what he was about, did his job in an efficient manner.

"Heard you are going to Oundle," Donald remarked.

Logan guessed at the source of the information. "I gather Wat stopped by to tell you."

"On his way to the brewer. A tavern in Oundle is always pleased to buy Mistress Brewer's spiced mead. Ain't often anyone makes the trip so she can sell it."

Logan wondered if there would be room in the cart for kegs of spiced ale, but decided that wasn't his concern.

The smith used a pair of pincers—of the same form Joanna had used to remove his stitches, only several times larger—to pluck the red-hot shoe from the coals. Not hot enough, apparently, for he put it back.

"Do her ladyship good to go to Oundle." Donald turned the shoe over. "Take her mind off her problems."

Meaning the thieves. Did the smith think the same as the reeve, that the mercenary had failed their lady? Didn't matter.

"I gather she does not go often."

"Never, far as I know. Sir Bertrand, he liked to make a good time of it, did not take her ladyship along. Would not surprise me if she bought some of those fripperies the ladies like, hair ribbons and such. She has done without them for a good long time."

The more he heard about Bertrand, the more Logan wished . . . but the man was already dead, and how he'd treated Joanna was no longer a concern.

"Lady Joanna is a beautiful woman. Lack of ribbons for her hair makes her no less so."

The smith smiled and again removed the shoe from the fire, this time placing it on the anvil.

"That she is. Deserves a bit of happiness, methinks. Says she does not want to marry again, but a beautiful widow with a nice piece of land to add to the bargain— hard for a man looking to wed to pass by."

Logan's heart burned as red as the iron. "Perhaps she is content with the way things are."

The smith picked up his hammer. "Maybe. But her ladyship sure misses the two children she lost to the plague. Mourns them something fierce. Could use another one or two to fill the emptiness in her soul."

Hammer sang against iron in a steady rhythm. Logan watched, barely seeing, his thoughts focused elsewhere. On Joanna, grinning, holding a newborn babe.

Maybe she didn't want Sir Gregory, perhaps not even the Sir Edgar whom Harold had mentioned. But someday she might happen across someone she considered worth marrying, a man to keep thieves from her door and plant babes in her belly.

That man would be a knight, at the least. Possibly a higher lord. Not a mercenary.

Donald plunged the hot iron into a bucket of cold water, a sharp hiss rising with the cloud of steam. A few moments later he pulled the shoe out, inspected it, and with a satisfied nod placed the shoe on the anvil and fetched a file with which he scraped at the edges.

"Never been to Oundle myself," he said. "I hear one can purchase most anything from the merchants."

"If one has the money."

"Think Lady Joanna will be able to sell the chain mail?"

"Depends on who is in the city. I hope so. She is certainly set on flooring the tithe barn."

"So Wat said. Take a lot of coin, but might be worth the doing. Said something about a tapestry, too."

Apparently Wat had related the entire conversation to Donald. Complained, most likely. About the tapestry, certainly. About Logan's accompanying them? Most probably. Too bad.

The smith ran a hand along the shoe's now smoothed edge, then handed it to Logan. "Tell Oliver to use a longer nail on the right edge. Better chance of it staying on the whole trip."

"I will tell him."

"Good journey to you, and to her ladyship. We will all pray for good weather and her safe return."

"I am sure she will appreciate your prayers. Might I ask a favor of you while we are gone?"

The smith crossed his meaty arms. "Such as?"

"Lady Joanna is concerned about the security of the manor in her absence. Clarence goes with us also, leaving Harold short a guard. Might you and some of the village men take a turn at augmenting the garrison?"

"You are concerned about the thieves?"

"Nay, I am concerned for Lady Joanna's state of mind. If she knows the manor and village are well guarded, she may not worry herself to distraction the entire time."

Donald scratched at his beard. "I can mend a sword, but I cannot say I know how to use one."

"I am sure the guards would be willing to show you." Logan smiled. "Besides, you are such a big man, a villain would hesitate to challenge you."

"Think you?"

"I know so."

"How long do you expect to be gone?"

"Nearly a sennight. Too long for her ladyship to be worried over Lynwood."

Donald lowered his hand. "Then might I ask a boon, too?"

"Certes."

"Guard her well, Grimm. Lady Joanna is very special to us."

Logan didn't hesitate. "On that you have my word."

Shoe in hand, horse in tow, Logan made his way back across the green, his promise to Donald sitting easy on his shoulders.

Joanna might now wish to keep her distance from the mercenary she'd hired. There would be no more late-night talks over spiced mead, no more trysts in the woods. Much had changed between them.

Going into the hall that morning he'd feared she might be ready to pay him off and send him on his way. She'd been cool and a bit aloof, but even that had been reassuring.

She still expected him to do as he'd been hired to do—

catch the thieves. More importantly, she didn't doubt his ability to escort her and Ivy safely to Oundle.

He might never possess Joanna's heart, but he had her trust and a measure of her regard, and by damn, he would prove himself worthy of both.

The cart held together. The weather cooperated. By the end of the second day, with Oundle in sight, Joanna wanted nothing more than to stretch her legs and allow some feeling to return to her backside.

The deeply rutted dirt road only made matters worse, jarring the cart, bouncing her on the seat. Enjoying her arrival in the city she hadn't seen in years wasn't possible. By the time their party stopped in front of a tavern, she was sure she'd never walk again.

Wat handed her the reins. "I will be but a moment, milady. We will soon be rid of the kegs and can then move on."

The reeve jumped down and dashed into the tavern. Logan eased his stallion alongside, and Joanna truly envied Ivy's seat in front of him. Even if seated high up on a stallion, the perch on Logan's thighs had to be more comfortable than bare plank.

Whenever the little minx had complained over the hard seat, or that she felt too confined in the bed of the cart, Logan hefted her up into his saddle. Ivy had complained often.

"Nearly there," Logan said, as if he'd read her mind. "The inn Harold suggested is on the next street. Once the mead is unloaded, we will get you and Ivy settled into a room before we deal with stabling the horses and storing the trunk and the cart."

Joanna nodded, grateful the ordeal was almost over and that the men would take care of the arrangements. All she wanted was a bite to eat and a tub of hot water in which to sink.

Then Logan heaved an aggrieved sigh, snatched Ivy from his lap, and set her down in the cart beside the large trunk.

"Stay by your mother." His order brooked no argument, and to Ivy's credit she didn't try.

When Logan rode out several yards in front of the cart and dismounted, Joanna had the strange sensation of something amiss. He crossed his arms and looked up the street, his stance firm and tense as if expecting trouble.

Joanna looked where he did, and saw trouble strolling toward Logan in the form of a man. A huge man, garbed in leather covered by chain mail. He wore a sword similar to Logan's angled across his back. His dark hair was long and shaggy, his beard full and wiry, his eyes set close together, mouth set in a snarl.

The closer he came, the more Joanna wished Logan would draw his sword and warn the man off.

Ivy's hands landed on Joanna's shoulders, her small frame pressed up against her mother's back. Joanna reached up to cover Ivy's hand with hers, trying not to hold her breath.

"Logan!" The punch delivered to Logan's shoulder would have felled a lesser man. "What do you in Oundle? Thought you were wasting away in London!"

The hearty shove Logan gave the other man barely budged him. "And leave the field open to you? Never!"

The fight she'd begun to envision never happened.

The punches and words flung were good-natured. A friend, then. Perhaps a fellow mercenary?

Joanna exhaled. Here she'd been frightened for Logan, and now the two men stood with their heads close together, merely talking.

Wat stepped outside of the tavern's door, pointed two men in her direction, then stepped back inside. Joanna held tighter to the reins, keeping the horses still while the two men pulled kegs of spiced mead from the back of the cart, hefting them up onto their shoulders to carry them into the tavern.

"I cannot just yet, but here . . . " she heard Logan say. He led his "friend" past her to the back of the cart and put a hand on a keg. "Guard one of these. I will be back later to introduce you to the finest spiced mead in the kingdom."

The man's smile didn't improve his appearance, to Joanna's way of thinking.

"Now there is a bargain I will take you up on. Try not to tarry."

"Once I get her ladyship settled, I will be back."

The man hefted a keg up to his shoulder and carried it into the tavern.

"Who is that?" Ivy asked Logan.

Logan heaved himself back into the saddle. "Conrad Falke."

Joanna barely suppressed a shiver, thankful she'd not remembered Falke's name first when deciding which mercenary to hire. But if she'd hired Falke, she would never have met Logan, and wouldn't now be suffering pangs of remorse for how badly she'd treated him since remembering that horrible tale.

With all the time she'd spent in her own thoughts during the journey, she'd come to realize Logan wasn't guilty of all she accused him of the other night. Unfortunately, the opportunity to apologize hadn't yet presented itself.

All the kegs unloaded, Wat climbed back into the cart, slapped the reins against the horses' rumps, and bounced them down to the next street and a tidy inn.

Joanna climbed down, not waiting for Wat's assistance. By the time her legs were steady enough to help Ivy down, Logan had already entered the inn to inquire about rooms. Wat fetched the small satchel containing the few items she and Ivy required for their comfort. Joanna hoped to put the bar of lilac-scented soap to immediate use.

Logan came out of the inn, and with a courtly bow waved her and Ivy toward the door. Joanna accepted the invitation without qualm or question, entering the taproom to be greeted by the innkeeper and the odor of stale ale. Whatever bubbled in the hearth's cauldron, however, smelled delicious.

Arrangements made for hauling up the trunk and cheese, the company's meals—and her bath—Joanna followed the innkeeper up the stairs and into a private room nearly as large as her bedchamber at Lynwood.

"I hope you will be comfortable here, milady," the innkeeper said, opening the windows that looked out over the main street.

Joanna took in the thickness of the mattress, the plumpness of the bolsters, and the rich sheen of the coverlet. Pure heaven.

"I am sure Ivy and I will be fine."

"Then I will see to your meals and bathwater."

The innkeeper bowed out, and Logan entered. The room closed in around her.

For the entire trip they'd been civil, but rarely had a word passed between them that didn't have to do with some aspect of the journey. He kept her apprised of their direction and progress, but saved idle conversation for Ivy. That was what she'd wanted. Distance. A lack of familiarity.

'Twas driving her mad.

He glanced around as he had at last night's inn, ensuring the room suitable for the lady he escorted and felt responsible for. There wasn't a thing wrong with his demeanor—except she hated how he treated her, with bows and manners, and that he never used her name anymore, always giving her a title.

She wanted to shove "milady" down his throat.

"Where is the bear?"

Ivy leaned out the window, bent far forward to see up the street. Heart in her throat, Joanna strove for a calm tone.

"Ivy, come away from the window."

"But where is the bear?"

Logan answered. "It grows late, so the bear needs his sleep. I am sure your mother will take you in search of it tomorrow."

Ivy backed away from the window, sighing, allowing a mother's heart to again beat in her chest.

Logan took another glance around him. "You are satisfied with the room, milady?"

Her irritation returned. "The room is fine. I am sure the food and bath will also be acceptable."

"Then I will take my leave. Be sure to bolt the door and latch the window before you sleep."

"I will."

"Then I bid thee good night."

He bowed out of the room before she could protest. But what could she say? Truly, under other circumstances she would have no complaint. Logan was behaving exactly as he should.

And dammit, she missed him.

The spiced mead went down as smoothly as it did at Lynwood, except in the tavern Logan had to pay for it. Oddly enough, he didn't mind. Conrad made for good company—sometimes. Tonight happened to be one of those times.

They'd spent the last hour steadily emptying the keg, making excellent progress, and catching up on each other's lives.

"Not an offer I would expect you to accept," Conrad said of Logan's chasing down a band of thieves for the lady of Lynwood Manor.

"Damn leg still hurts a bit. Did not want to take anything more strenuous until it healed fully."

Conrad didn't need to hear the whole of it, especially that there had been no other job in the offing. Logan would not reveal the tale of his stitches for anything.

"Heard you lost the leg."

"Your hearing never was too good."

Conrad chuckled. "How much longer you expect these thieves will evade you?"

"They will enjoy their freedom for at least another

sennight, until after we return to Lynwood. After that, a few more days at most."

"Looking at another fortnight, then. Timing might be just about right."

"For what?"

"Army gathering along the northern border. I might be persuaded to put in a good word for you with the earl."

The prospect of war with Scotland—a delight to any mercenary's ears. Good pay, decent loot, a chance to win a few honors and bonuses.

Logan expected he'd be ready for a good fight by then. He was already close to putting his fist through a wall nearly every time Joanna spoke to him with "her ladyship's" air. A few days more, and he just might go mad.

"Keep in mind who pays for your mead, Conrad. Which earl?"

"Essex."

Not a bad man to sign on with. "Let me know where and when."

Conrad nodded. "So . . . part of your assignment was to bring the lady shopping?"

Logan smiled at the taunt, glad Conrad didn't know about the significance of a dancing bear. "The journey worked to both of our advantages. How long have you been in Oundle?"

"Few days."

"Know of anyone who has complained of having horses stolen?"

"Nay."

"How about a merchant who boasts of purchasing a recently stolen chalice?"

"Now I know you have gone mad."

"And you are no help at all. Unless you know of some-one looking to buy a suit of chain mail. Lady Joanna wishes to sell one, including spurs, daggers, and a sword."

Conrad's brow scrunched in thought. "Now there I may be able to help. How big?"

"Too small for you or me, but made for a large, if shorter, man."

"Her husband's?"

"Got rid of his stallion first and is now looking to be rid of the rest of it."

"No sentiment, hmmm?"

"From what I hear she has no reason for sentiment."

Conrad upended his tankard, draining it of mead, then set the tankard aside and leaned forward. Logan mistrusted the sparkle in his fellow mercenary's eyes.

"Getting a bonus from the lady?"

Logan didn't mistake the meaning. He growled the word "Nay."

"Too bad. Pretty thing, and methinks you could use a good boffing. What say we find us a few wenches and have us a lecherous night?"

Logan couldn't remember how many times he'd taken Conrad up on the offer, in several countries. Conrad always seemed to know where to find inventive entertainment.

"Not tonight. Knowing you, we would not be done until dawn, and I have a chalice and a horse owner to hunt down first thing."

"Getting old are you?"

"Getting smarter."

Conrad tossed back his head and laughed. "Never. But suit yourself." The punch on the arm wasn't as hard as before. "I will let you know about the chain mail. Here. Same time, same brew."

Logan remained seated several minutes after Conrad left, finishing the last of the spiced mead in his tankard, mulling over what he hadn't told Conrad, his true excuse for refusing to go wenching.

He simply couldn't see himself rutting, making love to, or boffing anyone but Joanna. And he had to get back to the inn soon and spread his pallet in the hallway in front of her door as he had last night.

Perhaps tonight, if the Fates were kind and the mead worked its magic, he might even be able to get some sleep—but he wasn't counting on it.

Chapter Seventeen

From her youth, Joanna's memories of Northampton-shire were of rolling green hills spotted with white sheep, of Oundle a collection of pretty buildings clinging to a slope along the River Nene. She'd remembered correctly.

At the market, held in the center of town, one could purchase most any item one would ever need, and some things one would never find a use for. Wares brought in by merchants from all over England ranged from the mundane to the exotic.

The locals sold ales, cheeses, and eggs, and one enterprising young woman sold hot, fragrant meat pies. There Joanna had planned to sell her rounds of cheese, but was spared the task by the innkeeper, who took one sniff of them, declared them divine, and made the purchase.

So instead of hawking cheese, Joanna and Ivy wandered through the market, several extra pence jingling in the leather pouch tied to Joanna's belt. She hadn't yet found anyone selling wheat seed, but the day was young, and Wat was somewhere in the market looking, too, so she held her concern at bay.

Clarence was back at the inn, caring for the horses and guarding the trunk containing the chain mail. Where Logan had gone off to Joanna didn't know, though she hoped he made inquiries about a chalice and stolen horses and a buyer for the chain mail.

While she'd remembered most things correctly, including the gaiety of color and thrill of spying oddities— like a brass turtle the seller claimed was fashioned by a sculptor in far off Constantinople—she'd forgotten about pushing her way through crowds of intent shoppers and the stench raised by too many people pressed together.

Joanna guided Ivy around a group of people gawking at a merchant's collection of seashells, only to be forced to give way for a party of nobles passing by.

Oh, the gowns! Wondrous fabrics in beautiful colors, the hems of skirts and sleeves decorated with embroidery. She tried not to envy the lady and her bevy of hand-maidens, but 'twas damn hard.

"Who is she, Mama?"

"I know not her name, dear, but she must be noble if she can afford to wear silk."

"Are we noble?"

"Nay, merely gentry."

Ivy giggled and pointed at a girl not much older than herself, garbed much the same as her elders. "Look, Mama, she has ducks on her skirt."

Indeed, along the hem of a gown the hue of emeralds marched an entire flock of little yellow ducks. Ivy, of course, had never seen the like.

Joanna placed her hand on Ivy's shoulder, covered by a dark brown linen tunic with no decoration to soften the stark declaration of their lack of wealth. Ivy might be the daughter of a knight, but might never have a gown of silk. The girl could, however, know the joy of color.

She looked up the street, spotted what she sought, and hurried Ivy over to inspect an array of ribbons neatly arranged on a blanket.

"How much?" she asked the older woman sitting cross-legged beside the blanket.

"Halfpenny each."

"Choose two," Joanna told Ivy, and dug into her pouch for the necessary coin.

Ivy took her time before finally choosing one of emerald green, the color of the noble girl's gown, and one of the deep red of summer roses.

"What say we wind one of these into your braid before we go find the dancing bear?"

Ivy agreed and chose the green ribbon, so Joanna found a patch of grass out of the crowd's path where they could sit. She folded the red ribbon and placed it in her pouch, then gently unwound Ivy's golden braid.

"So what do you think of the market?" Joanna asked.

"Where is Constan . . . tin?"

Joanna smiled. "Constantinople is a great city far, far to the south. One must travel all through England, cross the channel, go through France and over some mountains to get there."

"Logan has been to France."

Joanna wasn't surprised. Whenever England wasn't at war with Scotland she was at war with France, giving the knights, soldiers, and mercenaries plenty of opportunity to get themselves killed. Well, some knights. Bertrand had always evaded death.

So had Logan, but she doubted Logan had also evaded battle.

"Logan told you about France?"

"When I rode with him yesterday. He said they make good wine there, but he prefers Mistress Brewer's spiced mead."

Joanna's smile widened. "Does he?"

"Uh-huh. I think he likes being at Lynwood, Mama." Ivy tilted her head back far enough for Joanna to see the girl's grin. "I know he likes us. He said so."

Joanna's fingers fumbled with the twisting ribbon. The lump forming in her throat nearly choked off her words. "Did he?"

"Aye. I told him we liked him, too."

"Oh, Ivy." Joanna pulled her daughter against her, the hug as much for herself as Ivy. "That was good of you. I do not think he hears that from many people."

Ivy remained cuddled and quiet for as long as her restless nature allowed.

"After he catches our thieves, Logan will go away, will he not?"

Joanna didn't want to think about that day. "Aye."

"Will he come back?"

Probably not. "Perhaps someday."

"Oh."

She purposely shook off maudlin thoughts, determined to let nothing ruin her day with Ivy. "Sit up straight now, so I can tie this ribbon. We have a bear to find."

They found the dancing bear at the far end of the market. Ivy watched, entranced, as the owner prodded the old, muzzled, mangy-furred bear to rise up on its back legs and hop around to entertain the crowd. When Joanna began to feel sorry for the poor beast, she tugged at Ivy's hand.

"Ready to go? We should find Wat and see if he has found any wheat seed."

Naturally, Ivy didn't want to leave. "Can we come back later?"

"Maybe."

But not if she could help it. The bear was such a pitiful sight.

Keeping watch for Wat, Joanna went with the flow of the crowd, sometimes stopping to inspect a merchant's wares, tempted by many, especially by the brightly colored yarns. Oh, what a lovely tapestry she could make with those, but she resisted, consoling herself with three lengths of linen for which she wondered if she had paid too much. Except she couldn't withstand the merchant's description of their quality, and they were so very pretty and she hadn't worn a gown of fine fabric in so very long.

The blue she would make into a gown for Ivy to wear to church and on feast days. The saffron and green were for her, would serve her well for several summers.

Then a comb of ivory caught her eye and ended up in her hand. A fitting gift for Maud, as thanks for everything the housekeeper had tried to do for a young bride caught in a thankless marriage, then for a hapless widow trying to rule a holding without truly knowing how.

Temptation abounded at every turn. Just when she was about to give in to a girdle of leather woven in an intricate pattern to replace the single, thin strip of leather she wore around her waist, she spotted Wat coming toward her.

His look of relief told her he might have been searching for her for some time.

"I have found seed, milady. Four sacks' worth. I had hoped for six, but we shall have to make do."

Not as good news as she would have liked, but better than nothing. She grabbed Ivy's hand—and heard a drum, the rap of fingers on taut hide.

Several men and women, swarthy-skinned and dark-haired, made their way down the center of the market. A young woman led the group of musicians, jugglers, and tumblers. Garbed in bright colors, her loose skirts flowing around her, drum in hand, the harem dancer smiled seductively.

Everyone turned to stare. Some whispered excited comments to companions. Mummers. Jugglers. *Dancers.*

All Joanna could see was fantasy in a woodland clearing and hear the pounding of her heart as she'd danced for Logan. Felt again his hands on her skin, his chest pressed to her breasts, that exquisite moment of possession.

She felt a tug on her hand—Ivy craning her neck to see what all the fuss was about. Not wanting to answer questions about the entrancing dancer, Joanna turned to Wat.

"Where is our seed?"

"Other end," he said, distracted by the girl with the drum.

"Shall we go, then?" Joanna prodded.

"Aye. Of course, milady." He walked backward a few steps before finally coming to his senses, turning away from the bewitching dancer.

Soon Joanna could no longer hear the drum and once

more focused on her purpose. Wat led them to where a man stood beside a cart piled high with sacks.

Wat made the introductions, Lady Joanna of Lynwood Manor to Master Woodside of Lincoln.

He patted a sack near his hand. "Four sacks of prime wheat is all I have left, my lady. Been a hard year. Yer lucky yer reeve here found me when he did. I was about to hitch up me team and head west."

Joanna recognized the opening round of bargaining.

She let go of Ivy's hand, shifting the fabric becoming heavy in her arms. "Prime, you say. How old is it?"

Woodside huffed. "Why, from last fall's harvest. I'd not sell old seed."

Joanna smiled at his indignant stance, knowing better than to believe everything he said. Back and forth they bartered, Joanna insisting on inspecting a handful of the seed before offering what she considered a good price.

"Robbing me blind, you are, milady."

"Have we a bargain?"

"Aye, why not. For a beautiful lady I am willing to forgo a meal or two."

Woodside didn't look like he missed a meal often.

"You are most kind, Master Woodside. Wat, go get our cart. Ivy would you hold this fabric while—"

Except Ivy wasn't at her side.

"Ivy?" she called, glancing around for a green ribbon coiled through a golden braid.

No green wound through gold. No Ivy.

Logan wasn't sure if what he held in his hand was actually a chalice or just a goblet. He wasn't even sure if it was made of gold.

"I can give you a good price on that one," the merchant declared.

"Truly?" Logan countered.

"Have not had the chalice long. Man I bought it from said he got it from a Crusader, who picked it up in the Holy Land."

Logan knew he'd just heard the merchant's good price rise.

"A relic, then."

"Very possible."

"Too bad. Not the one I am looking for."

The merchant's eyes narrowed. "You look for a particular chalice?"

"I am told it is made of plain gold, no jewels or engraving, much like this one. But unlike your relic here, it comes from a church in a little village in Leicestershire."

"Stolen?"

"About a sennight ago. The seller would have an ugly scar across his forehead."

The merchant looked relieved. "Nay, not the chalice you seek then. I have had this one for nigh on a month. However, if you wish to replace the stolen one—"

Logan set the chalice down on the merchant's blanket. "Not for me to do."

"I see. Might I inquire—"

Logan walked away, disappointed, unwilling to give any more details on the chalice's ownership or get talked into buying the chalice, donating it to the church, thereby procuring several indulgences for his sins.

The morning was almost gone. He hadn't found the stolen chalice, and no one he talked to knew of anyone in the area who'd had horses stolen. He hoped Conrad was having better luck locating a buyer for the chain mail and Wat had found wheat seed.

As for Joanna and Ivy, he hoped they were enjoying the market, buying trinkets and having a good time. He'd seen the dancing bear and hoped Ivy wouldn't be too disappointed in the old, half-blind, mange-riddled bear. He'd also seen the harem dancer and wondered if Joanna had, and if the dancer reminded her of shared passion on a forest floor.

He didn't have to be back at the tavern to meet Conrad for a few hours yet, and was pretty sure he'd visited every merchant in Oundle, both honest and questionable, who dealt in gold, silver, and jewels.

Tempted to stroll through the market to find Joanna, he turned the other way. The rap of the dancer's drum yet beat in his head, the swirl of her skirts reminding him too vividly of a tryst he'd give most anything to repeat. Given his wayward thoughts and the ache in his private parts, he couldn't trust himself to keep his distance from Joanna if he found her.

So he went into the tavern—and found Conrad sitting at a table, a tankard of spiced mead in hand.

Conrad tilted his tankard in Logan's direction.

"You were right. Best spiced mead in the kingdom."

Logan eased onto a stool and called for his own tankard. "Glad you agree because today you are buying. I did not expect to see you until nearly nightfall."

Conrad shrugged a shoulder. "Small town, not much to do."

"I never did ask why you were here. Thought you preferred Oxford."

"Not much to do in Oxford, either. By the by, I believe I know where you can sell the suit of mail."

"Wonderful. At least one thing goes right today."

"No luck with the chalice or horses?"

"None, though for a moment I thought I had found—"

A loud bang from the front of the tavern turned his head, and it took him a moment to identify the woman standing in the now open doorway, paler than cream, her eyes wild with panic.

"Joanna?"

She let go the door and ran toward his table.

He was off the stool before she was halfway across the room. She hit him square and hard, clutched fistfuls of his tunic.

"What is wrong?" he asked at the same time she announced, "Ivy is missing. I cannot find her. Dear God, Logan, if anything happens to her . . ."

His arms wrapped around Joanna, his heart slamming against his ribs. "She cannot be far. Oundle is not very big."

Except there were too many people about who didn't live there. Merchants, shoppers, entertainers—and villains who preyed on the unwary or inattentive.

"Ivy was at my side one moment and gone the next."

"We will look. So can Wat. Where is he?"

"I sent him back to the inn with the fabric to fetch the cart for the wheat."

That almost made sense.

"Where did you see Ivy last? Never mind. Show me. That is where we will start."

"I already looked there. Twice. Logan, where can she *be*?"

Anywhere. Just about damned anywhere.

Conrad put his tankard on the table. "Would she have gone back to the inn?"

Joanna's head rose from Logan's chest. "I do not know. I . . . perhaps."

"What does she look like?"

Logan put his hand waist high. "So tall. Brown tunic. Blond hair."

"Green ribbon," Joanna added. "We bought ribbons. I wove one into her braid."

Conrad rose up to his full height. "Should not be hard to find. Might I suggest, milady, you check the inn first, then begin your search at the south end of the market and meet us somewhere."

"By the dancing bear," Logan suggested, hoping that's where Ivy had gone.

Logan loosened his hold but didn't let go of her. She looked too damn fragile to stand on her own. Then Joanna took a deep breath and gathered her strength.

"I will go to the inn. If Ivy is not there, I will set Wat and Clarence to the search, too." She looked up at him, tears close to flowing. "What if—"

"We will find her, Joanna. Go."

The hug was brief and hard. Joanna turned heel and ran out the door, Logan and Conrad not far behind her.

They headed for the market.

"Lot of people around who do not belong," Conrad said.

"Thought of that. We need to hurry."

"Call out the watch?"

The question surprised Logan. He and Conrad didn't tend to get along with the men of the town watch.

Besides, between the two of them, they could take care of any trouble . . . God, he hoped Ivy hadn't found trouble.

"Not yet. They may only get in our way."

"Your decision. East or west?"

"Take west. I want to check the dancing bear. 'Twas the one thing Ivy wanted to see in Oundle."

The bear was nigh on the only thing she'd talked about the entire journey, and Joanna had probably already looked there, but he had to look himself.

"Thought you said you were not getting a bonus from the lady."

"Shut up, Conrad. Brown tunic. Blond hair. Green ribbon. My thanks."

"Remember that when it is your turn to buy again tonight."

They separated in the middle of the market.

The crowd wasn't as thick as that morning. Logan supposed people were downing their noon meal, preparing for another round of bargaining in the afternoon. He walked briskly, but not so fast he would miss a blond braid done up in green ribbon.

He passed by merchants he'd spoken with earlier, slowed down when he saw a blanket full of ribbons, nearly stopped when he reached where the dancing bear had performed that morning.

Damn. He'd hoped Ivy would be there.

As the minutes passed by, he began to worry about hours, about nightfall. Strange people, strange city. Was she scared? Hungry? In the clutches of someone she couldn't get away from?

What if he never found her? What if he couldn't hand

her back to Joanna? Ye gods, Joanna. She'd be devastated if she lost Ivy, too.

Then he heard the light rap on a drum and the chimes of little bells. The harem dancer. Several men and a few women had gathered to watch her perform. Would the spectacle also catch the fancy of a little girl?

Logan closed the distance at a fast clip, and there, at the edge of the crowd, he spotted Ivy.

His relief almost overwhelmed him, making it hard to speak when Conrad sidled up, and asked, "Ivy?"

Logan settled for one word. "Ivy."

"Cute."

She certainly was. Unable to see over the grown-ups, she strove to take peeks between them while trying to imitate the dancer. Like mother, the daughter swayed to the rhythm of the drum, but unlike mother, didn't have the grace to seduce—yet.

In her little brown tunic, with the ribbon in her braid coming undone, he'd never seen a cuter, more precious girl in his entire life. And by damn, if he ever caught Ivy dancing in the woods to entice some idiot swain, he'd slice the bastard in two.

The thought brought him up short, and he might have shouted Ivy's name if at that moment Logan hadn't realized how much he loved her. And her mother.

Sweet heaven above. He locked his knees so they wouldn't give way.

"Now what?" Conrad asked.

Logan's mind reeled, and settling it took brutal effort.

Conrad, of course, meant about Ivy, not about loving Joanna or the obstacles Logan faced in winning her. Could he win her? Would she even let him try?

Concentrate, dammit! Fetch Ivy, give her to Joanna, then . . . what? He wished he had half a notion of how to proceed in convincing Joanna the two of them belonged together.

"Pray for me."

Logan heard Conrad chuckle, but continued to walk toward Ivy.

The minx truly deserved punishment for putting herself in danger and scaring Joanna half-witless. But it wasn't his place to punish, which he probably couldn't carry through with anyway because he was too damn glad to see her. Better just to deliver her up to a higher authority.

When close enough, he planted his feet, crossed his arms, and said her name in as stern a voice as he could manage.

She turned around, her braid and ribbon flying. Eyes wide, her little mouth formed an astonished "O" before her hand rose to cover it.

"Your mother is most peeved with you."

Ivy glanced around, and must have decided she wasn't in immediate danger because she merely clasped her hands behind her back and drew lines in the dirt with the edge of her sandal.

"Mama was taking so long to buy the wheat, and I heard the drum, and I thought I could be back before she missed me."

"You were wrong to leave her side, Ivy. She thinks something bad has happened to you. She even cried."

Ivy frowned. "I will have to beg her pardon."

"Several times. As I said, she is *most* peeved with you."

Having done all the scolding he dared, given he had no

right at all, he opened his arms. As he knew she would, Ivy jumped into them to be carried. Once he had her safely against him, he pressed her close.

"You must never scare us this badly again."

"Sorry."

With a sigh, he turned around and headed toward the inn. Conrad fell into step beside him. They hadn't gone far when he saw Joanna coming toward them.

He halted and jiggled Ivy. "What are you to do?"

"Beg Mama's pardon. Several times."

"What else?"

"Vow never to scare her again."

"Good girl. Go."

He set Ivy on her feet, and she ran straight into Joanna's open arms. First there were hugs, then Joanna's inspection of Ivy for hurts, and lastly the scold.

Conrad cleared his throat. "Not interested in seeking entertainments tonight either, I suppose."

"Nay."

"Then if getting smart means what I think it does, you ought to get smarter."

"How so?"

"Ask again for that bonus."

"Shut up, Conrad."

Joanna and Ivy apparently made their peace and were, hand in hand, coming toward him.

Logan nudged Conrad. "Prepare to be gracious."

"Always."

'Twas Logan's turn to chuckle.

Ivy made Conrad a pretty curtsy. "Mama says I must beg your pardon for putting you to so much trouble."

Conrad nodded. "Pardoned, with the condition you mind your mother from now on."

Poor Ivy. She was getting scolds from all sides. To her credit, she accepted Conrad's condition.

"I thank you, too," Joanna said, her voice shaky, her face too pale for Logan's comfort. She might be relieved, but her fear yet showed. "We would be pleased if you would both join Ivy and me at the inn for nooning. The least I can do is feed you after . . . after your showing us such kindness."

"I would be pleased to accept, my lady. You will also be pleased to know I may have a buyer for your chain mail."

"Truly? Well, we can talk over our meal then." Joanna gave Conrad an unsteady smile, then turned Ivy around and led her across the market.

Logan and Conrad followed a few steps behind, Logan noting the graceful sway of Joanna's hips, his thoughts far from food.

"You are sure you want to know when Essex calls his army together?"

Logan had no strategy in mind as yet. The idea of winning Joanna was too new and fragile, and he knew had little chance of victory. At present, he still had every reason to believe that after he caught her thieves, he'd be leaving Lynwood.

"Aye, let me know."

Chapter Eighteen

Almost home, milady. Be good to sleep on my own pallet tonight."

Joanna smiled at Wat's sentiment. They'd pushed hard all day, resting only when necessary for the horses, to arrive at Lynwood by midafternoon.

"Aye, that it will. Traveling is exciting, but returning home is comforting."

The cart's wheel bumped on a rut. Joanna didn't mind so much because her backside wasn't too sore, thanks to the long length of wool folded several times over that served as a buffer between her backside and the cart's hard seat.

"I must say I believe you did rather well in Oundle."

The compliment took Joanna off guard. Of late, Wat so rarely approved of anything she did, or planned to do. An unexpected and pleasing change to have the reeve's sanction.

"Why, thank you, Wat."

"Deserved, milady."

If pride was indeed a sin, then she'd have to confess to

Father Arthur that she took great pride in what she'd accomplished, though she hadn't done it all by herself.

Thanks to Conrad Falke—whose size and looks had frightened her a bit but he'd proved to be a nice man—she'd sold the entire contents of the trunk. With the hefty profit she purchased more fabric, some spices she had never heard of before for Maud to try, then filled the rest of the trunk with colorful yarns for a tapestry.

Not only was the trunk full, but the cart as well.

Surrounding the trunk were four sacks of wheat seed and the emptied kegs the tavern owner had pleaded to have refilled with spiced mead. Joanna planned to talk to Mistress Brewer about supplying the tavern regularly.

More kegs would be needed and cartage arranged for, but then Joanna could also send along cheese to the innkeeper, who'd professed willingness to purchase any rounds she could spare.

Perhaps as Logan had once suggested, she should hire a steward, especially someone more familiar than she with the ways of trade and how to take advantage of them. A notion to mull over later.

Right now she yearned for home, to see if the oats were in the ground, if the shepherd was ready to begin the shearing, and if the thieves had struck in her absence.

She knew Logan was disappointed in his lack of success. He hadn't found the chalice, nor learned of where the thieves had stolen their horses. But he'd certainly been there for her when she needed him most.

Joanna glanced to her right, where Ivy again took advantage of Logan as she had for most of the trip home. Because the cart was so full, there was barely any room left for Ivy, giving the girl more excuse to ride with

Logan—where she now slept snug and secure across his lap.

Sweet mercy, what would she have done without Logan when Ivy went missing? Every time Joanna thought of that terrifying moment when she realized Ivy had wandered off, her heart beat faster and her palms began to sweat. Her panic had been absolute, and after a frantic, unsuccessful search of the market, she'd run straight to Logan.

He'd given her the assurances she desperately needed to hear, then he and Conrad had done exactly as Logan promised—found Ivy.

She'd paid for the mercenaries' noon meal, thanked them both profusely for finding Ivy. That afternoon had been taken up with selling the chain mail and her subsequent added shopping. That evening Logan presented her with four men he deemed suitable soldiers. All four now walked behind the cart, and Harold would have the final say in their hiring.

The following morning they'd left for Lynwood, and with so many people around, she'd hesitated to broach sensitive issues. So they were still a bit formal with each other, the distance she'd once thought advisable still between them.

Joanna now wanted the distance closed.

She'd put her doubts to rest. Logan's past was his past and couldn't be changed. 'Twas the confident, caring—and aye sometimes stubborn—man he was now whom she loved.

She kept her smile and the glow in her heart to herself. Imagine, Lady Joanna of Lynwood, who'd informed everyone within hearing she wanted nothing to do with men or marriage ever again, had fallen fast and hard for a mercenary.

Visions of the future had once included only herself and Ivy, with Joanna ruling Lynwood until Ivy came of age to inherit. Now she wanted Logan to share that future. Somehow.

Joanna knew Logan desired her, knew he cared about her well-being and Ivy's. But did he care enough to want to stay after the thieves were caught? When she handed him the two shillings she still owed him, would he bid her fare-thee-well, climb aboard Gideon, and leave for London without looking back?

She wouldn't know until she told him she wanted him to stay, but above all she feared hearing she had no place in his life or affection. She'd hired Logan to provide peace and security, which she'd believed the capture of the thieves would provide. Now she wanted more, Logan's love, and didn't know how to secure it.

"Ah, the oats must be in the ground."

Joanna came out of her musings with a start, a quick glance at the furrowed fields confirming Wat's observation.

Home spread out before her. The manor, the church, the village in between. Was it only five days ago she'd been delighted to escape? Now she could hardly wait to pass through the gate.

"That is good." She raised a hand high in the air to wave at the shepherd on the hillside, who lifted his crook in greeting. "The sheep are yet too white, so shearing has not started yet. Tomorrow or the next day, perhaps?"

"I see no reason why not. Shall we stop at the tithe barn to unload the seed?"

The new guards had walked the entire distance and looked ready to drop. Her backside might not be too sore, but her legs were stiff. Logan's arms must be weary from supporting her sleeping daughter for league upon league.

"Nay. Pull the wagon into the bailey. We can sort out and put things in their proper place later."

"As you say, milady."

No argument from Wat? She would have to figure out what she'd done to gain his cooperation. Of course, he might just be tired and looking forward to his pallet, then be back to old form after a good night's sleep.

Joanna looked out over the village. Quiet and peaceful. No one seemed to be about. Which struck her as disquieting.

Too quiet. Too peaceful. Something was amiss.

Joanna clasped her hands in her lap, wondering if she should say something to Wat. The reeve watched the road, didn't seem concerned about a lack of activity in the village.

Perhaps her imagination had run amok, and she looked for disturbance where there was none.

Except Logan's expression echoed her concern. With narrowed eyes he peered at the village, expecting to see something he didn't see, as she had.

The gate swung open. She could hear the guard on the wall walk shouting down to others, announcing her return. Her concern heightened as they crossed the bailey, noting the lack of activity there, too. Wat no more than halted in front of the manor when she sprang from her seat and climbed down. Within moments she was inside the hall.

A more sullen gathering she'd never seen.

Maud rushed up, her relief evident. "Praise be ye returned safely, milady."

"My thanks, Maud. What goes on here?"

The housekeeper glanced toward Harold, who rose from the bench. No relief there, but simmering anger.

"Our thieves struck again, nigh on two hours ago."

They'd taken more than a goose or firewood this time, she could feel it.

Behind her, Logan handed Ivy over to Maud. Wat, Clarence, and the new soldiers filed through the door.

She asked the question uppermost in her fears. "Was anyone hurt?"

"Robert Brewer and his wife. Both are alive but sore. The thieves punched Robert around a bit before tying up both."

"Lord have mercy." The thieves had never hurt anyone apurpose before. This didn't bode well. "Did no one see them, try to raise the hue and cry?"

"Unfortunately, no one did. By the time Margaret Atbridge found the Brewers tied and gagged in their cottage, the thieves were long gone, along with two kegs of ale, bacon, and bread."

'Twas little wonder nobody roamed about the village. Everyone must be holed up in their cottages, the doors bolted tight.

Wat had gone pale. "I had best get to mine own cottage, milady."

"You are welcome to remain in the manor."

"Nay, milady," he said quickly. "'Tis best I am out in the village, should anything more happen and I am needed."

Joanna understood his reasoning and appreciated his attention to duty. "As you wish. Have a care."

"I doubt I am in any danger. The thieves will not be back today."

"You are so sure of that, Wat?" Logan asked.

"They have never struck twice in the same day. I have no reason to believe they will this time."

"They have never entered a villager's cottage, either."

"Milady, I do not worry for myself, and truly, I should visit the Brewers to see if I can help them in any way."

Joanna thought that a very good idea. "Then I shall go with you."

Logan put a hand on her shoulder. "Nay, Joanna, you should not."

"He is right, my lady," Harold agreed. " 'Tis not wise or necessary. Margaret and Greta are both with the Brewers, and Donald will visit them a bit later. If they are in need of assistance, we will hear."

She wanted badly to go, but couldn't disregard her captain's advice, or Logan's. 'Twould be foolhardy to put herself at risk, and therefore others.

"All right, then," she relented. "Wat, tell the Brewers they are in my prayers, and I will see them on the morrow."

With a nod, he left.

Joanna's shock and concern gave way to anger. "You must find them, Logan. These thieves become far too bold and dangerous."

Logan addressed Harold. "Do you know which path they took to the river?"

"We found fresh prints on the path behind the church."

"Tell the guards to bolt the gate behind me."

Then he was gone before Joanna could tell him, too, to have a care.

For the next few hours, Joanna tried not to worry over Logan. An impossibility. As evening shadows lengthened, she was nigh on ready to go out and find him, tell him to come home, to hell with the thieves.

Just at nightfall, a shout from the gate saved her from going mad.

Logan strolled into the hall with a grin on his face. "They were not so careful this time. I know where they came out of the river. Pray the saints for a clear dawn."

At a bit after midnight, Wat tied a piece of twine to the branch of the tangled oak, hoping one of the band would see it in time for a meeting tomorrow.

The thieves had become too brazen, too violent. They'd invaded Robert's home, bloodied his face, and cracked two ribs.

"Get rid of them," Robert had whispered with a cut and badly swollen mouth.

Wat agreed. He just wasn't sure the thieves would obey.

The band had taken things other than what they'd been given permission to take—the chalice, which he didn't think they would give back, and two kegs of ale, which they would drink.

No one was supposed to be hurt. Then Ivy had been injured—unintentionally, but injured all the same—and now Robert, the beating given deliberately when he'd tried to interfere with the theft of the kegs stored in the shed behind his cottage.

What had begun as a simple plan to prod Lady Joanna

into marriage had become complicated and unmanageable, and had to come to an end.

Perhaps serving a lady instead of a lord wouldn't be so bad. Lady Joanna had proved a keen bargainer with the seed merchant and kept a cool head when dealing with Ivy's disappearance. After speaking with a wool merchant, Wat was coming around to the idea of flooring the tithe barn, though he still wished her ladyship hadn't sold the chain mail.

Only one thing was certain. Edward and his band must move on. With them would go the possibility of more loss and injury. With no thieves to chase, Logan Grimm would go back to London. Only then would Wat and his coconspirators be safe from discovery.

Logan heard the groan of leather hinges and looked up to see Joanna come out of her bedchamber. She saw him sitting at the table, mug in front of him. For a moment he thought she would retreat, but she smiled softly and came toward him.

How beautiful she was, especially in the middle of the night, sleepy-eyed, her hair flowing around her in a golden veil, her body covered only by a thin nightrail.

His body reacted as it had that first night, when she'd walked out into the hall, trying to escape her upset. That his desire for her had strengthened over the weeks didn't spark pangs of panic. And unlike that first night, when he'd been so eager to leave Lynwood and Joanna behind, now he wanted to stay, for a lifetime.

She slid onto the bench beside him. "I thought I heard you out here. Can you not sleep?"

"Always a bit restless before battle."

"You expect a fight."

"I doubt the villains will come peacefully."

She rested her head on his shoulder. "You and Harold have a care."

He wouldn't bother to tell her she worried about the wrong men, too thrilled she deigned to touch him again. They'd exchanged harsh words, been very formal these past few days. Joanna couldn't have forgotten, but if she was willing to put aside their differences for the nonce, he'd be a fool to bring it up. Nor did he want to talk about the thieves, not with Joanna pressed up against his side, her hair teasing his cheek.

"What brings you into the hall, milady?"

"Restless. I often pace when I cannot silence my demons."

"Ah, Joanna, would that I could slay all of your demons."

She moved her head to look up at him, a soft smile on her face. "Some will never go away, but there is a particularly vexing one that rears its head when you are near, and only you are able to banish it."

Logan didn't misunderstand. Lust could be vexing. While he might wish for more, he didn't question his good fortune. He kissed the woman he'd come to adore. Passion flared as his heart swelled.

"Hard work, banishing demons. Could take most of the night."

"Are you up to the challenge?"

In answer, he spun on the bench, picked Joanna up, and carried her into the bedchamber. Bolting the door without putting her down proved awkward.

"You *could* put me down," she suggested.

"Not yet. Lift up on that end."

With her support, he slid the bolt in place, even managed to do so quietly.

A single lit candle cast flickering light over the bed, the coverlet slightly mussed. He tossed Joanna down atop the thick feather mattress, heartened by her light laughter.

"I gather you like a challenge."

He made quick work of removing his boots and short hose. "Depends on the challenge and who presents it. I admit I am eager to wrestle with this demon of yours."

She turned onto her back and stretched out, raising her knee and shifting her nightrail, granting him a tantalizing view of her calves.

"Since this demon arrived on the same night you did, I believe you should silence it."

Logan tore off his tunic and dropped it on the floor. "That same night?"

"I admit to an awareness of you."

His breeches joined his tunic. "And I you," he admitted while climbing onto the mattress. Not until he took her in his arms and kissed her thoroughly did he add, "I swore I beheld a goddess."

Her blush enchanted him.

"Flattery is not necessary."

"Has no one ever told you how beautiful you are? How you brighten a room merely by your presence?" He slid his hand up her leg, bunching up the nightrail, uncovering the woman beneath, an incredible sight to behold. "Sweet mercy, Joanna. Your face alone could stop a man's breath, and the rest of you could halt the beating of his heart. Pray I have the strength to survive this night."

Again she laughed lightly, a sound he would never

tire of. "You survived once, so I am confident you will again."

So was he, until he tugged the nightrail over her head, tossed it to the floor with his clothes, and beheld Joanna in her full glory. Reverently, he stroked her from knee to breast, taking the time to admire her sleek lines and gentle curves.

She'd closed her eyes and laid a hand across her stomach, the fine lines beneath her fingers a woman's battle scars, evidence of having given birth. He felt a twinge of envy for the man who'd given her those children before he purposely laid her dead husband in the grave where he belonged.

Logan twined his fingers with hers, over her womb, selfishly hoping their union would prove fruitful—which could create profound problems for Joanna.

Joanna's hand squeezed his. "Is aught amiss?"

He should say no, take what she offered him. Surely she'd considered the possibility of getting with child before inviting him into her bed. She might even know of a method to keep her womb from quickening.

"Demons come in all shapes and forms. By vanquishing one we could be creating another. I do not want to cause you pain or strife. I love you, Joanna. Should what we do hurt—"

She put fingertips to his lips. "You could never hurt me, Logan. 'Tis one of the many reasons I love you."

Speechless, on the verge of tears, he gathered her into a full embrace—arms wrapped, legs entwined, hearts beating against each other. With Joanna pressed this close, knowing he possessed her heart, he could barely think much less talk, but the words must be said.

"On my oath, Joanna. To hurt you would be to hurt myself beyond bearing."

She kissed his neck. Her soft lips and wet mouth tasting, teasing.

"I know," she said, between licks of tongue and nips of teeth. "I did not invite you to my bed lightly, Logan Grimm. I know more of wrestling with demons than I care to, and we shall deal with any new ones as they appear. For tonight, love me, Logan, just love me."

So many demons to deal with, but most were best dealt with in daylight with a clearer head. How could he do aught but obey the lady's command?

Logan vowed to go slow. He'd taken her once in a fury of heat, hard and fast, thinking he would have only the one chance to join with Joanna. Now they had all night, and surely they would have other nights. No need to rush.

His loins burned, and his penis screamed a protest at the delay of the coupling, but he refused to heed either. Instead, he engaged in a campaign to ensure Joanna's needs were thoroughly met first, her demon silenced.

He began with kisses, gentle ones, which somehow deepened and lengthened. Through the haze filling his head, he became aware of Joanna's little gasps, of his own breath growing short, of how heated the kisses had become as he hadn't intended.

Logan abandoned that course in favor of worshiping every inch of her, gliding his hand along her sleek curves. His palm delighted to the rise of her nipples, going hard and yearning. Joanna's hand slid to the back of his neck, seeming to press his head down and down until he took a rosy nipple into his mouth and suckled.

Her moan announced her delight, urging him to pull

harder and deeper, first on one breast and then the other. All the while his palm sought the skin of her inner thigh, his fingers itched to test the readiness of her sheath.

Joanna twisted, her thighs parted, and he saw no sense in refusing her whatever she wanted. He slid a finger through her moist heat, teasing the little nub at the apex, then seeking the depths. She curled her fingers in his hair, then grabbed at his shoulders, her gasps telling him more than words ever could that she was ready to accept him, to caress him and drive him wild.

And damn, he was ready to let her.

He removed his hand. Joanna turned into him and somehow flipped him onto his back. She hovered over him, her hair wild, her eyes shining with—mischief.

Demon driven mischief.

Dare he allow her control?

"My turn," she said, low and throaty. "You have taught me several things, Logan. From you I have learned daring is no bad thing when the need arises."

He swallowed hard, his need hardening and rising at the thought of which direction her daring might lead.

"I thought you wanted me to silence *your* demons."

"You will. Soon," she promised, then sprawled atop him, her mouth on his, and proceeded to muddle his senses. One of his last coherent thoughts was of surrender to a force mightier than he—to Joanna's loving touch.

This was what she'd wanted since their tryst in the woods, the chance to thoroughly explore Logan's body. Bone and muscle shaped his ruggedly sculpted form. A variety of scars marred his dark-toned skin, the newest one on his thigh, healing nicely now that the stitches had been removed.

Joanna looked her fill, not fearful of his great size nor repelled by the evidence of his profession.

True, she'd seen parts of him naked before, but not the whole banquet spread out for her enjoyment.

Daring definitely had its place. Fetching him from the hall had taken a bit of courage, and enticing him into her bed even more bravery. Rolling him over and seizing control . . . well, she wasn't sure whence she'd gotten either the idea or strength. But now she had Logan where she wanted him—in her heart and in her bed.

Whatever ugly demons raised their heads on the morrow, and she was sure one or two would, could be dealt with then. For tonight she intended to be both selfish and brazen, neither of which she'd had much opportunity to practice and recently learned she liked them both within limits.

She raked fingernails through the hair on Logan's chest, her lips toying with his nipples, seeking to arouse him in the way he did to her. His long, indrawn breath told her she succeeded, feeding her boldness, daring her to test her newfound power.

Joanna lowered to plant kisses along his stomach, making it quiver, eliciting a low moan and pressure on her shoulders. Guessing at what he craved, she lowered farther yet, to kneel between his legs and stare at his fully ready shaft. She wrapped her hand around it. In answer it twitched.

"Demon slayer," she whispered, and kissed the tip.

The second kiss sat him up in the bed. He grabbed

her upper arms and pulled her against him, kissing her fiercely all the way back down to the mattress.

And she didn't care, very willing to take his weight, to open to his possession. He entered with a swift, deep stroke, raising her off the bed. With each lunge he pushed her closer to the ecstasy she'd never known existed until he'd guided her there on that first journey. With each withdrawal time stood still in anticipation of again being filled, of again reaching that painful point of rapture.

Then it came, the mystifying, satisfying pulse of her core. With a groan Logan dived to the hilt and joined her in bliss. Exhausted and replete, all she could do was hold him to her and savor the contentment.

He brushed what must be very tangled hair from her face, wearing a smile that could only be called smug. "May I assume the demon is vanquished?"

"Only silenced. I have no doubt it will pester me again. Soon."

"No doubt." He nuzzled in her neck, and whispered, "Must I leave you now?"

So that on the morn the guards would find him on his pallet in the barracks, and the manor servants wouldn't see him leave her bedchamber. His consideration touched her deeply.

"Only if you wish to."

"I would stay if you will have me."

"I love you, Logan. I would have no other."

"Heaven help me, Joanna, I love you, too." He sighed. "We need to talk about those other demons."

She also needed to offer him an apology for judging him so harshly, but feared if they began talking, they'd lose this rare, wondrous closeness.

"If you think the demons will stay silent until daylight, I would rather you just held me tonight."

He made no protest. Not long after, cuddled into Logan's side, within the circle of his arms, Joanna slept so soundly she didn't hear or feel Logan slip away at dawn.

Chapter Nineteen

Logan hunched down to run his fingertips over the hoofprint he'd found late the day before, hardly believing his good fortune, and a bit disgruntled he hadn't paid better heed to this path before.

He turned to Harold, who'd been waiting for him in the stable, unwilling to be left behind.

"The thieves take the path to the hunting lodge."

"Or close to it," Harold agreed.

"Have a care for noise."

Approaching the hunting lodge silently couldn't be done, given the natural noise of moving horses, but Logan thought he and Harold did a fine job of getting near with little sound.

They tied the horses well back in the woods and approached the lodge on foot.

Logan studied the one-room timber building. Enough of the thatched roof remained intact to provide scant shelter from rain. Its single door stood ajar, and only one horse was tied to a bush off to the side, a blanket roll behind the saddle.

He'd hoped to see three horses.

"Damn, they are not all here." Harold echoed Logan's irritation. "Should we wait?"

"Hard to say when the other two might come back. What say we take the one, then decide about his companions?"

Logan drew his sword, hearing Harold do the same. They couldn't cross the clearing without possibly being seen. Best to do it quickly and quietly and hope the thief in the lodge wasn't keeping watch.

Logan reached the door first and took a moment to listen for sounds of activity. He heard the faint shuffling of feet, telling him the thief was on the roofed end of the lodge, near the hearth. After a quick hand motion to give Harold the information, he pulled the door open and rushed inside, Harold at his heels.

His dark-haired, raggedly garbed quarry knelt near the hearth rolling up a blanket. A few steps away were five kegs. On one side of the hearth lay a pile of picked-clean bones, probably the remains of the piglets. Two mugs sat on the hearth's mantel.

The thieves must have taken up permanent residence in the lodge about the time he left for Oundle.

Unfortunately, before Logan could cross the room, the thief had time to get to his feet and pull out his short sword.

Logan looked for a scar across the man's forehead. No scar, only smudges of dirt. This wasn't the band's leader, and from the way he held his weapon, he wasn't adept with a sword, either.

Logan pointed at the short sword with his broadsword,

blatantly exhibiting the inequity between the two weapons.

"Put your weapon down. You have no hope of escape."

Wide-eyed, the thief glanced between Logan and Harold, still unwilling to surrender. "What do you want of me?"

"We take you to Lynwood to face charges of thievery. Where are your companions?"

He shook his head. "There is only me. I am no thief, am merely passing through and used the lodge for shelter last night. If I trespass, I beg your pardon and will be on my way."

Logan gave him credit for audacity, given the number of blankets and mugs. He didn't bother pointing out the man's error.

"Harold, do you recognize this one?"

"Nay, I did not get a good look at the thieves, but Lady Joanna and many of the villagers did. We will know soon enough if he is one of them or no."

Logan turned back to the man he fully intended to take prisoner and present to Joanna for judgment. "I would prefer you come peacefully—"

The thief cut off the rest of the warning, attempting to reach the door by bolting past Logan. Three sword strokes later, the thief again knelt on the floor, this time clutching his side in a futile effort to halt the blood from seeping out of the wound to stain his tunic.

Logan didn't feel pity, merely annoyance at having to wound the man to stop his escape.

"Harold, find something to bind his wound, and while you're at it, look for the chalice."

While Harold set about the task, Logan stood over the

thief, ignoring the pain-filled expression and gasps for breath.

"I might consider helping you if you tell me where the others are."

"Edward will . . . kill me if I do."

Glory be. A name. Edward. The leader.

"Your wound needs tending. You may very well die if it is not cauterized soon."

The thief held up a blood-coated hand, stared at it, and Logan sensed the moment he relented.

"At tangled . . . oak. Meet a . . . villager."

Logan didn't have time to ask the villager's identity before the thief's eyes rolled back in his head, and he slumped to the dirt floor.

Logan had a good idea of who the villager was.

He glanced over his shoulder to see Harold coming toward him, a strip of blanket in his hands.

"No chalice. Did I hear him correctly? The others meet a villager?"

Harold's disbelief echoed Joanna's when Logan had suggested that the thieves were being helped.

"You have good hearing."

"Ye gods."

Ye gods, indeed. While Logan helped Harold bind up the thief's wound, he glanced back at the five kegs, which must belong to Mistress Brewer. They hadn't been there the last time he'd searched the lodge. Only two kegs had been reported stolen the previous day, so someone had provided the thieves with the others.

Robert Brewer?

Had he been too suspicious of Wat to see other

possibilities? Perhaps both Wat and Robert were involved. And if two conspired, there could be three, maybe more.

The thief yet breathed when they tossed him over his horse, and Logan hoped the thief lived a while longer, if only to repeat the accusation against a villager to Joanna.

Father Arthur darted into the hall, his mouth set in a thin line.

Joanna rose from the bench, expecting to hear another complaint about one thing or the other. Instead, he handed her a battered piece of parchment.

"I found this on the altar this morn, my lady. I would have brought it sooner, but it took me nigh on an hour to make out the meaning."

Said as if put out by the interruption to his day, as if she should be grateful. In truth, she admitted the priest had committed an impressive feat. The parchment was a mess, the letters badly done markings, like scribbling with a charred stick.

"Shall I assume this is a message?"

The priest took a long breath. "Best I can make out, the thieves are holding Wat Reeve and demand thirty shillings for his ransom. They require the mercenary to meet them at noon with the money, at the old mill south of the waterfall; otherwise, Wat will die."

Joanna eased back down on the bench, tossing the offensive parchment on the table. Her shock quickly gave way to anger. Damn thieves! They'd begun with pilfering a chicken and had now advanced to stealing people!

She put fingertips to temples, desperate to sort through the myriad questions begging answers.

How had the thieves gotten hold of Wat? 'Struth, 'twas

probably not too hard. As reeve, his duties took him all over the holding. They had only to snatch him up when he left one place to go to another.

Though she'd left most of the coin from selling the chain mail with a reputable banker in Oundle, she'd brought a portion of it to Lynwood. Thirty shillings was a lot of money, and paying the ransom would nearly empty her coffers. But what was thirty shillings compared to Wat's life?

But that was not all that bothered her.

The questions and her temper beginning to settle, she looked to Father Arthur, who'd sat down on the bench across from her. Some of the manor folk had gathered around, too.

"Logan is not here. He and Harold are following tracks left by the thieves after they robbed the Brewers. He may not be back in time to ransom Wat."

"The message says the mercenary is to deliver the ransom."

Another puzzle.

"Why Logan, I wonder?"

The priest shrugged a shoulder. "Perhaps they assume him the one you would send in any event."

Perhaps. Logan would be the logical choice to send on such an errand. Still, the request proved bothersome.

"If Logan does not return on time, will the thieves take umbrage if I send someone else with the ransom?"

The priest shrugged a shoulder. "I cannot answer that, milady."

Given the silence in the hall, neither could anyone else.

Poor Wat. Was he frightened? Had the outlaws hurt him? Where was he? At the mill?

Too many questions with no answers, none of which she'd know until they got him back. And she would get him back, somehow.

If Logan didn't return, then someone else must deliver the money. The next logical choice was Harold—who was out with Logan. A guard, then? One of the villagers? Whoever she sent she placed in a position of risk. If the thieves—now outlaws—took offense at another's taking Logan's place, they might hurt or even kill both messenger and hostage.

For a brief moment she considered going herself, then winced at how Logan, Harold, and the men of the village would upbraid her for such a foolish idea. The outlaws could decide the lady of Lynwood a better hostage, hold her for a far richer ransom than thirty shillings.

Send Father Arthur? Perhaps. If she could get the priest to agree. And only if she had no choice.

There was time yet before she must act. For the moment, she would prepare a pouch full of coins and pray Logan returned soon.

'Twas nigh on noon when Logan rode through the gate—thief-bearing horse in tow—hungry and still disturbed by the morning's events. Naturally, as he rode through the bailey, people noticed and began coming toward him to satisfy their curiosity.

He stopped in front of the manor and barely had time to dismount when Joanna came running out of the door. She stopped abruptly when she saw the thief draped over the horse.

"We caught one. He needs a wound cauterized. I sent Harold for Greta."

"Will he live?"

"I am hoping he does so long enough to tell us who his companions are."

More importantly, he wanted the thief to wake and repeat to Joanna what he'd said about his companions meeting a villager. 'Twould not be hard to find out who. Simply round everyone up and see who was missing. Logan would wager several weeks' fee on Wat.

Joanna beckoned forth two of the new guards. "Take him down and put him on a table in the hall." Then she handed Logan a piece of parchment. "Father Arthur found this on the altar this morning."

Logan gave it back. "I cannot read. You will have to tell me what it says."

She did, and he didn't like what he heard. Thirty shillings for a mere peasant? An absurd amount. Especially for a peasant who'd been working with the thieves. Except Logan hadn't proved Wat's involvement to Joanna yet, and she seemed determined to have the reeve ransomed.

"Give this some thought, Joanna. Once you give them what they want, they may try something like this again."

She raised an eyebrow. "I cannot leave Wat to their mercy!"

Logan was quite willing to allow noon to pass with no attempt to ransom the reeve. Joanna, however, wasn't willing.

Her compassion wouldn't allow her, and Joanna's compassion was one of the many reasons he'd fallen in love with her. She would never understand if he simply refused to fetch Wat.

"All right, if you want the man back, I will go get him, though I think your money and mercy misspent."

She sighed. "I know you do not like Wat, but he is my reeve, and the money is mine to spend."

"Then feed me and give me the money and I will see what can be done."

Her smile was worth the aggravation. He followed her into the manor.

The guards had done as Joanna ordered—laid the thief on a trestle table. The man's pallor boded ill. She placed fingertips over the blood staining the blanket, then jerked them back. For a moment, she went pale.

Logan pulled her away from the table, thinking he knew what was amiss. "You need have nothing to do with the villain. Leave him for others."

She shook her head, as if clearing away haze. "This is beyond me. Perhaps beyond Greta, too."

"Harold and the guards should have enough field training to know how to cauterize a wound. If Greta cannot do it, I am sure one of your guards can."

"Could you?"

"Aye, if needs be. But that will take time and—"

She waved a dismissive hand. "You need to ransom Wat. Come eat, and I will get you the money."

Joanna headed for her bedchamber. From a nearby table, Logan grabbed a chunk of cheese from a platter and plunked it between two slices of bread. He was on his way toward the ale keg when he spied Ivy standing beside one of the guards, staring at the thief.

Logan held out his free hand. "Ivy, come away."

She glanced at him, then stared at the thief a moment more before finally obeying. Quiet, deep in thought, she took his hand and accompanied him to the ale keg. Not until they took a seat did she ask, "Will he die?"

" 'Tis between him and God and Greta's skills."

In her eyes he saw her mother. Though young and prone to mischief, Ivy didn't lack compassion or tolerance, even for a thief. Even for a mercenary who'd wanted nothing to do with either female in the beginning. Now he couldn't imagine his life without them.

He pulled Ivy close and ate his meal, glad she asked him no questions he couldn't answer.

Joanna came out of the bedchamber at the same time Harold and Greta walked into the hall, the midwife calling for scissors and a hot poker. Logan picked up Ivy and escorted mother and daughter outside, preferring neither of them witness what would either cure or kill the thief.

Once outside, he put Ivy down and raced back to the thief on the trestle table.

Greta lifted an eyebrow. "You intend to help?"

"Nay, steal a boot."

With a quick jerk he pulled the boot from the thief's right foot, then hurriedly joined Joanna and Ivy outside.

Naturally, both females looked askance at the boot.

"On my way through the village I will stop at Margaret's cottage, compare it to the boot print near her woodpile."

Joanna said, "Ah."

Ivy tilted her head. "He does not look like a thief."

Joanna ran a hand over Ivy's hair. "I fear he is, though. I recognize him as one of the men who rode through the green. One cannot tell by looks, dearest. One must always look deeper."

She spoke to Ivy, but looked at him.

Deeper, hmm? Meaning he shouldn't judge Wat so harshly?

They were so different, he and she. He quick to assess and judge, Joanna wanting to believe the best unless proved otherwise.

As she'd believed in him, trusted him when most others at Lynwood advised her against it. She'd even given him her love when she must know it ill-advised. Now she entrusted him with Wat's ransom. He suddenly didn't want to prove her unwise.

Damn you, Wat.

Logan held out his hand; she gave over a money pouch.

"Have a care," she said softly, love in her eyes, hope in her heart.

Knowing he probably shouldn't, Logan leaned over and kissed her cheek. "I will. Have the guards close and bolt the gate, just in case something goes wrong."

Logan rode out, knowing why when the minstrels sang of love, they also sang of woe.

Joanna was going to be disappointed when she learned of Wat's involvement with the thieves. And when he brought in the other two—which he fully intended to do—his job would be done. She wouldn't need him anymore.

By fulfilling his oath to Joanna, did he jeopardize his chance of keeping her love? A cheerful thought. Still, he could do nothing other than what Joanna asked him to do. Well, almost.

Never once had he intentionally disobeyed an employer's order. 'Twas ironic that for the first time in his life, he was about to do just that. No way in hell was he handing Joanna's thirty shillings over to Wat's kidnappers. Not if he could help it, anyway. Doing it without getting Wat hurt or killed would be the difficult part. A challenge.

But then, he'd always loved a challenge.

Margaret's eyes narrowed when she saw him coming, then lit with glee when he held up the boot.

"Ye caught the thieves?"

"Only one. The other two yet elude me, but perhaps not for long." He handed the boot down into her outstretched hands. "See if this fits."

She ran for the crate, flipped it up, put down the boot.

"Damn. Does not fit. Too big."

"So we look for a thief with smaller feet?"

"Not too much smaller," she said with a slight smile, offering up the boot.

"Do me the favor of returning it to the manor. No sense my taking it with me."

Margaret's head tilted, studying him. "Heard you were the one chosen to deliver Wat's ransom. Poor man must be at his wit's end. You on your way now?"

Logan nodded.

"Have a care then. And do try to bring me another boot."

Joanna paced the hall, quiet now that a thief no longer lay on one of the trestle tables. Greta's treatment had been swift, and the man carried out to the guards' barracks immediately afterward, there to recover or die as

God willed. The odor of blood and stink of charred flesh yet lingered in the hall.

Logan had been gone only a few minutes. Hours could pass before he returned. She'd tried turning her hand and mind to various tasks to make the minutes pass more quickly. Nothing as yet had worked.

She wasn't alone in her unease. The manor folk went about their tasks in near silence. Even Ivy's spirits were dampened.

Waiting. Wondering. Hoping. Praying.

Joanna put a hand to the cheek he'd kissed. A brazen thing to do, claiming her as his own in front all and sundry in the bailey who might happen to see. If anyone had doubted that morn that she'd taken Logan as her lover, they doubted no more.

She smiled, thinking the whole lot of them had best become accustomed to seeing the mercenary kiss their lady. Or sharing her bedchamber. If she could convince Logan to stay.

She spun to the sound of the door opening. Donald entered, carrying the shears he'd promised the shepherd would be sharpened and ready the next day. Maud pointed him to a spot near the hearth, where he put down his burden.

Then he came toward her, his expression troubled, his shoulders slumped.

"Milady, I just heard from Margaret of what all has gone on this morn. I believe 'tis time you and I talked."

His tone set the back of her neck tingling.

Joanna waved him to a bench, sure she wanted to be sitting down for whatever he was about to say.

Donald crossed his arms on the table. "This is not an

easy tale to tell, and I offer you no excuses—" he began, then proceeded to tell her a disheartening tale.

Stunned, she learned of a night when four men she'd thought she could trust consumed too much ale and concocted a scheme to prod her into marriage.

"Not that you had done anything wrong, milady. We merely preferred to serve a lord."

She heard echoes of Logan's initial refusal to enter the service of a woman. Men!

"So deciding to hire a thief to harry the village was done on a whim?"

Donald grimaced. "Aye."

"How did we then get three thieves instead of one?"

"Wat's doing. Three men came looking for day work in the fields, and Wat took it into his head that the three should be the thieves."

Wat again. Sweet mercy, she'd sent Logan off to ransom the very man who caused all the problems to begin with, from the very thieves the reeve had hired!

Joanna fought her rising fury, held firmly to her composure. "So now Wat is in the hands of these men over whom he apparently no longer has control. Or does he? Is he truly being held under duress, or is this part of the scheme?"

Donald splayed his hands on the table. "I believe Wat is being held against his will, milady, though 'tis also possible the exchange for ransom might not go well."

Her heart beat faster. "How so?"

"When Wat feared the mercenary might actually find the thieves, he . . . asked the thieves to kill Logan Grimm."

Horrified, Joanna leaned against the table.

"Wat asked them to kill Logan?"

"I fear the mercenary could be riding into a trap."

Dear God in heaven, had she sent Logan to his death? Nay. Not Logan Grimm. Not the mercenary of fearsome reputation. Surely he knew enough to take precautions. Surely he was more than a match for two day laborers turned outlaws.

Unless he had no idea the two could be lying in wait somewhere along the path, planning to take him by surprise. Logan might not realize the danger until too late.

Someone had to go after him. Her. But she wasn't foolish enough to go alone.

Joanna ran out the door and spotted a guard nearby. "Clarence, see to the saddling of three horses. My mare, Harold's, and the thief's horse for you. Where is Harold?"

The guard's eyes narrowed. "On the wall walk, milady. We go somewhere?"

"Aye. Now hurry."

Clarence might think she'd gone witless, but she had no time or intent to explain. Besides, though confused, he turned heel and headed for the stable.

Joanna scanned the wall walk, spotted Harold, and shouted his name. He spun to look down at her.

"To me! The stable!"

Never doubting he'd obey, she ran across the bailey to find Oliver and Clarence in a flurry of horses and tack. Harold soon burst into the building.

"What goes on, my lady?"

"We are going after Logan. Have we time to catch him before he reaches the mill?"

"Perhaps. But why?"

"I have reason to believe the ransom may go badly. Logan may need help."

Harold rubbed at his forehead. "Our presence could be taken as a show of force. If they feel threatened, the outlaws may kill Wat."

Oliver led her mare to the mounting block, Clarence following with the other two horses. Joanna took the reins with trembling hands and threw herself onto the mare's back.

Better Wat's blood than Logan's.

Better to leave the one who'd schemed against her to his fate than endanger the one who'd always been on her side.

"So be it."

Harold stared up at her. "As you say, milady. But perhaps 'twould be best if you stayed here, let Clarence and I—"

Impatient, she snapped, "Were I your lord and not your lady, would you even question my decision to go?"

He opened his mouth to answer, then closed it.

"I thought not."

Joanna gave her horse a kick and rode out of the stable.

Chapter Twenty

Logan rode slowly as he approached the mill, his senses tuned to the sounds around him, hearing nothing but the rustling leaves and the bubbling stream.

He saw no horses where he expected to see two, which presented several possibilities.

The horses could be hidden in the brush, with all three men waiting inside the mill. Or the outlaws held Wat someplace else, watching for Logan to arrive—alone—before showing themselves.

He'd searched the mill once, on the day he began his service to Joanna. Finding nothing in the building to indicate the thieves used it as shelter, trusting the people in the hamlet to report seeing unfamiliar men or horses, he'd not come back. That might have been a mistake—or not.

Fact was, no matter where the outlaws had hidden all this time, they would soon regret making Lynwood Manor their target.

Logan dismounted and tied Gideon to a bush on the edge of the river. He peered under the mill's huge wheel, tilted off its axle so it no longer turned with the water passing beneath. Assured no one hid there, he studied the roof, still intact atop the sturdy timber building.

The thought passed through his mind that the axle could be fixed and converted to a more efficient overshot wheel, and that Joanna might now have the funds to make the repairs and improvements. 'Twould be an excellent source of revenue for the manor, and ensure Joanna of income even when other ventures might fail.

He smiled to himself. Perhaps he was ready to settle down after all if he was thinking like a landholder rather than a mercenary. The conversion no longer seemed so strange. But first he had to complete the task he'd been hired for before dwelling on the rest.

Perhaps he should hand the money over to the thieves and be done as Joanna expected him to; but verily, thirty shillings was an outrageous amount to demand as ransom for a peasant, reeve or no. And allowing the villains to escape didn't sit well. At all.

Logan listened at the door and heard no sound. He opened it slowly, to see Wat sitting on the floor against the opposite wall—hands bound behind him, mouth gagged with a strip of cloth, uncomfortable and distressed.

Logan stepped across the threshold, purposely leaving the door open.

The other man in the room—garbed in ragged black, a scar marring his forehead—leaned against the millstone. This must be the band's leader, Edward.

Logan assumed the other thief must be out guarding their horses.

Edward pulled himself upright, his dark eyes narrowing. "Who are you?"

Considering the content of the message, Logan thought it an odd question. "Logan Grimm, mercenary, currently in service to Lady Joanna of Lynwood."

"Mercenary?" he spit out. "She was supposed to send one of her guards! Can the woman not follow simple instructions?"

Logan took umbrage on Joanna's behalf. "I was told the note said to send the mercenary, meaning me, so here I am."

Edward's mouth thinned, then he spun and kicked Wat in the shin. "You fool! I should slit your throat for your trickery. What else did you write that I know naught about?"

Gagged, Wat didn't answer. Logan wondered if Joanna realized her reeve had been forced to write his own ransom note. Likely not, or she would have said so. He also found Wat's change of instruction interesting. Was the reeve unwilling to risk any of Lynwood's people, or did he have another reason?

Edward gathered himself. "No matter. Did you bring the ransom?"

Logan wanted to say nay, but the thief was angry and too close to Wat. Angering him further might get the reeve killed, which would upset Joanna. Contriving to allow the thief's ire to wane and to gain a better position in which to control the situation, Logan stalled for time.

"Thirty shillings is a damn high price for a mere peasant, especially one who has proved faithless."

Wat's guilty expression was all Logan needed to know

he'd guessed aright about the reeve's involvement with the thieves.

Edward crossed his arms. "We ask a pittance of what her ladyship is able to pay."

"Only if I allow her to pay. Verily, I have advised her against it."

"She does understand the reeve dies if the ransom is not paid. Or did he change that part of the note, too?"

"Lady Joanna understands. Unfortunately she has a soft heart and wants him back. What I propose to you is a compromise. I take Wat with me, and I allow you to live."

Edward didn't react, at first, waiting for more. When he realized no money settlement was involved, he tossed back his head in laughter.

"You bargain badly, mercenary. My men and I have gone to too much trouble to leave with naught. Better we should kill you both and take the money."

Logan moved two steps sideways, slowly, away from the door and nearer to Wat.

"You are welcome to try, but I urge you to take my offer."

Edward pulled his short sword, similar to the one used by the thief in the hunting lodge, and shouted toward the door. "Joseph! Hugh!"

Using Edward's momentary distraction, Logan took another step toward Wat.

The last member of the band entered the building, his sword drawn. He stopped just inside the building and closed the door, shutting out most of the light. Damn. Logan blinked several times, willing his eyes to adjust quickly.

"Where is Hugh?" Edward asked.

"He has not come as yet."

Logan settled the matter. "Nor will he. We captured Hugh at the lodge earlier. He rests uncomfortably at Lynwood."

A portion of Edward's bravado slipped. "Damn. Well, then only Joseph and I share in the ransom. 'Tis time you handed it over, Grimm."

From the way the thieves held their short swords, Logan knew them as inept as Hugh. He made a show of pulling out his broadsword, then twisted his wrist to cut several whistling arcs through the air.

Logan took his fighting stance, and smiled. "I think not. I suggest you lay down your weapons and come peacefully."

They didn't listen to his good advice. They rushed him, awkwardly brandishing their weapons. Even together they were no match for him, and Logan struggled not to kill them outright. He met their ungainly attack with a flurry, hoping they would realize they were badly outmatched and retreat.

He blocked stroke after stroke, fending them off one after the other, allowing them to expend their vigor.

Then Joseph tripped, and Logan pulled back hard to check his slice—to no avail. The edge of the sword slashed through cloth and skin, laying open the inside of the victim's forearm from elbow to wrist. Joseph fell, bleeding heavily, his screams reverberating through the mill.

Logan stepped away, his attention where it belonged, on his remaining foe. Horrified, Edward stared down at Joseph, whose screams weakened into moans.

"Time to surrender, Edward."

Edward bolted for the door.

Well, hell. He'd given Edward several chances to realize his peril, and the man refused to see reason.

Logan drew his dagger from his boot and aimed low. The dagger flew true and bit deep into Edward's calf. He fell forward with a shout of pain and soon lay on the dirt floor, writhing and cursing.

With a shake of his head at Edward's foolhardiness, Logan quickly judged the severity of both wounds, determining Edward in the least danger of death. Joseph wouldn't last long without immediate aid.

Having learned a valuable lesson several weeks ago and leery of more stitches, Logan kicked the thief's sword well away before he knelt and rolled the now quiet and very still Joseph onto his back. His eyes were closed, his breathing shallow. Blood poured from his arm at an alarming pace. Even as Logan used his sword to cut off a strip of Joseph's tunic to bind the wound, he doubted his ministrations were of any use.

Having done all he could for Joseph, Logan rose and wiped his hands on his already bloodstained tunic, glanced at Edward to make sure he wasn't going anywhere—he wasn't—and turned his attention to Wat.

The reeve had wisely kept to his seat. Logan untied the gag binding Wat's mouth.

The reeve let out a rush of air. "I cannot feel my hands."

After a quick glance at the rope securing Wat's hands, Logan fetched Joseph's short sword to cut the bonds.

"'Tis the least of your concerns. Verily, you are fortunate to be alive. Hold still."

The sword was so dull Logan had to saw at the rope to cut it loose. Freed, Wat immediately wrung his hands to regain feeling.

"I know. My . . . thanks."

Logan tossed the short sword aside, picked up his broadsword, and slid it into its scabbard, resisting the urge either to strangle or lecture the dolt of a reeve. 'Twas Joanna's right to deal with Wat.

"Why did you change the ransom note? Edward might well have slit your throat if he realized beforehand."

Still rubbing his hands together, Wat glanced at Edward before answering. "Because one of the guards would have handed over the money without question. I hoped you would not."

Before Logan had the chance to mull that over, the door crashed open. He spun, hand on sword hilt.

Harold burst into the room, with Clarence close behind.

Logan lowered his hand. "There were only two of them, Harold. You need not have come."

Harold smiled slightly. "We were not given a choice."

Then Joanna had sent them, and Logan wasn't sure if he should be pleased she sent reinforcements in the event he needed help, or annoyed she wasn't aware he didn't need any.

He waved at the men on the floor. "As long as you are here, you can help me toss them over their horses. I imagine they are tied nearby."

"We already found their horses," Joanna said from the doorway.

Shocked that she'd come, too, Logan watched Joanna enter the mill. She glanced at Edward where he lay on the floor with a dagger stuck in his leg, her nose wrinkling as if catching a foul odor. She paled as she passed Joseph and the large pool of blood next to him. Her eyes went wide at the sight of Logan's bloody tunic, and her bottom lip trembled when she reached out to touch his chest.

He could almost hear her fears.

"Joanna, 'tis not—"

He didn't have a chance to finish the reassurance. Joanna's eyes rolled upward and her knees gave way. Logan barely had time to catch her before she could hit the dirt.

Joanna roused to the sound of Logan calling her name, the distinct sensation of rocking, and the unmistakable feel of her cheek pressed against warm skin.

"Wake, dearest. We are nearly returned to Lynwood."

Since he insisted, she opened her eyes and blinked away the haziness. Indeed, the voice belonged to Logan, and they swayed together atop his stallion—Lord have mercy!

More awake, she looked down from that great height, wondering why she didn't feel afraid. Probably because Logan's arm was snug around her, cradling her against his bare chest.

Logan's bloody chest.

The memory shoved her upright, her hand flying to cover his heart, only to find a sprinkling of raven hair over olive-toned skin stretched taut over sculpted muscle.

No blood. No wound. Her long sigh of relief and collapse against him set him to chuckling.

"I tried to tell you 'twas not my blood, but you swooned before I could finish."

"So I see." His amusement annoyed her even as it assured her of his well-being. She also thought him rather gallant for stripping off his tunic so she would neither see nor smell the blood again. "Is everyone else all right?"

"Harold and Clarence are fine. I fear I killed one of the thieves, and the leader is wounded. As for Wat, he suffered no wound other than to his pride."

From behind them she could hear the thud of hooves and the jangle of tack, alerting her to the presence of the others. She didn't look back, knowing very well who followed. For the moment, she was content knowing that Logan was alive and unharmed and held her close.

"What the devil possessed you to come after me?" he asked.

Displeased, was he? Well, that was too bad. She'd done what she felt must be done and would make no apologies. Again her anger flared at what Donald confessed of the villagers' plot, of what they might have robbed her of—Logan.

"Donald feared the thieves might be planning an ambush. I could not allow you to ride into one without trying to warn you."

He squeezed her hard. "My dear, two men cannot execute much of an ambush."

"Three men. 'Twas possible Wat had not been kidnapped but was involved in the plot."

"Truly?"

Joanna snuggled into him and told him of all Donald confessed, ending with the smith's fear that Wat might actually be planning Logan's death.

She shivered, but as far as she could tell Logan never twitched a muscle. As if he suspected all along and had been prepared, or he didn't fear death at all—which was quite possible given his profession, having seen death too many times for it to have power over him anymore. He said nothing, so she continued.

"I hoped to catch you before you reached the mill. When we saw no signs of mishap along the road, my fears eased—until I heard the screams."

"Not my screams."

"So Harold said, but I ordered him to go into the mill anyway. I could no longer bear the thought I had sent you to the mill and put you at risk. Had the screams been yours, the blood yours—"

The words caught in her throat. Logan's arms came firmly around her, the embrace so encompassing she could barely breathe—and she didn't care.

"Hush, love. All turned out as it should."

All had, but long moments went by before she regained her composure fully. Meaning to let him know she'd recovered, Joanna turned her head and kissed him beneath his ear.

Her fearless, battle-hardened, usually composed mercenary reacted with the barest of shivers and lowest of groans.

"Joanna, you do realize we are not alone."

"Aye." She kissed him again, breathing in the scent of his bare skin, aware of his next reaction, proving all of his parts still whole and in working order.

"We are nearing the village."

"Must we?"

"Minx." Laughing, he reined in and called over his shoulder. "Harold, her ladyship has awakened. Bring her mare alongside."

"I would rather ride with you," she grumbled.

"Best the lady of Lynwood return on her own horse, upright and venerable, not wantonly sprawled across the lap of a half-naked mercenary."

He made sense. Except she wasn't ready to leave Joanna the woman behind to become the lady of Lynwood, who must now pass judgment on the villagers seeking to undermine her authority as well as on the outlaws.

Worst of all, she must soon pay Logan the remainder of his fee, releasing him from her service. Setting him free.

With assistance from Logan and Harold, Joanna slid from atop the stallion down onto her mare. Gown and veil arranged, her chin held high, she led the company through the village.

The tenants stopped what they were doing to gawk at the outlaws, both draped across their horses, one alive, one dead.

Margaret raced to catch them. "Milady, their boots!"

Knowing why Margaret wanted the boots, Joanna reined in, halting the company.

Margaret almost had the dead thief's right boot off when Wat told her softly, "There is no need, Margaret. I stole your wood."

Joanna couldn't remember ever seeing Margaret speechless, nor had she ever thought to hear such an admission from her reeve. Angry and sad, she urged her mare onward.

Many of the villagers fell into step behind the company. By the time Joanna passed through the gate, a large crowd followed.

She halted near the manor's door, knowing she should be elated the ordeal was almost over, relieved finally to have the peace she craved, proud her plan to hire a mercenary had proved sound.

Verily, all she felt was alone.

Logan admired Joanna's style.

As soon as she dismounted she'd shouted orders, making it clear she intended to hold court immediately in the bailey, where she required the attendance of every man and woman who had reached the age of majority.

Servants scrambled to haul out a table. Others dashed out into the village to gather those people who hadn't followed the company through the gate. Within the space of an hour, all was ready.

Hands bound behind him, Edward sat in the dirt off to the side of the table. Beside Edward sat Wat—legs crossed, elbows on knees, face in his hands. Two guards hovered above the pair.

In front of the table lay Hugh and Joseph, a blanket covering them, and Logan couldn't summon remorse for causing both men's deaths.

In the crowd Logan spotted Donald Smith, Otto Carpenter, and Robert Brewer, who must know their part in Wat's scheming wouldn't go unremarked.

Logan didn't know what Joanna intended to do with any of the men awaiting her judgment, though he hoped she didn't allow her tendency to show mercy to overcome her too forcefully.

The crowd quieted as she used a stool to aid her climb onto the table. His heart ached as he beheld the lady of

Lynwood. Joanna. The widow he'd once refused to serve and now loved deeply.

He held her heart, he knew. But gaining her love didn't mean he possessed the woman. Last night he'd granted her request to leave demons lie until daylight, and now wished he hadn't. Uncertainty over their future gripped his innards, squeezing the life out of his confidence. The insecurity was killing him.

Joanna raised a hand for silence. The crowd hushed. A smile touched her lovely mouth.

"People of Lynwood, our outlaws are caught!"

A cheer rose, but without enthusiasm. Likely most of them now realized a few of their own had been involved in the thefts.

Joanna stretched a hand toward Clarence, who gave her the chalice found in the blanket roll strapped to Edward's horse.

She held it high. "Father Arthur, I believe this belongs to the church."

The priest burst through the crowd. "Praise be!"

"I expect my goblets returned on the morrow."

He clutched the chalice to his bosom and bowed. "As you say, my lady. My thanks."

The priest hurried to rejoin the villagers, giddily holding up the chalice for all to see.

Joanna again reached down, this time to Maud. What the housekeeper handed up Logan couldn't tell.

"Logan. Harold. Step forward, if you would."

Logan obeyed, belatedly realizing he hadn't put his tunic back on, which was probably for the best given Joanna's previous reaction to the bloodstains.

Along with Harold, Logan bent at the waist, giving the lady of Lynwood her due.

Joanna gave him a pouch fashioned of a square of cloth tied up with yarn. He knew immediately it held his fee. From the weight he knew the pouch contained more than he and Joanna had bargained for, possibly the full fee for three weeks.

Fifteen shillings.

She'd once told him she wouldn't cheat him, and now she proved her word good. Too, she could now send him on his way with her conscience clear.

"Accept this payment with my appreciation for your good service. Today you proved your worth by ridding us of the outlaws. Well done, Logan Grimm."

To his surprise, a smattering of people echoed Joanna's "well done." The praise touched him, especially when he heard the phrase uttered by a young but hearty female voice. Ivy's. He turned his head to see her standing next to Maud with the rest of the manor folk.

Ivy's broad smile set his heart to aching. Not only had he fallen deeply in love with Joanna, but tumbled over the edge for Ivy, too. Exactly how and when they'd engaged his affection he couldn't say, nor did it matter. All he knew was that he wanted them both more than he wanted anything else in his life.

How odd to hold his fee in his hand and not be making plans to leave, but to stay. He looked up at Joanna. Her smile was nearly as wide as Ivy's. It gave him hope, but didn't banish his uncertainty.

For the time being he could do nothing. The lady had duties to attend which couldn't be put off.

Again he bowed. "At your service, my lady."

He stepped away from the table, leaving Joanna to address the captain of her guard.

"I owe you a debt, Harold, for your unswerving loyalty and the invaluable assistance you provided Logan." She handed him a pouch, too. "A small token, only. I also offer you the position as Lynwood's steward. Will you accept?"

Logan thought the offer an excellent reward, but the expression on Harold's face didn't bode well for acceptance.

"My lady, I am truly honored, but I must refuse. Verily, I ask for release from your service."

Joanna's eyes widened with surprise, and Logan remembered a conversation with Harold on the wall walk. The man had ambitions beyond the stewardship of a small holding, and apparently now felt comfortable about leaving Lynwood.

"Release? Are you so unhappy here?"

"Nay, milady, not unhappy but unfulfilled. Since the day I became Sir Bertrand's squire, my goal has always been to attain my knighthood. Now that Lynwood is no longer endangered, I beg your leave to pursue that goal."

"Then I suppose you must go," she said quietly. "Know that I am sorry you leave us, but you do so with my blessing and good wishes. I do have another task or two I wish you to perform first."

Harold gave her a bow fit for royalty. "For the nonce, I am still yours to command, Lady Joanna."

Logan knew Joanna hadn't counted on losing the captain of her garrison that day, and several heartbeats passed before she gathered her resolve to continue what she'd begun. She'd handled the blow very well, but the worst was yet to come.

He wished he could spare her the judgments, but only Joanna could punish her errant villagers and Edward.

Her voice rang with authority when she called Wat forward.

If the reeve had looked forlorn in the mill, he looked pitifully wretched standing before her. From out of the crowd emerged Donald, Otto, and Robert to stand behind Wat, and Logan gave the three credit for willingly taking responsibility for their actions even before Joanna called them.

She gave the three a mere glance before she crossed her arms and stared down at Wat.

"I cannot tell you how much it pains me to learn a man in whom I placed my trust was not worthy of my trust. You betrayed me, Wat Reeve. Not only me, but your fellow villagers. Have you aught to say in your defense?"

"Didn't mean no harm, your ladyship," he mumbled.

"No harm? You hired three men to harry us, to pilfer food and wood from your fellow villagers and the manor folk, and you have the gall to say you meant no harm?"

"Weren't supposed to go so far."

"But it did, did it not? And even when you were advised to desist, you pressed to continue. You could have stopped it all, merely by giving Harold the information he needed to drive the thieves off. Instead, your stubbornness put lives at risk, including your own."

She turned away and addressed Harold. "Assign two guards to escort Wat to the reeve's cottage. He is allowed to remove only those personal possessions he can carry on his back. The rest I seize as the fine for his misdeeds against both manor and village, to be used as reparation for the thefts suffered. He is then to be escorted off Lynwood lands, never to return."

Stunned, Wat finally lifted his head. "I am *banished?*"

"Since you so much prefer serving a lord rather than a lady, pray go find one to your liking."

"But my lady—"

Before Wat could further protest, Harold grabbed the reeve's sleeve, shoved him away from in front of the table, and tossed him toward two guards, who none too gently hurried Wat across the bailey and out the gate.

Joanna then turned her attention to the three villagers she had yet to deal with. "For your part in Wat's scheme, I fine you each six pence to be added to the fund used for reparations. For your disloyalty, I require from each of you added service to the manor. Donald, from now until after harvest you will sharpen all of the manor's plows, knives, and shears for no fee. Otto, you will floor the tithe barn as soon as I can arrange for the lumber. Robert, I expect an added keg of ale and two of spiced mead delivered to the manor each week from now until Michaelmas."

Nary a one of them uttered a word, well aware their punishment could be much worse.

Joanna glanced over the crowd. "A sennight from today, the villagers must elect a new reeve. That man will *not* be one of these three."

No villager objected to Joanna's restriction.

Apparently satisfied, Joanna walked to the end of the table, where Edward still sat in the dirt.

"I am not sure who was more the fool, Wat for coming up with this scheme or you for accepting his offer.

Perhaps if you had stayed within the limits he first gave you, we would not have come to this pass. Your companions might still be alive, and you might have found acceptable employment and homes elsewhere. But you allowed greed to overrule your good sense. I accuse you with the theft of a chalice, the beating of Robert Brewer, and the unlawful abduction of Wat Reeve. On all counts you are guilty. Your companions have already paid for their crimes with their lives, as will you."

Once more she turned to her captain. "I understand Wat and Edward used an oak tree as a meeting place. I think it a fitting gallows. Hang him. Now."

If she heard Edward's protests and curses, she gave no sign. Lady Joanna of Lynwood Manor merely stepped down from the table and strode into the hall.

She'd handled the entire affair swiftly, decisively, and fairly. Without giving in to emotion or seeking advice or needing support. She'd proved to all she could rule with the dignity, wisdom, and fortitude of any man.

And drove home to one heartsick mercenary that she didn't need him at all.

Chapter Twenty-one

Following Robert Brewer's directions to the tangled oak tree, Logan went with Harold and a few guards to ensure Edward met his end. Efficiently, Harold carried out his orders. Logan doubted Edward even felt the jerk that snapped his neck.

His job now finished to his satisfaction, Logan went to the village to borrow a tunic from Donald Smith, the only man whose clothes were large enough to cover him. Promising to return the tunic as soon as his own was cleaned, Logan headed back to the manor, well aware this could be his last night at Lynwood.

Ye gods, his future relied upon a yea or nay from one woman's lips. He knew precisely how to present himself as a sword for hire, but not as a suitor for a lady's hand.

How best to approach her? Straight out or roundabout? Must he ply her with gallant words or present her with bouquets of flowers?

Did he first give an account of his redeeming qualities—of which he had a few—and point out how he could be of use to her? In bed and out. After all, she did need a captain for the garrison.

If that was all he could be to her, a soldier and lover, could he accept it?

And what of Joanna? If she stood fast to her decision never to marry again, would her sense of propriety allow her a relationship of which few would approve?

Selfishly, he wanted Joanna as his wife. But he also wanted what was best for her and Ivy, and that might mean he should leave. Many at Lynwood still thought of him as "that mercenary" and might never accept him—a situation that would wear on Joanna, cause strife between the two of them and between her and her people.

His head in a muddle and his stomach in knots, Logan passed through the gate to see a strange horse in the bailey.

A visitor? Lynwood's last visitor had been Sir Gregory. 'Twould be just Logan's luck if the horse belonged to Sir Edgar, the other suitor to Joanna he'd heard about.

Logan ran into the manor's hall to spy Adam, nephew of Conrad Falke, enjoying a mug of ale. His presence meant Essex must be forming his army.

Relieved he hadn't come face-to-face with Sir Edgar, Logan joined the lad of ten-and-six who sought to follow in his uncle's footsteps.

"Greetings, Adam."

"Logan." He handed over a rolled parchment. "I bring you tidings from Conrad."

"Conrad knows very well I cannot read. Waste of ink and parchment, this. You will have to tell me what it says."

Joanna sidled up next to him and held out her hand. "I can read it, if you will allow."

Logan hesitated to hand over such a stark reminder of how he made his way in life. 'Twouldn't do for her to recall the appalling tale of him she'd heard in her father's hall. Not now when he wanted her to dwell on how well they suited each other, how their bodies melded in perfect accord when coupling, of the love they'd both professed.

But if Joanna couldn't accept his past and put it behind her, then he wouldn't need a bouquet of flowers or to list his finer qualities. Her reaction would determine which path to choose, either to ask for her hand in marriage or leave with Adam.

He gave her the parchment.

Joanna smiled at Adam and urged him to partake of more ale and food, and offered a pallet in the barracks for the night.

Adam graciously accepted the manor's hospitality and went out to take care of his horse.

She unrolled the parchment, and after a few moments rolled it up and tossed it on a table.

"Come walk with me," she ordered, her manner distant, her upset too obvious to deny.

His heart fell on hearing the words he'd used a few nights ago when he'd taken her up to the wall walk and had his past thrown in his face. Still, he followed, hearing his death knell when she led him to that same spot on the walk.

She leaned against a timber post, looking out over the village she ruled and the people whose well-being must always come before her own—and his.

"Hard to believe the ordeal is over," she said. "The

outlaws are dead. No one will rush in to report another theft or injury. Verily, Ivy is certainly pleased she will be allowed to play on the green with the other children tomorrow."

If naught else he'd given Joanna the peace she sought, given Ivy back her favorite place to play. Praise for a job well-done, however, belonged to the lady of Lynwood.

"You did them all proud, Joanna. No one will ever again question your ability to rule."

A brief smile touched her mouth. "Oh, I am not so sure. A man surely would have remembered to ask the leader from where he stole the horses before sending him out for . . . hanging."

It struck Logan that today was the first time Joanna had passed judgment on anyone. She'd imposed fines and demanded added labor from Donald Smith, Otto Carpenter, and Robert Brewer, the easy part when compared to the rest. Banishing Wat must have been hard on her. Sending Edward to his death could only have been akin to torture.

"You did what you had to do. Sometimes that is not pleasant."

"Sheer agony."

"Rule or be ruled."

She nodded and took a deep breath. "The message from Conrad entreats you to meet him in a fortnight in York. He is especially pleased to inform you that Essex has agreed to a weekly fee of seven shillings for each of you."

Taken aback, Logan raised an eyebrow. "Seven? Are you sure you read that aright?"

"I know the difference between a five and a seven. The missive says seven."

He whistled low. "A very good offer."

"Will you accept?"

His work here was finished, and he'd been paid. The lady he loved didn't seem to need him, would do admirably on her own. Only her love could hold him in Lynwood, but apparently love couldn't banish the demon of his past.

Letting her go was the hardest thing he had ever done, would ever do.

"Likely."

"For how long would you enter his service?"

"One never knows with wars. Two months. A year. Depends upon whether Essex actually marches into Scotland. Verily, sometimes peace is negotiated before an army takes to the field. 'Tis quite possible I could travel to York for naught."

"Ah." She bit her bottom lip. "Will you go back to London before going to York?"

Back to the Red Rooster. To sit on a stool and drink ale and think of what might have been.

"May as well."

"You could stay at Lynwood. I see no sense going all the way south to London just to retrace part of your route."

An offer of hospitality. A comfortable pallet, good food, and spiced mead. Perhaps a night or two in Joanna's bed if her demons needed slaying. A good offer, but one he couldn't accept and hold on to his sanity.

"My job here is done. The thieves are dead, Wat will

no longer press you to marry, so you have the peace and security you craved. Time I moved on."

"Actually, I have been giving the whole affair much thought. This afternoon proved to me that ruling this holding may be more of a challenge than I first thought. Not that I cannot do it, but now I wonder if I want to. Perhaps I should marry."

Jealousy reared up and raged.

"Have you someone in mind?"

"I do. Unfortunately I am not sure he will have me."

"The man would be a fool not to."

She shook her head, then finally tore her gaze from the village to look at him. A single tear ran down her cheek, and without any hesitation he thumbed it away, hating that some fool possessed the power to make Joanna cry.

"Not a fool, merely a mercenary who may not wish to take on the burden of a holding, who needs no wife or child clinging to him when he would rather be off in Scotland with Essex."

Logan's heart slammed into his ribs. He couldn't breathe and doubted his hearing. But the love in her eyes brooked no doubt. Sweet mercy, he'd been a thickheaded dolt. All along she'd been working her way to a proposal of marriage—to him—and caught him blindsided.

The possibility of his leaving upset her, not the reminder of his past. She brought him here, where she once railed at him, to begin anew.

Somehow, he managed to answer, "I never did like Scotland."

"France?"

"Decent wine, better mead here."

This time her tears flowed from eyes glittering with

joy, over a grin that pierced his heart. Every day, from then until he breathed his last, he would do whatever he must to keep that smile on Joanna's face.

He caught her up in an embrace, careful not to crush her. "Be sure, my love. Many of your people will not approve of their lady marrying a lowly mercenary."

"Approve or not, they have no choice but to accept."

A firm, almost fierce stance she might regret later.

"My past is bloody, my reputation savage. You may ask too much of them."

She sighed and pulled away far enough to look into his face. "I owe you an apology for condemning you for deeds of another's doing. I realize your past is strewn with violence, but you are no savage, and I admit I did not understand the difference fully until I was forced to end a man's life. Now my hands are bloodied, too, and for that I make no apology."

She waved a dismissive hand, pushing aside a demon before she continued. "Perhaps I am being selfish, but the only other opinion I considered was Ivy's, and she will be elated. No one else but the three of us has any say in this."

So proclaimed the lady of Lynwood, and Logan began to think that maybe she was right.

Ivy. Sweet mercy, this offer of Joanna's included a girl who would look to him as a child looks to a father. The prospect sent him reeling again, and widened his smile.

"I love Ivy, too. I will be good to her, I vow."

"I know, or I would not have asked you to marry me."

Hearing the words set his heart thumping again, so he pulled her closer. "Here I was ready to leave for York because I love you too much to ruin your life. I swear, Joanna, I will forever try to do right by you."

"And I you." She sighed. "Getting married will put another dent in your reputation, and seven shillings a sennight is a huge sum to pass up. Perhaps you should reconsider."

So he did, for the space of a heartbeat. His days of wandering from one place to another and hiring his sword to one lord or another were over. Instead, he would henceforward learn when to plant and harvest crops and how to shear sheep.

All for the love of a woman. And he didn't mind at all.

What he did mind was being stared at by the crowd of people in the bailey, some smiling knowingly, others utterly horrified to see their lady in the arms of a mercenary.

Then he spotted Ivy in the crowed, hands on hips, utterly confused, and knew what he must do. The best way to meet a challenge was head-on. For all three of them.

He slipped out of Joanna's arms, grabbed her hand, and pulled her toward the stairway. "Have you parchment and ink?"

Her eyes narrowed. "Aye. Why?"

He didn't answer until they'd scurried down the stairs. "Need to send a message to Conrad, but there is something I must do first."

Now halfway across the bailey, he let go of Joanna, scooped up Ivy, and settled her on his hip.

"Too soon you will be too big for me to carry."

Little arms tightened around his neck. "But not yet."

Her gentle but firm protest brought a lump to his throat and squeezed his heart.

"Nay, not yet," he quietly assured her, then again seized Joanna's hand and headed for the hall.

Joanna squeezed his hand. "What do you wish to tell Conrad?"

"Inform him that I will not be going to York, because her ladyship has made me a better offer—with a bonus."

Which brought Joanna's smile back. "Has she?"

Logan crossed the threshold, family at his side, peace in his heart.

Logan leaned down and kissed the woman who'd given him what he'd never wanted and always needed. A home. A family. Her love. Treasures beyond measure.

"She has. Therefore, I will accept her generous offer and will remain in her service for as long as she will have me."

Joanna laughed lightly. "At what cost this time?"

"Only your love, Joanna. And the occasional strawberry tart."

About the Author

SHARI ANTON'S secretarial career ended when she took a creative writing class and found she possessed some talent for writing fiction. The author of several highly acclaimed historical novels, she now works in her home office where she can take unlimited coffee breaks. Shari and her husband live in southeastern Wisconsin, where they have two grown children and do their best to spoil their two adorable little grandsons. You can write to her at P.O. Box 510611, New Berlin, WI, 53151-0611, or visit her Web site at www.sharianton.com.

More
Shari Anton!

Please turn this page
for a preview of
Midnight Magic
available in mass market
December 2005

Chapter One

England 1145

When the royal temper raged, prudent men held their peace.

Alberic of Chester considered himself a prudent man. With his helm securely tucked under one arm, he stood quietly near his fellow soldiers, holding a sword still too bloody to sheath.

A skirmish shouldn't have been fought in this field where sprouting oats were now ruined. So many men shouldn't have died a mere hour before nooning. A frightful waste.

Alberic watched tall, robust King Stephen pace the road alongside the freshest battlefield in the ten-year-old dispute over the rightful possession of England's crown. Unconcerned for either the rain wetting his woolen cloak or the mud splattering his leather boots, the king focused his fury on two men: Ranulf de Gernons, the earl of Chester, the living, stoic target of his wrath, and Sir Hugh de Leon, a baron who lay face down in blood-soaked grass, now beyond hearing and earthly cares.

"An unfortunate death, Chester."

The king's deceptively placid statement reeked of ire and accusation.

With nearly as regal a mein as the monarch's, Chester retorted, "His death could not be avoided, sire. Sir Hugh refused to surrender when given the chance."

The king gestured toward a young, fair-haired man sprawled not far from the baron. Alberic tensed, aware of whose blood dried on his sword, and prepared to confess his part in the senseless carnage if need be. But the king continued to address the earl.

"The son, also?"

"Young William followed his father's foolhardy example. Had they allowed, I would have captured both and held them for ransom."

"So instead you allowed them both to die!"

Chester tossed a hand in the air, his usually unshakable composure fraying. "Their goal was to attack the camp and take your majesty as their prisoner. What would you have us do, sire? Not defend our own lives? Stand aside? Perhaps allow them to escape and return to the Empress Maud?"

"We would *prefer* that land-rich subjects be captured and brought before us! Sir Hugh might have been turned to our service if given sufficient enticement."

The twitch of Chester's jaw made Alberic wonder how long the recent, brittle alliance between the earl and the king would last. Chester's reputation for acting only in his best interest was well earned and widely known. And given the king's mistrust of Chester, a breech could come at any time, for any reason, split asunder by either man.

"As I said, Sir Hugh gave us no choice," Chester stated, firmly indicating he would argue no more.

Wisely, King Stephen didn't push the earl further. Instead, he glanced around him at the field littered with dead, at the wounded men-at-arms being tended, and finally at the few poor souls who'd been taken prisoner. They were all that remained of Sir Hugh's small force.

Too small of a force to prevail against the earl's. Alberic still didn't understand why Sir Hugh, vastly outnumbered, hadn't surrendered. Or why William had fought with such vicious determination, even when knowing his father had fallen and their mission doomed to failure.

All pondering over the de Leon men's actions halted when King Stephen's gaze settled on him. Alberic was forced to endure the full force of the dark-eyed, measuring stare for several uncomfortable moments.

Then the king asked of Chester, "Your whelp?"

Alberic almost smiled at the earl's obvious chagrin.

For several years now, Chester had dismissed the familial similarities between himself and Alberic as slight and utterly no proof of paternity. To have the king notice the resemblance so quickly and accurately must be irritating. Alberic also knew better than to hope for the answer he'd waited nigh on half a lifetime to hear—full acknowledgment. Even so, his heart beat quickened.

"So his mother claimed," Chester finally answered.

"Have you provided for him as yet?"

"He has a place in my household."

A place grudgingly given and not the one Alberic had hoped for as a lad of twelve. After his mother's death and with no means to support himself, he'd shown up at Chester's castle and confronted the earl. While Chester might not have acknowledged Alberic as his son, neither had the earl tossed him out the gate. Unhappy but needful of shelter and sustenance, he responded to Chester's scant generosity by working hard to earn the earl's respect, if not his affection.

Most days Alberic believed he made strides in winning the earl's acceptance. On others he fought the feeling of being that skinny lad, raw with grief, needing to belong *somewhere* and fearful he never would.

"Is he knighted?" the king asked.

Alberic's heartbeat kicked up another notch. That longed

for event hadn't occurred yet, though he was already beyond the age when most squires acquired their knighthood. Chester, however, was decidedly reluctant to bestow the honor.

"Not as yet."

Scowling, King Stephen squatted next to the corpse and slid a large, gold ring from the baron's hand, pausing to study it before clenching it in his fist.

"The seal of the dragon," the king said softly. "We remember the first time we saw this unusual ring many years ago, on an occasion when Sir Hugh attended our uncle's court. He said he wore it in honor of his wife, a Welsh princess, whose family claims lineage from that of Pendragon."

Pendragon? The fabled King Arthur?

All around him Alberic heard both awed murmurs and snickers of disbelief. All muttering stopped when the king rose from beside Sir Hugh.

"Disbelieve, do you?" Stephen called out. When no one answered, his attention again returned to where Alberic didn't want it. On him.

"What of you? Do you believe?"

Alberic quashed a twinge of nervousness, blaming it on his inexperience in addressing royalty. He considered his answer carefully, well aware he was being judged.

"I know naught of the descendants of King Arthur, sire, so cannot come to an informed judgement."

The king came toward him, his steps purposeful, his intention impenetrable, stopping a mere arm's length away. "What is your name, lad?"

"Alberic of Chester, sire."

"And on your sword dries the blood of William de Leon?"

Said mildly, but with an undertone of cold steel.

Apparently the messenger who Chester had sent to camp

to inform the king of the skirmish had described how the baron and his son had met their end.

"Aye, sire."

"Do you now consider yourself the better man?"

"William fought with both zeal and skill. He had already vanquished several of the earl's soldiers before he and I crossed swords. I consider myself blessed to have come away the victor."

"His equal, then?"

Only by citing legitimacy of birth could anyone make a case of William de Leon's superiority over Alberic of Chester, and he chose to ignore that unfortunate circumstance of birth whenever possible.

"As you say, sire."

The corner of the king's mouth twitched with humor, and approval softened his eyes.

"As we say, is it? Then we believe you may be ripe for what we have in mind." The king drew his sword, a fighting weapon instead of the fancy blade one might expect a royal personage to wield. "Kneel before your king, Alberic of Chester."

Doubting Stephen had lost his wits and intended to behead a man who'd committed no crime, Alberic could think of only one other reason for the king's drawn sword and the accompanying order.

Knighthood.

Alberic hesitated, overjoyed at the prospect of receiving the coveted rank, but wary of why Stephen had singled him out. Kings didn't confer knighthood as an act of kindness, and Alberic suspected Stephen of an as yet unfathomable selfish motive.

Chester frowned in stark disapproval, and Alberic knew their fragile relationship might suffer if he accepted the king's offer. Dare he risk what the earl might consider betrayal?

Misgivings brushed aside, Alberic got down on one knee

and on a muddy road in Bedfordshire. Ignoring the unrelenting drizzle, he felt the weight of the king's sword land on his right shoulder.

"We dub thee knight, Alberic of Chester, with all the rights and responsibilities that come with the honor. We charge thee to uphold the laws of our beloved England, to serve as protector for widows and orphans, to hold fast to the teachings of Holy Church and praise Almighty God for his blessings. Do you so swear?"

His mouth dry as dust, he answered, "I do so swear."

The king's sword lifted from his shoulder, and Alberic tensed, steadying for the *colee*. The king's open-handed buffet to the side of Alberic's head nearly knocked him over, fixing it in Alberic's memories of this day, of the men involved and the oath given.

Of the day Alberic of Chester became *Sir* Alberic.

Through the ringing in his ears he heard the king continue. "And now, Sir Alberic, we propose to grant you a living to support your new rank. For your homage and fealty to our royal person, we shall bestow upon you Sir Hugh de Leon's castle at Camelen, along with all his other holdings."

Stunned, Alberic stared at the ring the king held out, eager to grasp it but wary of accepting.

"What of Sir Hugh's widow?"

"His Welsh princess died many years ago. William was his only son. Three daughters remain. We charge you to take one as your wife, send another to our court and give the last to the Church."

Alberic's curiosity nearly burst with questions about the extent of the lands, where they were located, and the income he could expect. Verily, for wont of a simple oath the king meant to make him a rich and powerful man.

He gave fleeting thought to the daughters. Surely one of the females was tolerable enough to wed and bed, and the marriage would firmly establish his claim to Camelen.

Only a witless fool would hesitate longer or argue further.

Alberic put down his sword and helm, slipped on the baron's ring, then raised his clasped hands for the king to enfold. When next he stood, only two men within sight outranked him—the earl of Chester and the king of England.

Ye gods, how quickly men's fortunes rose and fell given the vagaries of war.

The king slid his sword into an intricately tooled leather scabbard belted at his waist. "Take de Leon and his son home. Bury them with the honor due them, then hold Camelen in our name."

"As you say, sire."

The king spun and called for his horse, and the unease Alberic felt earlier returned. Why in the name of all the saints had the king granted a knighthood, and the wealth and power of a barony, to the earl of Chester's bastard?

Definitely something amiss here.

He stared down at the uncommon gold ring King Stephen had called the seal of the dragon. A small, sparkling ruby graced the face of faceted black onyx, the mounting held securely by gold prongs fashioned as dragon's claws.

"A handsome gift," Chester commented, still frowning in disapproval and envy? Though the earl stared at the ring, clearly he meant the entire royal gift.

Alberic bent over and wiped the blood from his sword in the long grass, his stomach tightening as it always did when he spoke to Chester.

"A handsome gift, indeed. My mind would be easier about accepting it all if I knew what game the king plays."

The earl shrugged a broad shoulder. "Simple enough. He believes he has now purchased your loyalty, and thereby firmly fixed mine."

Then the king believed wrongly, the grandiose gift given for naught. Alberic glanced at the baron and his son, who'd fought and died together for the same cause, loyal to each other to the very end. With one or the other the king might have struck a bargain and gained the cooperation of the other. The same could not be assumed about the earl of Chester and his bastard son.

"Then the king does not know you very well."

"Nay, he does not. I wish you good fortune in claiming your prize."

The earl walked off, shouting orders to his men to fetch carts to carry the wounded, to begin burying the dead, to march the prisoners back to camp.

Prisoners Alberic would soon have to take charge of.

He took a deeper than normal breath, the problems associated with his new position beginning to surface. The faces of the men he'd recently fought against twisted with varying degrees of defeat, anger, resentment and despair. He needed only one of Sir Hugh's soldiers to lead him to Camelen. Surely, if one man of Camelen swore allegiance to the new lord, others might too, if only for the chance to return home.

Not that he could wholly trust the word of a one of them.

Accepting the king's gifts had been as easy as taking an oath. Gaining possession of them wouldn't be so simple. Not only did he have to get to Camelen, but somehow get through the gate without someone on the battlements taking umbrage and shooting an arrow through his heart.

Alberic again inspected the ring, the ruby winking at him from atop the onyx, the dragon's claws seeming to dig deep into his gut. He told himself he'd come by the ring and Camelen fairly and honestly, but couldn't completely banish the sick feeling he'd somehow stolen them and was about to pay the penalty.

Atop Camelen's battlements, Gwendolyn de Leon saw no immediate danger to either Camelen or her person, merely two men coming across the field separating the castle from the woodland beyond, one of them Sir Garrett, whose rotund form and limp-marred walk she had no trouble identifying.

"I do not like the looks of this, my lady," Sedwick grumbled from beside her.

Her attention forced back to the field, Gwendolyn conceded that Sir Garrett shouldn't be walking, but riding. Nor should the elderly knight even be here, but with her father and brother defending Bedford Castle.

"Perhaps Father sent Garrett home with a message and something happened to his horse."

In answer to her optimistic conjecture, Sedwick snorted through the battle-marred nose on his round face. "Perhaps something happened to both knights' horses? Nay, my lady. The very air stinks of trouble."

Gwendolyn bit her bottom lip to hold her peace. Sir Garrett certainly meant Camelen no harm. As for the knight who walked by his side, how much harm could one man do against thick stone walls and an armed garrison?

The knight was big certainly, towering a full head above Garrett, who she could look straight in the eyes. A young man, she judged, from the swagger in the knight's long-strided amble over the grassy field. His broad shoulders carried the weight of gleaming chain mail with ease. The belt of his scabbard circled a trim waist over narrow hips. Black leather riding gloves covered his hands.

He wore a helm, of course, concealing his hair, the nose guard obscuring his facial features. Except his jaw. Which from this distance she couldn't judge as strong or weak.

As the men traversed the field, Gwendolyn's curiosity kept pace with her rising impatience until, finally, the men had no choice but to halt at outer edge of the moat.

She could see the young knight's chin now, square and bold, strong. Gwendolyn caught herself wondering about the coloring of his hair and eyes when Sedwick's shout stopped the silly musing.

"You return to Camelen in strange manner, Sir Garrett."

Garrett removed his helm and ran a hand though his steel-gray hair. Sweet mercy, the man looked weary unto dropping where he stood!

"Not the manner of my choosing, Sedwick." The weariness in Garrett's voice matched his appearance and, for the first time since she'd been called to the battlements, Gwendolyn felt a twinge of apprehension. "We bear news best not shouted over the wall, so would be most grateful if you would lower the drawbridge."

Sedwick made no move to signal an affirming command to the guards posted near the giant winches that controlled the bridge's thick chains.

"Who do you bring with you?"

"Christ's blood, Sedwick, I will explain all after."

Abruptly silenced by the young knight's hand to his forearm, Garrett leaned slightly to the side to listen to whatever the knight was saying. When he finally righted, Garrett's visage was grimmer than before.

"He is Sir Alberic of Chester. By my oath, I warrant that he means Camelen no harm."

Sedwick's eyebrow arched sharply. "My lady, if this Sir Alberic is of Chester, then he is our enemy. Yet Garrett bids us allow him entry! I like this not."

Her father firmly believed in the right of King Henry's daughter, the Empress Maud, to the English crown. For in his mind, King Stephen was an usurper and traitor for having swiftly claimed his uncle's crown after swearing years ago to uphold Maud's right to inherit. Ranulf de Gernons, the earl of Chester, had recently thrown the weight of his earldom behind King Stephen, infuriating her father, who'd vowed to one day present Chester's head to Maud on a gold platter.

Nay, Sir Hugh de Leon wouldn't be pleased if a man of Chester were allowed inside Camelen. And yet, if Sir Alberic was in the company of Sir Garrett, a man her father trusted completely who was willing to enter a fully garrisoned hostile castle, he must have a very good reason. The news the two wished to impart must be important, and she feared grave, indeed.

"Truly, Sedwick, what harm can come of Sir Alberic's

entry? Garrett vouches for him, and I doubt any knight is slow-witted enough to challenge an entire garrison. I say we allow him inside."

Sedwick hesitated a moment before tossing up a hand, signaling the guards to lower the drawbridge. The winches groaned and chain clanged as the heavy door of thick planks began its decent.

The bridge thudded to the earth, sending her scurrying down the stairway, with Sedwick and several guards close behind. By the time she reached the bailey, Garrett and his companion had crossed the bridge.

She halted at the base of the gate tower, her curiosity centered on the young knight who now carried his helm he struck her as arrogantly confident to believe he wasn't endangered, but she had to admit he wasn't, yet. Much depended on the next few minutes.

Sweet mercy, Alberic possessed a riveting countenance.

He looked about him, taking in his surroundings with eyes as green as summer grass. Dark brown hair skimmed the wide shoulders she'd noted earlier, and framed a swarthy-skinned visage that undoubtedly quickened the beat of careless maiden's hearts.

Gwendolyn wasn't careless, having learned at her mother's death bed the importance of holding her heart on tight rein. So she appreciated Alberic's handsomeness as if admiring a finely sculpted statue, choosing to ignore the faster beat of her pulse.

She could tell nothing of his thoughts save for his interest in the arrangement of the castle and contents of the bailey.

Garrett, who'd looked weary from a distance, looked nigh on haggard up close, but not for all the gold in the kingdom would she embarrass the proud knight by fussing over him.

He attempted a smile. "Thought that was you on the

battlements, Lady Gwendolyn. A welcoming sight to these unworthy, weary eyes."

Now wasn't the time for smiles and gallantry.

"You bring news, Garrett. What has happened?"

Garrett took a long, steadying breath. "The worst news, I fear. My lady, I have the sad duty of informing you that your father and brother have . . . fallen.

Nay! Sweet Jesu, nay!

For several long moments Gwendolyn could only stare at Garrett, unable to breathe, struggling to deny what she couldn't possibly have heard. Then Sedwick cursed, mocking her feeble attempt at disbelief. Grief hit hard and hot, as if she'd been struck by lightning. Tears welled up and spilled down her cheeks. To hold herself upright, she grabbed hold of Garrett's arm.

"Fallen? Both?" she asked, damn near choking on the words.

"In battle, near Bedford Castle. I am so terribly sorry I must bear such horrible tidings."

Briefly her thoughts flew to her sisters. The elder, Emma, lying in the bedchamber all three sisters shared, suffering one of her sick headaches. The younger, Nicole, in the nursery with the priest, attending her lessons. *Orphans, all of us.*

But not poor, and not without resources. Father had been most specific on her course of action should the worst happen.

Gwendolyn palmed away her tears, forcefully setting aside her grief. Later she would mourn, especially for William, but she must now see to her duty both to Camelen and to the legacy left to her by her mother.

"Where are they?" she asked of Garrett, glad to hear her voice sounded stronger.

"On a cart in the woodland." Then he sighed and put his free hand over Gwendolyn's. "We brought them home for burial. However, we cannot bring them into the castle until assured all at Camelen are ready to accept their new lord."

Shock left her speechless, even as her thoughts and feelings chased round in circles. Soon they settled, and through her subsequent anger and defiance, Gwendolyn reasoned out who that supposed *new lord* must be.

Sir Alberic of Chester.

She glared at the knight she'd foolishly allowed entrance. "You have no right to Camelen. My father's will clearly states that if William does not survive him on his death, Father's estates should be divided between his three daughters."

"In time of peace, or had Sir Hugh supported the king, then his will might have stood," Alberic said in a deep, rumbling voice that held a surprising, unwanted note of gentleness, even sympathy. "Unfortunately, your father rebelled against the king from whom he held the charters for his estates, which gives the king the right to seize and dispense the lands as he chooses."

Garrett's hand pressed down on hers where she still clutched his arm. "Sir Alberic is right, my lady. I witnessed the gifting myself. We have no recourse."

She snatched her hand away, distraught Sir Garrett could so blithely abandon his loyalty to her father in favor of an upstart knight, stopping short of labeling him a traitor. "What if we do not accept this new lord, Garrett? What stops us from tossing him out the gate and raising the drawbridge?"

Garrett, damn his hide, looked to Alberic, who answered.

"The king was kind enough to allow a company of his soldiers to accompany me. They are in the woodland, guarding the men of Camelen who survived the skirmish and the cart that bears your father and brother. If I do not give my troops the signal to bring all into the castle, they will take everyone back to Bedforshire and King Stephen, to dispense with at his whim."

Gwendolyn's heart sank, her defiance snuffing out under the blow of his cruelty. Alberic held the bodies of her loved ones hostage to her cooperation, and Camelen's men-at-arms prisoner to her decision. If she wanted them all back, she must admit the king's soldiers, assuring Alberic's possession of Camelen.

Sedwick's hand landed gently on her shoulder. "My lady, your father always knew he might one day suffer retribution for his part in the rebellion. It appears the day has come, and 'tis we who must pay the price. If what Garrett and Sir Alberic say is true, then we have no choice but to bow to our fate."

Gwendolyn closed her eyes and willed the tears of despair not to fall. If Sedwick and Garrett were both willing to concede the battle to Alberic, then he'd won the day.

For the nonce, she had no choice but to acknowledge his lordship of Camelen, but damn, she would never, ever, recognize Alberic as *her* lord. Thanks to the same father who'd lost Camelen to another man, she had resources of her own with which to leave and a safe haven awaiting her.

As soon as she retrieved the ring from her father's hand, she must escape. The fate of all England, in particular the rebellion on behalf of Empress Maud, might depend upon it.

THE EDITOR'S DIARY

Dear Reader,

Whenever life throws lemons at you, make lemonade, right? But even the best lemonade isn't any good without a little sugar to sweeten things up. So grab our two Warner Forever titles this January—I promise even the sweetest of sweet tooths will be satisfied.

New York Times bestselling author Cathy Maxwell raves **Kathryn Caskie's** writing "sparkles with wit and humor" so prepared to be dazzled. Pick up her latest, **LADY IN WAITING**, and you'll never look at facial cream the same way. Jenny Penny is a lady's maid to the matchmaking Featherton sisters and a lover of all things fine—and expensive. But soon her debts pile up, forcing her to secretly sell her homemade facial cream. Jenny could never have anticipated the sensation it would cause...or that women in the ton would use her tingle cream in the most intimate of places to boost their libido. As if that weren't enough, the Featherton sisters have made Jenny their project. Passing her off as Lady Genevieve, they are determined to see her wed sexy Scottish marquis Callum Campbell. Being wooed by day and churning out tingle cream by night, Jenny is leading a double life and she's about to get caught. But will Callum's feelings change when he learns she is not a lady but an entrepreneurial lady's maid?

How far would you go to protect your daughter? Lady Johanna from **Shari Anton's AT HER SERVICE** would risk anything to protect her little Ivy. The plague devastated the village, killing Johanna's abusive husband and two of her three beloved children. Determined to keep Ivy safe from harm's way, Johanna has pledged her life to her daughter. So when outlaws raid her village, threatening their safety and injuring Ivy, Johanna is forced to hire a fearsome mercenary to stop them. Though she dreads the presence of a hulking, aggressive, and completely uncivilized man in her home, she has no choice. But when Logan Grimm arrives, he's nothing like Johanna thought. With his broad shoulders and kind eyes, she sees a gentleness she never expected—and one that she fears more than anything. For while Logan is protecting them against the outlaws, who, pray tell, is guarding her heart? *Rendezvous* calls Shari Anton a "master who weaves magic onto every page" so get ready to fall under her spell.

To find out more about Warner Forever, these January titles, and the author, visit us at www.warnerforever.com.

With warmest wishes,

Karen Kosztolnyik

Karen Kosztolnyik, Senior Editor

P.S. Here are two reasons to believe in true love again: **Annie Solomon** presents a powerful romantic suspense about a blind man and the sole witness to his attack who must save themselves from the assassin on their trail in **BLIND CURVE;** and **Candy Halliday** delivers the hilarious and outrageous tale of a woman determined to create the perfect virtual soulmate and the very real man who starts to seem more perfect every day in **DREAM GUY.**